Down in the Zero

DOWN IN THE ZERO

by Andrew Vachss

Alfred A. Knopf   New York   1994

THIS IS A BORZOI BOOK
PUBLISHED BY ALFRED A. KNOPF, INC.

Copyright © 1994 by Andrew Vachss

All rights reserved under International and Pan-American
Copyright Conventions. Published in the United States by
Alfred A. Knopf, Inc., New York, and simultaneously in
Canada by Random House of Canada Limited, Toronto.
Distributed by Random House, Inc., New York.

Library of Congress Cataloging-in-Publication Data
Vachss, Andrew H.
Down in the zero : a novel / by Andrew Vachss.
p. cm.
ISBN 0-679-43328-7
I. Title.
PS3572.A33D69   1994
813'.54—dc20   94-12312
                                    CIP

Manufactured in the United States of America

FIRST EDITION

When winter vanished
I searched, only to find you
Missing and presumed

Down in the Zero

The first two kids stepped off together, holding hands.
By the time I got mixed in it, they had company down there.

I'd been quiet a long time. Since I went into that house and killed a child.

Killed a child. I can say it now. Every word.

I took out each word and played with it. Over and over again, the way I used to do in prison. The way you try and take something apart, see what makes it work. Words. Like . . . in war, they call the bodies "casualties." I was in a war. Casualties. Casual. You think about it, it makes sense. No, that's wrong. It doesn't make sense. But it fits.

Each word. One at a time. Over and over again.

Facing it.

I went into that house. Me. I knew what I was going to do in there.

In Africa, I served with this Aussie. Malcolm, his name was. A cheerful guy, I once saw him greet a man in a bar by butting heads with him. An old mate, he told me, from Rugby days. I didn't know what he was doing in the middle of that miserable war—one of the rules was that you didn't ask. Malcolm was telling a story once, about someone who had done something to him. When he was just a kid, in Sydney. "I got my own back," he said. I finally figured out what he meant. Revenge. Get your own back.

I went into that house to get my own back. When I was done, I left a dead kid as a monument to my hate.

I told myself all the stories. Ever since. Every damn dead day. They were going to kill the kid anyway . . . had him all trussed up for the film they were getting ready to shoot. Shoot . . . a funny word for making a film. Not the films they were making, though. The right word, for them, what they were doing.

Words. More bullshit, cold-comfort words.

It was a gunfight, a shooting war—I told myself that too. But I went into that house to kill every last one of them. Whatever, whoever I found there, it was going down.

I did it to defoliate the jungle of my childhood. To rip out the roots. I went in shooting.

I wasn't trying to rescue the kid—I didn't know he was there. They were going to sacrifice him. Kill him and film it. Sell the films.

Killing them, I sacrificed the kid myself.

I got shot, getting out, took one in the shoulder. It didn't seem like enough.

The kid was a casualty of war. Very casual. Gone.

He didn't have a life to live anyway—I told myself that. Probably would have killed himself if he had the chance. Committed suicide. Gone over.

That's how this last business started. With kids killing themselves.

The old street dog shook himself and snarled at Spring, knowing he'd beat the odds for another year. In a wild pack, Winter takes them. He looked like his ancestors had been German shepherds, but a dozen generations later, he was a City Dog: lean, dirt-colored and sharp-eyed.

I was his brother, hunting. I was watching the tall redhead—covered to her ankles with a long, quilted coat, but moving with the confidence that said she was packing something potent under it. Her hips, probably, from the brassy-sassy look on her face. On the other side of the street, a black kid, with a geometric design cut into the side of his fade. Wearing a white leather jacket with a big red STOP sign on the back. He was walking just behind her, tapping his heart, making sure the pistol was still there.

A dead giveaway, no matter how it played out.

He wasn't my problem—I was there for the redhead.

"**I** want to see if she's cheating on me," the client had said, looking me dead in the eye. "I'm a hard-core bottom, but whoever owns me, I own *that*, understand?"

She was a short, delicate little brunette with improbable-violet eyes. Probably contacts.

"Rena disciplined me with this," she said, brushing her close-cropped hair back from her forehead. "It used to be shoulder-length. You understand?"

I nodded, holding her eyes.

"I'm pierced too. Down there." Looking at her leather-wrapped lap. I didn't follow her eyes, waiting.

"I want to know where she goes, who she meets, what she does. And I want to know soon."

"Okay."

"I don't need pictures, tapes, anything like that. Not legal proof. This is a lot of money for just watching—I expect you to watch *close*, agreed?"

"Yeah."

"I don't like dealing with men," the brunette said. "But Michelle said you were all right."

"Michelle tell you I get paid for what I do?"

"Yes, she told me everything."

If I had a sense of humor left, I would have laughed at that.

She slid an envelope across the tabletop. "There's five thousand dollars in there," she said. "What am I buying for that?"

"What you said you wanted," I told her.

Michelle came back a few months after I killed the kid. I don't know how she knew, but she did. She stayed with me for a couple of weeks. Pansy was still up at Elroy's, trying to get pregnant, so it was safe for Michelle to live in my office. Days, she visited Terry and the Mole in the junkyard bunker—nights, with me.

I was up on the roof, looking into the Zero. She came up behind me, one red-taloned hand on my forearm, tracer-bullet perfume all around her. I had forgotten how pure-beautiful she was. I'd never asked her if she'd gone through with the surgery when she came back—never asked her why she came back at all.

She stood close to me, wrapping her arms around me like a referee with a beaten fighter, whispering the same words. "You can always do it, honey," she crooned. "Tonight's not your night."

Not this one, anyway.

I stayed to myself. In my office. My cell. Did a lot of reading, the way I did when they had me locked down. Built up all this vocabulary I had no place to use.

I didn't have the heart for any of my usual scams. I waited to save it for the pain.

More than a year passed, and they never came around. Maybe they knew and just didn't care.

It could be. I knew, and *I* didn't care.

I twisted the ignition key and the cab's engine kicked over. I put it in gear and pulled away from the curb on Franklin Street, circling the block, canceling the rooftop OFF DUTY sign with a flick of my thumb. When I came back around, the redhead was still striding along. She hailed my cab and I pulled over.

She climbed in the back seat, keeping one hand on a big black leather pocketbook.

"Where to?" I asked her.

"Central Park West and Seventy-seventh," she said in a hard, measured voice. "You know where that is?" she challenged, glancing at my hack license framed on the dash. Maybe she thought Juan Rodriguez didn't speak English.

"Yes ma'am," I told her. "West Side Highway to Tenth okay?"

"Isn't straight up Sixth shorter?" she asked, a hostile overtone to her throaty voice.

"Lots of traffic now, ma'am. It's quicker the way I said . . . but anything you say, that's okay."

"Oh, go your way," she snapped, lighting a cigarette, blowing a jet-stream at the yellow decal I had plastered on the partition between the front and back seats. The one that said **No Smoking Please—Driver Allergic** in bold black letters.

When I pulled over on CP West, she tipped me two bucks—I guess she liked docile drivers.

I watched her go into the high-rise. The doorman smiled as if he'd seen her before.

I parked the cab at a hack stand, pulled my gym bag off the front seat and walked along until I found a bar that didn't have ferns in the window.

"Absolut rocks," I told the bartender. "Water on the side."

The place was nearly empty. I left the change from my twenty on the bar, waited until the bartender was down at the other end, drank most of the water, poured some of the vodka into the water glass. I picked up my gym bag and carried it into the Men's Room. It was empty.

I took off my leather jacket, pulled the sweatshirt over my head, took off the oversize chino pants. Underneath, I had on a pair of dark gray wool slacks and a light gray silk shirt. I took an unstructured navy blue linen jacket from the gym bag, shrugged into it, checked for fit. Then I peeled off the phony mustache, squeezed some gel into the palm of my hand, ran it through my hair. When my hair got heavy and greasy enough, I combed it straight back, secured the little ponytail with a rubber band. I put the cabdriver clothes in the gym bag, walked out of the Men's Room and out the front door of the bar.

The doorman was still at his post, dressed like a lieutenant in some banana republic, standing with his hands behind his back.

I closed up the space between us, hands open at my sides, palms down.

"How you doing?" I asked him.

"Okay, man. What's up?"

"I'm looking for a little information. Lightweight stuff. Thought maybe you could help me out . . ."

"You the po-leece?"

"The police this polite?" I asked him, holding out my hand to shake.

He did it, palmed the three twenties I had folded up.

"Woman came in maybe twenty minutes ago. Tall redhead. You smiled at her—she's been in before?"

"I'm not sure, man."

"Yeah, you're sure. You didn't know her, you'd have to play the role," I said, glancing at the sign posted at the door: ALL VISITORS MUST BE ANNOUNCED.

"I don't know her name, just . . ."

"I know her name, pal. Which apartment does she go to?"

He tilted his head back, looked into my eyes.

I looked back.

He took his hand out of his pocket, looked over the money I'd passed him.

"It's enough," I told him.

"She goes to twenty-seven-G, man. Every time."

"Who's there?"

He looked back at the money in his hand.

"Fair enough," I told him. "I got a couple more, make it a flat yard, okay?"

He nodded. I handed him two more twenties.

"Miss Kraus," he said.

"Just her?"

"Yeah, she lives alone, man. Suzanne Kraus. She does something in advertising, I think."

"Yeah. She a good tipper?"

"Not as good as you, man."

The redhead came back twice more in the next five days. There's a nice bench across the street on CP West—you can sit there for hours, your back to the park, taking the sun. Nobody pays much attention.

I met the brunette in a Village tearoom on a Friday afternoon. Her eyes were a blissful blue this time. I went over every place the redhead had been in the past few days. When I got to the CP West address, her mouth went into a flat line.

"Suzanne," is all she said.

"Twenty-seven-G."

"Yes, I know."

I sat there, waiting. Finally, she leaned over, dropped her voice. "I need something else done," she said.

"I don't do that kind of work," I told her.

"What happened?" Michelle asked me that night.

"She wanted me to take the redhead out," I told her.

"Burke, you didn't . . . ?"

"No."

"I'm getting a place, honey. I've got to go back to work. On the phones."

I didn't say anything. Got up and walked outside to the rusty old fire escape. Climbed to the roof. Pansy used to dump her loads up there every day, but she'd been gone for a while and the hard chemical rains had done the job—the smell was almost gone. I leaned over the railing, looking down.

"What is it, Burke? You've been up here for hours." Michelle . . . I hadn't heard her come up behind me.

"Nothing."

"What nothing?"

"*Nothing* nothing. I'm just looking into the Zero."

"What's this 'zero,' honey? You said it before . . . I don't get it."

"Nothing. Zero is nothing. That's what's down there. Nothing. After you're done. Nothing. It's not good—it's not bad. Just . . . zero, see? Maybe there's people there, I don't know."

"Who knows? Who knows those things? What do you care? It's not for you."

"You ever think about dying?" I asked her.

Moonlight bounced on her cheekbones, never touching her big, dark eyes. "I have," she whispered.

"Me too. I thought about it a lot. I always thought, I had a fatal disease or something, knew it was gonna do me soon, I was gonna take a whole lot of motherfuckers along for the ride, you know? There's places I could go. Like Wesley. Walk into the room strapped to a satchel of dynamite. Let 'em see what was gonna happen first."

"Wesley was crazy."

"What am I, Michelle? Dead already, I think. I don't even have that dream anymore. Like it's too much trouble. I could just go into the Zero, be done with it."

"Nobody's there, baby. Nobody's waiting."

How could she know? The last time I went hunting, I killed that kid. But I'd never made a promise to him before he died. I never knew his name. There was nothing to do.

I flipped my cigarette over the railing. Watched the little red dot spiral into the Zero.

W hat I really miss is fear. It used to be my friend, fear. Been with me ever since I could remember. It kept me smart, kept me safe. I worked the angles on the edges of the corners. Lived on the perimeter, striking from cover, sneaking back over the border. A guerrilla without an army. A wolf without a pack. Tried to take my piece out of the middle. Walked the underbelly without a flashlight, fear coming off me like sonar, keeping me from stepping on the third rail.

I was always scared. They taught me that. I think maybe it was the first thing anybody taught me.

I used to feel the electricity in me. Fear-jolts. Zip-zapping around inside me, jumping the synapses, making the connections.

Keeping me safe.

When I looked at that house of beasts in the Bronx, when I started my walk, the fear wasn't with me.

It hasn't been there since.

I just don't fucking care.

The betrayal business was booming. Michelle found me work all over town. I was always a patient man, but now I was a stone. It didn't matter how long anything took.

Peter was a hardworking guy, nervous and jumpy, always doing the same things. A rabbit of habit. Every morning, he caught the 5:05 from Bethpage, out on Long Island. I picked him up there a couple of times, eyed him over the rim of my newspaper, dressed in a commuter suit, invisible. He never talked to anyone. Always caught the E or the F train from Sutphin Boulevard in Jamaica, rolled it all the way into Fifty-third and Fifth, walked the rest of the way to his office. He worked for an insurance company, something with numbers.

His wife told her hairdresser that Peter had something on the side. She could tell, she said. The hairdresser told his friend, and his friend told Michelle. She made the arrangements.

He didn't do anything on the LIRR. Nothing. I started to wait for him on the subway, down the line a few stops at the Union Turnpike station.

The mornings had a held-over night chill to them, as refreshing as the air conditioning in a morgue. I'd wait on the platform, dressed like a city nomad, my nostrils stuffed with Vicks so I could handle the smell.

On the subways now, the scariest sound isn't a gun being cocked— it's that liquid-center TB cough.

Sometimes he was on the E, sometimes on the F. Always in the last car. The F isn't as good as the E for skells to sleep. Homeless riders hate the new R-46 cars—the seats are orange and yellow, hard plastic, with indentations for your butt, splayed all around the cars with no more than three seats in a row at any point. Most of the E trains have the old-style cars, with flat-bench seating for six in a row—much easier to stretch out and snooze.

I got to know the regulars. A pair of Latins with impressive mustaches—they always sat next to each other, never spoke, never read the paper. Central Americans, not Puerto Ricans, their posture was military. They just watched—one to the right, the other to the left. Maybe for the roving gangs of dead-inside kids who never go out without their squeeze bottles of gasoline to set fire to sleeping bums. A smooth-faced black woman with two little kids, dressed in a nurse's uniform—I guess she dropped them off at the babysitter's before she went to work herself. A young white man with a shaved head, always reading karate magazines. A Korean woman, only her sloe eyes visible above the surgical mask she wore . . . a fresh white one every day. A huge black man, palms on knees, knuckles so torn lighter skin showed beneath . . . as if he was wearing star sapphires on his hands.

Once you get a seat that early in the morning, you want to stay there—nomadic psychos use the space between the connecting doors at the end of each car as a urinal.

The homeless always ride to the end. Then they wait for the train to head back the way it came. They never get where they're going.

I always stayed on the train past Peter's station. The F makes its last useful Manhattan stop at West Fourth. I got off, switched to the A. Lots of people do that—the A stops at Chambers, same as the E, but the E goes much deeper into the station . . . all the way to the World Trade Center. You switch to the A, you save about a half-mile of walking if it's Chambers Street you really want.

I watched everything. On the platform, one of the steel girders has a metal flap covering a faucet. I watched a homeless man take a plastic bottle—the kind yuppies keep in their refrigerator to have pure spring water always available after their workouts—out of a tattered duffel. He carefully removed the spigot from the bottle, turned it face up, and filled it from the faucet. Finished, he replaced the spigot, picked up the bottle by its carrying handle and shuffled along. He saw me watching.

"At least I got fresh water, amigo," he cheerfully informed me.

On the white tiles surrounding the stairway leading up to the street, a proclamation in black Magic Marker:

> I, Lizette,
> has to be
> punished, for
> disobeying Angel.
> $

I wondered if Angel was a man or a woman—they both pimp in the city now. Or maybe it was an S&M game.

I got on the A train. Sat right next to a white man who'd shaved only half his face that morning. His eyes were spinning in their sockets. One wrist was bandaged, the other had a watch tattooed on it, beautifully detailed. The maniac looked down at his wrist, saw it was 7:15. By the third stop, he'd checked it three more times, tapping his fingers impatiently.

I walked home from Canal, got some sleep. Around noon, I strolled over to the Brooklyn Bridge stop on the Lexington Avenue line. Took the local uptown so I could be ready for Peter's lunch hour.

A man with shoulder-length hair had the corner of the car to himself. He smelled like rot, dressed only in a baggy pair of blue jeans and a torn red T-shirt. Gym shoes, no socks. He was muttering, a vicious dialogue with an invisible enemy. Two black teenagers watched him, awestruck. I could see what they were wondering at—the man's upper body was bulging with sharply cut muscle mass—he looked like an ad for bodybuilding.

I could have solved the mystery for the kids: psycho-isometrics. The poor bastard had been raging against the chemical handcuffs for years before they "de-institutionalized" him.

It was hard to get a seat on that train—a pain for some, a chance to vogue for others. A pair of pretty-girl teenage twins got on, dressed in matching green sheaths so short you could see the heavy black bands around their thighs where their stockings stopped. One took an open seat, the other sat on her lap, kicking her legs, smiling, showing off. They chattered to each other like they were the only ones there, but they registered it all. At Fourteenth Street, they switched places . . . so they'd each have a turn on stage.

I got off at Fifty-first, took a short walk. Had a couple of cigarettes. Waiting for Peter.

A bubble-butted model pranced on the sidewalk, holding the pay phone at the end of the cord in one hand like a rock singer with a microphone. A trio of flash-dressed young execs watched her, dreaming of trophies you could buy with gold cards. A limo driver waited at the curb, bored. A bag lady shuffled past, pushing a baby carriage full of returnable plastic bottles.

Most days Peter just walked around. Sometimes he'd buy a hot dog from a street-corner vendor, sit on a bench, munch it slowly. Sometimes he didn't eat at all. He made a decent salary—maybe he was just cheap.

A whole week went by, same routine. It was a Tuesday when Peter started walking. Up Fiftieth, against the traffic flow. By the time he crossed Sixth and turned left, I had it figured out.

The topless joint served overpriced meals, but nobody was there for the food. Peter ordered a drink and a sandwich. He spent the rest of the lunch money he'd been saving on a tall girl with long black hair who danced for him. Right on top of his little table. Her high breasts stayed unnaturally stiff no matter how much the rest of her bounced. He looked up at her, never moving his face. Tipped her good too, stuffing a few bills down the front of her G-string. She acted like she knew him, gave him a little kiss before she walked off, switching her marriage-wrecker hips.

The black-haired girl worked hard for her money. In those joints, management doesn't pay the talent—they're all independent contractors, renting space to do their work. They keep their tips, management gets the booze and meal money. It doesn't bother the yuppies—they can put the whole thing on their business account as long as they don't eat alone. It's easier for them to watch for-sale flesh in packs anyway.

Extras are extra.

In the back, in the VIP Room, they have lap dancing available. It's just what it sounds like. Peter didn't go back there. Didn't go for the shower room, the slow-dance body rubs . . . any of the extras.

It was just before rush hour when I headed back. The subway car was almost deserted. A slender, light-skinned black kid with a short, neat haircut got on. He was wearing a resplendent soft leather jacket. The front panel was maroon, ballooning white sleeves ran over the top of the shoulders with a black circle on each one, a white 8 inside the circle. The back was a red triangle tapering to the waist, with blue filling in the gaps, a huge eight ball smack in the middle.

An 8-Ball jacket is a major prize for ratpacking teenage gangstah-bandits—they cost a few hundred dollars. I caught the kid's eyes, shook my head, telling him he was a chump for being such a target. The kid looked back, calm, tapped his waistband, gave me a sweet, sad smile. You want his jacket, you ante your life.

That's what it costs today.

I t's easy to stalk—all you need is the time and the focus. It was a little past four in the morning when the tall black-haired girl hailed a cab in front of the topless joint. A couple of other girls stood on the sidewalk next to her. Not talking, tired from the work.

I pulled out behind the cab, my old Plymouth an anonymous gray shark, a moving block of dirt in a dirty city. The yellow cab crossed town, heading east. I followed to the Fifty-ninth Street Bridge, trailed it all around the loop to Queens Boulevard. It settled down then, rolled straight ahead.

She got out in front of a squat old building in Rego Park. There was no doorman to greet her.

T he table dancer was named Linda. Lynda, she spelled it now, but it was Linda on the lease she signed. Linda Sue Anderson. The apartment was a one-bedroom. She paid $650 a month, utilities separate. She'd been there seven months, never caused any problems. I TRW'ed her through a guy I know. It was easy—her righteous Social Security number was on the credit application she'd filled out for the apartment. Date of birth too. She was twenty-nine, right on the border.

Linda Sue was a college girl. LSU, class of 1986. Drama major. Came to New York in 1987. Big dreams, dying slow, dancing on tables instead of the stage. Her legs weren't long enough for the Rockettes, I guess. And the implants wouldn't hold the stealing years back forever.

Her apartment was on the same subway line Peter took every day, a local stop. Peter would have to switch to the G train to get off where she did.

He never did that, coming or going.

I could have braced her someplace, got her to tell me all about Peter.

But I already knew all about Peter.

I told Michelle to tell the customer it was a false alarm—Peter didn't have anything on the side.

I've gone dead before. But this time, it didn't feel like it would cycle out.

When it got real bad once, I went over to Max's temple. Worked the heavy bag in his dojo until I couldn't see straight, until I couldn't lift my arms to throw another vicious shot.

I never laid a glove on the sadness.

Betrayal was around. A piece of the environment, like winos sleeping on park benches. I didn't check with Mama much, just enough to keep her from thinking I was gone. Belinda kept calling. I'd met her working the last job. She was jogging in the park, stopped and said she liked my dog. Turned out she was a cop. Maybe she was working undercover in the park, maybe she was working me. I never did find out. Never returned any of her calls.

I might have gone on like that forever, just numbing my way through until the finish. Now I didn't even want to try. Didn't want to die either—at least not enough to just do it. In prison, the scariest guys were the anesthetics—once they went off, you could club them, mace them, it didn't matter—they just kept coming. Maybe they didn't feel the pain. Maybe it was like you get in a gunfight ... the blood-adrenaline rush blocks your ears so you don't even hear the shots.

I was walking around like that.

I was in Mama's restaurant, waiting for Michelle. I'd promised to drive her up to the junkyard. Max was there, trying to be with me. Max the Silent, not even talking with his hands now, a warrior lost without an opponent. But lost only with me—he had another life. His woman, Immaculata. And their baby, Flower. Not such a baby anymore.

We still played at our life-sentence gin game once in a while, but I couldn't get with it. Max had been on a winning streak for months, even with Mama's occasional dumbass advice.

I felt . . . institutionalized. Used to it. They didn't need the Wall—I wasn't going to make a break.

Michelle came in, made a big show of kissing Max, bowing to Mama. At first, they had walked soft around me, giving the pain plenty of room. But that passed. For them, anyway. Now I was furniture.

"You ready to go, baby?" Michelle asked me.

I nodded, started to make my move. One of the pay phones in the back rang. Mama got up to answer it.

"For you," she said. "Money man."

With Mama, it's all in the inflection—she meant a man who came from money, not a man with cash.

"Tell him I'm not here," I said, not looking up.

"You not going to work?" Mama asked. "Not make money?" Her tone was confirmation of my madness.

"I got enough."

"Don't be crazy, Burke."

I could see this wasn't going to end. So I did what I'd been doing . . . just moved with it. I got up, went to the pay phone.

"What?"

"Mr. Burke?" A young, thin voice, tremolo with something worse than nervousness.

"What?"

"I have to talk to you."

"Talk."

"Not on the phone. Please. I . . . I think I'm next."

"Next for what?"

"I can't . . . my mother said to call you. If I ever got in trouble, big trouble. She said to call you."

"Tell your mother she made a mistake, kid."

"I . . . can't. She's not here."

"Where is she?" *Dead? Which one of them is gone, now?*

"In Europe. Switzerland. In the clinic. She goes every year. There's no phones there, nothing."

"Look, kid, I . . ."

"Please! My mother said . . ."

"Who's your mother?"

"Lorna. Lorna Cambridge."

"I don't know her."

"She said to tell you it's Cherry. Cherry from Earls Court. She said you'd remember."

I did.

I did, and I owed her. I guess I had that much left. I answered on auto-pilot.

"I'll talk to you, kid. *Talk*, you understand?"

"Yes. Sure! Just tell me . . ."

"You know Grand Central?"

"Grand Central Station?"

"Yeah."

"Sure, I can—"

"Be there tomorrow morning. Before ten. Stand under the clock. You know the clock?"

"Yes, I—"

"Just wait there. Someone'll come up to you, ask you your mother's name. Just go with them, understand?"

"Yes. Sure, I'll . . ."

I hung up on him. Went back inside. Told Mama to find the Prof, have him sheep-dog the kid in from the station tomorrow.

I drove Michelle to the junkyard. She goes there on her own all the time—I'm just easier than a cab. We slipped through the city, over the bridge to the South Bronx, the Plymouth finding its own way to Hunts Point. Terry opened the gates, shooing the dogs aside. He walked around to my side of the car—I started to slide over so he could drive the rest of the way when Michelle barked "Hey!" at him through her window.

The kid stopped dead in his tracks. Walked around to the passenger side, said "Hi, Mom," gave her a kiss. She tried to look fiercely at him, reminding him of his manners, but it was no go—love beamed out of her eyes, bathing the kid in its glow.

Terry got behind the wheel. He didn't adjust the seat, just worked the pedals with the tips of his toes. He piloted the big car expertly, not showing off anymore like he used to, just a man doing a job.

After the car was hidden, we switched to an old Jeep they keep there as a shuttle—Michelle ripped the Mole one hell of a speech last time about having to walk through the junkyard in her spike heels.

The Mole was sitting on the cut-down oil drum he uses for a chair, looking into the middle distance where he spends most of his time. A tawny shadow flitted at the edge of my vision—Simba, boss of the wild dog pack. The beast came closer, sat on his haunches, tongue lolling, watching with more interest than the Mole showed.

Terry went into the bunker and came out with a chair for Michelle. A real one, black leather, sparkling clean. She sat down, lit a smoke, took the glass of mineral water Terry brought for her. At home like it was a cocktail lounge.

Terry sat next to her. They talked, close in. After a while, the Mole would come down from wherever he was, and he'd talk too—as much as the Mole ever does. I didn't wait for that.

I walked back to the Plymouth, feeling the dog pack around me. I drove slow, meandering my way back downtown.

Before I went upstairs to my place, I grabbed a pay phone, rang the restaurant.

"It's me," I told Mama when she answered. "You find the Prof?"

"Just now. He say he bring the boy tomorrow, okay?"

"Sure."

I drove by the restaurant early the next day. Checked the window. Only the white dragon tapestry was standing there . . . the all-clear flag flying.

I parked in the alley behind the joint, tapped on the flat-faced steel door, walked through the clump of gunmen masquerading as cooks, went past the bank of pay phones into the dining area.

I took my booth in the back. Mama detached herself from her cash register, walked over to me, snapping something in Cantonese to the men in the back. She'd gotten tired of me saying no when she asked me if I wanted food . . . now she just brings it. She sat across from me, served me a portion of her infamous hot-and-sour soup from the tureen, served herself. I blew on my spoon, took some of the potion into my mouth, feeling her eyes.

"There's something different," I told her.

She bowed slightly, so slightly I could still see the little twitch at the corner of her mouth.

"Good. You pay attention."

"Yeah. What is it?"

"Ginseng powder."

"How come . . . ?"

"Ginseng for wounds."

"I'm not wounded anymore," I told her, tapping my shoulder where the bullet had taken me coming out of that house in the Bronx.

She bowed again, expressionless.

I finished the soup. Waited for her to refill the bowl, sipped it more slowly this time—if I emptied it too fast, she'd just deal another round. I looked at my watch: 9:30. Plenty of time.

"You work soon?" Mama asked.

"Maybe."

She left me after that, going back to her wheeling dealing stealing.

The bell over the front door sounded. Too early for customers, especially with the CLOSED sign displayed. I looked up. The Prof stepped in, a tiny man with the face of an African prince. He was wearing a white and blue poncho that looked like an Indian blanket . . . it trailed almost to his feet. Behind him, a white kid. Gawky, tall and skinny, pasty-faced, dark hair long in the back, spiked straight up in the front. The kid was dressed in a black chino sport coat two sizes too big, worn over black baggy pants gathered at the cuffs around black Reebok hightops. The huge tongues of the sneakers had little orange circles on them . . . Pumps . . . the only spot of color anywhere on him. Clarence came in behind the kid as if his mission was to take up the chromoslack with a canary yellow silk jacket that draped almost to his knees. A heavy gold bracelet dangled from his left wrist—his right hand was in his pocket.

The convoy rolled over to my booth. The Prof slid in first. Clarence ushered the kid into the next seat, then sat next to him, boxing and blocking. One of the waiters walked past, ignoring us, taking up a position at the front. The place started to bustle. It might have felt like a restaurant gearing up for customers if you'd never spent time in a guerrilla base camp. A stranger was inside—time to see if he'd brought friends with him.

"It's done, son," the Prof said to me. "This here's Randall Cambridge—he's lean and he's clean."

So whatever the kid was, he wasn't wired.

"You wanted to talk to me?" I said to him.

"I . . . thought we could speak . . . alone."

"We can't."

"This is kind of . . . personal."

I reached for my pack of cigarettes on the tabletop but the Prof was there first—he had hands faster than Muhammad Ali. Always did. I cracked a wooden match, fired both our smokes, blew some in the kid's face. He blinked rapidly, started to touch his eyes. Clarence shifted his weight, twisting the shoulder next to the kid. The kid's hands stayed on the counter—the Prof would have schooled him about the rules for a meet on the way over.

"Tell me about your mother," I said.

"She's . . . Lorna Cambridge. Like I told you. Cherry, that's the name she said to give you. Cherry from . . ."

"Yeah, I know. When did she tell you about me?"

"Before she left. Before she left the first time. I asked her not to go, but she has to. She always goes. Every year. She said, if you didn't believe me, I should tell you something. A man's name. Rex. Rex Grass."

"Okay, you told me. I got it. Now tell me what you want."

"It's . . . hard."

"So's life, kid. Me too. I'm not a fucking guidance counselor, okay? Spit it out or go back where you came from."

Clarence slid out of the booth, moved over to a seat directly across from us. The kid didn't move.

"Shove over, Rover," the Prof barked at him. The kid moved to his right, breathing easier. Clarence watched him the way a pit boss watches the dice roll—any way they came up, he'd deal with it.

"I think I'm next," the kid said.

"You said that before. On the phone. Next what?"

"Next to die," the kid said, a ready-to-break bubble under the surface of his voice.

"You do this a lot?" I asked him, leaning forward. He wouldn't meet my eyes.

"Do what?" he muttered, surly now.

"Tell melodramatic stories to people you don't know."

His hands gripped the counter but he wouldn't look up, mumbled something I couldn't catch.

"What?"

"Fuck *you*! I didn't come here for this . . . you don't care . . ."

"You got *that* right, kid. I *don't* care."

"My mother said . . ."

"It doesn't matter *what* your mother said. She thinks I owe her, I just paid it off. I said I'd listen to you, not hold your little hand, wipe your nose for you. All your mother knows, I'm a man for hire. You understand what I'm saying? Not a goddamned babysitter, okay? This is a simple deal—even a punk kid like you could get it. You want to talk, talk. You don't, walk."

The kid jumped up so suddenly that Clarence had the automatic leveled at his chest before the waiters even had a chance to pull their own hardware. The kid gasped, flopped back down like his legs had turned to jelly. He put his face in his hands and let it go, crying.

Clarence watched him for a minute or so before he reholstered his gun. I exchanged a look with the Prof. He shrugged his shoulders.

We waited.

The kid sat there crying, ignored. The rest of the joint moved into what it does: phones rang, people came in and out the back door, Mama's messengers and dealers and traffickers went about their business. The kid sat through it all, unmoving, a stone in a stream.

Starving to death in a restaurant.

When he looked up at me, his eyes were yellow-flecked with fear. If he was faking it, he was the best I'd ever seen.

"They have a way of coming for you. Getting inside. I didn't believe it at first. When Troy and Jennifer did it, everybody said they just wanted to be together. You know what I mean? Together forever. Kids talked. Like, maybe, she was pregnant or they wanted to get married and their parents wouldn't let them. But those kids . . . they don't know us. Our parents . . . it wouldn't matter. They wouldn't stop us from do-ing anything. Then Lana did it too. And Margo. They all did it."

"Did what?" I asked him.

"Died," the kid said. The way you explain something simple to someone simpler.

"They got done?"

"Huh?"

"Somebody killed them?"

"No. I mean . . . yes. I don't know. Suicide, that's what they called it. In the papers. Suicide."

"And you think it wasn't?"

"It was . . . I guess. I mean . . . they did it to themselves and all. But I think, maybe, they *had* to do it. And I will too."

"I don't get it, kid. People kill themselves. Kids kill themselves. They go in groups. Couple of kids, they're so sad, they play around with the idea, push themselves over the edge. The next kid sees all the weeping and wailing and special funeral services and how everyone knows the dead kids' names for the TV coverage. He doesn't focus on how they won't be around to bask in the light. He puts himself in that place . . . like he could have the funeral and be there too. And then goes to join them. It's a chain reaction—they call it cluster suicide. It's okay to be scared—that's a natural thing. But you don't need a man like me, okay? What you need, you need someone to talk to, like . . ."

"That's how it *started*!" the kid blurted out. "In Crystal Cove."

The Prof threw me the high-sign. I got up, left the two of them alone.

Clarence followed me out the back door. I stood there, watching the alley. It was empty except for my Plymouth and Clarence's gleaming British Racing Green Rover TC, both moored under a NO PARKING sign. The sign didn't have any effect on the community, but the graffiti did. You looked close, you'd see the spray-painted scrawls were really Chinese characters. Max the Silent, marking his territory with his chop.

I lit a smoke, thinking about Cherry. I left it alone—I'd play the tapes later.

"That is one weak sissy whiteboy, mahn," Clarence said, the Island roots showing strong in his young man's voice.

"He's just scared, Clarence. It happens."

"Yes, it happens to us all. Fear is a devil, for sure. But that boy, he is on his knees to it."

"It's not my problem," I said.

"Whatever it is, my father will find out. No man can hide the truth from him."

I glanced sideways at Clarence. I knew how he felt about the Prof, heard the pride in his voice. But I'd never heard him give it a title before.

"Yeah, the Prof is a magician."

"A magician, yes, but with the heart of a lion. He sees it all, but he never fall."

I started to tell this young man that I had come up with the Prof. He was the closest thing to a father I ever had, too. Made the jailhouse into my school, turned me from gunfighter to hustler. Saved my life. But Clarence, he knew all that. He was another savage cub whose heart the Prof found.

He'd been a pro even then—a young gun, working muscle for Jacques, the Brooklyn outlaw arms dealer. Up from the Islands he was, but he dropped straight into the pits, where the money was. The only thread that bound him to the straight side of the street died when his mother did. He was a quiet, reserved young man—his gun was much faster than his tongue. Jacques had him marked for big things, but Clarence got caught up in my war.

Clarence was there—waiting for me when I came out of that house of killing. He lay in the weeds, a few feet from the body of a cult-crazed young woman who would have taken him out with her long knife but for the Prof's snake-quick shotgun. Lay there in the quiet, lay there after the explosion, lay there during the gunfire. He asked the little man then, what do they do? Wait, the Prof said. Wait for me. And if I don't come out? Wait for the cops, the Prof told him. And die right there—die like a man.

After that night, the Prof had his heart. They bonded tighter than any accident of birth, flash-frozen together forever.

Me, I had a body. A baby's body.

I smoked through a couple more cigarettes in silence. A slope-shouldered Chinese stepped out the back, jerked his thumb over his shoulder. We went back inside.

The Prof was sitting next to the kid, holding an earless teacup in both hands. The kid had one too.

I took my seat. The Prof made a flicking gesture with his hand. Clarence walked over, put a slim, immaculately manicured hand on the kid's shoulder.

"You come with me, mahn," he said softly.

The kid got up. Clarence made an ushering gesture with his hand, and the kid started off to the back, Clarence shadowing. They'd be heading to the basement.

The Prof watched them go. Then he turned his milk chocolate eyes on me. I waited to hear what he'd pulled out of the kid, but he wasn't having any.

"Tell me what you know, nice and slow," the little man said.

"Already told you."

"Not about the boy, about his momma. You really go back with her?"

"Yeah. I guess. Maybe. There was a girl. Cherry. A long time ago. In London. Just before I went over to Biafra."

"She didn't have a kid then?"

"I don't know. Wouldn't be *this* kid, anyway . . . he's in high school, right?"

"Yeah. Just finished in fact. He's got a weak rap, but it's not no trap. The fear is real, bro."

"Lots of people scared."

"His nightmares could be gold, partner. Could be cream in those dreams. Tell me the rest."

"She was a waitress, or whatever they call those girls work in the clubs."

"Runway dancer?"

"No. It wasn't a nightclub, one of those Playboy-type restaurant things. Everybody dressed up, fancy . . . but Vegas-glitz, not real class, you know what I mean? All matching little outfits for the girls . . . not topless, but just about . . . little black things, laced up the back, fishnet stockings, spikes, look-but-don't-touch, you got it?"

"That fluff-stuff won't play today."

I nodded my head in agreement, thinking of Peter, that poor sorry bastard, saving up his lunch money for weeks to buy a few minutes of delusion.

"Yeah. I was in this cheap hotel, staying low, waiting. We had to fly out of Lisbon, something about the Portuguese government backing the rebels . . . I never did understand it all. Anyway, I knew the man who was supposed to come for me . . . the same guy I'd met over here, right? But two guys knock on the door, call me by name, ask if they can come in. I figure, it's a new passport or something, but they were outsiders. They knew all about the Biafra thing, but that wasn't their play. What they had, what they *said* they had, was a whole bunch of diamonds. Handfuls, they said. Right out of the mines in South Africa. They gave me a whole lot of stuff about some mercs who wanted to pipeline it back to the States, how I could hook up with them on the island before we jumped in."

"What island?"

"São Tomé. Little tiny island, just off the coast of Nigeria. Biafra was landlocked by then, it was . . . you sure you want to hear this?"

"Play it out till it shouts, son."

"All right. They asked me to have a meet. At this club. Where Cherry worked, only I didn't know her then. I went every afternoon, for about ten days. One guy was always there, this guy Rex."

"Rex Grass, the kid said."

"Grass, that's just the way Limeys say 'rat,' Prof," I said, glad for once to be telling my teacher something he didn't know. "That wasn't the name he gave me."

"Motherfuckers talk some strange shit, don't they?"

"I guess. We had this corner table, like regulars. It was always this Rex, but one day there was a couple of Chinese guys, from Macao. Another day it was an Indian . . . like from India. Rex was the middleman, putting it all together."

"The guys who sent you over, you didn't tell them anything about this?"

"There wasn't any way to tell them, even if I wanted to. They gave me the cash in the U.S., the passport, told me they'd make contact at the hotel. That was it."

"Ice, huh?"

"That's what they said. I was just listening. I was a kid myself, right? But I was trying to do it right."

"So . . . ?"

"So this Cherry, she was the regular girl on that table. It wasn't the kind of joint where they'd stuff tips into her bra, but her butt was always bruised from the pinches. I never tipped her myself—I wasn't picking up the tab. I get back to my place one time and I find a slip of paper in my jacket pocket. Just her name and a phone number. I called her, and we spent some time together."

"She was a player too?"

"I don't know . . . now. I sure didn't think so then. She was a bit older than me. I thought she just wanted some fun. That's all we did. She never asked me a word about business, didn't ask what I was doing over there, nothing. I asked her once, why she worked there. She said she was gonna meet a rich man, get married. It was a good place to meet a rich man, I remember her saying that."

"Look like she scoped the dope."

"Yeah. The last time I was in the joint, she gave me the high sign. I went to the Men's Room and she was there. Inside. I thought she wanted to get it on, but she wasn't after sex. She told me she saw this Rex the night before. Meeting a government man. I asked her how she knew. She told me I wasn't the only boyfriend she'd ever had. 'Don't come back, love,' is what she said. And I never did."

"What happened?"

"I don't know. I went back to the hotel, packed my stuff and got out. Called a number back in the States, left word where I was. I just waited on the recruiters. When they came to the new hotel, I told them I got nervous . . . spotted a *federale* in the place where they'd put me up. They took it okay—said I was smart to be spooky—made me describe this Rex. They didn't get mad about me looking to score for myself . . . like they expected it. Couple of days later, I went over to Cherry's house. The landlady said she moved out. I was there maybe another week, then I shipped out."

"Never saw her again?"

"Never."

"So what finally happened?"

"They bounced me around. London to Geneva to Lisbon, then to Angola, then to the island. I found the plane easy enough. Then I went over. After a while I came back. Never saw any of them again. It didn't come up until those South Africans came to me with that end-user certificate scam . . . the phony gunrunners, remember?"

"Yes, my brother," the Prof said, serious now. That was when Flood came into my life.

She won't be back either.

"I wouldn't know her . . . this Cherry . . . if she walked in the door. It was a long time ago."

"Want to ride the rocket?" the Prof asked, leaning forward. "Here's what the kid told me—get down to the sound."

The Prof reached over, glommed another of my smokes. Took a minute to fire it up to his satisfaction, like it was a five-dollar cigar, working with a convict's sense of time, killing it the way it was trying to kill him.

"They all rotten-rich, where this kid lives. Got all the *things*, you know what I'm saying? They all do everything the same way—there ain't but one kinda vines to buy, one kinda way to wear them, one kinda car to drive, right? It's all groups. Some of them ride horses, some ride Mercedes. Their folks are all someplace else. With their *activities*," he sneered. "They got crews, but they got no loyalty, see? Savage little bastards. Our boy, he was a tanker—the same nitrous they slip you in a dentist's office. Other ones, they played with Jello-shots. Some tranq'ed it through. Whatever makes your head dead, Fred."

"So what's he scared of? There's no more draft . . . and his kind don't go to jail."

"You ever watch TV? Ever see those ads . . . your kid's fucking up big-time, maybe he needs some of our fancy psychotherapy? A few weeks in our little hospital, you get yourself a brand-new kid. No more drugs, no more booze, no more bad temper. That's this Crystal Cove joint he was talking about."

"He's afraid they'll send him there?"

"Maybe. They sent his pals, a whole bunch of them. And they all come back. Talk about how great it was. They don't seem no better to him—they go right back to whatever lightning they was riding before they went in. But they're different."

"How?"

"The kid don't know. Here's what he says: half a dozen kids . . . kids he knows, kids he ran with . . . they checked out on the do-it-yourself plan. Stepped over. First two went out from an exhaust pipe. One drowned herself. Couple more overdosed on downers. And the last one, he ate a gun."

"They do that . . ."

"None of them left a note, bro."

"So?"

"He won't say why, but he thinks they got done. And what he's scared of, it's gonna happen to him."

"So the move is . . . ?"

"He can't run, son. Something's going down in that town, and he thinks it's coming for him, Jim."

"He wants . . . what?"

"A bodyguard, way he says it. Make sure he don't have himself an accident. But that plan don't scan, man. Got to be something else . . ."

"Where's the money?"

The Prof's voice dropped. He was talking without moving his lips, out of the side of his mouth. In the jailhouse, you talk two ways: loud when you're selling tickets, quiet when you're plotting. I leaned forward, tuned in.

"You be fucking *surrounded* by money, schoolboy. Up where the kid lives, the whole scene is green."

"Yeah, but . . ."

"You don't like the bet, you can always jet," the Prof rapped. "Take the case, Ace."

It didn't take me long to pack. Michelle dogged my steps, harassing me with questions. All I had was an address—told the kid I'd be there by nighttime.

"I don't know how long this is gonna take," I told her. "You can stay here, long as you want."

"About a New York minute is as long as *I* want, baby. This place is creepy enough with you here—I'm not staying one single night alone."

"Whatever you . . ."

"Yes, I know. I'll find a sweet little crib someplace, don't worry about me. Soon as you have a safe number, get it to the Mole."

"Okay."

"Now remember what I told you to watch for?"

"Yeah, yeah. What they wear, how they wear it, what they wear it with . . ."

"Don't be such a sarcastic bastard. How am I going to help you if I don't know the territory?"

"I said okay, Michelle. Soon as I know, you'll know, all right?"

"Shut up. And pack this too," she snapped, tossing a package at me.

It was a silk jacket, midnight blue. Soft as down, almost weightless. A pair of pleated pants of the same material, a slightly lighter blue.

"It's beautiful, Michelle."

"You got *that* right, dummy. That jacket's a genuine Marco Giallo. You can wear it with a pair of jeans, over a T-shirt, you still make a statement. Put on a nice shirt and a tie, you can walk in anywhere. Understand?"

"Yes. Thanks, honey."

"It gets crumpled, you just turn on the shower, all hot water, fill the bathroom with steam, hang it up for a couple of hours, it'll be good as new."

"Okay."

"Take the alligator boots too. Just wear them all the time, like a trademark. They'll never know you don't belong if you stand apart . . . got it?"

"Yeah."

"And don't do anything stupid."

"I *got* it, Michelle."

"I love you, baby," she whispered, standing on tiptoe to kiss my cheek.

After she left, I packed the things she bought for me. And threw in a gray summer-weight business suit and some other stuff, just in case I had to work a straighter crowd.

I crossed the Triboro through the Bronx, took 95 North to the Connecticut Pike, rolling east, driving just past the speed limit, staying with the Exact Change lanes. The Plymouth's tach never saw three grand, its monster motor bubbling, so far within itself it was almost asleep.

Just off the side of the road, the carcass of a dead dog. Couldn't cross the highway, but he made it to the other side.

I threw one of my Judy Henske tapes into the cassette slot just past the bridge—I was already across the state line by the time I heard it stop to switch sides. I hadn't heard a note. If her flame-throwing angel's voice couldn't get through to me . . .

Stay focused, I told myself. Stay inside. Think about the money.

I kept with the Pike to Exit 18, turned north, following the kid's directions. Soon it got real empty, even for the suburbs. Big pieces of land, wood fences that wouldn't keep anyone out, street signs on high posts with names that were supposed to make you think of colonial America and horses.

The roads got narrow. Curvy blacktop. Like moonshine country without the hills.

The house was set back only a short distance from the road. I drove just past it, like the kid said, turned back into a crescent driveway and parked. I could see a big garage through the rearview mirror, on the other end of the driveway. I popped the trunk, grabbed my duffel bag and walked through the quiet night around to the back door.

The lights were on. I rang the bell. The door jumped open—the kid must have been waiting.

I stepped past him into a huge kitchen. It had a nook with a round table set into a bay window, a restaurant-size stainless steel double-door refrigerator, a matching triple sink, more built-ins than I could count.

"Anybody else around?" I asked him, walking through the kitchen, past a dining room dominated by a long, rectangular table, going down a couple of steps into the living room.

"No. Just me. I've been waiting . . ."

"Yeah. Okay. I'm here now. Like I said. Just relax."

"You want a drink or something?"

I shook my head no. Kid probably thought I swilled rye by the quart. Next thing he'd ask me if I was packing a rod.

I sat down on a long, cream-colored couch, facing a panoramic window that looked out toward the road. I looked around. The Prof was right—the joint stunk of money. I half closed my eyes, thinking about being alone in the place for a few hours. Jewelry, cash, gold coins, bearer bonds, who knew? Sure, I'd be a suspect, but so what?—I was born a suspect.

A phone rang, a soft, insistent trill. The kid reached over behind him without looking, came out with a white cordless. He pulled out the antenna, said "Hello" in a shaky voice. Like he was waiting on bad news. Expecting it.

As soon as he heard who it was, his face switched from fear to petulance. He held the phone to his ear for a minute, listening. Occasionally, he tried to get a word in edgewise, but the caller wasn't having any.

"It's late . . ."

The kid cocked his head, listening.

"I have company and—" he said.

More listening, shaking his head.

"No, you *can't* come here. Not tonight. Just find some other fucking place to party, okay?"

He put the phone behind him, still watching me.

"My . . . friends. They know nobody's going to be home for a while, so . . ."

"They gonna listen to you?"

His face flashed white, like it never occurred to him that his pals wouldn't stay away.

"Yeah. Sure! I mean . . . there's other places, right?"

"I don't know."

"Well, there are." Pouty little creep.

"Whatever you say, kid," I assured him. "Is there a garage or something . . . where I can park my car?"

"Sure. Out by the stables. Come on, I'll show you."

As we walked around, I got a better sense of the place. Behind the house was a big slab of land, rising up to a flat plateau. "Three and a half acres," the kid told me, like I had any idea of what an acre was. "That used to be the stable," he said, pointing to a two-story thing that looked like a barn. "We use it for a garage now."

He opened the door and I backed my car in between a beige Lexus sedan and a red Mazda Miata roadster. The Plymouth looked like a rhino at a tea dance.

"Yours?" I asked him, pointing at the Mazda.

"Yeah. Graduation present. It's last year's," throwing it off.

He closed the wood doors to the garage. No lock. I saw a flight of steps around the side of the building.

"What's this?"

"It's to the caretaker's apartment. Above the stables."

"Caretaker?"

"For the stables. When we had horses. There's nobody there now."

I looked up at the dark windows. "You got electricity up there?"

"Sure. It's real nice, actually. Mom says we're gonna rent it out, one of these days."

I lit a cigarette, thinking how peaceful it was out there, when I heard the thump of rap music on the move. Gravel crunched in the driveway. It was a white Suzuki Samurai, a topless little jeep, loaded with people. The driver stomped on the brakes, cutting a Brodie in the dirt. A big blond kid vaulted over the side just as a dark BMW sedan pulled in behind.

"Oh fucking *shit!*" the kid half moaned next to me.

The blond kid muscle-walked over to where we were standing, a brawny, cocky guy, moving with a linebacker's menacing grace.

"Hey, Randy! Heard you were lonely, so I brought you some company."

"You can't—" the kid started to say.

The blond cut him off with a chop of his hand. "Hey! I got it. No problemo, pal. We're just gonna use the upstairs, okay? We're not going near the house, don't get yourself all excited."

"Not here," I said, stepping forward.

"Who the fuck are you?" the blond kid asked, head swiveling on a thick neck, giving me a stare that might have frightened a quarterback.

"The caretaker," I told him. "Mrs. Cambridge hired me to look after the place while she's away. I'm living there . . ." jerking my thumb at the upstairs apartment.

"Oh yeah? Then we'll just—"

"Leave."

The blond kid stepped closer, expanding his chest. He was wearing a loose T-shirt over surfer baggies, barefoot. "Look, man, you don't . . ."

I caught his eyes, smelled the beer. Thought about my steel-toed boots and his bare legs, wrapped my hand around the roll of quarters in my pocket. Reminded myself to get off first if he dropped a shoulder . . . and not to hit him in the head. Feeling how good it would be to hurt him—letting him feel what I felt.

"Nice babysitter your mommy hired for you, Randy," he sneered. "Some old dude asshole rent-a-cop."

Somebody laughed, behind him.

He eye-tested me for about five seconds—as a bully, he was a rank amateur. "See you around," he finally said, turning his back on me, climbing into the jeep.

The little white car tore up the driveway on the way out, the silent BMW in its wake.

The kid wasn't overcome with gratitude. "Now you've fucking done it," he said, nasty-voiced.

"What's the big deal?" I asked him.

"They'll be back. Nobody says no to Brew . . . he's an animal."

"Brew?"

"Brewster Winthrop. He's like the . . . leader around here."

"The leader of what?"

"Of . . . us, I guess. I dunno."

"What's he do?"

"Do?"

"Yeah. Besides his little drive-bys. Does he work, go to school, what?"

"He's in college. Or he was, anyway. Now he's home."

"Don't worry about it."

"That's easy for you to say."

"Look, kid, it isn't all that important, all right? It bothers you so much, give him a call, tell him to come back and trash the place to the ground. I'll go over to the other house and get some sleep."

"I *can't* do that. My mother would . . ."

"Yeah. Okay. Just let it rest."

I lit a smoke, feeling the knots in the back of my neck relax.

"You weren't scared of him?" the kid asked.

"No," I told him.

He gave me a funny look—I let it slide.

We walked back over to the house. "Maybe I should sleep over the garage tonight," I said. "In case your pals make a comeback."

"No! I mean . . . I thought you were gonna stay . . ."

"You can sleep over there too, all right?"

"I don't . . . I mean, it'll be okay. There's an intercom, anyway."

"Intercom?"

"I'll show you," he said over his shoulder, flicking on the stereo in the living room. Soft string music flowed, so faintly I could barely hear it. He walked up the stairs, me right behind. The second floor was bigger than it looked from the outside, four bedrooms, two of them master-size. I followed him to the end of the house. "This is hers," he told me, tilting his head in that direction.

The room was huge, with high ceilings, one of the walls almost all glass. A side door opened into a bathroom: stall shower, separate tub with Jacuzzi jets, a phone set into a niche in the wall within easy reach. A double sink with an elaborate makeup mirror surrounded by tiny lights. All pink marble with a faint white vein running through it. The floor was the same motif in glistening tile.

"Here," he said, opening a walk-in closet full of enough clothes to stock a small store. Just past the door was a control panel, a small round speaker set into the top, a double row of buttons beneath it, each button numbered. He pushed one of the buttons. The string music from the stereo flowed out of the speaker.

"See?" he said. "She has the whole place wired."

"Every room."

"Yes." Something in his face, couldn't tell what in the reflected light.

"Is this the only control panel?"

"Yeah."

"So if I stay over there, how will you . . . ?"

"I'll sleep in here tonight," he said, his face down.

I shouldered my duffel, headed back across the yard alone. Climbed the wood stairs along the side of the garage. The door to the apartment had a glass pane next to a dime-store lock. A clear message to burglars about what was inside—either nothing worth stealing . . . or a Rottweiler who hadn't been fed in a while.

I used the key the kid gave me, stepped inside and flicked on the lights. It was nicer than I expected, the living room furnished with substantial, expensive-looking pieces that had aged out of chic. Even the living room carpet was deep and decent, a muted blue with a thick pad underneath. Against one wall was a stereo-tape-CD combo with bookshelf speakers. The kitchen was small, but all the appliances looked serviceable. The bathroom was small too, a plastic curtain turned the tub into a shower on demand. I crossed over to the bedroom, which was dominated by a heavy, carved wood frame for the double bed and a matching dresser with a mirror.

I kept looking. The refrigerator was empty except for some bottled water, but the kitchen cabinets had a good supply of canned goods. Pots and pans too. The pilot light was working on the stove. The hall closet had towels and sheets. No security system that I could see. I spent another fifteen minutes searching the living room for the microphone that would connect to the house intercom. No luck. I finally found it in the bedroom, a thin wire with a bulb tip running under the base of the window frame. The window looked out over the back area—the three and a half acres the kid had been bragging about. It slid open easily when I shoved. Maybe twenty feet to the ground. Okay.

I poured myself a glass of cold water, lit a smoke and sat on the couch. A white telephone sat on an end table. Probably recycled from the main house too. I checked the number—it was different from the one over there. I picked it up: dial tone.

Okay.

I was up at first light the next morning. Made myself some prison-tasting orange juice from powder I found in a kitchen cabinet, walked around inside a little bit, getting a daytime feel for the place.

I shaved and took a shower. When I got out of prison the last time, I took a bath every chance I got—something you couldn't get inside the walls. After a while, the pleasure wore off. After a while, a lot of pleasures do.

Whoever lived there before me left some stuff behind. An old leather jacket on a coat stand in the living room, just past the door. A stack of magazines: *Penthouse*, *American Rifleman*, *Road & Track*. Maybe they had expensive tastes. In one of the dresser drawers, I found a green and black plaid flannel shirt, a couple of wool pullovers. And a black leather riding crop.

I left the drawer the way it was. Unpacked my own stuff. Hung the jacket Michelle gave me in the bathroom, letting the steam run to refresh it.

I went downstairs, opened the garage doors, started the Plymouth. I pulled out quietly, then I cruised in increasing circles, smelling the wind, making notes inside my head. I found some of the things I'd need: a bank of pay phones in the parking lot of a mini-mall, a deli with a coffee shop up front that was open at that hour, an underpass to the highway where I could pull the car in, make it disappear.

It was a little past ten by the time I put the Plymouth back in the garage.

The kid was still asleep when I went through the back door to the main house. I found him in his mother's bedroom, face down, covers to his waist. I left him there, went looking around.

The basement was like an old-fashioned storm cellar, not the finished rec room I'd expected. Just an oil burner in one corner, some sagging wood shelves gray from dust, a collection of rusty old garden tools, some suitcases with stickers on them, a steamer trunk.

I prowled through the house, looking for whatever. Didn't find it.

He came downstairs a little before noon, wearing a red terry-cloth bathrobe, hair wet from the shower. I was in one of the leather chairs in the living room, having a smoke, thinking.

"Anything happen last night?" I asked him.

"No. Not really."

"What?"

"Phone calls. Hang ups, that's all. Just somebody playing with my head."

"They do that a lot around here?"

"I . . . guess so. I don't know."

"When does your mother get back?"

"Around Labor Day. That's when she always comes back. When school starts."

"School for you?"

"Yeah, I guess. College. If I go."

"Yeah. Well, look, I can't stay that long. Just sitting around here, understand?"

"You said . . ."

"I said I'd come up here, and I did. Hang out with you a while, and I will. But I don't know where to go with all this. You're not doing any work."

"Work?"

"Yeah, kid, *work*. You said you were scared of something—I still don't know what that is."

"Neither do I . . . exactly."

"Your friends died, right?"

"Yes."

"And you said you thought it could happen to you, right?"

"Yes."

"And that's it? That's *all* you fucking know?"

"I . . ."

"Look, either you know more than you're telling, or you don't know enough. Either get off it, or get on it. Otherwise, I get on out of here, you're gonna be the same as before I came, see?"

"Yeah." Sulky now. Sullen. I left him that way.

Darkness drops softer in the suburbs—I couldn't feel it coming the way I do in the city. I changed my clothes, walked over to the main house. The kid was sprawled on the floor in front of the big-screen TV in the living room, smoking a joint, flicking the remote rapid-fire, getting off on the images.

I sat down on the couch, pulled the remote out of his hands—it was making me dizzy. The screen image stabilized. CNN. Some twerp was talking. He had an Opie face, but his eyes were weaselly little beads. I hit the volume toggle, listening to the twerp squeak about family values. Lousy little Senator's Son. I had his family, I'd be all for family values too—wasn't for his family, he'd be kissing ass to be assistant manager at McDonald's.

The kid giggled. It wasn't a political statement—he was halfway stoned, blissing.

"Let's go for a ride," I told him. "You can show me the sights."

We walked out to the garage. He started to climb into the Miata. I shook my head. The keys were in the Lexus. I got behind the wheel, fired it up. He got in the passenger side, cranked the seat way back so he was almost reclining.

I backed out, pointed the car's nose toward the street, hit the gas and pulled away. The beige car handled like graphite—quiet and slick.

"Which way?" I asked him.

"To where?"

"Wherever you all hang out."

He made some vague gesture with his left hand. I turned left at the corner, tracking. The kid turned on the stereo. Too loud. I found the knob, dropped it down. I kept driving, following his hand waves every time there was a corner-choice.

The town wasn't much—a long, wide street with little shops. Service stops for the locals, atmospheric joints for the summer people. The street had no pulse.

When we hit the water, I turned right, following a winding road. Seafood restaurants, couple of one-story tavern-types, some smaller office buildings.

A squad car came toward us at a leisurely speed, too fast for prowling but not in a hurry. The kid toked on his joint, unconcerned.

"What's in there?" I asked him. We were rolling past a freestanding building with a big parking lot full of cars, some of them covered with college-age kids. It looked like an upper-class version of a drive-in hamburger joint.

"The Blue Bottle. A nightclub, like."

"You ever go there?"

"Sometimes. It's not really down."

"Where do you hang out, then?"

"Houses, man. In the houses. If you know the circuit, it's always party time."

In the morning, there was a fat housefly buzzing around on the inside of my window screen. I found a plastic squeeze bottle with a spray top—the kind you use to mist houseplants—and filled it from the tap. I gently misted the fly until it stopped moving. Then I picked it up carefully, opened the window, put it outside on the ledge. I watched, smoking a cigarette. Finally, it shook itself and took off. You can't drown a fly.

I dragged deep on the smoke, playing it in my head. Burke, he wouldn't hurt a fly.

Just kill a kid once in a while.

I got dressed slowly. Last night had been a waste. Driving around, looking at not much of anything. The kid didn't seem scared anymore, but every time I mentioned leaving, the panic danced in his eyes. He was going to make a list for me, give me a place to start.

I'd seen his kind before—a herd animal, with no drive to be the bull of the pack.

There was a strange car in the driveway. A black Acura NSX, gleaming in the sun, standing like it had been there awhile—I hadn't heard it pull in. I opened the back door. A woman was in the kitchen, playing with the coffeemaker, her back to me. She was maybe thirty, thirty-five, hard to tell. Medium height, with short black hair cut in a blunt wedge, wearing a white tennis outfit. She didn't turn around, just glanced at me over one shoulder.

"Want some?"

"Some what?"

She made a little snorting noise. "Coffee. That's all I cook."

"No thanks," I told her, opening the refrigerator, tapping the plastic water bottle into a glass. I sat down at the kitchen table, sipping the water. She finished what she was doing, turned to face me, leaning against the counter.

"I'm Fancy," she said.

"You sure are."

"That's my *name*. I already know yours."

I looked a question over at her.

"Burke, right?"

"Yes."

"You're the caretaker, aren't you? Yes. You look like you could take care of things."

I didn't answer, watching her face. Her eyes were light gray, heavy with mascara and eyeliner, set wide apart with a slight Oriental fold at the corners. Her nose was small, too perfect to be factory-stock. Her chin was a tiny point, emphasized by the broad, square shape of her face. Her mouth was small, the lips almost too thick, slashed with a dark carmine that ran against the light bronze of her skin. A lamp, I figured—this one would know all about skin cancer.

"I was going to wake Randy up, get him to play some tennis with me. Work some of this off," she said, slapping a plump thigh hard enough to leave a welt, a sharp crack in the quiet morning.

"Seems a shame," I told her.

"Playing tennis?"

"Losing any of that."

She flashed a smile. "You like fat women?"

"I like curves."

"Ummm," she said, deep in her throat. "Your mother ever tell you you were cute?"

"No." As pure a truth as I'd ever tell a stranger.

She walked over to the table and sat down, holding her coffee mug in both hands. A diamond bracelet sparkled on her wrist. No rings on her fingers—the nails were long, carefully crafted, the same color as her lipstick. I took out a pack of cigarettes, raised my eyebrows.

"You have nice manners," she said.

"It's not my house."

She nodded, reaching over to push an ashtray in front of me. I fired up a smoke, took a drag. She took the cigarette from my hand, held it to her lips, sucked in so deeply that her breasts threatened the white pullover. When she exhaled, the smoke only came out one nostril. She put the cigarette in the ashtray, turned it toward me so I could see the lipstick smear on the filter.

"Your turn," she said.

I took another drag.

"How does it taste?"

"Hard to tell from such a little piece."

She made that sound in her throat again. Leaned forward. "Let's see if . . ." just as the kid stumbled through the door.

"Z'up?" he greeted us both.

"I thought we were going to play," the woman said.

"Maybe later," he mumbled, helping himself to coffee.

"Then I'll come back," she said, getting up. As she walked toward the door, I could see the harsh red mark where her hand had marked her thigh.

"She's a bit old for you, isn't she?" I asked the kid.

"Kind of young for you, though," he grinned back.

I tipped my water glass toward him in acknowledgment.

"She's really my mother's friend," he said.

"Kind of drops in when your mother's not around, keeps an eye on you . . . like that?"

"She keeps an eye on everything, the bitch."

"You don't like having her around?"

"Not really."

"So . . . ?"

"She's gonna do what she wants anyway."

"Okay. You got that list we talked about?"

"Not written down, exactly. But I could tell you stuff about them if you want."

"Who cleans the house while your mother's gone?"

"Juanita. She comes in three days a week."

"Un huh. And who cooks?"

"I can always call take-out . . . there's a lot of different restaurants."

"You got a summer job?"

He gave me one of those "Are you crazy?" looks kids his age specialize in.

"So what you do is dress yourself, make a few phone calls, watch TV . . ."

"Get high . . ." the kid supplied.

"And wait for the summer to be over?"

"You got it."

"Make the list, kid. I'm not your fucking secretary, understand? You want this done, you got to do your piece."

"Okay, okay. It's no big deal. I just thought . . . if you wanted to get started right away, it'd be easier."

"Just make your list," I told him. "Do some work."

I went back over to the garage. The NSX was gone—deep ruts in the bluestone where it had peeled out. I dialed Mama's joint.

"Gardens," she answered.

"It's me."

"That woman call again. Two times."

Belinda. Nothing to do there.

"Anything else?"

"No strangers."

"Okay. Tell the Prof it's quiet up here. Did Michelle call in with a new number yet?"

"No."

"Okay, take this one down . . . I'll be here for a while."

"Good. Okay. Be careful."

"I am."

I sat there for a while, working it through. Nothing. The kid was a field mouse, that's all. Spooked by the headlights. His list would be useless—cold ground doesn't hold tracks.

The Prof was right about one thing—the whole town was lousy with money. I couldn't see an easy way into any of it. Sooner or later, the kid would need to go out, do something. If I could get him to go alone, I'd have time to look through the house.

I walked back into the bedroom. A stiff white card sat on the pillow, a few words in careful calligraphy on its face.

Call me.
After dark.
F.

There was a number in the lower right corner.

Back at the big house, the kid worked on his list. I watched TV. Every half hour or so the kid would come into the living room, bitching and whining about how it would be easier for him to concentrate in front of the TV—he always did his homework that way. I ignored him each time and he finally stopped.

He made a couple of phone calls. I didn't pay attention. A knock at the back door. The kid got up, came back with a couple of meatball heros, handed me one. I got myself a glass of cold water, sat down to eat. The bread was doughy, with no real crust. The sauce was thin and weak. The meat tasted like aged basset hound. In the city, the only people who'd visit that restaurant would be holdup men.

The kid didn't seem to notice, munching away, washing it down with a couple of Cokes.

It was late afternoon by the time the list was ready. He had the names for all six checkouts, phone numbers for three, a street address only for one.

"It was all in the papers, the other stuff," he said, handing it over, not meeting my eye.

"You didn't really know these kids, did you?"

"Not . . . close, you know. But I knew them."

"Yeah. You tell anyone why I'm here?"

"No. I told them you were the caretaker, like you said."

"Your mother had caretakers before?"

"Once. Once she did. Last year."

"What happened to him?"

The kid shrugged his shoulders. People come, people go. Cleaning women, pool boys, groundskeepers, caretakers . . . all the same to him.

That's what you get in a town where their idea of fighting racism is giving the maid a raise.

"Whose idea was it . . . to call me in?"

"Mine, I guess."

"Your mother didn't say anything?"

"She always says the same thing. Every time she leaves. If I get into trouble, I should call you. It just never happened before."

"Okay. I'll take this, get started tonight."

"Started?"

"To look around, that's all. I'll only be gone a few hours."

"Can I . . . ?"

"It'd be better if you didn't come along . . ."

Troy and Jennifer. Lana. Margo. Brandon. Scott.

Just names. Nothing in the kid's list to make them into people. Maybe he was right—the papers wouldn't cover this up—it wouldn't affect property values like a killer shark haunting the beaches. Tomorrow, I'd see if the local rag had a morgue.

I picked up the phone, punched in the number for the restaurant. It wouldn't matter if it appeared on their long-distance bill—the kid already knew it.

It rang three times. Then . . .

"Gardens."

"It's me."

"That woman call again. Say for you to leave an address next time."

"Address?"

"She say, you not talk to her, then she write you a letter, okay?"

"Yeah. Give her the Jersey box, okay, Mama?"

"Sure."

"Anything else?"

"The Prof . . . see if you have message for him."

"Just tell him nothing yet, okay?"

"Sure. You finish soon?"

"I don't know. Maybe."

"Maybe not so good, there."

"Maybe not."

"Okay."

I hung up the phone. Belinda, still calling. Even if she could keep Mama on the line long enough to run a trace, she'd only get the number in Brooklyn. We ran a series of bounces to the restaurant, changed them all the time. The Jersey P.O. box wouldn't help her either. It's a dead-drop—I've never been there. Every couple of weeks, one of Mama's delivery guys cleans it out, leaves everything at one of the noodle factories off Broome Street. Max stops by at random, picks up the load. He brings the mail back to his temple—I look at it whenever I have a chance. It's not fast, but it's safe. The lady cop wants to write me a letter, I'll get it. And the best she'll get is an answer.

I sat and smoked a couple of cigarettes. Not even thinking, just waiting for dark.

I watched the bands of light shift across the back fields. When the last thin strip fell into the ground, I closed my eyes.

It was just past ten when I came around. It was country-dark outside then. Rich and quiet-feeling, no neon-knives to dice it into pools of shadow.

I tapped the keys on the phone, holding the stiff cardboard in my hand. It was picked up on the second ring.

"Hello?"

It sounded like her . . . but not quite. As if she was a little juiced.

"Could I speak with Fancy please?"

A muffled giggle. Then . . . "Sure. Hold on . . ."

"It's been dark for a while," she said, coming on the line.

"So?"

"I said to call after dark."

"Oh . . . that was an order, then?"

"Sure. Don't you like orders?"

"No."

"You'd like mine."

"Not so far I don't."

"Don't be such an adolescent. You're too old for boy-games, aren't you?"

"What do you want?"

"Ouch! I don't like cold things."

I lit a cigarette, not saying anything. Closed my eyes. It was no contest—she didn't know about waiting.

"You want to start over?" she whispered.

"Tell me what you want."

It was her turn to sit quiet. I could hear a faint undertone, like a humming . . . couldn't tell if it was her or the line. I ground out my cigarette. Heard her take a breath. Then . . .

"You're no caretaker. And I know why you're here."

"Do you?"

"Yes. Want me to tell you?"

"Sure."

"Maybe I will. Tonight. Late. You know where Rector's is?"

"No."

"It's a club. Private club. Get the address from Randy."

"Okay."

"In the back, the parking lot makes a kind of bulb . . . like in a thermometer? Pull in there and wait for me."

"When?"

"I'll be coming out around two."

"*Around* two?"

"Yes, *around* two. You wait for me, understand?"

"I'll be there at two."

"Look, you . . ."

I hung up the phone.

I went back over to the big house. Music came from upstairs . . . loud . . . but I didn't see any sign of the kid. I found a Yellow Pages near the phone in the kitchen. No listing for any joint called Rector's. I tried 411—nothing.

I made my way upstairs. The kid was blissed out across his bed, staring at the ceiling. The marijuana stench was heavy. Sticks of incense on his bureau, unburned—no reason for him to mask the smell with nobody around, I guessed. No point asking him any questions.

I went back over to the apartment. Showered, shaved, put on the outfit Michelle told me would open all these lush doors. In the garage, I helped myself to the Lexus.

I was in town just after midnight. Passed a few restaurants, scoping it out. Didn't feel right, so I turned toward the highway. Found the Blue Bottle. Pulled in. I didn't get a second glance making my way to the entrance—maybe Michelle was right.

A blonde girl in a sequined halter top was taking money at the door, a bouncer hovering over her right shoulder in case someone's ID didn't check out. He was strictly Amateur Hour: big, sharp-cut muscles bulging out of an orange silk T-shirt, but his hair was too long, too easy to grab in a fight. And his hands looked like he only used them to pat on his cologne.

I gave the woman the ten bucks she asked for, moved past her toward the dance floor. As I passed by the bouncer, I tilted my head in a "Come over here" gesture. He moved with a bodybuilder's strut, rolling his shoulders with his hands clasped behind his back. When he got close, I turned my shoulder so he came into a space just for us.

"I was supposed to meet some friends. Not here. At another joint. And I lost the address. Thought maybe you could help me out."

"What's the place?" he asked me, a practiced hardguy edge to his voice.

"Rector's."

He shot me a look. "I'm not sure I know where that is."

"Sure you do," I told him, opening my hand quickly, letting him see folded green.

He glanced over his shoulder, turned his attention back to me. "That's a private club, pal. I can't get you in there."

"Don't worry about it. That's covered. Just give me the directions, okay?"

He leaned close. "Follow the water to forty-one, take it north a couple of miles. You'll see the sign for Calm's Corners. Just turn in there, follow the road. It's a white house, big driveway out front. You can't miss it."

"Thanks," I said, shaking his hand, passing the cash.

I found the sign for Calm's Corners, whatever the hell that was. Turned in, followed a two-lane blacktop ribbon. The house was there, like the bouncer said. Good-sized house, three stories. The driveway was one of those half-moons. From where I sat, I could see a couple of men in tuxedos standing at the front of the house, between two thick columns. Valet parking—that wouldn't work.

I drove on, looking for an opening. It took me three slow passes before I saw it—a side road that merged with the back parking lot. I nosed the Lexus in cautiously, but nobody was paying attention. The very back of the lot was just like Fancy had said. And empty. I backed the Lexus into the spot she said, checked my watch. 1:19.

I got out of the car, looked around. The parking lot had no fence—it ran right up against a forest in the back, following the tree line.

I returned to the car, dropped the driver's side window, watched. I saw cars being parked maybe fifty yards away. The guys in the tuxedos did it mostly, but once in a while somebody would do it themselves. Traffic all coming in . . . nobody leaving. No pattern to it: mostly male-female couples, but there were some singles too, and some same-sex combos.

The night was clear, but I couldn't hear anything. Either they ran a real quiet joint or it was soundproofed.

I waited there until twenty past two. No sign of Fancy. I drove the Lexus out the front way. Nobody paid me a glance.

I stashed the Lexus next to my Plymouth. The red Miata was gone. I went upstairs, changed my clothes. Almost four in the morning, a good time to have a quiet, leisurely look around the big house. The kid probably wouldn't come back until well past daylight. Whatever had sent him into a panic didn't seem to have much staying power.

I had just opened the back kitchen door when a pair of high beams flashed against the garage. I slipped away from the house as Fancy's black NSX spun into the driveway, scattering stones as she stood on the brakes, skidding to a stop, the headlights aimed across the back yard. The lights went out, I saw her jump out of the car and slam the door, a long black coat trailing behind her as she marched up the stairs to the apartment.

I moved out of the shadows behind her, crossing to the bottom of the stairs just as she unlocked the door and stepped inside. I followed, moving quiet.

I stood outside the door. Heard the sound of glass breaking inside. I stepped in, breathing shallow. The long black coat was thrown over the back of the sofa. The TV screen was cracked, pieces of a heavy glass ashtray scattered all around. From the bedroom, sounds of someone rooting through the drawers. Harsh, heavy breathing.

I went down the hall. Fancy's back was to me. She was poured into a black leather mini-dress over dark stockings, standing there in bright blue spike heels, wrecking the place.

"You having a good time?" I asked her.

She whirled without a word, the black riding crop in her hand, slashing. I spun away, let her momentum carry her past me when she missed, slammed my shoulder into her back and took her down to the carpet. She squirmed, snarling something I couldn't make out. I locked my arm around hers, pinning it close, letting my weight hold her.

Finally . . . "Let me *up!*"

"Let go of the stick first," I told her.

Her fist unclenched, the riding crop slipped from her fingers. I shifted my weight from her hips, still keeping her shoulders pinned. Her dress was around her waist. I saw a flash of dark nylon over bronze skin. There was only a slash of black silk between the cheeks of her butt, some kind of thong.

"Nice, huh?" she whispered over her shoulder, calm now.

I rolled away from her, letting go my hold. She got to her feet, tugging down the dress, breathing hard.

"What's all this about?" I asked her.

"What?"

"Breaking in here, busting up the place, tearing through my things."

"I didn't break in here—I have a key."

"Who gave you . . . ? Ah, never mind. What about the other stuff?"

"I was angry. You stood me up. People don't do that."

"I was there. At two, like you said. You never showed."

"Why didn't you wait?"

"For what?"

"People do what I tell them," she said, bending over and picking up the riding crop. She tossed it on the bed, turned to me. "They *love* to do what I tell them. You think you're something? You're nothing, Mr. Caretaker. I know your secrets."

"Okay."

"Okay? That's it? Okay? I know why you're here. I know what you want."

"Sure."

"Don't be slick—you don't have the looks for it. I could save you a lot of time, point you straight. That's not your secret—that's mine. You want it?"

"Maybe."

"People wait for me, I told you. You can wait too. You know how it works—you want something, you have to pay, yes?"

"How much?"

"A lot. Not money. I don't need money. You want to pay, you have to play. Play with me, get it?"

"No."

She walked over to the bureau, rummaged around, like she knew what would be in there. Came up with a fat white hurricane candle. She held it out to me.

"Light this," she said, her voice rough-edged, insistent.

I cracked a wooden match, held it to the wick. Her hand was steady. When the candle flickered into life, she went back to the bureau, held it in one hand over her head as she swept everything onto the floor with the other. She planted the candle, stepped back, watched the flame in the mirror over the bureau, adjusted it until she was satisfied.

"Go turn out the lights," she said, still giving orders. "Do it now."

I stepped back, hit the switch, still watching her.

The black dress had a wide zipper all the way down the front, anchored with a silver pull-ring the size of a half-dollar between her breasts. It made a metal-singing sound as she pulled it down. She shrugged her shoulders and the dress fell away. Then she stood facing me, hands on hips. Her breasts were bare. A humming sound came off her, not from her mouth. She hooked her thumbs in the waistband to the thong, pulled it slowly over her hips. When she had it worked down to just above her knees, she wiggled her legs and it dropped to her ankles. She stepped out of the little piece of black silk, hooked the toe of a blue spike heel into the pile and kicked the thong over in my direction. I felt it brush against my feet but I never dropped my eyes from her face.

She turned her back to me. Put one knee on the bed, looked over her shoulder. Climbed the rest of the way onto the bed, on her hands and knees, facing away from me.

"You want to play now?" she whispered.

I took out a cigarette. Walked over to the candle, got a light. I took a deep drag, put the cigarette on the dresser top. Her butt looked like a piece of white marble, the dark stockings setting it off like a center-piece. The spikes of her heels were pointed back at me.

I took off my clothes, watching, breathing through my nose, something telling me I needed to keep a control card in my deck.

I hung my clothes over the back of a straight chair. Stepped to her. I put one hand on her hip, touched her deep with the other. She was wet. I entered her slowly. She snapped her hips to the side, throwing me out.

"Kiss first," she said, not turning around.

I put my hands on her shoulders to pull her around. She locked her arms rigid, resisting.

"Kiss my ass," she ordered. "Kiss it good."

I stepped back. "Not this year," I told her. Calm, not arguing.

"Make you mad?" she challenged. "Here!" handing me the riding crop, still not turning around.

I tossed it onto the floor, still watching her. The marble glistened in the candlelight.

I went back over to the bureau. Took another drag from my cigarette. She didn't move.

A piece of time passed. I walked back to her, put one hand on each of her cheeks, stroked with my thumbs.

"No!" she snapped. "Kiss it or whip it, that's all there you get. I don't do vanilla sex."

I stepped back again. Finished the smoke. Ground it out on the dresser top.

"Well?" she demanded, her voice thick.

"I don't like the choices," I told her.

She looked over her shoulder, still on her hands and knees. "It looks like you do," she whispered.

"That's my body," I said. "Not me."

She dropped her face to the sheet, arched her back. Her dark sex bloomed in the candlelight, framed in marble. "Last chance," she whispered. Sugar threats.

I shook my head. It was as though she could see it without looking. She backed toward me, backed all the way off the bed. Stood up. Walked over, put the dress on like it was a coat, bent at the waist and zipped it up. Snuffed out the candle with two fingers and stalked out to the front room.

I followed her. She was pulling on the long coat. I grabbed her from behind. She ground her hips into my crotch. I slipped my hands into the side pockets of the coat. Pulled out a bunch of keys, stepped back. The keys were all anchored to a piece of wood in the shape of a tiny cane. I rifled through the keys, picked out the one to the apartment, pulled it off the ring. She turned to face me. I handed her the rest of the keys. She held the keys so the tiny cane dangled.

"You know what this is?"

"No."

"It's birch. Get the idea?"

"Yeah."

"You think so? Maybe I'll tell you about it sometime. When you're ready."

She walked out, leaving the door open. I stood in the doorway, watching her walk to her car. It started up, moved off, no headlights.

I walked back through the wreckage to the back room, turning on the lights. Her black silk thong was on the floor of the bedroom. I picked it up.

It smelled like handcuffs.

I got dressed, putting rich-bitch games out of my mind, centering on the job. I crossed the yard back to the big house. A burglar's dream—I had a key, and the cops wouldn't stop even if they saw lights on. I slipped on a pair of surgeon's gloves—all I'd need to slice this piece of cake.

It had to be her room. Whatever she was now, Cherry was a working-class girl—she'd need to keep the good stuff close. I worked the teakwood chest of drawers first, moving from the bottom up the way I'd been taught. It saves time—that way you don't have to close one drawer before you move on to the next. Nothing. I pulled out each drawer completely, checked for something taped underneath. A blank. I couldn't find an inset panel anywhere. Tapped the wood frame—it rang solid.

I went over the carpet section by section. It was seamless, a double-thick pad underneath. The nightstand by the bed supported an ice blue telephone in some free-form futuristic shape and a black clock with green hands, no numbers. The hands pointed to 4:45. In the base of the clock was a window with a digital readout—7:45. I let it roll around in my head, kept working.

Inside the nightstand I got lucky. A thick stack of bills, all hundreds, neatly banded. I quick-counted it—ten large. The bills looked Treasury-fresh, but the serial numbers were random. Toward the back of the little drawer, a black leather address book. I tossed it on the bed, kept looking.

I took the mattress off the bed. Nobody home. The box spring was next. Another blank. I checked the headboard for a compartment, using my pencil flash to spot a seam. It was made from the same teak as the dresser, and just as solid.

Only one picture on the wall. A sepia-toned photograph of a woman, her back to the camera. She was dressed in a dark Victorian suit, some kind of velvet it looked like, with a long skirt and long sleeves. Her hands were clasped in front of her, head slightly bowed. I took it off the wall, hoping for a safe. The paint was undisturbed—whoever cleaned the joint removed the picture every time they dusted.

Nothing left but the closet. I did the footwear first. She had everything from thigh-high boots to running shoes, but they were all empty. Then I went through the clothes, piece by piece. Found a string of pearls in one coat pocket, a pair of used theatre tickets in another. Tissues, a blue chiffon scarf, a lipstick-size spray atomizer. I pointed it away from me, pressed the tiny button. Some kind of citrus perfume.

Against the back wall, I found a black silk cape with an attached hood. The lining was red. In a side pocket, a gray business card. Normal size, but twice the weight. In steel blue copperplate script: "Rector's." And a phone number. I put it on the bed next to the address book.

There was no lock on the bedroom door. I walked quickly through the rest of the floor. No locks anywhere. It wasn't doors that covered that house's secrets.

Back in Cherry's bedroom, I opened the address book. Nearly every page was filled with distinctively shaded block letters. The ink was a dark blue—looked like a fountain pen. I found the culprit in the nightstand drawer, a fat black Mont Blanc.

None of the names meant anything to me at first. I took it page by page. Nothing under "Burke." "Fancy" was under "F," but the phone number wasn't the same as she'd written on her After Dark card. Not quite the same.

Page by page. I came to a strange listing. "MERC" is all it said. I looked at the number. Looked at it again. It was the pay phone that rings in Mama's restaurant, written backwards. A man for hire, that's what I must have seemed like to her back in England a lifetime ago. Some people grow, some just age.

I turned back to the page with Fancy's number. Read it backwards. It matched her card.

Was the code that simple? I found a listing for Rector's. Compared it to the card. It didn't match, backwards or forwards.

I went over to the control panel in her closet. Pushed buttons at random. String music came from the speaker again. Not the longhair stuff this time—Santo and Johnny's "Sleepwalk"—'50s steel guitar spooling softly strange in that lush room.

I laid down on her bed, staring at the ceiling, surprised not to find a mirror. Glanced over at the clock again. 5:19 on the dial, 8:19 on the digital. Three hours' difference.

Where the hell would that be?

I reached for the phone. Dialed the number on the card I'd found in the cape. A woman's voice answered, pleasant but loaded with the promise of something harder: "Rector's."

I hung up. Dialed the number under that name in her address book. A recorded message: "Your call cannot be completed as dialed. Check the number and . . ."

I hung up on that one too. It's the message Ma Bell sends when the exchange isn't local.

I checked the book again. No area code. Maybe she didn't use them at all. But . . . no, she had a lot of them—Chicago, L.A., Houston—even some foreign ones.

I closed my eyes. *What's your secret, bitch?* I asked her.

When I opened my eyes, the clock said 5:51. A long time to be out. I got up, put everything back the way it was. The closet speaker was playing something slithery . . . something I didn't recognize.

I went back to the bed, picked up the book, started to punch the number she had listed for Rector's into the control panel. Four buttons into the sequence I heard a sliding noise. I looked in its direction. A panel was opening in the seamless pink marble of the bathroom tile over the tub.

I went over, took a close look, not touching anything. I've been trained by the best—if you don't figure out how to close the wound, the autopsy will be too easy. I pushed the buttons again, in the same order. I heard the faint sound of an electrical motor, but the panel stayed open.

Okay. I tried it in reverse, last digit first. The panel slid back, closing with a barely audible click. From where I stood, I couldn't see where it had opened. You don't get craftsmanship like that from a local handyman—it had to be the work of the original architect.

Even up close, I couldn't find the seam. The white veins in the pink marble pulled my eyes into a swirling pattern, the recessed lighting bouncing off the slick surface blurred my eyes. Like the random stripes of a herd of zebra, making the lions dizzy, distracting the hunters from the target.

A four-digit code. Ten thousand chances to hit it by luck—no chance at all. I punched the Open Sesame again, one slow button at a time. The panel was about six inches wide. Inside was painted a flat black, a matte finish that would eat light, no reflection.

I pulled a thick white towel from a standing brass rack, laid it down in the tub in case something spilled. I started to reach my gloved hand inside the compartment when I remembered this was too elaborate a setup for a rich woman to hide her pearls. And remembered where Cherry came from, what she'd know.

I walked downstairs, looking around. What I really wanted was a pair of needlenose pliers, but the kitchen didn't have anything like a tool kit. Finally, I settled on a pair of long barbecue tongs, heavy steel with a rosewood handle.

Back upstairs, I used my pencil flash to check out the inside of the compartment. I could see some plastic cassettes, a padded jewelry box, and what looked like a black drawstring pouch. I wasn't worried about a burglar alarm—if I was right, the cops were the last thing Cherry would want if somebody got this far. I probed the air space inside the compartment with the tongs, testing.

Nothing happened.

I extended the tongs toward the pouch again, as delicate as plucking a butterfly off a flower. I closed the tongs slowly, standing well back. I felt the tips touch something and there was a sharp *clang!* It almost knocked the tongs from my hand. I pulled them back, used the pencil flash. A curved metal wand hung just over the pouch, still vibrating, three separate hooked tips pinpointing the light. An L-shaped lever dangled from the far corner of the compartment. I pushed it back toward the wall with the tongs. Watched as the wand retreated. Whatever it was, it could be reset.

The tips of the wand looked surgical. I could guess what she had painted on them—curare lasts a hell of a long time, but it only takes a few seconds to do its job. I shoved the lever back to disable the wand. Then I worked the stuff out of the compartment like I was defusing a bomb, working front to back. My hands were calm, but my knees were locked against the trembling. I dropped each piece lightly on the heavy towel in the same position it was inside the compartment.

Three VHS videocassettes. Blackmail maybe?

Seven audiotapes, premium-grade metal, ninety minutes each. The blackmail scenario looked better than ever.

A round disk I didn't recognize.

A pair of three-and-a-half-inch computer diskettes, Teflon coated, one red, one blue.

A mini-cassette backup computer tape.

Business records, maybe? Of somebody *else's* business? Had to be some pretty hot data to be this well protected. Industrial espionage?

No matter what all the stuff was, there was no way I could tell just by looking.

But then I found the black velvet pouch.

I gently pulled the drawstring, tipped the pouch upside down. Fire inside: red, white, green. Gems. Big ones, all faceted. And some smooth black stones.

I glanced over at the clock. 6:39. Enough.

I took one of each of the gems, one of each of the cassettes, both diskettes. Put everything else back in reverse order. If you took a quick look inside, it would look pretty close to normal. I pushed the lever home, watched the poison wand disappear, heard it snap into place. Then I went back to the control panel, pushed the buttons, and made the compartment disappear.

I carefully wrapped the gems in a piece of dark blue felt I carry with me for emergencies. The loot disappeared into the pockets of my jacket. The towel went back on the rack. I pulled off the surgeon's gloves and headed downstairs.

It only took me a few minutes to lock the stuff in the false bottom of the Plymouth's truck, right next to the fuel cell. I never went back to the upstairs apartment.

I was getting a traffic report from the all-news station by 7:08, heading for home base.

As soon as I crossed the bridge into Manhattan, I found a pay phone and started to work. Left messages for Michelle and the Prof. Called Mama, told her I'd be on my way before nightfall.

By eight, I was in my office, sacked out on the couch.

It was almost three in the afternoon as I worked the Plymouth through the maze of Chinatown's back streets. Clarence's immaculate BRG Rover was parked in the alley behind Mama's.

They were in my booth. The Prof had three playing cards in front of him, folded lengthwise, face down, showing Clarence the finer points of three-card monte. Mama was at her cash register. The joint had the usual number of customers—none.

I sat down in my booth, ignoring the questions in the Prof's eyes. Mama strolled over just as I was pulling the blue felt from my pocket. She nodded, snapped something in Cantonese to one of the hovering waiters, and sat down.

The blue felt sat between us on the table—Mama made no move to touch it. In a couple of minutes, the waiter came back. He cleared the table, wiped it down, spread a brilliant white bolt of heavy cloth over the top. Then he placed a black metal cube near Mama's left hand, spread a red silk square next to her right. Mama bowed her head, fingertips together, waiting. The waiter opened the top of the black metal cube, telescoped a long stem with a tiny quartz halogen light at the tip. He pressed a button on the side of the cube and a circle of pure light showed on the tabletop. On the red silk square, he carefully assembled a jeweler's loupe and several different-size tweezers. From one of his apron pockets, he took a miniature scale with an electronic dial. He placed it at the far corner of the table and stepped back.

Mama raised her head, opened her eyes. Nodded an okay at me. I unwrapped the gems. Mama plucked the diamond first, placed it on the table in front of her. Then she screwed the loupe into her right eye, picked up the gem with a pair of tweezers and took a look.

Nobody spoke.

Mama turned the gem back and forth with the tweezers, her fingers precision machinery.

"You remember what I teach you about diamonds? Five C?"

"Sure," I told her, remembering the lesson from so many years ago, when I came back from Africa and told Mama about new smuggling opportunities. Four C was the world standard: color, clarity, cut and carat. The last C was Mama's own—cash.

Mama nodded acknowledgment as she worked. After a couple of minutes, she put the rock down. Her smile was brighter than the light.

"Very fine stone."

"It's for real?" I asked her.

"Oh yes. Blue-white, brilliant cut. Maybe VVS, VS for sure. Three carats, pretty close."

"How much?"

"A hundred thousand, quick." Meaning it was worth a quarter million.

"What about the others?"

Mama didn't reply. She reluctantly put the diamond on a corner of the cloth, reached for the green. She did the same routine, switched to the red. Finally, she took up the smooth black stone, rubbing it between her fingers. After a few minutes, she switched off the light, looked across at me.

"All perfect stones. Ruby is pigeon blood, probably from Burma. Emerald is Colombian for sure. Very big stones to be so perfect."

"What's this?" I asked, touching the smooth black stone with a fingertip.

"Girasol," Mama said. "Black opal. From Australia."

"There's more," I told her. "This is just a sample."

"Passport," Mama said. I knew what she meant. There's no harder currency than fine gems. A universal language—you could turn these into cash anywhere from Bermuda to Bangkok.

"I told you, bro, I know what I know. We tap that vein, we feel no pain."

"It's not that easy, Prof. She had something else too." I showed him the diskettes. "You know what these are?"

"Sure, schoolboy. That's the cake—the rocks are the take."

"That's the way I see it too. We Hoover the place, she knows it was me. And she's got enough juice to buy trouble."

"But if we know what she knows . . . "

"Yeah."

"Let's ride, Clyde."

We picked up Michelle on the corner of Twenty-ninth and First. She climbed into the back of the Rover like it was a limo, gave me a quick kiss on the cheek, settled back into the leather and lit a smoke.

"What's on?"

"I'm not sure yet. The Prof was right—the joint is rotten with money. I took some samples . . . gems. Mama says they're true blue. She's got seven figures stashed in the house."

"Oh honey, you know just what to say to make a girl crazy."

"It's trickier than that, Michelle." I showed her the disks.

"Blackmail?"

"That's my guess. I'm not sure. There's some tapes too. But either I put everything back or we're stuck with hit and run, see? We need a way to take a look."

"My man can do it," Michelle said, confident.

Terry let us into the junkyard, greeting the Prof and Clarence with elaborate courtesy as Michelle looked on proud.

"Damn, boy, you getting *big*!" the Prof told him.

The kid flushed. "I told you, Mom," he said, holding his back real straight. "How tall am I gonna be?" he asked the Prof.

Clarence stepped forward, took both the boy's hands in his, turned them over, looked at the backs.

"You be taller than me before you a grown man," he said quietly, the Island lilt clear in his rich voice.

"For real?" Terry asked, joy all over his face.

Clarence nodded gravely.

The Mole was nowhere in sight when we pulled up to the clearing. Simba was lying down in front of the underground bunker, calm and watchful.

"You want me to get him?" Terry asked.

"We'll need to be in his lab for what we got to do," I told the kid. "Just go downstairs, ask him if it's okay, all right?"

"Sure," the kid replied, pushing Simba to one side like the killer beast was a stuffed animal.

I lit a cigarette in the South Bronx air, feeling safe like I always do around the Mole's base. Simba watched without interest.

The kid stuck his head out of the bunker. "He says to come down."

I went first, Michelle right behind. Clarence came last, walking backwards, one hand on his pistol . . . he doesn't feel the same way I do about the junkyard.

The Mole was at his workbench. Michelle kissed him. His pasty skin turned a mottled red, his lank hair falling over his forehead. Michelle slapped at his upper arm in pretended disgust at the Mole's lack of romance.

I put the computer disks on the workbench. The Mole looked at them and shrugged.

"Can you read them?" I asked.

He shrugged again. Picked one up, plugged it into a slot on his computer as he simultaneously kicked it into life. The screen flickered, settled down into a paper-white blank.

The Mole tapped some keys, watched the screen. We found places to sit, left him alone to work. Terry showed Michelle some experiment they were working on—something about heavy water, whatever that is. The Prof settled back into a jailhouse wait-state. Clarence's bright eyes flicked over the bunker, taking in the strange machinery, a glazed look on his smooth young face. He'd been raised on Carib legends, but he never imagined voodoo like this.

The Mole turned his head slightly. I bent to listen—the Mole never talks loud.

"It's passworded," he said, pointing at the screen where it said **[Locked]** in bold black letters.

"Can you get in?"

"Eventually. Password could be anything. I can run a random program, try every combination."

"How long would that take?"

He shrugged again. "I don't have a big enough machine here. Could take a couple of weeks, even longer."

"Damn! Can you copy the disk so I can replace it while you run through the combos?"

"No."

"Great." I stood for a minute, trying to think it through. People get lazy with stuff they have to remember, use their birthdays for safe combinations, like that. Maybe she . . . ?

"Try Cherry," I told him.

His stubby fingers flew over the keys. The machine beeped. "No," the Mole said.

"Try Rector's."

"Spell?"

I spelled it for him, with and without the apostrophe.

"No," he said.

I took a few more shots, all blanks. "I'll start it on random," the Mole said.

I nodded glumly. Then I thought of the safe. "Could it be numbers?" I asked him.

"What?"

"The password, could it be numbers instead of letters?"

"Yes."

I gave him the combination to the safe. Watched his fingers as he tapped it in.

"Yes," the Mole said as the screen flashed and words popped out on its surface like invisible ink when you hold the paper over a flame.

The Mole copied the blue and red diskettes, gave me back the originals. "The rest is storage media," he said, holding the round disk and the tiny cassette in his hand. "Probably the others didn't get added yet. Take them back too—what I have will be enough to see what they do."

I nodded agreement. "You have a VCR here?" I asked him.

He gave me a sour look, craned his neck in the direction of a small-screen TV in the corner.

"I *told* you it would come in handy, Dad," the kid said, a look of gleeful triumph on his face. He took the videotape from my hand, stuffed it into the slot expertly, hit some buttons.

The tape was black and white, streaky at the edges.

"Adjust the tracking," the Mole told him.

"I know, I know," the kid said, absorbed, playing with a tiny dial.

The camera opened on a pristine white bedroom. White walls, white sheets . . . even the bedposts were white. The camera zoomed in on one of them. A black leather strap dangled, waiting.

"Go upstairs, Terry," Michelle said, her voice calm.

"Ah, Mom . . ."

"Now!" she snapped. The kid turned his eyes from the screen, testing. Michelle stared him down, not saying a word. He gave her a baleful look over one shoulder as he climbed back to the outside air.

The only sound was the hum of the tape. A man entered the white bedroom, dressed in a conservative business suit. He sat down on the bed, hands on his knees, facing the way he came in. A woman walked in, her back to the camera. She was wearing a black-and-white-striped jacket with a peplum flare over a dark pencil skirt. Couldn't see her feet in the picture.

"Infrared camera," the Mole said. "High resolution. They wouldn't need lights."

A match flared as the Prof lit a smoke.

The woman removed the peplum jacket, tossed it away. A scoop-necked white blouse was underneath. The man watched as she unbuttoned the blouse to display a black push-up bra. She said something to him. He looked down.

The bra unhooked from the front. The woman dropped it to her side. The man looked up. The woman stepped to him, slapped his face hard with a roundhouse swing. She said something to him again. He dropped his eyes.

The woman turned her back to him, reached behind her to unzip the pencil skirt. As she bent forward to tug it over her hips, the man slyly looked up. The woman arched her back, looking full into the camera.

Fancy.

As she stood slightly to one side, the camera came in on the man's face, full and clear.

I didn't know him, but he'd recognize himself quick enough when they showed him the tape.

Fancy turned to the man, now wearing only a pair of black panties over a garter belt and dark hose. She stopped, walked off camera.

Came back holding a riding crop in one hand.

The man stood up and stripped, quickly. He lay face down on the bed as Fancy secured his hands with the restraining straps to the head-posts.

She worked him over with the riding crop. It went on for a while. Then she stopped, stood hands on hips, saying something to him.

The man turned his head. Fancy hooked her thumbs in the waist-band of her panties, slipped them down over her legs. She walked to the side of the bed, slapped the man's upturned face, bunched up the panties and stuck them in his mouth.

Then she went back to work.

The man finished lying on his belly, his back all lacerated, hips jerking in harsh spasms. The camera zoomed in and out erratically, sometimes focusing on a place where nothing was happening. When Fancy finally unhooked him, he rolled off the bed, the gleaming evidence of his orgasm displayed in the classic Times Square tradition— freaks hate it when you fake it.

The last shot was of the man sitting on the bed, looking into the camera with a dazed look on his sweaty face.

"There's more?" Michelle asked.

"A lot more," I told her.

"Audio too?"

"Yeah."

"This is some sophisticated operation, baby. That's a fixed camera with a remote—a setup like that, you could run it without an operator, so long as the action lasts long enough."

"I know. I met the woman."

"She want you to play too?"

"Yeah."

"It figures. This is the latest thing," Michelle said. "Super-safe sex. No penetration. In fact, no skin-on-skin, you get right down to it. You find a girl who works pro doing this, she probably likes it herself. Most of them, they just found a way to make it pay."

"That's what we need too . . . a way to make it pay," I told her. The Prof nodded agreement. Clarence watched us. The Mole was busy doing something at his workbench—he hadn't even watched the tape.

I packed everything up, walked topside with the Prof and Clarence, leaving Michelle downstairs. Terry wasn't around.

"What do you think?" I asked the man who taught me so much when I was a kid.

"I think they make a date, play it straight. Even a sap will turn off the tap, you push too hard. You can't keep going back to the well."

"You think they turn over the whole deal, no copies?"

"For that kind of cash? Sure. They must have a real solid rep."

"Like people *know* they pull this stuff?"

"Remember a few years ago . . . when that maniac was carving up gays down by the pier?"

"Sure," I told him. A serial killer, heavy into mutilation, stalking the sex-for-sale streets down by the river. The body count was getting up there, the headlines were screaming, and the homosexual community was in panic. A couple of them came to me, said there was good money in it if I could come up with the killer. They didn't have much faith in the cops.

"Remember that guy Robbie?" the Prof asked. "Remember how he ran it down."

I lit a smoke, bringing it back. Robbie owned a small art shop in the area—he was one of the first guys I spoke to when I started the job.

"Nobody's cruising anymore, right?" I'd asked him.

"Oh *please!*" he snorted. "That's not going to change. A maniac might scare the hustlers, but not those looking for love. Besides, you know someone like that's out there, it adds a little jolt, understand?"

"You think people into that let's-meet-and-beat stuff know somebody's playing with cameras, Prof?"

"Could be, schoolboy. Long as nobody actually got burned, it'd probably just be a turn-on for them. They know they got to pay for their play anyway, what's the difference?"

"It's a sweet racket. They get paid at both ends."

"Listen, homeboy, whatever that kid's mother is, she ain't stupid. We need some proof, and we need some truth."

"I'm going back there tonight. I'll replace all the stuff."

The Prof stepped close, put his hand on my shoulder. "Burke, listen good—if you got the right climate, the weather don't matter, see?"

"No. What's it mean?"

"Take a look, but be ready to book. If you can't walk light, stay outta sight."

"Look, Prof . . ."

"I mean it, bro. I'm not liking a damn bit of this."

It was around midnight when I pulled into the garage. The red Miata still wasn't there. I couldn't tell if the kid had come and gone, or hadn't come back at all.

The apartment over the garage looked the way I left it.

I walked back over to the main house. It was empty. The hair I'd plucked from my head and anchored with a tiny dot of spit was still in place across the marble seam of the safe. I put everything back.

I had just walked into the apartment over the garage when the phone rang. I picked it up, said "What?" and waited.

I heard some breathing, then the line went dead. I closed my eyes, drifted off.

Later that night, I heard a car pull in. My watch said 3:15. I heard a door slam, walked over to the glass panel in the door. The kid was moving across the lawn, not too steady.

I gave him five minutes, then I went across. The back door was standing open. The kid was sitting at the kitchen table with the lights off, staring at the far wall.

"You okay?" I asked him.

"I called," he said. "I kept calling. You weren't here. I didn't want to come back until I knew."

"That was you on the phone before?"

The kid nodded. "I was going to go up to your place, but I didn't want to wake you up."

"What's going on?"

"Diandra's dead. It happened . . . I guess a couple of days ago. We just found out."

"Who's Diandra?"

"Diandra Blankenship. She jumped. Off the Old Mill Bridge. Onto the rocks."

"How do you know?"

"They were all talking about it. At the party. We were going to do a couple of tanks, just chill, listen to some tunes. But nobody could really get into it."

"You knew her?"

"Yeah. A little. She was a year behind me in school."

"Didn't the cops come around?"

"Not to the party. They talked to some of the kids. Myron said Brew said they talked to him. She didn't leave a note or anything."

"Get some sleep," I told him.

"Are you going to . . . ?"

"I'm going to be right here. Downstairs on the couch. All right?"

He nodded, getting to his feet, moving like he was carrying too much weight.

I didn't know enough. That's where the real risk is—that's why the hardest currency in the world is information. I knew people who had killed themselves—suicide isn't a rare thing in jail. I knew some who did it on the installment plan too—there's hustlers who turn street tricks, use the money to buy dope to make themselves forget. I remember asking one about it once. I was looking for a runaway—he was looking for some cash, so we made a deal.

"Spell 'needle,' " he told me, like it was a secret code.

I played it straight. "N-e-e-d—"

"Stop right there," he said, looking through my face.

I got it then.

But it didn't add up. Rich kids get bored enough, they might do damn near anything, but you don't snuff yourself because there's nothing else to do that day.

And there were too many of them doing it.

Maybe an hour passed. I smoked a couple of cigarettes, watched the occasional car flit past the front window. I took the pencil flash, found my way upstairs. The kid was asleep, face down on his own bed, still dressed.

A light rain started to fall. I lay on my back on the living room couch listening to it tap against the windows.

A burring noise, soft, like an expensive phone. I picked up the nearest receiver . . . dial tone. The sound kept repeating, so faint it barely registered. I got up, closed my eyes so my ears would work better. Maybe it was some fancy alarm clock. The wall phone in the kitchen had two lines. I switched between them . . . dial tones on both. The sound kept coming. I stood dead-still, trying to sonar it out. A narrow closet was built into the archway between the kitchen and the living room . . . there! I opened the door—the sound was louder. I went through the stuff in the closet and found it. In the side pocket of a black leather coat—a cellular phone, as thin as a paperback book. I pulled up the antenna, flipped it open.

"What?" I said into the speaker.

"Where's Charm?" A man's voice, suspicious.

"You got the wrong number, pal," I told him, growling like I'd been interrupted.

He hung up. I put the phone back where I got it, sat down and lit a smoke. Before I was finished with it, I heard the phone again.

I let it ring until it stopped.

Charm? Another player . . . or just another name Cherry used?

Two more hours, three more cigarettes, the phone in the closet stayed quiet. Maybe it was a wrong number for real.

I was up with the first light, wondering what day it was. Hard to tell out there—people who don't work a regular nine-to-five don't have a good sense of weekends. I looked out the front window. At the head of the driveway there were two mailboxes. I walked out there. Turned out one of the mailboxes was for the local newspaper. It was empty. The regular mailbox only had some bills . . . no personal letters. I brought everything inside, left it on the kitchen table.

I wanted a shower, but I checked on the kid first. He was in the same position. I moved close, some little flicker warning me he might be gone. But he was okay, breathing deep, his mouth hanging open, slack.

The garage door was standing open, the cars untouched. The keys were in the kid's Miata—maybe he was expecting valet parking.

I walked through the apartment, watching close this time. Nobody had been there.

I showered and shaved, thinking about kids killing themselves. About the kid I'd killed.

I was at the kitchen table by the time the kid came downstairs. His face was blotchy from sleep, eyes wary from his dreams.

"You stayed here last night?" he asked.

"On the couch, in the living room."

"I'm sorry . . . I didn't mean for you to—"

"That's okay. You want some coffee or something?"

"I'll get it," he said, turning his face away from me.

He put a couple of Pop-Tarts in the toaster, hit the switch on the coffeemaker, took a long pull at a wax carton of orange juice. I found a box of rye crackers, poured myself a big glass of water from the bottle in the refrigerator.

"What's those?" he asked me, nodding his head in the direction of the pills I had taken out of my pocket.

"Vitamin C, beta carotene, Vitamin E."

"You take them every day?"

"Sure."

"How come?"

"An old girlfriend of mine, she's a doctor. Told me if I was gonna smoke, this is what I needed to do."

"Be better to quit smoking," he said, with all the superiority of someone who fucks up his life twelve ways from Sunday but doesn't share *your* bad habits.

I didn't say anything, just crunched my crackers, popped the pills, chased them down with the water. The kid joined me at the table, started on his meal without much enthusiasm.

"You expect the cops?" I asked him.

"No, they didn't come around before, why should I?"

"I don't know. I don't know how things work around here. It's just that if they do, you may need to explain me . . . what I'm doing here, see?"

"Sure. I'll say you're the caretaker. It won't be any big deal."

"It could be if they run my sheet."

"Huh?"

"I've got a record, kid."

"Oh. I mean . . . I kind of figured that."

"Did you?"

"Well, from what my mother said . . ."

I looked a question at him, waiting.

"She didn't say you were a *criminal* or anything. Just that you could . . . take care of things. I know in her business, she had to deal with some pretty heavy people, so . . ."

"Her business?"

"When she was young. Before she had me. In England, where she lived."

"What business was that?"

"You know," he gave me a quizzical look. "She was a gem dealer. Traveled all over the world. That's when she met you, right? When you worked as a bodyguard?"

"Right," I told him.

"Were you . . . close with my mother?"

"It was a long time ago, kid."

"I know, but . . ."

"What? You want to know if we were lovers?" Softening it for him if that's what he needed.

"Lovers? Like romance? No. I want to know did you have sex with her?" he asked, looking at me head-on for the first time that day.

"That's your mother's privacy you're talking about," I said.

"Privacy? My mother? You have to be kidding. I was just curious, that's all. She never has sex with men."

"She must have . . . at least once."

"Yeah, with a turkey baster," he laughed, a feathery undercurrent to his voice. "Artificial insemination. My mother's gay. She told me, a long time ago. She said she wanted a baby, but she didn't want a man. That's why I was wondering . . . if she ever did."

"I get it," I told him, not answering his question. "Your father, was he . . . ?"

"No. It was an anonymous donor, she told me. She was married once, but it was for money. The guy was gay too—he wanted her for a beard. I guess the joke was on him, huh? I don't know who my father is."

"You mean your biological father?"

"That's what I mean—I don't know whose genes I have in me."

"Neither do I," I told him.

"You were adopted?"

"No."

"Then how . . . ?"

"I was raised by the State. In an institution."

"Like a foster home?"

"Like a jail."

"Oh." He got up, busied himself with loading the dishwasher for a minute. "You ever wonder about it? Who your father was?" he asked over his shoulder.

"No."

"I do," he said, coming back to the table. "All my mother could tell me was that he had a very high IQ. It was a special sperm bank. Very expensive. She had it done in Switzerland."

"You already got all you're going to get from him," I told the kid.

"What do you mean?"

"The color of your eyes, your hair, maybe your height, I don't know. Physical characteristics. And your basic intelligence. Some hard-wired personality traits, stuff like that."

"What's 'hard-wired'?"

"You know how some folks have a basically happy temperament, some are more stubborn than others . . . like that. Nothing major."

"You mean that?"

"It's true. You can pass along DNA, but not behavior, understand? Blue eyes, blond hair . . . sure. But if a rapist and a murderer got together and made a baby, and if that baby got raised by good citizens, the kid would be one too, see? You get what you raise, not what you breed."

"But with horses, they always breed the champions. To get better horses."

"Those aren't better *horses*, kid. They're horses better at doing the stuff *people* want them to do, see? If you put those blueblood, inbred nags out on a prairie, they'd be the first ones the wolves would take down."

He sat there for a couple of minutes, playing something around in his head, more alert and focused than I'd ever seen him. "In school, we had that. Genetics. I don't remember much about it. Hell, I don't remember much about any of it."

"You passed all your courses?" I asked him. Shifting gears, setting up to blindside him.

"Sure," he said, with a "Doesn't everybody?" look.

"What are you going to college for?"

"I don't know. My mother says if I learn anything, it will be good. You can always use what you learn, that's what she said."

"But she doesn't care what?"

"I don't think so. She never said."

"What does your mother do now?"

"I'm not exactly sure," the kid said. "Something with international finance—that's why she travels so much."

"She travels alone?"

"I . . . guess so. She never said."

The kid was relaxed, talking. Softened around the edges from all the guidance-counselor questions. I lit a smoke, blew a stream at the ceiling. "Who's Charm?" I asked.

"She's Fancy's sister. Her twin sister, actually, but they don't look alike. She . . ." He gave me a puzzled look. "How do you know about her? Was she here?"

"No. There was a phone call for her. Last night. On this," I said, getting up and bringing the cellular phone back from the closet.

"That's one of Mother's phones," he said, recognizing it.

"One of them?"

"Yeah, she has a whole bunch. She gives them to people who work for her on jobs. So she can reach out for them anytime she wants. They have special batteries and all."

"Does Charm work for your mother?"

"Charm? No. What would she do for her?"

"I don't know. What about Fancy?"

"Her either. I mean, they don't really work, either of them. Charm rides, and Fancy has her plants."

"Rides?"

"Horses. Like in shows. She jumps them too. I think she was supposed to be in the Olympics, but she hurt herself last year."

I opened the cellular phone—there was no number on it. "Do you know the number for this phone?" I asked him.

"Let me see it."

I handed it over. He turned it so he could see the back. "Yeah, this is hers, for sure. See?"

On the back was the number 4, stenciled on in white paint. "She left a list somewhere around here," he said. "Let me think for a minute."

He got up, went into the living room. I could hear him opening drawers in the antique desk, rummaging around. He came back with a piece of paper in his hand, gave it to me. It was a list. Next to number 4 there was a local phone number. "Let's try it," I told the kid, handing the phone to him. I walked over to the wall phone, punched in the number from the list. The cellular phone buzzed. The kid opened it up, said "Hello." I could hear him through the receiver.

"Bingo," I told him. "Do you know where she keeps any of the others?"

"Well, I guess some people have them with them. But maybe there's another one or two around. How come?"

"Well, if we each had one, we could keep in touch while we're working."

"Working?"

"Yeah, Randy, working. You and me."

The kid flashed me a shy smile, as if he liked the idea.

While the kid was getting dressed, I walked out to the mailboxes again. This time, the newspaper was there. I carried it back inside to the kitchen table. Some local rag, a real good-news special. The local Little Theatre was doing *Guys and Dolls*, there was a big dressage event—whatever that was—coming next weekend. Somebody's kid won a scholarship. Another was spending the summer in Europe on a museum tour. Mr. and Mrs. Whoever announced the engagement of their daughter to Somebody's Son. A section of some road was going to be regraded. A bunch of ads for car restorers and restaurants—no personals. Most of the paper was about real estate, some of it with pictures. Not a word about suicide.

The kid came downstairs, wearing jeans and an oversized Rugby shirt. He was holding another one of the cellular phones in his hand.

"I found this upstairs. It's number seven—we can check the list."

"Okay," I told him. "Now here's the deal. The phone rings, you answer it. If it's me, fine. Anyone else, just tell them it's a wrong number. You get an immediate callback, just let it ring. Got it?"

"Got it."

"Okay. Now you said the other suicides were in the paper, right? This paper?" I asked, holding up the one I'd taken from the mailbox.

"No," he laughed. "Fat chance. The Bridgeport papers, I meant."

"They deliver here?"

"No, but we can buy one in town. They sell all the papers there."

We took the Lexus—it was as anonymous there as my Plymouth was in the city. It drove so silky I couldn't tell how smooth the roads were.

"What happened after the first time?" I asked him. "When the first kids died, didn't the town put something together? Counseling, whatever?"

"Yeah, down at the high school. They got everyone together. And they had counselors come in from someplace. You could talk to them if you wanted."

"Did you do that?"

"No, I was out of school by then. I know they had a big meeting, the parents. With a psychologist. He, like, answered their questions and all."

"A psychologist from the school?"

"No, from Crystal Cove. They have a lot of experience with that stuff."

"You go to that one?"

"No, I told you, it was really for the parents."

"Did your mother go?"

"I guess so. She told me it happens a lot, suicide. She said the important thing was, if I had anything I ever wanted to tell her, I could do it. Not to keep secrets, they eat at you."

"You think those kids had secrets?"

"Everybody has secrets," he said.

The paper we bought in town had the girl's name. Her parents' names too. They played it like tragedy, not crime. Apparently they held back the news a couple of days . . . maybe the cops didn't want it released? The paper interviewed this Dr. Jubal Barrymore, from Crystal Cove. Gave a phone number for him, in case anyone wanted to know more about the subject of teen suicide.

"Was this the guy?" I asked the kid, pointing at the doctor's name in the paper.

"I don't remember," he shrugged. But his face was guilty.

"Is the library open in the summer?" I asked the kid.

"Library?"

"The town library . . . I want to see if they have back issues of this paper on file."

"I guess so," he replied.

At least he knew where to find it. We parked and went inside. It was fuller than I expected, mostly women jockeying for position in front of the shelves that held the Seven Day books. The librarian was a woman in her late forties, with graying hair and a prominent nose. She got up as we approached her desk, standing over me by a good four inches.

"Do you keep back issues of the *Bulletin* on file?" I asked her politely.

"We have eighteen months only. We rotate the stock. There's no microfiche. But we do have the *Times* all the way back," she added hopefully.

"It's the *Bulletin* we need," I told her.

"Is there something you're looking for in particular?" she asked.

"It's a research project," I told her. "Real estate."

"Oh, I see." She led us over to the reference room, showed us a few dozen issues suspended on wooden racks. "The rest are in the back. Do you know which dates?"

"We need to go back about seven months," I told her.

"Well, that would be a pretty heavy stack," she said doubtfully.

"I'll carry them out," the kid said.

She flashed him a smile as I nodded approval. They went into the back room as I sat down and started to work.

The kid was a help. He knew the names, cruised through the back issues looking for the suicide stories. It took less than two hours and we had everything the papers had printed. With the parents' names, it was easy enough to get the addresses from the bank of local phone books the library had.

"Did you find what you wanted?" the librarian asked.

"Pretty much," I told her.

"You can just leave the papers on the table," she said. "I'll have one of the—"

"I'll put them back," the kid said, earning another smile.

D riving back, I heard the chirp of a phone. I pulled the cellular out of my pocket. Nothing. The phone sounded again. The kid laughed, reached over and popped the console open, pulling out a car phone.

"Hello?" he said into the receiver. I couldn't hear the person on the other end.

"It's Randy."

. . .

"I just felt like driving her car," he said, an edge to his voice. "What's it to you?"

. . .

"He's around somewhere," the kid said, glancing over at me. "I don't know. How come you—?"

. . .

"Okay, I'll tell him. So long."

He replaced the car phone, looked over at me.

"That was Fancy," he said. "She wanted to know if you were still working . . . being the caretaker."

"How come you didn't tell her I was right here?"

"I don't know. I just thought . . ."

"You thought right," I said.

The kid nodded gravely, a slight flush on his face. Embarrassed that he'd done something right. "She said to tell you to call her."

"Exactly that?"

"Yeah. 'Tell him to call me,' that's what she said."

I didn't say anything. I made the turn onto the road for the house, shoved in the dashboard lighter, fitted a cigarette in my mouth.

"She's a bossy bitch, isn't she?" the kid said.

"Not mine," I told him. *Not my bitch—not my boss either.*

I spread out my notes on the kitchen table, working with what I had. The kid watched me for a few minutes. I expected him to get restless-bored the way they do, but he hung in, quiet.

"You want me to do something?" he finally asked.

"We're looking for a pattern," I told him.

"A pattern?"

"Yeah, stuff all these had in common, you understand?"

"Sure. Like on TV, when they're trying to catch a killer."

"I don't know if we got a killer here, kid. But one thing's for sure— we got enough bodies."

He got to his feet, rubbing his head with both hands. "You want some food?" he asked.

"Sure. Whatever you're having."

He went into the living room to use the phone. I kept my head down, concentrating.

The back doorbell startled me. Randy opened it up, signed something the deliveryman gave him. He opened a couple of paper bags, started assembling stuff on plates.

"I figured you might like Chinese," he said. "I mean . . . that restaurant in the city and all."

"Sure," I told him. "You didn't give the guy any money. How come?"

"My mother has an account with them. With a few others too. It makes it easier. She says I really won't need cash while she's gone."

"Un huh."

The food was hot. And limp. The soup was thin. The rice clumped, the vegetables sagged. The pork was undercooked. "You like this?" I asked him.

"Yeah, it's great. They don't use any MSG either."

"You need to try some of Mama's cooking someday," I told him.

"What's the difference?"

"Same as between Debbie Gibson and Judy Henske."

"Which is the Debbie Gibson?"

"This stuff."

"Oh." He took a deep mouthful of the food, chewed it experimentally. "So who's Judy Henske?" he asked.

It was getting dark by the time I was done playing with the charts I had made.

"You going anyplace tonight?" I asked him.

"Not really. I was just gonna . . . hang out, you know?"

"Yeah. Okay, I'll see you in the morning."

"Are you gonna do something?"

"Yeah. Take a look around."

"Can I . . . ?"

"I'll be back before you," I told him. "And I'll sleep here again tonight, you want me to."

"No, I didn't mean that. I just meant . . . maybe you want me to come along."

"I'll meet you in the garage at ten," I told him. "Wear some dark clothes."

He was there on the dot. Dressed in black pants, black hightops and a black satin Raiders jacket with silver sleeves.

"You have any fluorescent paint around?" I asked him.

"I don't think so. Why?"

"I was worried maybe that outfit wouldn't stand out enough," I told him, pointing at the jacket sleeves.

He nodded his head, turned around and went back to the house. If he was sulking, I couldn't see it. Good. He was back in a minute, this time wearing a heavy black sweatshirt with a hood.

"It was all I could find. Okay?" he asked.

"Perfect," I said.

He started for the Lexus. I held up my hand. "We'll take this one," I told him, pointing toward my Plymouth.

He gave me a dubious look, but climbed in without another word. I turned the engine over. The kid gave me a look. "That doesn't sound stock."

I pulled out of the garage, turned onto the main road. "You know where the bridge is? The one that girl jumped off of?"

"Sure. Take the next left."

The Plymouth tracked flat around the curve, its independent rear suspension communicating to the wide tires. I fed it some throttle coming out of the turn, swooped past a white Cadillac and slipped back into the right lane.

"All right!" the kid said, so softly it was almost to himself.

I gave him a sideways glance. "You like cars?"

"I *love* them. For my eighteenth birthday, Mom let me go to racing school. It was great. They had Formula Fords and everything. That's why I got the Miata—that was one of the cars they used in the school."

"You want to race?"

"Oh yeah! More than anything."

"You gonna do it?"

"Well, not *professionally*. I mean . . . my mother says I could race on weekends, maybe. Like a hobby. Some of the guys here do it. Like rallyes and gymkhanas and stuff. But that's not real racing."

"You any good?"

"I . . . think so. It *feels* good, you know? I can't really explain it."

"Am I going the right way?"

"Yeah. You turn at the crossing . . . I'll show you where it is."

I followed the kid's directions, slowing down when we got close. The bridge was really a concrete overpass between two pieces of rock. It looked like the gap had been hacked out a hundred years ago. No water underneath. No road either, just dark stone. We parked the Plymouth, got out and walked over.

The barrier was stone too. It looked old, weathered, with big pieces chipped away. The railing had a bubble in it, where you could stand and look down—maybe it was scenic in the daytime. The railing was waist-high—you couldn't just fall over, it would take a real commitment.

A car swept by behind us. Not even eleven at night and it was pretty deserted. The paper said the girl went over sometime after two in the morning.

I took out my pencil flash, flicked it over the stone barrier. Nothing. The top of the barrier was flat. It was so clean it looked scrubbed. No graffiti, no chiseled hearts. I bellied up to it, looked down.

Into the Zero.

"**Y**ou okay?" It was the kid's voice.

I turned around. "Sure. Why?"

"You were . . . standing there so long. I thought you were . . ."

"What? Gonna jump?"

"No! I didn't mean that."

"I'm okay. I was just trying to feel it."

"Feel it?"

"What she felt."

The kid nodded like he understood. But his hands were shaking. I lit a cigarette. Smoked it through. Snapped the red tip into the Zero.

"You want to drive?" I asked him.

He started tentatively, getting the feel of the controls—the way you're supposed to. He gave it too much gas coming out and the Plymouth got sideways on the dirt. The kid didn't panic, just turned the wheel in the direction of the skid and powered right out.

"Wow! This bad boy's got some juice!"

"All right, don't get us arrested now."

"I'm okay," the kid said, leaning into a curve. "Where do we go now?"

"We're done for tonight," I told him. "Just head on back."

The Plymouth reached the main road. The kid gave it the gun, the torque jamming him back against the seat. He adjusted his posture, a grin slashing across his face.

"Okay if I take the long way?" he asked.

I nodded. The kid pulled off the highway, found a twisting piece of two-lane blacktop. He kicked on the high beams, drew a breath when he saw they were hot enough to remove paint.

"Can you downshift it?" he asked.

"Stomp the pedal and it drops down. Or you can flick the lever one stop to the right. But watch it, the rear end gets loose easy."

"This is great! How'd you get a car like this?"

"It was supposed to be the prototype for a super-taxi," I told him. "Got an over-cored radiator, oil and tranny coolers, steel-braided lines. It won't overheat even if it sits in traffic for an hour. It weighs almost five thousand pounds—the bumpers will stop a rhino."

"Yeah, but underneath . . . I mean, the way it grips and all."

"There's no beam axle back there, Randy. It's an IRS, understand?"

"Sure. And big tires. But that wouldn't make it grab the way it does. I'll bet this is what a NASCAR stocker feels like."

"I never drove one."

"Me neither—they don't have those kind of races around here. But I've seen them on ESPN."

"You like that kind of racing too?"

"*Any* kind," the kid said.

He had the Plymouth wailing by then, flitting over the surface of the blacktop. We might as well have been in the West Virginia mountains with a trunk full of white lightning. I reached into the glove compartment, popped a cassette into the slot, turned it on. "Dark Angel" throbbed through the speakers, darker than the night outside, with more hormones than the monster engine.

"Jesus!" the kid yelled. "What's that?"

"*That's* Judy Henske, kid."

He gunned the Plymouth around a long sweeper leading back to the highway, a huge grin plastered across his face, Henske's sex-barbed blues driving right along with him.

"I gotta try some of that Chinese food," he said.

T he kid parked the Plymouth expertly. It's a gift, driving like that— he already handled the big car better than I did.

"You want me to—?"

"No, that's okay," he said. "I'll be all right over there. I'll just leave the intercom open, okay?"

"Sure."

Upstairs, I called Mama's. She told me it was all quiet, nothing happening.

"You want Max?" she asked.

"No. Not now, anyway."

"Okay."

I lay back on the couch, closed my eyes. I'd told the kid about the car, but not where it came from. A young man gave his life for that car, a long time ago. Spent every minute of his time, every dollar he could lay his hands on—it was his dream. He hired me to find out if his wife was stepping out—he knew something was wrong between them, just didn't know what it was. It was an easy job—the wife copped to it right away. She was stepping out all right. With another woman. Told me all her husband cared about was that damn car—she needed dreams of her own.

I didn't tell the guy the truth. He was a young guy, maybe a year or two older than Randy. I figured he might do something stupid.

It was me who did something stupid. His wife told him the truth, even told him she'd told me. He got hot about it. Told me he wasn't going to pay me for my work. I walked away.

Next time I saw him, he was in the Tombs. Killed his wife. He didn't want to hire me—he just didn't want his bloodsucking lawyer to get his car. Told me he understood why I did it—because I thought it was the right thing. That's why he did what he did, too.

But he knew it wasn't.

I told him he could do the time. It'd probably get busted down to manslaughter—it wouldn't be so bad. He didn't want to hear it. He signed the Plymouth over to me, said goodbye. They had a suicide watch on him, but it didn't do any good. He went into the Zero.

That bridge where the girl had gone over . . . I could feel the pull.

When I came downstairs the next morning, I saw the kid sitting on the back step to the big house.

"Want some breakfast?" he asked. Looked like he'd been up for a while—his eyes were fresh and bright, hair combed.

"Sure," I told him. "You gonna cook it?"

He gave me a funny look. Opened the door and stepped inside. He showed me a few different kinds of cold cereal. "They delivered milk," he said. "And I could make toast. There's orange juice too, okay?"

"Great."

"What are we gonna do today?"

"I think I need to talk to some parents. Of the kids who died. I got the addresses, figured I'd start around ten."

"It's only eight now."

"So?"

"So . . . I was wondering . . . do you think I could take a look at the car? In daylight?"

"Let me just finish this first," I told him, nodding at my breakfast.

"Take your time," the kid said, bouncing with impatience.

I opened the garage doors. The kid backed the Plymouth out onto the bluestone. Then he made a slow circle of the car, as respectfully as a child approaching an unknown dog he'd like to pat. He crouched low to the ground next to the rear tires, running his hands over the tread. He got up, went into the garage, came back with a canvas tarp. He laid that on the ground, slid himself under the car. I smoked through two cigarettes by the time he came up for air.

"I wish we had a lift," he said. "I asked my mother about it—we got plenty of room. But she said she didn't want a mess."

"Couldn't you rent one someplace else?"

"Yeah!" he said, as if the idea had never occurred to him before. "Could we open the hood?"

"It doesn't open," I told him, sliding behind the wheel. I threw the switch from under the dash, opened the hinges on each side of the car, and swiveled the whole front end forward, exposing everything from radiator to firewall.

"Oh man!" the kid said. "I knew a guy who had a setup like this. With an old Spitfire. But I never saw it on a big car."

"I gotta make some phone calls," I told him, starting for the steps.

He didn't answer, lost in the engine bay, muttering something to himself.

I slid a cassette into the stereo, adjusted the volume down low, let the music flow over me as I did a final run-through, trying to match the addresses I had with the street map I'd bought in the city—I didn't want to have to bring the kid with me when I went calling on the dead girl's parents, but I didn't want to drive around their neighborhood and call attention to myself either.

Seven kids by now.

I needed a cover story too. I'd have to ask the kid if his mother's name was known around there.

The door opened. Fancy. In her white tennis outfit. She walked over to the couch, sat down, crossing her legs, displaying a round thigh all the way up to her hip.

"I see you have Randy working," she said. "I asked him if he wanted to play, but he said he was doing something with you."

"Maybe some other time," I told her.

"He used to be such a nice boy."

"You mean he used to do what you told him?"

"Yes. That makes a nice boy. A nice man too."

"You already figured out that I don't qualify, right? So what can I do for you?"

"You didn't . . ." she started to say, just as Randy walked in.

"Burke, where's the battery? I could see the lines, but they just go back. Is it under the back seat?"

"In the trunk," I told him. "Next to the fuel cell."

"You got one of those too? Listen, I got this dynamite idea, okay? Now don't say no before I—"

"We were *talking*," Fancy told him, throwing a hard look his way.

"*You* were talking," I told her.

The kid chuckled. Two bright red dots popped out on her cheeks, dark under the tan. "Yes, master," she purred, her voice thick with sarcasm.

I lit a smoke. The kid shifted his feet awkwardly.

"What's that song?" Fancy asked, cocking her head toward the stereo.

"Judy Henske, right?" the kid piped up. He was on the money. Her fire-throated version of Champion Jack Dupree's ground-zero blues, "My Real Combination for Love." I held up an open palm. The kid slapped it in acknowledgment, a delighted grin on his face.

"You're quite the expert," Fancy said.

The kid ignored her. "Burke, what I was gonna ask you—"

I shook my head. He got it, dropped whatever he wanted. Fancy got it too. "I need to talk to your 'caretaker' for a minute, Randy. How about if you go back downstairs, play with your cars?"

I nodded an okay at the kid. He took off without another word.

"What?" I asked her. "I don't play tennis."

"You don't play much of anything, do you?"

"No."

She stood up quickly. "I could *help* you," she said softly, turning her back to me, leaning her elbows on the top of the couch. "You don't want some of this," she purred, flipping up the short white skirt to flash a pair of red panties. "You'll want some of that." She turned around, facing me, hands on hips. "I know this place. Randy doesn't. You have questions, a man like you. Come over tonight. To my place. And I'll answer them."

I held her eyes, watching for the game.

"What time?" I asked her.

She told me midnight, gave me the address.

I stood next to the kid, watching Fancy's sleek black car whip out of the driveway.

"That's a costly ride," I said. "What's she do for a living?"

"Do? Nothing, I don't think. I told you—she just plays around with her plants and all. Her folks were rich, probably left her a bundle," he shrugged. Like it was an everyday thing.

"Okay," I told him. "Here's what I need you to do. I'm going to pay a call on that girl's parents. The Blankenships. Maybe they know something, maybe they don't—it's worth a quick look. I'm going to take the Lexus. I want you to lead the way, in the other car, see? Once I go in, you take off. Head back here . . . the guy may call to check on me. What I'm gonna tell him, I'm working for your mother, okay? She hired me to look into the suicides 'cause she has a kid of her own that knew them, see? They call, that's the story you tell. When I come out, I'll call you, arrange a place to meet. Got it?"

"Sure."

"Okay. I'm going upstairs to change. Be down in fifteen, twenty minutes."

He threw me a half-salute. Then he went back to mooning over the Plymouth.

I shaved carefully. Put on the gray business suit with the chalk stripe. White shirt, wine-colored silk tie. A black leather attaché case and I was in business. I checked through my stock of ID's, found the business cards that listed me as a private investigator, complete with telephone and fax numbers. I knew a lawyer who let me front him off in exchange for some favors. One of his phone numbers was a dead line—his secretary would answer any calls and cover for me no matter who was asking.

I walked downstairs, ready to ride. The kid looked me over.

"How do I look?" I asked.

"Like a cop. A mean cop."

"Close enough. You ready to ride?"

"Sure. Uh . . ."

"What?"

"Could I . . . take the Plymouth?"

"Drive carefully," I told him, handing him the registration papers.

"Juan Rodriguez?" he asked, looking at them.

"A close personal friend of mine," I told him.

The Blankenship house was small, almost a bungalow, but set well back from the road on a big piece of ground. The curtains were drawn in front—no signs of life. A blue Saturn station wagon sat in the driveway—the garage door was closed.

I pulled into the driveway as the Plymouth moved away ahead of me, the kid driving sedately while I had him in my sights.

The house was white shingle with a gray slate roof. The front door was painted a dark shade of red. I tapped gently with the iron knocker. I was just about to try again when the door opened. The man standing there was about my age, shorter than me, slim-built. His light brown hair was cut short, receding at the temples. He was wearing a white shirt with a button-down collar over a pair of chinos. One of the buttons on the collar was undone. He wasn't wearing a belt. And he'd missed a few spots when he shaved that morning.

"What is it?"

"Mr. Blankenship?"

"Yes. What is it? Are you from the police?"

"No sir. I'm a private investigator. Could I come in and talk to you for a few minutes?"

He stepped back, but not far enough—I had to brush against him as I walked by. The living room was trashed: overflowing ashtrays, containers of take-out food, a raincoat thrown carelessly over the back of a chair. It looked like it hadn't been cleaned in a month. I sat on the green cloth couch, facing a brown Naugahyde easy chair, figuring the chair for his. I reached in my coat pocket, took out a small notebook and a felt-tip pen, looked up with an expectant expression on my face. He was still standing, hands clasped behind him, watching.

"A private investigator? Who hired you . . . one of the other kids' parents?"

"Yes sir. Mrs. Lorna Cambridge."

"Cambridge? That wasn't one of the names."

"No sir. Her son Randall went to school with some of the kids. He's the same age. She was concerned . . . frightened, really. And she thought I might be able to look around, maybe be of some help."

"What could you do?"

"I don't know, to be honest with you. It's a mystery. There doesn't seem to be any reason . . ."

"There's got to be a reason," he said, sitting down in the brown chair. "There's got to be."

"Yes sir. Could you tell me, was there anything in your daughter's behavior that might have led you to suspect . . ."

"You mean like drugs?"

"That. Or alcohol. Problems in school. With a boyfriend. A pregnancy. Anything."

"Diandra had problems. All kids that age have problems, right?"

I nodded, waiting.

"Her mother and I, we used to get into it about her grades. And she had a smart mouth . . . at least to her mother." He fumbled in a shirt pocket, came up empty. He felt around with his right hand, located a pack of cigarettes. He put one in his mouth, lit it with an old brushed aluminum Zippo. "I haven't smoked in fifteen years," he said ruefully. "Before this happened . . ."

"She fought with her mother?"

"Not fights, exactly. Arguments, more like. Her grades were slipping, she broke curfew a few times. And they'd go round and round about the clothes she wore."

"Did she have one of those arguments just before . . . ?"

"No. It wouldn't have been possible. My wife hasn't lived here for months. We separated just after Christmas. She kept after me to send Diandra for counseling, but Diandra didn't want to go. She was screwing up, I admit that. Flunking a couple of subjects. Stayed out all night once. I figured . . . kids. This neighborhood and all. It's a pretty fast crowd. We don't have the kind of money some of her friends' parents do . . . maybe she was trying to keep up, you know?"

"Yes sir."

He dragged on his cigarette, not tasting it. "Anyway, my wife was hot to send her to this hospital they have for kids with problems. Crystal Cove. Diandra didn't want to go. And I wasn't crazy about it either.

But my little girl was really going over the line. I was worried about her too. We met with the director there. Dr. Barrymore. He's a pretty young guy, but I got to admit, he made a lot of sense. Said Diandra needed a time-out period. To decompress, get away from the pressure. So, we finally sent her. The insurance on my job covered most of it. Diandra was dead against it, but the people at Crystal Cove told us that was normal. They said they have lawyers—they could get her civilly committed if she didn't volunteer."

"I see."

"So she went. Last fall. It was supposed to be for only six weeks, but they kept her longer. They said she had deep-seated problems, maybe clinical depression, maybe a chemical imbalance—they wanted to run more tests." He ground out his cigarette without looking, eyes down now.

"She came home for Christmas. She didn't want to go back. The hospital said to expect that. I didn't want to send her. After she went back, I was real down. My wife and I fought all the time about it. She always said Diandra was my girl, not hers. We were . . . close, her and me. Anyway, that's when my wife left."

"When did Diandra come home?"

"Valentine's Day. That's how I remember it. I bought her a giant teddy bear, a white one with a red ribbon around its neck. She loved it. Put it right on her bed . . ." His control cracked then—he wiped hard at his eyes, but the tears still came. I lit a smoke, kept my eyes down. I was almost down to the filter before he got it managed.

His eyes came up to mine, red-rimmed but hard. They didn't spare me—his voice didn't spare himself. "Things were going so great," he said. "She was doing good in school again, not running around. I have to work. Long hours, sometimes. Diandra used to say she was a latch-key kid, like a joke between us. She got much more responsible after my wife left . . . did her share of the housework and everything. And she didn't go *near* drugs, I know that. When I'm wrong, I cop to it. I called my wife, told her that Crystal Cove had saved our daughter. She'd been right. I thought . . . maybe she'd come home. But she said it really wasn't Diandra that broke us up—it'd been coming a long time, hiding under the surface. She stuck with me through everything before, but . . ."

"Diandra was doing fine just before she—"

"Yeah! She *was*, goddamn it."

"I'm not doubting you, sir. I know she didn't leave a note . . . ?" making it a question.

"No," he said, watching me now.

"But maybe she . . . I don't know, kept a diary or something. The way girls do. Have you . . . ?"

"I tore this place apart," Blankenship said. "The police opened her locker at school too. There was nothing. Even when she was . . . messed up before, she wasn't suicidal."

"I understand," I told him soothingly. "But sometimes, when a loved one searches, they let certain . . . emotions get in the way. Do you think I could . . . ?"

His face came up again, a different focus in his eyes. "Who did you say retained you again?"

"Mrs. Cambridge, sir."

"Right. You wouldn't mind if I called her myself, just to be sure?"

"No sir."

He got up, walked over to a small table near the TV, picked up the phone. "What's the number?" he asked.

"Sir, I don't mean to sound like a wiseguy or anything, but anybody could give you a phone number, have somebody standing by in a pay phone, you understand? Perhaps you'd feel better if you checked the number in the local phone book?"

His eyes were even more sharply focused, watching me without a flicker. "What'd you say your name was?"

"It's Burke," I told him.

He punched some buttons, got information, asked for the Cambridge residence phone. Hung up, dialed again.

"Could I speak to Mrs. Cambridge, please?"

. . .

"I see. When will she be back?"

. . .

"Okay, well, maybe you can help me, Randy. Do you know anything about your mother hiring a private investigator? Name of Burke?"

. . .

"Thank you. That's very helpful. Yes. Thank you, we're doing the best we can under the circumstances. And please tell your mother . . . tell her thanks for what she's doing, all right? Goodbye."

He hung up the phone. Walked back to his brown chair, lit another smoke.

"You ever do any soldiering, Mr. Burke?"

I rapid-processed the various stories I could tell, but none of them fit just right. Something about the way the man looked at me said he wasn't going to take no for an answer.

"Not for the U.S.," I said.

He raised an eyebrow as a question, waited for my answer.

"It was a long time ago," I told him. "In Africa."

"The Congo?"

"No. Biafra."

"You were a mercenary?"

"A freedom fighter," I told him, not even a hint of a smile on my face.

He dragged deep on his cigarette. "You have rank over there?" he asked.

"No sir."

"Get paid good?"

"Not like the pilots did."

"Yeah. I could tell. I can always tell a man that's been a working solider."

"How can you do that?"

"You relax inside the fire. It goes around you, and you know there's not a whole hell of a lot you can do about it. You know your real job is getting out alive. There's no rules."

"You did that?"

"In the Nam. Surprised?"

"No," I told him truthfully. "Infantry?"

"That's right," he said, nodding his head. "A ground grunt. I was just a green kid, but I saw a lot of working pros. Especially when we went over the border. I've seen the look before."

"You can see it in prison too," I said, not even thinking about why I was breaking the rules . . . telling a source the truth.

"You've been there?"

"Yes."

"And now you work as a private eye?"

"Yes sir."

He took a deep breath, hands clasped in his lap. "Her room's in the back. Look around all you want. You can't miss it—there's a big teddy bear on the bed."

I went over the room with a microscope. No diary, no address book . . . maybe the cops had them. I checked inside Diandra's clock radio, slit open a tube of toothpaste, opened every book, even checked the teddy bear for seams.

When I came back out, he was still sitting there.

"I didn't find anything," I told him.

"I know. But this isn't the only place you're going to look, is it?"

"No sir."

"If you find anything, you'll tell me?"

"I will."

He got to his feet, moving slowly like there was a piece of broken glass inside his gut. His handshake was way too powerful for his slender frame, pulling me close. "You think something happened to her, don't you?" he whispered.

"I don't know."

"I still know how to do things," he said in the same whispery tone. "You find out anything, I'll be here."

In the Lexus, I raised the kid on the car phone.

"Hello," he said.

"It's me. I'm on my way back."

"He called. Did I . . . ?"

"Not on this phone," I told him.

As I turned into the bluestone drive, I spotted the kid. He had a green garden hose in one hand, a big clump of sponge in the other. The Plymouth was shining in the afternoon sun, as close to its original dull gray color as it ever got. I parked the Lexus, got out and walked over to him.

"What's going on?" I asked, pointing at the Plymouth.

"I just thought I'd clean her up a bit. Man! When was the last time you washed her?"

"I generally *don't* wash it. The idea is to blend in, not call attention to yourself. This is a working car, kid, not a showpiece."

"Oh. Hey, I'm sorry. I was just trying to . . . I don't know."

"I know. You were trying to show respect, right?"

His chin came up, a bit of strength edged into his voice. "That's right, I was."

"Good," I told him. "Doesn't matter around here anyway . . . no way this beast is gonna blend in."

"I know. It's . . . cool. I mean, she doesn't look like much of anything, but . . ."

"There's people like that too," I said. "You don't know what's under the hood until you hit the gas, right?"

He nodded, not sure who I was talking about—never thinking it could be him. "That guy called," he said. "Like I told you."

"Blankenship? Yeah, I was in the room when he did."

"I told him my mother had hired you, before she went to Europe. I said she'd be back soon—she hired you because she was concerned that maybe the police weren't doing everything they could."

"You did good," I told him. "But, listen, remember when I told you not to talk on the cellular phone?"

"I was on the regular line."

"But I wasn't. Anyone can listen in to those calls. Some geeks do it with scanners—they got nothing else to do with their lives, so they stick their nose into other people's. Used to be CB's they listened to, now it's these cellular phones. So when we use them, we keep it short, right? No names, no information. Got it?"

He nodded gravely.

"I'm going upstairs to change. And I'm going to work again tonight. When I come down, we'll get some dinner, okay?"

"Okay. Uh, Burke . . . ?"

"What?"

"What kind of oil do you run in her?"

"The synthetic stuff—you don't have to change it so often."

"Yeah. Is that a dry sump underneath?"

"That's right," I said, looking at him in surprise.

"I read about them all the time, cars," he said, a grin on his flushed face. "I wished they had auto mechanics in school, but they don't. But

I sent away for books. I do all the work on the Miata myself. I thought maybe I'd change the oil and filters, put in some new plugs . . ."

"It's running fine, Randy."

"I know, but . . ."

"What the hell," I told him. "It could always run better."

He took off like a kid with a puppy.

"What is this stuff?" I asked him, spearing a bite-size chunk of white meat off my plate.

"It's coq au vin. Like chicken with sauce on it. There's a French restaurant in town. They deliver too. I thought maybe you'd rather have something like a real meal."

"It's good," I said. "That was thoughtful of you."

The kid ducked his head again. We ate in silence for a bit, part of my brain still working over what Blankenship had told me.

"You know what a gymkhana is?" the kid asked.

"Where they race around in a parking lot?"

"Well, sort of. A real one, it's like a slalom, only flat. They set up pylons for the course, and you run through it for time. If you hit a pylon, they add time to your score, see? It's tricky. Not like real racing. I mean, they only let one car at a time go through. But it's slick. All kinds of cars do it, 'Vettes, Ferraris, one guy even has a Lola he brings."

"What do you get if you win?"

"Trophies. I mean, it's not for money or anything. But it's real serious—the drivers really go at it."

"You ever do it?"

"Sure. In the Miata, once. It was . . . okay. I mean, all the kids go there just to hang out."

"Do they bet on the races?"

"Bet? Gee, I don't know. I mean, we don't. But maybe the older guys do . . . we don't mix with them much."

"Did any of the kids who killed themselves race there?"

"No. At least I don't think so. I mean, that's not why I asked about it. I was thinking . . . maybe . . . if you wouldn't mind . . ."

"What?"

"Could I run the Plymouth in one? There's one next Sunday. I never saw a big American sedan run one—it would be boss, you know?"

"Can you get hurt doing it?"

"Nah. You could spin out, that's the worst. They make you wear a helmet, that's all."

"You really want to do it?"

"Yeah! *Big*-time. It would be—"

"Okay."

"You mean it?"

"Sure."

"Great! We could drive over early, get in a couple of practice laps, then we could—"

"Hold up, kid. What's this 'we' stuff?"

"I just thought . . . seeing how it's your car and all, you'd want to . . ."

I watched his face, seeing how different it looked from when I first met him. Thinking about why kids kill themselves. "Good idea," I said. "Let's do it."

"**G**ardens," Mama answered the phone like always.

"It's me. You hear anything from Michelle?"

"Yes. She say, take Mole longer to read what you show him."

"Longer than what?"

"I don't know. You ask, okay?"

"Okay. Anything else going on?"

"Very quiet. You?"

"I'm not sure."

"Very pretty stones," Mama said. "Look careful."

I learned to sleep in chunks a long time ago. Grab it when you can. I know that REM is the true deep sleep, the only kind that restores you. That's where you dream. I don't remember most of my dreams—it's one of the few things in my life I'm grateful for.

It was after eleven when I came around. I took a shower, thought about shaving again, decided the hell with it. I listened to some music while I was getting dressed in the outfit Michelle bought for me. The broken blank eye of the television stared at me—I guess I really only watch it with Pansy—she loves it.

I held my pistol in my hand, turning it over like it would tell me something. I couldn't leave it in the Plymouth with the kid driving it around, and there was no good place in the Lexus to stash it either. Finally, I just wiped it down, wrapped it in a sheet of heavy plastic and put it inside the toilet tank. It wasn't a world-class stash, but even if someone turned it up, it wouldn't connect to me. The piece was ice-cold—came right off the assembly line at the factory, never went through a dealer's hands. The serial number would never have been registered. I got it from Jacques, Clarence's old boss. Specialty of the house, guaranteed not to alert any law enforcement computer. If they found it, they'd have a hell of a time proving it didn't belong to whoever stayed here before me.

Fancy's house was in the same neighborhood as Cherry's, that's what she said, anyway. The same neighborhood turned out to be about five miles away—people measure differently out here. I found it easy enough: a big modernistic spread, all redwood and glass in front. It was midnight plus two when I pulled into the long drive. I angled the Lexus toward a long, wide building that looked like a six-car garage . . . where she'd told me to park. The doors were closed. I opened the car door and stepped out, getting my bearings.

"You're late," a voice said from the darkness. Fancy. In a pale blue T-shirt that draped to mid-thigh, standing barefoot a few feet away. She stepped forward, no real expression on her face.

"Come with me," she said, turning to walk away.

I followed her along a slate path around the back of the garage, past an Olympic-size swimming pool glowing a muted gold from underwater lights. The big house was to our left, but Fancy moved in the opposite direction, past a low structure that looked to be all glass.

"Is that a greenhouse?" I asked her.

"No, that's the pool house. Where people change into their bathing suits before they swim."

"It looks too big for just that."

She made a face over her shoulder, kept walking. One more turn and we were facing three little houses standing in a triangle maybe a hundred feet along each line. Two were dark; one had a soft orange light glowing next to the door. As we walked closer, I could see it was some kind of Japanese paper lantern over a bulb.

Fancy opened that door, stepped inside. "Over there," she said, pointing to a long white leather couch.

I sat down. Fancy went to the far corner of the room, did something with her hand, and a small cone of light hit the dark carpet. I could see it was a long black floor lamp with a gooseneck top bent toward the floor. Fancy stood watching the light for a second, hands on hips. Satisfied, she turned and came over to the couch. She sat, then curled her legs under her, turning so she was facing me.

"Could we start over?" she asked.

"Why?"

"You liked me when you first saw me. You did, didn't you?"

"Yeah, I did."

"How come?"

"I liked your look."

"My face? My body? What?"

"Not your looks. Your *look*. Understand?"

"No. Tell me. Please tell me," she hastily amended, like she'd made a fatal slip.

"You looked like a . . . merry girl. Bouncy. Sweet. A true-hearted girl."

"And I . . . showed you how I play. So you don't like me anymore?"

"I don't care how you play. I just don't have people playing with me."

"Are you scared?"

"Of what?"

"That you'd like it."

"I like a lot of things—the only things that scare me are the ones I need."

"And you don't need much?"

"I've had a lot of practice."

"Because you were poor?"

"I was born broke," I told her. That's the best way to lie to strangers—tell them the true truth.

She got up, walked over to a big-screen TV facing the couch. She bent over at the waist, cued a VCR, ran her finger down a stack of cassettes. When she found the one she wanted, she shoved it into the slot. Then she plucked a remote from the top of the TV set, came back over to the couch holding it in her hand.

"You want a cigarette?" she asked.

"Sure," I said, waiting.

"I don't have any," she said. "I just meant it was okay to smoke here. That's an ashtray," pointing to a flat silver dish on the top of a black lacquered coffee table.

I took the pack from my jacket pocket, shook one out, put it in my mouth. I opened the little box of wooden matches, the one with the name of the nightclub in Chicago I'd never been to. I leave them places, throw trackers off the scent. She put her hand on mine, said "Let me do it." I handed her the matches. She pulled the cigarette from my mouth, put it between her lips, struck the match. When she got it going, she handed it to me.

"Thanks."

"You didn't say anything about the taste this time," she said, soft-voiced. "I really liked it when you did that. Flirting. It's sweet fun. People don't do it much anymore. What you said . . . that was a line, right?"

"No. I never said that before in my life. It just happened."

"I bet."

"*Don't* bet. You haven't learned to tell the truth when you hear it by now, all you'll ever be able to do is play—you'll never be for real."

"I'm sorry," she said, dropping her eyes. "Did you mean the other stuff, what you said before? About me looking like a merry girl?"

"Yes."

She shifted her body so she was facing the TV set. "I don't just play—I work too," she said. "Watch."

She hit the remote. Chamber music came from the speakers. The screen background was a neon blue. Black letters popped up: A LESSON FOR MELISSA. Credits rolled over the music. CANE PRODUCTIONS, trick lettering—the "P" in "PRODUCTIONS" formed a stylized cane. Some other stuff. The camera dissolved to . . . Fancy. In a high-necked, long-sleeved, dark velvet dress with a gathering of white lace at the throat, tight bodice, full skirt. She was seated on a flat bench, both hands in her lap. "Get in here, young lady!" her voice cracked out from the speakers.

"Yes, mistress," said the woman walking on screen. A young woman, medium-height and slender, with long straight hair. She was wearing a schoolgirl outfit—dark plaid jumper over a white blouse, long white socks almost to her knees, flat-heeled shoes with Mary Jane straps.

"It's a standard script," Fancy said, pushing a button on the remote. MUTE appeared in yellow letters at the bottom of the screen.

There was some exchange of conversation between the two women, then the slender girl lay across Fancy's lap. Fancy pulled up the other girl's skirt and spanked her for a long time, occasionally stopping to say something. The camera shifted, zooming in from screen left to display the other woman's underpants. Back to a closeup of the woman's face, contorted in mock pain. Pulling away to a long shot: Fancy pulling down the other woman's panties, now smacking her with a hairbrush. The cameras danced around the show—at least three of them, an expensive setup.

The scene seemed to go on and on, with the slender woman turning her head once in a while to say something. The camera lensed lovingly over her bottom, now a bright red. Finally, in response to something Fancy said, the woman slid off Fancy's lap, Fancy hooking a thumb into the panties so they slid off the other girl's legs as she stood up. Fancy pointed screen right. The other girl walked off. The closing shot was of the other girl, standing in a corner, her face to the wall.

There were no actors' credits at the end. Just the Cane Productions sign and a P.O. box in Atlanta where you could order a catalog.

Fancy hit the remote and the screen went dark.

"That's me," she said.

I lit another smoke, waiting for the punch line. Fancy got up, rewound the cassette, popped it out of the VCR and put it back into a plain case. The case went into an open spot on the bookshelf. She came back over to the couch, sat down again.

"What do you know about me now?" she asked.

"I know you're a pro domina," I said. *And a blackmailer—where were the cameras hidden in the little house?*

"That's right. You think it's so bad?"

"Bad how?"

"Bad like . . . sick, okay?"

"It's a fetish," I told her. "There's lots of them. They're bad if they hurt you inside—if you hate yourself every time you do it. Or if they get in the way of what you have to do. Or if you use force to make someone do it with you. Otherwise, what's the difference? Some people get pumped up by high-heeled shoes, some like to dress up like cowboys. If you have to pay for it, it just costs more, that's all." *What a risk to be so needy. If you have a special way you need to play, how do you meet others like you? Coded ads in the personals columns? Advertise in the freak sheets? How could you ever trust them with your secrets?*

"You know about it?"

"Not a lot."

"It's a great business. Completely legal too. It's not just the videos—we have still photos, audiotapes, even custom stories."

"Stories?"

"Yes, a customer can set up a scenario, and we have people who will write them a special story. Just for them. Even put their name in it if they want. It's all on computer, in different fields. We can give the customer any setting he wants: schoolmaster, girls' dorm, sorority house, husband-wife, daddy-daughter . . . anything. And we have standard ones too, not custom. Like pamphlets."

"What does it cost?"

"It varies. The videos are forty-five dollars, the pamphlets are five. The custom stuff costs the most."

"Yeah. Always does. Special costs more than straight on the street too."

"I'm not a whore," she snapped. "And I'm not a degenerate. I don't slam dope, I don't booze, and I didn't get this shape from snarfing sweets. Don't you *dare* look down at me."

"I'm not, I—"

"Just listen," she interrupted. "I'm an actress. A role-player. I'm like a therapist too, for some of them. It relieves tension . . . like a massage. The girl-on-girl stuff is the most popular. Everybody in the scene says I'm a star."

"Whatever you say." *There's plenty of honest whores — whores who don't take your picture with hidden cameras.*

"It's true. It's a business. A good business."

"Most of your customers are men?"

"For the live scenes, sure. But we get women too. Couples, even. And we have plenty of women buyers for the videos. Some mostly buy . . . kid stuff."

I turned my head so I was looking deep into her eyes. She held my stare for a minute, then she nipped at the palm of her hand, just below the thumb, and cast her eyes down. "Audio and custom," she said. "That's mostly what they want. There's a woman in Iowa, she advertises in all the magazines. You want to see?"

I didn't react. Why would I want to see? This was coming too quick, secrets piled on secrets. When that happens, there's always a trade lurking close.

She got to her feet, walked out of the room. She was back in a minute, holding a slick-paper magazine with a black&white photo of a woman bending over on the cover—there was another person in the photo, but all you could see was the paddle in their hand. I stood up, joined her under the light. She thumbed through rapidly, looking for the ad. It was marked with a red ink star, hand-drawn. I held it close to read the small type:

> Proverbs 13:24 (!)
> Next time your kid has a good one coming, make a
> full-size cassette of the chastisement and send it to
> me. I pay $50 for fifteen minutes, more for longer.
> Good sound quality a must. I travel frequently, with
> my own equipment. Write to make arrangements.

Only a P.O. box was listed, no name. A new kind of kiddie porn, legal too—I'd never heard of it before. Freaks carefully recording their own children getting whipped. To entertain other maggots. For money. I felt ice-picks of fire in my chest.

"Why did you show me this?" I asked her, my voice flat and level.

"Cherry told me. A long time ago. She said that's what you do."

"That?"

"No. She said you . . . hunt people like that. She knew you a long time ago, that's what she said. And she ran across you a few times. Not in person. Your name, what you do. She said she had your number, but I was always afraid to call. When you walked in the kitchen, I knew it was you. Even before you said your name. I thought you'd be . . . bigger."

"Why?"

"Cherry always said if Randy got in trouble, she'd call you," she finished, ignoring my question.

"You think Randy's in trouble?"

DOWN IN THE ZERO

"I think *he* thinks he is. He's a cowardly little kid, always scared of something. All those suicides, I know they made him afraid—he told me once."

"So what's this whole show about? Where do you think I fit in?"

She turned away from me, walked back over to the couch. "I hate them," she whispered, almost choking on the words.

"Who?"

"People who hurt kids. Especially their own kids. I know all about this stuff. Spanking. I'm an expert on it. It's not for discipline, it's for sex. Some people get turned on by it, some people get off on it. A good submissive, she can come just from getting spanked. There's men like that too. They whip their kids for fun. Their own fun. And it *hurts* the children. Because they *know*. They know why they're getting it. It's a sex game. And it stays with them. I know a woman, she's over thirty and her father still spanks her. What's that for?"

"You know what it's for."

"That's right, I do. And I hate them. I thought if you knew about it . . ."

"You want to hire me? Is that it?"

"Hire you? You mean, you do it for money?"

"I do some things for money."

"I thought . . . I mean, Cherry said . . . you did that. She told me. About that mercenary who raped kids. He wanted to go to South Africa. And you . . . made him disappear."

A thin, cold fluid ran up my spine right into my brain, freezing my face into show-nothing survival.

Cherry had my number. Had it all this time.

Cherry. South Africa. Diamonds. Sure. She wasn't getting rich with hanky-spanky blackmail, that wasn't her game. But how much would a man pay for a tape of him confessing to homicide?

I could *feel* the tape recorders. Voice-activated, reel-to-reel with overlapping backup, microphones planted all around. Felt the fever-spike of fear whip through me and land in my gut, screaming *Stay safe!* I turned to Fancy and chuckled. "Yeah, sure. That's me all right. Burke, the masked avenger."

"But . . ."

"Hey, give me a break," I said, laughing harder now. "I'm not saying I never did anything wrong in my life. I'm a hustler. A thief. But *kill* somebody . . . forget it. That's not my speed. Cherry was just pulling your chain. I haven't seen her in a hundred years, but even then she was a world-class bullshit artist."

Her face was white under the artificial tan, hands shaking. "I thought . . ."

"What? That I was some kind of vigilante for kids? Because fucking *Cherry* told you?"

"Yes!" she sobbed, her face in her hands. I watched her cry for a minute, her body shaking under the blue T-shirt.

"Cut it out," I told her. "That's a fairy story. You're too old to think there's a Santa Claus."

She leaned her head against my chest, still crying. I put my hand on her shoulder, pulled her into me. Held her while she cried.

The outfit Michelle bought for me would look good in the movie the blackmailers were making, but even a Grand Jury of cops wouldn't indict Ice-T on the contents of the audio track.

The light was on in the kid's bedroom—I could see it as I turned into the garage. Maybe he was scared of the dark.

I took off the camouflage clothing. It was about two-thirty in the morning. I wasn't sleepy—too much to sort out.

What Fancy told me was true. It takes a player to know the game. Even the child molesters who call what they do "intergenerational sex" know what "domestic discipline" is all about. But why would Cherry tell Fancy about what I do? What I did. How much did she know? Or was it all a bunch of guesses, needing my own words to drop me for the count.

Today, people don't think about working to get rich. Or stealing either. It's all upside down now. People hear someone they know was in a car accident, they envy them . . . what a great lawsuit. Lawsuits and lottery tickets, that's the way you do it now.

You don't run across straight blackmail much anymore. Why risk doing time when you can make a bigger score from selling secrets to the media? Treason is fashionable today. You have an affair with someone famous, there's a cash market for letters. For tapes, whatever. It helps if you're willing to pose nude later—show the people what the famous man wanted so bad.

The important thing is to do it for the right reasons—because you got this desperate need for the public to know the truth—the media likes its whores better when they dress up.

There's a bounty on famous people. Everybody knows where to go with the tapes.

A celebrity's sister sells her diary to the garbage press. Sells her own sister. A young man writes a book about how some industrialist needed bondage to get off—a private game turned public for cash. A spoiled-stupid little girl pleads guilty to attempted murder of an older woman. She says she was having an affair with the woman's husband, that he told her to do it. He says it never happened, the girl is delusional. She's out on bail before she goes away to prison. She goes to see her boyfriend, another older guy. They talk, play with each other. She says spoiled-stupid stuff, jokes about the shooting, tries so pitiful-hard to be cool, sound tough. The boyfriend has a video going the whole time, sells it to a TV show.

I guess that makes him famous too.

It's not against the law, selling secrets. Why bother with extortion? Threats to expose are a waste of time when you can score more by actually pulling the trigger.

Save those letters. Tape those calls. When I was first coming up, the worst thing you could be was a rat. Now it's a respected profession.

There's a bull market in betrayal.

But the tape I took from Cherry's hidden safe . . . I didn't recognize the man in the video—whoever he was, he wasn't *that* famous. Private blackmail. Leave the cash in a drop and you'll get the negatives . . . you don't see that stuff much anymore. There's money in it, sure. But not enough to buy fistfuls of gems.

Unless it was a pyramid. Show some sucker who works for the government the tape. You want the tape back? Maybe we need to talk about being the low bidder on a defense contract. Or a judicial appointment. Or . . .

No, it didn't add up. You can't be sure your target has any particular fetish. It takes years of work to set something like that up.

So why would Fancy show me her video? Why would she talk about kids?

I didn't have enough. Like trying to cross a fifty-foot chasm over a forty-foot bridge—I could be jumping to conclusions.

If I did that, I didn't want it to be an accident.

The kid was outside when I got up the next morning, waiting around downstairs like he had something on his mind.

"I saw your light when I got in last night," I said. "You leave it on when you went to sleep, or what?"

"I was awake. I was going over some stuff I had."

"About race cars?"

"Yeah." He shot me a smile. "I was wondering—"

"Look, I gotta make a run into the city, okay? I won't be long, probably be back before this afternoon. Can we talk about it when I get back?"

"Sure, I was just—"

"Randy, is it important, kid?"

"Not *that* important."

"You get a call? Somebody say something to you?"

"Nothing like that. It can wait, all right?"

"Sure. Keep the phone with you if you go out."

"I will. Uh, Burke . . .?"

"What?"

"Could you take the Lexus. I thought I'd . . ."

"You got it," I told him.

The Lexus was right at home in the commuter traffic, common enough among humans who worship products. I took my time, not pushing it. When I turned off at Bruckner Boulevard for Hunts Point, the Lexus fit in just as well—they're as popular with the dope boys as Mercedes used to be.

I motored past the deadfall near the filthy water, watching the rapacious gulls circling. Meat-eaters all, they battle with the wild dog packs for the refuse from the nearby meat market, unafraid of earthbound humans who occasionally trespass.

"Nice car, Burke," Terry greeted me, running his palm over the sleek flanks of the Lexus. If the dogs noticed the upgrade in my transport, they didn't let on. I told Terry the Lexus wasn't mine, but I'd be driving it for a while. He nodded, holding his eager kid questions, imitating the Mole's way of doing business. I showed him the pistol. He nodded again, sagely pondering the obvious problem. "I got something that'll work. Wait here, okay?"

I fired up a smoke, watching the dogs work their way across the junkyard in the studied Z-pattern of the predator pack. They were like the Mole too—they were used to humans, but didn't like many of them.

The kid came back with a flat piece of black metal. It had a pair of black rubber grippers bonded to the back, two heavy suction cups on the front. He walked around the Lexus, finally found the place he wanted under the fender—he showed me the exact spot. I fitted the metal piece into the spot, pushed down. Nothing.

"Push real hard, Burke," he said.

I locked my forearm, shoved with all my strength. I felt it pop home, lock in place.

"You want to take it off, you have to push this little button on the side . . . see?" He guided my hand to the spot. I pushed, and the metal bar dropped into my hand. I put it back in place, shoved the gun's barrel between the rubber grips. It held like it was welded.

"Can I get the gun out without taking the whole thing off?" I asked him.

"Sure. Just grab the handle and pull in the direction of the barrel—it works like a fulcrum, see?" He pulled it out as easy as drawing from a holster.

"Pretty slick, Terry."

He blushed like a kid with a perfect report card. It was another minute or so before I realized he wasn't going to say anything. Waiting the way his father always did.

"Mole around?" I finally asked.

"He's got . . . someone with him."

I looked a "Who?" question at him. The kid shrugged. Whoever it was, it wasn't Michelle.

"Should I . . . wait, or what?"

"I'll see," Terry told me, moving off.

He was back quickly, mouth working so he'd get the message just right. "Mole says, the man with him is someone he works with. Not your business. You can trust him. Come down if you want."

I knew the only kind of people the Mole worked with. Knew where his priorities were. But I was just curious enough, just enough in a hurry.

"Let's go," I said.

Walking over, I handed Terry the key to the Lexus. "Can you make a copy?" I asked him.

He gave me another one of those "Are you kidding?" looks teenagers do so well.

The Mole was in his bunker, his pasty white skin shining like a mushroom in a cellar. His workbench was littered with printouts from the computer. A pad at his elbow was covered in his tiny, crabby handwriting, mostly with numbers and symbols I didn't recognize. A short, wiry man was standing next to him, dressed in a simple khaki summer suit. He was dark-skinned with thick, curly black hair and a mustache, dark brown eyes regarding me neutrally.

I greeted the underground genius—he grunted an acknowledgment, absorbed in another list of symbols scrolling down the screen.

I took the pad from his desk, puzzling over the Mole's strange writing.

"It doesn't print graphics," the Mole said, glancing over his shoulder at the printer.

"Ah, Mole . . ."

He turned to look at me. "This is Zvi," he said. "My cousin."

The dark-skinned man stepped forward, extending his hand. "Cousin" told me the whole story—Zvi was an Israeli, an operative in one of the dozen agencies they had working all around the world. High-placed too—if he knew where to find the Mole. Zvi was the Mole's *landsman*—of his blood, not of our family. Even his grip was neutral, promising nothing.

"Did you . . . ?" I began.

"I showed the disks to Zvi," Mole said, his eyes ready for a challenge. I didn't react—he'd told me the rules a long time ago. If his country could use something, he'd turn it over no matter what.

"One set of data is my area," Zvi said, his voice neutral as his handshake. "The other is not."

"Which is yours?" I asked.

"This one," he replied, holding up the red disk. "Look at the printout."

I picked it up. A fan-folded sheet with rachet-feed perforations along each side. It ran to dozens of pages all told. Looked like ID information: names, addresses, height, weight, hair and eye color . . . couple of hundred names, at least.

"What is this?" I asked.

"It's a before-and-after," Zvi said. "See this man," he said, indicating with a pointing finger.

I looked. R21\ANDERSON, ROBERT M.\669 EAST 79\33-C\ NYC\74\ 190\BRN\BLU\SMT=CAT2. Height in inches, weight in pounds, color of hair and eyes. More numbers followed: a pair of nine-digit sequences, one separated by dashes, the other solid. Social Security and passport, sure.

"What's this SMT CAT2 thing?" I asked him.

"Scars, Marks and Tattoos. I don't know what the Category means—it would be in their coding. If they're operating at this level, they'd have a way to alter things like that too."

"So?"

"So he could be this one now," he said, pointing to another name, different in everything but the height, with a Houston address. "Or this one," showing me still another, this time living in New Zealand. "This is a record of new identities. People who disappeared."

"What about fingerprints?"

"There's new technology. And even without it, people at this level don't get fingerprinted unless they're already caught—your local agencies don't really have a strong Interpol interface. They'd need a document generator too, probably on-line with government computers."

"How do you do the before-and-after? How do you know which is which?"

"There's a program that would do it. A sorting program. That's what the code is before each one. See? The R21 here. The MM8 there? That's what the computer would do, match them up."

"Could you crack the code?"

"It would take months, and even then we couldn't be sure, not without a reference point. We'd have to know at least one correct match to check."

"So what good is it?"

The Israeli lit a short, unfiltered cigarette with a butane lighter. Rubbed his face as though in concentration on my question, but I caught his glance at the Mole. The Mole moved his head maybe an inch, but it was enough.

"We know one of the people on the list," the Israeli said. "He vanished almost three years ago. We would like very much to locate him."

"How did you . . . ?"

"I called them," the Mole said, taking the list from the Israeli, his stubby finger touching the paper next to a name. The name didn't mean anything to me—the Mole was telling me what the Israeli's job was—Zvi was a hunter.

"A sorting program is a simple thing," the Israeli said. "It would be a macro . . . a series of keystrokes stored in sequence. When you invoke the macro, the whole sequence runs."

"I brought everything when I—" I said.

"I know," he interrupted. "It would be somewhere else. Did the . . . place where you got it have a computer? A small one would be enough, even a laptop."

"I didn't see one."

He looked at the Mole again. The Mole looked at me. "What was on the other disk?" I asked him.

"An experiment of some kind. A scientific experiment. This much I could tell, only—there are a number of subjects, each subject is given the same . . . thing. The thing could be a substance, a stimulus . . . I can't tell. Then there are results . . . something happened to some of the subjects, I can't tell what. The rest is all probabilities, chi-squares, standard deviations."

"Yeah, okay," I said, puzzled. "Do you know what . . . ?"

"I told you everything I know. The subjects have codes too."

"So there's a sorting program for them too?"

"Maybe." He shrugged his shoulders.

"I could take a look around," I said.

"You wouldn't know what to look for," the Israeli said. "You wouldn't recognize it if you saw it."

I lit a cigarette of my own, buying time, thinking about what I'd just learned. The Israeli sat stone-still, as if any movement would spook me into the wrong decision.

"What do you want me to do?" I finally asked.

"The . . . place where you got this from . . . could you give us the address?"

I exhaled through my nose, watching the twin streams of smoke in the underground bunker.

"The Mole can copy this for you," I said, handing over the key to

Cherry's house. "I'll call . . . here . . . when it's clear. You'll have a mini- mum of three hours. After dark better?"

"It doesn't matter," the Israeli said.

I gave him the address.

I left the two disks with the Mole, picked up the key to the Lexus, confirmed that Terry kept a copy for himself, and headed back to Connecticut. It was way ahead of rush hour—the drive didn't take long.

But I had time to chew on it, work it through. They hadn't told me the whole story—I didn't need to know it. That was their business, not mine.

I've got my own business too. I hadn't told them I recognized one of the names on the printout.

Bluestone dust was still dancing in the driveway when I drove up. The kid was lying under the Plymouth—I could see his sneakers sticking out. He pushed himself free, rubbing something off the front of his sweatshirt.

"I changed the oil and filter," he said. "Hey, what kind of injectors are you running? I checked my books—that's a four-forty in there, it came with carbs, right?"

"I guess so . . . I don't know."

"But . . ."

"Randy, I'm telling you the truth. The car's pretty much the way I got it. I didn't build it—I just drive it."

"Yeah, okay. Burke . . ."

"What?"

"She was here. While you were gone."

"Fancy?"

"No. Charm. She asked about you."

"Asked what?"

"How come you were here. What you were doing, you know."

"No, I don't know. What did you tell her?"

"That you were the caretaker. To, like, look after the place while my mother was away."

"So?"

"So she . . . didn't believe me, I think. She gave me a look, like I was lying. It was . . . I dunno . . . kind of scary."

"Did she go upstairs, Randy?"

The kid hung his head. "Yeah."

"You told her it was okay?"

"No. I told her she couldn't. She said I wasn't going to stop her . . . and I'd better not tell you she was there either."

"All right, take it easy. How long was she up there?"

"Just a few minutes. Then she went over to the house."

"You go over there with her?"

"No," he said again, his face still down.

"Stay here," I told him, heading for the stairs.

If she'd tossed the place, she was good. I could see the search-signs, but they were faint. Subtle.

It only took me a minute to find the listening device inside the handpiece to the telephone.

Downstairs again, I ignored the kid's look, walked past him over to the big house. The back door was open. I let myself in, moving quiet. Cherry's bedroom looked the same. I worked the buttons on the intercom and the sliding door opened in the marble wall to the bath. When I looked inside, the compartment was empty.

I stepped out of the bedroom, heard a noise downstairs. I moved back down the corridor, into one of the bathrooms, flushed the toilet, counted to ten, and came down the stairs.

The kid was sitting at the kitchen table pouring himself a glass of milk, a box of chocolate donuts standing open in front of him.

"Hey, Burke. You want a donut?"

"Didn't I tell you to stay by the car?"

"I thought . . . you meant until you were done in the apartment. I didn't . . ."

"Don't think so fucking much," I told him. Then I walked out the back door.

B ack in the apartment, I took out my notebook, started to go over the list of parents of the kids who'd died. Blankenship scanned legit to me—maybe I'd get lucky with one of the others.

I picked up my tapped phone, dialed Fancy's number. She answered on the second ring.

"Hello."

"Ten o'clock tonight," I told her, my voice flat and hard. "Get your fat ass over here. And don't be late, understand?"

"Yes," she breathed soft into the mouthpiece.

I hung up on her.

J ust past four, I heard a tentative knock on the door. I looked through the glass. Randy. I walked over from the couch, let him in.

"What?"

"Burke, I'm sorry. About Charm. And about . . . not staying where you told me. I was gonna . . . be different. The car . . . I can't explain it."

"Sit down," I told him gently, stepping back from the door.

He crossed over to the couch, leaving me the easy chair. He sat there for a minute, collecting himself.

"My mother told me about you," he said.

"Told you what?"

"She said she knew you a long time ago. When she did you that . . . favor, remember?"

"Yeah."

"My mother doesn't talk to me much. She never did, really. She said she wanted me . . . real special. That's why she went through all that, with the artificial insemination and all. She's not around here very much. She always says, someday she'll tell me things. She never says what things. Just . . . things. Things I need to know. I guess . . ."

His voice trailed off. I lit a smoke, not saying anything, letting my body language tell him it was okay, I was listening, patient, all the time in the world. He took a little gulping breath, got going again.

"Anyway, my mother told me you were a . . . tough guy. I mean, real tough, not like a weightlifter or anything. Dangerous, that's what she said. Burke is a dangerous man."

You tell a lot of people stories about me, don't you, bitch? I kept my face quiet, mildly interested, waiting for him to continue.

"She knew you when you were, like, my age, right?" the kid went on. "She said that's the way you were then, too. She said you were a man of honor—that you'd honor a debt. She really told me about you a long time ago. When she went away. I was just a little kid, like ten or something. She said, if anyone tried to do something to me, I should call you. Just call you and tell you, and you'd fix it. For the debt."

"Do something like what, Randy?"

"Like . . . I don't know. She didn't say. She would . . . leave me with people. Caretakers, she called them. She always did that. It was them she meant, I think. But I know what she said. If anybody makes me scared, I should call you."

"Did that ever happen?"

"No, not . . . really. But my mother thought it might, I could tell. I was in her room once, just playing around. I found a maid's outfit. You know, like a black dress with a white apron? I thought it was Rosemary's. She was the maid we had then. From Ireland. So I put it in her room, on the bed. My mother saw it there. I heard her yell for Rosemary. When Rosemary came upstairs, I hid. I was scared, my mother sounded so mad. She asked Rosemary why she took the outfit. Rosemary said she didn't, and my mother slapped her. Right across the face. She told Rosemary to put it back in her room. Then when Rosemary came back, my mother slapped her again. I never told her it was me."

"It was a long time ago," I said. "Don't worry about it."

"My mother asked me later, did Rosemary ever do anything to me? Like . . . punish me or something. I told her no, Rosemary never did that. That's when she said the thing about calling you, the first time."

I played with my cigarette, letting him drive his own car.

"When I called you, I was scared. Like something was gonna happen, but I didn't know what."

"The suicides?"

"I guess so. There's . . . something else too. I can't tell you. But I knew if you were around, it wouldn't happen."

"That kid Brew?"

"No!" he snorted a laugh. "Not him. Anyway, when I started to . . . do stuff with you, I thought I could . . . maybe help, I don't know. I don't smoke dope anymore," he said, looking straight across at me, eyes clear. "I don't booze either. And I'm not gonna tank, next time they have a party. I want to do . . . something."

"Drive?"

"Yes! When I drive, it's like *I'm* the car. It feels . . . connected. I don't know. You think I'm crazy, don't you?"

"No. No, I don't. All the great drivers, that's the way they talk about it . . . like it's all one piece."

"Did you know any? Great drivers, I mean."

I couldn't tell him. I started to lose it for a second, but I reached down and grabbed hold. I fussed with a cigarette until I had it under control. "I did time with one of them," I told the kid. "Long time ago. He was a great, great wheelman. Drove on some of the biggest hijacks in the country, bank jobs too. The Prof knew him better than me, but I talked a lot to him too."

"You mean like a getaway driver?"

"More than that, kid. He was stand-up, see? No matter what happened inside, Petey wouldn't leave you there. He'd be waiting at the curb when you came out."

"But when he drove . . ."

"Driving, that's only a small piece of it. I had this pal once, Easy Eddie. One time we were out riding, nothing special. But what he didn't tell me, he was holding dope. Heavy weight. And we got stopped. Now it worked out okay—the cops never saw it."

"Yeah?"

"Yeah. But if they had, it would have been Kaddish. Easy Eddie and me, we were as close as brothers. He was a stand-up guy. He didn't mean any harm—never thought about getting me in trouble. If we'd gone down for the dope, he would have taken the whole weight."

"So?"

"So he was real sorry about what happened. And I never rode with him again."

Randy's face changed colors as it hit him. "I get it," he said.

"Do you?" I asked. "Here's what a guy told me when I was just coming up. About working in a crew. You can't be counted *on*, you can't be counted *in*, understand?"

"Yes."

"Being a wheelman, it's not just about driving, Randy. Next time I tell you to stay someplace, you do it. Okay?"

"I will," he said, a bit of steel under the softness of his voice.

I had plenty of time before Fancy. "I need to make a phone call," I told the kid. "Want to drive me?"

"Sure," he said, starting for the Plymouth like there was no other choice. He didn't say anything about there being plenty of phones in the house—maybe he was a faster learner than I thought.

"Where to?" he asked, adjusting the rearview mirror, rocking gently back and forth in the driver's seat, getting the feel.

"What I need is a pay phone, all right? An outdoor phone, if you know where one is."

"There's some on the highway. In case someone has a breakdown."

"Let's ride."

He pulled out of the driveway without spinning the rear wheels, nursing the throttle, but as soon as we hit pavement he dropped the hammer, road-running at double the speed limit.

"Back it off," I told him. "The trick to driving, the real trick, you got to *blend*, understand? Any fool can drive fast—the game is to drive fast *smooth*, see? Especially in the city. A real pro, he can drive faster than it looks like he's going . . . the way a karate man can close space on you before you realize it."

"Okay," the kid said. He motored along in silence for a few minutes. "Can I try it?" he asked.

"Try what?"

"Blending. I'll go through town first, okay?"

"Sure."

The kid had a sweet soft touch with the wheel, piloting the big car in the light traffic with assurance. He pulled to a smooth stop behind a chocolate Porsche coupe, waiting patiently for the light to change.

"Give yourself more room," I told him.

"What do you mean?"

"You're too close to the Porsche. If he stalls, or just decides to sit there, you can't go around him without backing up first, see?"

"Yeah," he said, nodding.

"Drive with a zone around you, like a pocket of air. Another car comes in the zone, you adjust, understand? It's like you always leave yourself an escape route, never get boxed in."

He turned off to the highway, stayed just past the speed limit, looking over at me for approval.

"On the highway, stay with the packs, all right? Always keep cover around you. You want to pass, make sure there's another clump out ahead of you."

He nodded again, rolled into the middle lane behind a Subaru wagon. The kid held his position for a bit, then he pulled into the left lane, circled the Subaru and pulled in behind a three-car train in the middle lane.

"You got it," I told him. "Remember, this car is a crate. That's what it looks like, that's what people will see. Only time you show what it can do is when you got no choice."

The kid ignored the speedometer, driving by the tach and the oil pressure gauge. Another few minutes and he pulled over by a freestanding pay phone.

"See that switch?" I asked him, pointing to a toggle under the dash. "You throw that, the brake lights will disengage. You can leave it in gear with your foot on the brake, nobody watching will know you're ready to go."

He threw the switch as I got out, left the motor running.

I tossed coins into the slot, made the connection.

"Gardens," Mama answered.

"It's me. I need to talk to the Prof. Can you reach out, ask him to be at the phone anytime after midnight?"

"Sure. Everything okay?"

"Getting tricky. But I can see a light, maybe."

"You want Max yet?"

"Not yet, Mama."

I stepped back into the Plymouth. The kid had it rolling away before I had the door closed, merging with traffic like a pigeon joining a flock.

"Nice," I said.

He flushed, didn't say anything.

"Y ou need me for anything tonight?" he asked.

"No. I got stuff to work on. You?"

"There's a party. At Roger's house."

"Party?" This kid was so damn in-and-out . . . one minute panicked, the next partying.

"It's cool. There's a . . . girl I know. Maybe she'll be there. I thought maybe I'd ask her if she wants to come along Sunday. For the race."

"Why don't you just call her and ask her?"

"Well, I don't really know her that well. I mean . . . she doesn't exactly know who I am. I *met* her and all, but . . ."

"I got it. What's her name?"

"Wendy. She was in classes with me at school. Then I didn't see her when she went to college. She . . . writes poetry. I read some once—it was in the school magazine."

"You like her, huh?"

"I *always* liked her. But she doesn't hang with my crowd. I mean, she smokes dope and all, but she doesn't tank or anything. She's very deep."

"So what makes you think she'll be there tonight?"

"She's close with Scott's girlfriend Denise. I just figured . . . it's worth a shot, right?"

"Always is," I told him. "You want the Plymouth?"

"Oh no," he said. "I don't want anybody to know what I'm gonna be running on Sunday. That's a surprise. I'll take the Miata."

"Good luck, kid."

"Thanks."

"Take the phone with you."

"It's right here," he said, tapping the pocket of his jacket.

heard the rasp of the Miata's exhaust a little past nine. I prowled the apartment, probing the edges of my plan in my mind, looking for weak spots. The bugged phone—I couldn't tell if it was a line tap or a full-house microphone. There was the intercom too. Maybe the Mole could figure out what was what, but me, I'd play it like the whole thing was an audio zone.

Ten o'clock came and went. No Fancy. I smoked a cigarette, wondering if I'd miscalculated. A nervous tap on the glass. I went over, let her in. She was wearing a white T-shirt over a pink linen skirt, carrying a matching jacket in one hand and a big black leather purse over one shoulder. She stood there in white medium heels, head slightly down.

"I'm sorry I was late," she whispered.

I glanced at my watch: six minutes past the hour. I reached out and took her right hand, held it in my left with her chubby palm up.

"I don't want to hear your excuses, bitch!" I said, and slapped her upturned palm hard. The sound was clear in the quiet apartment—I hoped the microphone got it.

Fancy looked up, firelight in her big gray eyes.

"I'm sorry," she whispered again.

"Come over here," I told her, jerking her by the hand toward the couch. She came compliantly, breathing harsh now. I walked her past the couch toward the back bedroom. In the doorway, I pulled her to a halt.

"You know what, bitch? I think you'll get the message better if I teach you someplace else . . . like outdoors. Would you like that?"

"Yes," she said, real soft.

"Come along," I told her, switching my grip from her hand to her wrist. I walked her back to the door, pointed down. She took the stairs, stopped at the bottom and waited. I took her into the garage, opened the passenger door to the Plymouth. She stepped in, held the pose way too long. When she figured out I wasn't going to smack her offered rump, she sat down. I crossed to the driver's side, started the car and backed it out.

She didn't say a word on the drive, sitting like a girl in church, hands in her lap. I found the place I wanted, one I spotted on my recon visit a few days ago. A stand of high trees maybe a hundred yards off the highway with a creek running past. I guess it belonged to somebody, but I didn't see a fence. I turned off, parked so the Plymouth's nose was pointing back out the way we'd come, killed the engine.

"Sorry about all that," I told her, handing her my pack of cigarettes.

"I . . . don't understand," she said. "I thought you were going to . . ."

"People were listening," I told her.

"Where?" she asked, a shocked-scared look on her face.

"Back at the apartment. At least I think so. Cherry's got some kind of intercom hooked up," I told her, not mentioning the phone. No risk there, Randy knew about the intercom himself.

"But why . . . ?"

"If anyone's listening, they would have thought you and me were gonna play, right?"

"That's what *I* thought too."

"Light that for me, will you?" I said. She fumbled in her purse, came up with a silver lighter that looked like a lipstick. Fired it up, handed it over. "Thanks, girl. Look, did you mean what you said? About helping me?"

"Yes."

"If you did, now's the time," I said, putting it right to her while she was off-balance. "Can you get me into Rector's?"

"Rector's? Sure. I could get you a guest pass. But I couldn't go as your slave—they don't know I switch. I don't, actually."

"Switch?"

"Be a submissive. I don't do that. If any of my . . . clients saw me there wearing a collar, it might turn them off."

"I wasn't—"

"But I wasn't lying," she went on like I hadn't spoken. "I mean, in your bedroom, that first time. I gave you your choice because I thought it would turn you on but I . . . got wet when I made the offer. And I came tonight expecting . . . I don't know. I wanted to try it. And when you slapped me, it worked."

"The slap was for the sound," I said. "So anyone listening would think . . ."

"I was late on purpose," she replied, as if she hadn't heard me. "To give you an excuse. To punish me."

"Look, Fancy, I don't want to get into Rector's when they're having one of their parties. Isn't there any after-hours for a joint like that? In daylight or something?"

"It closes at four. There's a cleaning crew after that. And it doesn't open up again until eight at night. I . . . go there sometimes in the day."

Sure you do — nothing like a quickie during lunch hour when you're in the blackmail business. "By yourself?" I asked out loud.

"No . . ."

"So even if someone saw you go in with me, they wouldn't think anything of it?"

"Yes, that's true, but . . ."

"But what?"

"What do you want in there?"

"I want to look around. I think one of the people who goes there may be involved in the suicide thing," I told her, lying glibly. What I wanted was a good look—maybe Cherry had another hiding place. Or a laptop computer.

"How long would you have to be in there?"

"An hour. No longer."

"All right. I'll do it. I have the keys. It'll take a couple of days . . ."

"That's okay. Perfect." I put an arm around her shoulders. Her breasts strained against the T-shirt as she turned toward me. I dropped her hand to her hip, pulled her close.

"Don't," she whispered. "Please don't . . . kiss me. I hate that."

I snapped my cigarette out the window with my left hand, watching the red tip sail toward the creek. She put her face into my neck, I could feel her breath against my throat. "I don't want to neck," she said urgently. "It's too . . . innocent. Like kids. I don't want to be a kid. Tell me what to do. Tell me what to do—order me to do it."

"Fancy . . ."

"Please!"

I took a deep breath through my nose, smelling the mossy darkness. Then I slid across the seat toward the middle, touching her hips with mine.

"Get on your hands and knees," I told her.

She did it, facing out her window, back arched.

"No, stupid bitch," I said, hard-voiced. "Turn around."

She did that too, pulling herself around with her hands on the back of the seat.

"Unzip my pants," I said.

Her dark hair fell all around her face as she bent to do it. The zipper sound was like fabric tearing.

"Take it out." My cock sprung free, standing up rigid. I put my right hand on the back of her neck, shoving her down across my lap, flattening my cock against me. She moaned as I roughly pulled her skirt up around her waist. The pink silk bikini panties were just a thin strip across the width of her bottom—I hauled them down past her knees.

"Don't take them all the way off," she whispered. "It's better if they—"

"Shut up," I said, pulling the panties down more, leaving them hooked over one ankle. I turned slightly sideways, put my thumbs under her heavy breasts, wrapping my hands around her back. I picked her up, dragging her against my chest. Then I put my left hand on the inside of her right thigh and pulled her leg over so she was straddling me. She was sopping wet but it was still a tight fit. I set myself, rammed up hard. She grunted, penetrated. Her breasts pressed against me, her face next to mine, looking out over the back seat. I could feel the wetness all around me, smelled the blood beneath her skin.

"Wiggle your butt, bitch," I whispered.

She ground into me, humping like she was going to buck herself off, muttering words I couldn't understand. I stroked her back, then gripped her shoulders from behind, slamming her into me with each downstroke. I heard a deep, sharp intake of breath.

"Don't make a goddamned sound," I told her.

She let go with a rush, a split second before I did.

Holding her, I could hear the soft slapping of water over rocks in the creek. She was crying softly, gulping like a kid does, trying to get it under control. We stayed like that until my cock softened and gravity pulled it down . . . out of her.

She wasn't going to move. I gently pushed on her left shoulder, turning her around as I took her off my lap, felt the slight adhesive tear from the dried fluids bonding us.

She slumped against me. I zipped up my pants, ran my hand over the front of her thigh.

"Pull your skirt down, Fancy."

"Sleepy," she said softly, curling up, putting her head in my lap. I patted her back. She squirmed into a comfortable position, pulling her knees up to her waist.

I lit a cigarette. She didn't stir. I looked down. She was on her side, quiet, the pink panties around one ankle. I tugged her skirt down almost over her hips, the way you cover a sleeping child.

Sitting there, I went someplace else in my head, searching. There was a thread somewhere. A strong thread, so deeply woven that if you pulled it, the whole fabric would unravel. I knew it, but I couldn't see it.

When Fancy played her domina games in that white room, was anyone else in on the profit end? Even if there was, a blackmail racket didn't explain things. Not all of them, anyway. Blackmail's a high-wire act—one slip and they sponge you off the concrete. And blackmail wouldn't pay the kind of money Cherry was showing.

If she was on to the new identities of people who disappeared, that would buy her a whole lot more of those gems that I'd found. But how would she know?

And how did Charm know about Cherry's stash if she wasn't working with her?

Why would Cherry tell Fancy about me? Why did she tell Randy?

There's a tropical spider, I don't remember its name. What this spider does, it climbs into another spider's web. But it doesn't get trapped, it waits. The spider who spun the web feels the vibrations, runs over to wrap up its prey. Then he's lunch.

Fancy rolled her head back and forth in my lap like she was wiping her nose. She sat up, tugging her skirt down the rest of the way, smoothing it over her thighs. She reached down, plucked the pink panties from her ankle, put them into her purse.

"You were going to stay here all night?" she asked.

"I didn't want to wake you."

"That was sweet . . . but I wasn't asleep."

"You were . . . peaceful."

"Can we go outside?"

"Sure, if you want."

She took off her heels, slid over against me. I opened my door, climbed out. Held out my hand. She took it. We walked down to the creek in the darkness. Fancy found a fallen tree, the tips of its dead branches dangling into the creek. She tugged on my hand until I sat down next to her. Then she let go of my hand, spun so her back was against me, stuck her legs straight out on the tree, balancing easily.

"That was my first one," she said, facing away. "My first real one."

"Your first real what?"

"Climax. At least that's what I think it was. I could feel it inside. Hot bolts, like lightning crackling. Then . . . whooosh!"

"Good."

"Good? That's all you can say?"

"I don't know what to say," I said to her back.

"Did you really want me to help you?" she asked.

"Yes."

"Why?"

"Because you said you wanted to."

"Get you into Rector's? I didn't say anything about that."

"That isn't all of it," I told her, improvising, steering it away.

"What, then?" she asked, spinning to face me.

"I have to talk to some people. People from around here. The parents . . . of the kids who died. I figured, some of them would get suspicious. I'm going to tell them Cherry hired me. Because she was concerned about Randy and all. I thought you could back that up, maybe come along with me while I worked."

"You really do . . . want me to help?"

"That's what I said."

"When do we start?"

"Tomorrow," I said. "And, Fancy . . . don't tell anybody about this, okay?"

"Who would I tell?"

drove back to the apartment, Fancy sitting close to me the way girls did years ago, before seat belts.

"Can I come upstairs?" she asked.

"Not tonight, child. I've got to go out again."

"Don't call me 'child.' I *hate* that. I'm not a child."

"It doesn't mean anything, Fancy. It's just an affectionate term."

"I like 'bitch' better."

"Okay."

"In front of people, you understand? It's a property word."

She got out of the Plymouth, opened the door to her black NSX. "Tomorrow, okay?" she murmured, coming into my arms.

I gave her a squeeze, patted her bottom. "I'll call you, bitch," I told her, giving her a quick kiss on the forehead before she could protest.

The black car pulled off. I glanced over at the garage—the Miata was still missing.

I dropped the coins, dialed home base.

"You speak to the Prof?" I asked Mama when she answered.

"Right here," she replied.

"What you done, son?"

"I'm not sure, Prof. I got something . . . maybe a big score. Not on the phone, okay?"

"Keep it tight—we fly by night."

"You can get out here?"

"Name the place, I'm in the race."

I told him take the turnpike, grab the first gas station past the Greenwich tolls. Midnight tomorrow.

"I'll be at the spot. On the dot."

"How'd it go last night?" I asked the kid. He was sitting at the kitchen table, tearing into his third bowl of cereal like he needed the fuel.

"I'm . . . not sure. It was different. Not the party. I mean, that was like it always was. Me, maybe."

"You get to see that girl? Wendy?"

"Yeah. She was there. We . . . danced. Outside."

"I didn't think you all went in for dancing at those parties."

"We . . . they don't. The music . . . you really can't dance to it unless you're wrecked. We went outside, on the patio. I asked her to dance. Not to the music, just to dance."

"You can do that?"

"Dance? Sure. My mother sent me for lessons when I was a little kid. Ballroom dancing, like. I can do all the old stuff."

"Sounds pretty good."

"It was. Really good. We didn't stay there. I took her for a drive. We just drove around. I told her . . . about racing on Sunday. She said she'd be there. It was . . . I can't really explain it. She showed me some of her poetry. In this big notebook she's always carrying around. I never knew what was in it."

Something in his face. "What?" I asked.

He looked across at me. "One of the poems . . . it was about suicide. I got upset. Scared. I asked her, did she ever consider . . . doing it? She told me she didn't, not really. But she thinks about it. She said a lot of people do. Not 'cause things are bad . . . just 'cause there doesn't seem any reason. For anything."

"Randy, was she ever at Crystal Cove?"

"No. I asked her. She said it was none of my business at first, got mad at me a little bit. So I didn't say anything. But later, she asked, was I really scared for her? I told her I was. It was true. She . . . kissed me then. Just before I dropped her off at her car. And she told me she was never there."

"It sounds all right."

"I know. But that poem . . . it was all about suicide, I know it was. 'Sweet Darkness,' it was called."

"If she's a poet, she lives a lot in her mind, kid. It doesn't mean she's going over."

"I know. But . . . she's gonna be okay. I'm gonna . . . stay close."

"Good."

"Today, I mean. We're going to go to The Hills. It's like a park. Have a picnic. You think that's dumb?"

"I think it's righteous."

"You don't need me for anything?"

"Just take the phone with you."

He tapped his side pocket again. I finally realized where I'd seen that gesture before. The black kid with the 8-Ball jacket.

I considered my lawyer suit, finally rejected it in favor of Michelle's outfit. If Fancy was going to come along with me, I wanted to look like I might be in her circle.

She opened the door to her cottage before I knocked, holding a giant fluffy white towel in front of her, water beading on her shoulders.

"Am I early?" I asked, stepping inside.

"No, you're right on time. I was waiting . . . so you could tell me what to wear."

"Just put on . . ."

"No, come on—*tell* me." She walked toward a back room, still wrapped in the towel. I followed close behind. The cottage had an extension in the back, a greenhouse, built right in. The summer sun slanted through the sharply sloped glass. Fancy kept walking, all the way to a bedroom. The walls were a soft pink, the bed was covered in a quilt of the same shade. She opened a closet. "Tell me," she said again, a pleading undertone to her voice.

I pawed through the racks, picked out a rose silk outfit. It had a simple collarless bolero jacket, with a straight skirt underneath.

"This," I told her, holding it out to her. She stood there, holding the hanger. I found a plain-front white silk blouse with a loose turtleneck collar, held it against the rose silk. "This too," I said.

"Burke . . ."

"Get dressed, bitch. I want to get going."

She turned away, dropped the towel. I walked out of the room, heading for the greenhouse.

It was peaceful in there. The walls were lined with shelves, all kinds of plants. One shelf was a neat row of bonsai. Orchids were bunched in a corner, standing under a gentle mist from some kind of machine. I was fingering a big green plant loaded with small, hard buds, not quite ready to burst.

"What's your favorite?" Fancy's voice behind me.

"Favorite what?"

"Plant. What kind of plants do you like?"

"Blossoms," I told her. "Any kind of blossoms."

"Yeah . . ." she mused. Then she stepped between me and the plants. "How do I look?" she demanded.

"You look great, Fancy."

"You want some coffee?"

"No thanks."

"A drink?"

"No."

"Well, are we ready to go?"

"Just about. Let me look over my notes for a minute."

I walked back to the front room, sat down. She sat across from me, knees close together, hands in her lap.

"How's Randy doing?" she finally asked.

I looked up. "Seems like he's doing real good. Had himself a date last night. I think he took her dancing."

"Oh, he's a *good* dancer. I made him dance with me once, at a party Cherry gave."

"Yeah, he's got it all over me there." *I wonder why I never met a woman who couldn't dance. Maybe it's genetic.*

"What do you mean? You can't dance?"

"Not me. The only dance I ever learned when I was a kid was the Y dance."

"What's the Y dance? I never heard of it."

"Stand up—I'll show you."

She came over to me, stepping naturally against my chest, both hands going around my neck. I put my left hand around the back of her shoulder, dropped the other to her butt, pressed her hard against me. "Why dance?" I asked her.

Fancy giggled, rubbing against me.

"Hey, don't you think you should put on a bra if we're going out?"

"You didn't tell me to."

"What?"

"You didn't tell me to . . . just the dress and the blouse."

"Jesus Christ. All right, go put on some underwear."

"Come on, show me. I've got lots of stuff."

She did. "Aren't these uncomfortable?" I asked her, holding up a pair of black leather panties.

"No, they're good. They make you sweat when you work. Then I make the client put them in his mouth . . . like a gag," she said, gray eyes mocking.

I found a modest underwear set, pristine white. "This," I said.

"Can I wear a garter belt . . . please?" she asked, taking off the bolero jacket.

"Sure."

We took the Lexus. When Fancy said we were getting close, I turned slightly in my seat, making sure I had her attention.

"Listen to me, girl. You want orders, you got them. Here's one: I'm not calling you 'bitch' in front of people I'm trying to work, understand? What you're gonna do, you're gonna act like yourself—a smart, pushy rich girl. You're gonna use your head. I'm gonna be polite to you. You watch what I do, take your cues. Got it?"

"Yes sir."

"Don't be cute, Fancy."

"I won't."

The house was made up to look like a Cape Cod fisherman's cottage, but it was big enough to hold a convention. Set in the middle of what looked like an orchard, it was all weathered shingles and atmosphere, one wall nearly covered with ivy.

"These are the parents of Scott Lancaster," I told her. "You recognize the name?"

"No. But that house is real money."

"Okay. Remember what I told you."

"I'll be good," she whispered, wiggling a little bit in her seat, teasing, her skirt too far up on her thighs. I felt like slapping her, but I wanted her calm.

A woman in her forties answered the door, dressed in a dark blue pants suit, rich chestnut hair tied in a matching blue ribbon.

"Yes?" Her voice was tentative, not challenging.

"My name is Burke, ma'am. And this is—"

"Francesca Bishop," Fancy finished for me. "My father was Marlon Bishop . . . of Bishop Enterprises . . . ?"

"Oh, yes. What can I—?"

"I'm a private investigator, Mrs. Lancaster," I told her gently, trying to make my voice as rich as the house. "I've been retained by the Bishops and some other families—they're very concerned about the . . . recent incidents involving some young people in the area."

"You mean the . . . ?"

"Yes ma'am. Would it be possible to speak to you for a few minutes?"

"I guess so. If you . . . oh, come in. I'll get my husband."

She led us over to a navy blue velvet love seat with an elaborate carved back. It looked a couple of hundred years old. Fancy settled herself decorously, smoothing her skirt over her knees. I opened the attaché case, took out a notebook and pen. "I'll be right back," the woman said, leaving us alone.

I heard a murmur of voices from somewhere to our right. Then a man's voice, a vibrant baritone that any salesman would have killed for. "I've talked enough, goddamn it, MaryAnne! You can tell those people . . . ah, never mind."

He strode into the room like a ship captain ready to put down a mutiny. "Look, whoever you are, I've—"

He took us both in with one glance, stopped short like he'd hit a wall.

I saw the opening, pumped oil into the breach. "We're sorry to intrude, sir. Especially at this time. If you could just spare a few minutes . . ."

"Oh for Christ's sake, all right," he snapped, standing in front of us, hands locked behind his back. "Sit down," he said to his wife. "Would you like some coffee?" to us.

"No thank you," I said.

"If it's not too much trouble . . ." Fancy replied.

"MaryAnne," is all he said.

She jumped to her feet. "Would you like decaf or regular?"

"Oh, regular. Black if you don't mind."

"Not at all," she said, moving away.

"What can I tell you?" the man asked, taking the seat his wife had vacated.

"Did Scott give you any indication . . . before it happened?" I asked. "Was he depressed? In any kind of trouble?"

"The boy was *always* in trouble," his father said. "One damn thing after the other. He had two drunk driving convictions before he was eighteen. Suspended from high school. Kicked out of college. An alcoholic, that's what he was. Those parties they had . . . you know what Jello-shots are?"

"Yes," I said.

"That was his favorite. But he'd drink anything, from cooking sherry to fucking Sterno. Some kind of chemical imbalance in his brain, that's what the doctors said."

His wife walked back into the room, carrying a silver tray with a white china cup and saucer. She bent from the waist like a trained maid, serving Fancy, who said "Thank you" as if they had a long relationship.

"Do you mean the doctors at Crystal Cove?" I asked him.

"That's right. About time we got some straight answers, too."

His wife looked up from the tufted chair she was sitting on. "But Dr. Barrymore said—"

Lancaster shot her a look and she moused right out, looking down.

"Barrymore is a goddamned quack," he said to me. "Talked like a fucking queer."

"How long was Scott at Crystal Cove?"

"First time was thirty days. For the evaluation. Then he went back. Three months, the last time. Three months in, he didn't even make it three months out."

"Is it possible that . . ."

"What? That it could have been an accident? Like it was my fault because I keep some sporting arms in the house?" His eyes were hard, challenging, focusing only on me as if Fancy wasn't in the room. No question that his wife wasn't.

"No, I didn't mean that. I was just wondering . . . kids get ideas, you know? See something on television, like that. The papers just said it was a pistol . . . was it a revolver or semi-auto?"

"A revolver. Colt Python, .357 mag. What difference would that make?"

"Could he have been playing a game? Russian roulette?"

"How the hell would I know?"

"Well . . . how many cartridges were in the cylinder?"

"One. Okay, I see what you mean. But it only *takes* one, right?"

His wife muffled a sob, ran from the room.

"Sorry about that," he said to me. "She's a weak sister. Always has been. The boy took after her. Weak. That's what the boozing was really all about. Addicts are weak people. I don't smoke, don't drink. And I stay in shape. The business world, it's a tough racket, not for sissies. My wife thinks if I didn't keep guns in the house, he wouldn't have done it. That's bullshit!" he snarled vehemently. "Somebody wants to get hold of a gun, they can do it, am I right?"

"Dead right," I said.

His head snapped up. "Is that supposed to be some fucking kind of a joke?"

"No sir. It's my way of speaking. I apologize if I offended you."

"Yeah. Okay, anything else you want to know? I'm busy here, waiting on an important fax from Japan."

"He didn't leave a note, anything like that?"

"Absolutely not. And I'll tell you something else—his blood-alcohol level was sky-high when they did the autopsy. The boy was drunk, understand?"

"Yes sir. Sorry to have intruded. I won't trouble you further," I said, getting to my feet.

I offered my hand at the door. His grip was what I expected, a bone-crusher.

"I'm pleased to have met you," Fancy said demurely, holding out her own hand. He took it, expanding his chest, still staring at me.

"**D**id I do all right?" Fancy asked, buckling her seat belt.

"You did fine. I didn't think he was going to open up at first."

"I did better than you know, honey."

"What's that mean?"

"He wouldn't have said a word if I wasn't there."

"How could you know that?"

"I didn't recognize his name, but I knew his face."

"So?"

"So he was a client, Burke. Last time I saw Mr. Macho Big Business-man, he was on his knees, licking my boots."

Yeah, I thought, *and if I don't believe you, you can always show me the videotape.*

I took Fancy to lunch at a restaurant she told me about. It was just off the main drag, very high-tech, tiny portions on black glass plates, artfully arranged for appearance. Didn't taste bad, but it was more like samples than food.

Fancy had a good appetite, chowing down as if it was steak and potatoes instead of a thick disk of blackened tuna and a motley assortment of baby vegetables.

"You played it pretty good," I said, lighting a cigarette from the slim black candle sitting in a bud vase on the table. "No question that he recognized you?"

"He was the one wearing the mask. A black discipline hood with a zipper for the mouth. I made him put it on. It was a long session— he'd know me anywhere."

"So the rough-stud business tycoon bit—that was for my bene-fit?"

"Only partly," she said, reaching across and plucking my cigarette from the little round ashtray, taking a deep drag. "They never let you forget who's paying. It's not like it's a relationship. I'm a profes-sional—he'd *expect* me to keep his secrets. Discretion is part of the game."

I fell into her big gray eyes, held on tight. They reflected back guile-lessly—as if she'd never heard of blackmail. When she exhaled, the smoke shot out of the one nostril. Something there . . . I couldn't grab hold of it.

"They map out the scenes in front, then?"

"Most of the time. There's always a lot of crap about respecting lim-its, safety words . . . all that stuff. It's really hot now—all over the place. The hard-core magazines spell it out more, but even the upscale ones let you advertise. Some of them, you can't use words like 'dominant' or 'submissive,' but they always find a way. 'Role playing,' that's the fa-vorite."

"No surprises?"

"Not really. Except, maybe, for virgins. The first time, they're not sure what they want, and it can get silly."

"What happens if you mark them up?"

"Mark them up?"

"Whip marks, like that. Wouldn't their wives want to know what—"

"I know what I'm doing," she said defensively. "There's no reason for that to ever happen in a private scene, unless they want it to. In the videos, that's different . . . the audience wants to see the marks. That's why girls with light skin make the best submissives."

"You been . . . doing it a long time?"

"Since the beginning," she said, eyes glazing at some memory.

"If you only go one way, how come you . . . ?"

"I wanted to try it. See if it works. I . . . I'll tell you about it, someday."

"You don't have to—"

"I know. I never met a man like you before."

I finished my cigarette. "You want some dessert?" I asked her.

She nodded happily. I signaled the waiter. He rolled a four-tiered cart over. Fancy took three different pastries, gobbled them up, rolling her eyes, licking her lips. "I *love* sweets," she hummed. "They're perfect—'specially 'cause I can't have them too often."

I took out my notebook, showed her the list. "I got an idea," I told her. "Let's not hit the next one blind, all right? How about if you call, try and make an appointment?"

"What should I say?"

"Just introduce yourself, express your sympathy for their loss. Tell them a few families got together to hire me—to look into the suicides. Make it a kind of community concern thing."

"I can do that."

"So do it, girl."

"Is that an order?" she smiled.

"You want me to say 'or else'?"

"No," she said, grinning. "I'd be too hot to find out what the 'or else' was."

"Now, Fancy."

"Yes boss," she said, getting up and walking off, switching her hips hard enough to blow out the candles on the other tables.

S he was back in a few minutes. "I tried the Robinelles first. Got the mother. She said to come on over, right now."

"Good girl."

I paid the check. The waiter looked down his nose at cash, but perked right up when he saw what piece of it was his.

"Give me directions," I said as we rolled out of the restaurant parking lot.

"I don't give *you* directions," she told me, a heavy pout on her newly made-up lips.

I reached over, slapped her round thigh hard. "Tell me how to get there," I said.

She took me through town, out toward the water. "It's about another two, three miles down this road," she finally said.

I didn't reply, watching the scenery, trying to orient myself. Out here, you use landmarks, not street signs.

"I'm going to have a bruise," she said softly, touching a lacquered fingernail to the front of her thigh. "Look."

I flicked my eyes down and over. She was right.

The house was right on the waterfront, an architectural wet dream, skylights placed at odd angles on a steeply sloped roof of red Mediterranean tile, a tower of three stories cut right into the middle of a ranch-style design.

When the woman let us in, I could see the tower was a cathedral ceiling, like a hotel atrium without the fake waterfall.

The Robinelle woman was a blowsy blonde maybe fifteen pounds over the limit, a good deal of that spilling out the front of a sharply slashed V-neck blouse. She was wearing some kind of industrial-strength push-up bra, compressing her breasts into cartoon cleavage. Her blouse was red, the stretch pants a shiny black. A wide patent leather belt cinched in her waist, and the black spike heels exaggerated the jiggle as she walked toward the back of the house, telling us to follow.

She seated herself in a grotesquely curved white plastic chair that forced her back to arch, waving us toward a matching pair of green canvas director's chairs, spaced a few feet apart.

"I thought you'd be coming alone," she said to me by way of greeting. "Was it you that called me?" she asked Fancy.

"Yes."

"I don't feel comfortable talking in front of . . . neighbors. You *are* a neighbor, aren't you?"

"Yes. We live in the Crescent."

"That's nice. Well, perhaps Mr. . . . ."

"Burke," I told her.

"Perhaps, Mr. Burke, you can come back sometime."

"Go wait outside," I told Fancy.

"Look," she said, sitting up straight. "We hired you and—"

"And you're not calling the shots. Go wait in the car."

Fancy jumped to her feet, a flush under her dark tan.

"You don't have to do that," the woman said. "Perhaps you could just excuse us for a little bit? There's really a very nice library, just off the living room . . ."

Fancy looked at me. I nodded an okay. She flounced off, keeping the wiggle under control this time.

"I hope smoke doesn't bother you," the woman said, helping herself to a cigarette from a box sitting next to an ashtray on a black plastic cube standing next to her chair. "Lorenzo—that's my personal trainer—he'd kill me if he caught me."

"Not at all," I told her, taking out my own.

"Now . . ." she said, taking a deep enough drag to give her blouse a workout. "What can I tell you?"

"Well, I'm not really sure. With this kind of investigation, you can't be sure there *is* anything. Was Lana depressed in any way before it . . . happened?"

"Depressed? Mr. Burke, she was *born* depressed. Lana was always a strange girl. You know the type—dressed all in black, stayed in her room a lot."

"The . . . suicide wasn't such a shock, then?"

"Shock? Not to me. She'd tried it before."

"She tried to kill herself before?"

"That's what I just said. She wrote this long, incomprehensible poem first. A piece of drivel. Then she ran herself a warm bath, climbed in and cut her wrists. If my husband hadn't called the paramedics, she would have been dead then."

"How long ago was that?"

"Almost four years ago. She was still in high school."

"What happened after that?"

"She went into therapy, what else? Cost enough money, I can tell you. But it was a waste of time. This therapist, she wanted me and my husband to come in and talk about it. And we *did* that. But I wasn't going to spend the rest of *my* life in therapy because I had a sick girl for a daughter."

"Did she ever try it again?"

"She was *always* trying something. She and a friend of hers, another weirdo, they were always writing this sick poetry about death. She tried pills once, too."

"And . . . ?"

"And they pumped her stomach out at the hospital. And she went back into therapy. What a joke."

"You don't seem much of a fan of therapy."

"Why should I be? Everybody I know has been. They want to quit smoking, their husband has an affair, they're losing their looks . . . whatever it is, some shrink will do a number on you. You want a therapy fan, you need to talk to my husband—he loves the stuff."

"Your husband has been in therapy for a while?"

"Sure. Started when he was a kid. He's a rich, weak man. If that sounds like a contradiction to you, it isn't. He inherited the money. From his mother. He was a sensitive poet too, just like his precious daughter."

"Was?"

"Oh, he's alive. If you can call it that. We have a cabin. In Maine. That's mostly where he spends the summers. *Writing*," she sneered, the last word rich with contempt.

"He's a writer?"

"Some writer. He *pays* to have his own stuff published, can you imagine that?"

"I've heard of it."

"That's so lame. So weak. Him and his *literary* little friends. Fags, most of them, the way I see it. I intimidate them. The only kind of women they like are so skinny you could use them to pick a lock."

"I know what you mean."

"Do you?" she asked, squirming in her chair to make sure I couldn't accuse her of being subtle.

"Sure. It's a class thing. Working-class men have different taste."

"And what class are you, Mr. Burke?"

"Low-class," I told her, earning myself a wicked smile. "Was Lana at home when she . . ."

"Killed herself? Sure. She was only back from the hospital a couple of weeks. Crystal Cove. Another of these joints that charges an arm and a leg. To hear them tell it, we pay enough money, we'd get a brand-new kid."

"How was she when she came back?"

"The same. To be honest with you, I got pretty sick of it. My husband, he gives me my space. But not little Miss I'm-So-Depressed, not her. The shrink at the hospital told me the suicide crap was a cry for help. I never put up with it. I called her bluff all the time. Told her, you want to kill yourself, it can't be *that* hard."

"How did she react to that?"

"With a lot of babble. Like I said, I wasn't surprised. Only thing that surprised me was the way she did it."

"How did she do it?"

"She drowned. You know where Chalmer's Creek is?"

"No."

"It's maybe ten miles from here. It's not really a creek, more like a lake. But they call it a creek. They found her floating in it. The police said her lungs were full of water, so it was a drowning, I guess. But she didn't leave a note. That would have been the one thing I'd've expected from her—she always loved attention."

"The police tell you why they didn't think it was an accident?"

"They did think it was, at first. But when I told them all about her other attempts, they changed it."

"You've been very helpful, Mrs. Robinelle."

"Marlene."

"Marlene," I agreed. "Just one more question, if you don't mind. This friend of hers, the one she wrote poetry with . . . do you remember her name?"

"Wendy. Wendy something. She was only here a few times—I never really spoke to her."

"Would you have any of the poems?"

"No. The police took all that. They wouldn't even let me have her room cleaned until they were finished, can you imagine?"

"Yeah," I said, standing up to leave.

She got up too, standing very close to me. I could smell her over-ripe perfume, sweat running through baby powder. "If you need more information, you know where to find me."

"I appreciate that."

"My husband won't be back for a couple of weeks. It gets pretty tiresome, even with all this," she said softly, sweeping her hand to show me the water view through the picture window.

"I'm sure I'll have more questions."

"Then you come back. Call me first. But don't bring that nosy bitch with you."

I raised my eyebrows in a question.

"I like the way you handled her. I like a man who can take charge."

"She's paying the bills," I said.

"I can pay some bills too."

Fancy was sitting in the lush, paneled library, her face in an art book.

"Come on," I said to her.

She got up meekly and followed me. Marlene Robinelle didn't see us to the door.

"**W**hat did you find out?" Fancy asked me from the front seat of the Lexus.

"You first," I said.

"What do you mean?"

"Don't play games, bitch. I know you used that time to stick that perfect little nose of yours places."

"Do you really think my nose is perfect?" she smiled.

"Yeah. Cute as a button. Now what did you—?"

"I never left the library. I was afraid you'd come back and catch me. I didn't know how long you'd be."

"And . . . ?"

"She's a big phony. I found a list in a drawer. The last four, five weeks of the *New York Times* best-seller list, okay? And on the shelves, every single one of those books. Brand-new, never opened. You can tell, the spines were too tight. And inside each one, she had a photocopy of the review from the *Times*, see?"

"No."

"She doesn't read the books, just the reviews. So she can be with it at cocktail parties, see? What a tame cow she must be."

"Because she lets other people tell her what to do?"

"You can't be *that* stupid," she snapped at me. "I'm talking about your mind, not your body. Sex is different."

"Sex is only with your body?"

"What do *you* think it's with?"

"It's got to be with your mind. Otherwise, you could do a better job by yourself, right? Once your eyes are closed, once it's dark . . . how could you tell the difference?"

"Maybe there *is* no difference."

"Maybe not. But you have to throw the switch first."

She gave me a long look. "You scare me sometimes," she whispered.

"And you like that too, don't you?"

"Yes."

I piloted the Lexus back the way we came, not asking for directions, seeing if I could retrace my steps alone if I had to. Fancy wasn't talking, looking out her window, drumming her fingernails on the console between us.

"None of the books had been read?" I asked her. "In that whole huge library?"

"Oh sure, a lot of them. On a separate shelf. Like they were for separate people. Old books, you could tell somebody really loved them. And I'll bet my sweet ass it wasn't her."

"All that time alone, and that's what you found out?"

"Well, yes. It's a real clue to her character."

"Big fucking deal."

"Well, it could be. Did she offer you sex?"

"Kind of."

"That sow. If she ever climbed out of that girdle she calls an outfit, she'd flop around like a fish."

"Don't worry about it."

"I'd like to whip her fat ass. That'd be fun, but there's no market for it."

"What about—?"

"Nobody wants to see fat people being disciplined. They have to look good. And young."

"I guess you'd know."

"I'm a pro," Fancy said, turning her head so she could watch me.

"**W**hat can I get you?" she asked over her shoulder, crossing the threshold to her house.

"A glass of water."

"That's all?"

"Yeah. I don't have much time."

She moved off. I closed my eyes, playing the tapes of my conversations with the parents, mentally engraving the notes I hadn't taken. My eyes were still closed when I heard the click of high heels on the hard-wood floor, quick and close together, thinking: *Either a short woman or a real tight skirt*. It was both. Fancy, in a French maid's outfit right out of a porno movie. She had a glass of water on a wood serving board. She bent down, holding the serving board in both hands, just the trace of a smile on her lips.

"I always wanted to try this on," she said. "You like it?"

"It's very pretty."

"Pretty? *I'm* pretty—*this* is sexy."

"That's true."

"Wouldn't you like a maid of your own?"

"Sometimes . . . I guess I would."

"Here's your chance, mister."

"Not now," I told her. "I have to go."

Her gray eyes darkened. Sadness, not anger. "It's too good to rush-rush," I told her softly. "I'll be back."

"When?"

"Tomorrow."

"What about tonight?"

"I'm meeting some people. Late."

"Going back to fuck that sow?"

"What if I was?"

"I could come too. Did you ever—?"

"I'm not going there. It's business."

"Can't you come back? After?"

"It'd be way late. Three, four in the morning."

"That's okay."

"You sure?"

"Yes. I helped, didn't I?"

"You sure did."

"Well, if it's business, it's *this* business, right? Couldn't you come over, tell me about it?"

"All right."

She dropped to her knees, resting her chin on my knee. "Tell me to stay here," she whispered. "You know how to do it. Please."

I slapped her face, a short, sharp slap. It was louder than it was hard. "Stay here, bitch," I told her. "Don't leave. Right by the phone. I'll call you when I'm coming. And you better answer on the first ring."

"Yes sir," she said in a choky voice.

The kid was working on the Plymouth in the garage. He had the back end jacked up, the rear tires off. I wasn't worried about him finding the false bottom to the trunk—even the ATF had missed it once.

"What's going on?" I asked him, stepping out of the Lexus.

"I'm cleaning the tire treads," he said. "I tested it earlier. She corners better with forty-five pounds all around. You know you were only running thirty?"

"Yeah. Too much pressure and it rides like a truck."

"Sure, but for the race . . ."

"Okay. That's fine. However you want to do it."

The kid busied himself, intent. I lit a smoke, figuring out how to do what I had to do. First rule, get the other guy in a place where he's comfortable. Relaxed, so the knife goes in easier. I thought of taking him into the kitchen in the big house, where he couldn't hide his face. But when he had his hands on the car, he was a different kid, so maybe . . .

"Randy," I said, playing the long shot, "your girlfriend Wendy, how come you didn't tell me she was pals with Lana Robinelle?"

He dropped the tire pressure gauge, whirled to look at me, blood flooding his face.

"How did you . . . ?"

"You haven't been leveling with me, kid. Maybe not from the very beginning."

"I was! I mean, I told you the truth. Just . . ."

"Just what?"

He stood up, walked over to where I was standing. His hands were shaking, but he met my eyes. "I knew Lana . . . tried to kill herself. Before. A couple of times, even. Everybody knew it, at school and all. I tried to talk to Wendy about it, but she thought I was an asshole. A tanker, you know?"

"So when you called me . . ."

"I was scared. That was the truth."

"But not scared for you, huh?"

"I guess I was, maybe. I don't know. The hospital. My mother told me once that she'd send me there if I didn't straighten up."

"But you're eighteen now. An adult, right? She couldn't *make* you go."

"Nineteen," he said. "But you don't know her."

"Never mind that now. Just give me the whole story."

"I was at a party a couple of months ago. She . . . Wendy was there. She doesn't do dope, but she drops acid sometimes—it's coming back in now, a lot of kids do it. She was out in the back, on the lawn. Tripping. She got real scared. The rest of them thought it was funny, her jumping around and all. I . . . held her. A long time. When she stopped, she was dreamy. Spaced out, I guess. She told me she saw Lana. She was happy. Lana, not Wendy. Happy where she was."

The kid took a breath, still on my eyes. I could feel him willing me to understand how bone-deep important this all was to him. "I got . . . terrified. You see it, don't you? She was going there. With Lana. But the more I told her it was crazy, the more she said I didn't understand. I stayed with her, that whole night. She has her own car, but I wouldn't let her drive. When I took her home, it was light out. Her father was there, waiting up. He blamed it on me. Told me if he ever saw me around her again, he'd kill me.

"I couldn't call her on the phone. And I don't see her in school anymore. She sent me a letter. A poem. It wasn't a sad poem, like I expected. It was . . . I don't know, gentle. I read it and read it. But when I got it, I got scared. It's about dying, Burke.

"I watched her house. At night. The police stopped me one time. They were gonna take me in, but then they found out who I was. Who my mother was, really. They called her and she came and got me.

"Wendy found out. She told me it was sweet, what I did. But it didn't matter. She wasn't going to go until she was ready.

"I saw her a lot, after that. Different places. She was the only one I ever told about racing. She said that was my poetry, driving.

"Then my mother went away. For the summer. Right after that, Wendy told me. Her parents were gonna put her in Crystal Cove, to get her some help. She promised to stop the acid-tripping, but they didn't believe her. That's when I got so scared. That's when I called you. I thought you could . . . save her. And I could . . . help, like."

I felt it. So deep I didn't know there was such a place in me. This rich, spoiled kid. This punk I thought was a herd animal. I never saw anyone so scared for someone else, reaching outside himself like that, trying to pull her in with him.

"Come on, kid," I told him. "We got work to do before it gets dark."

We took the Miata. The kid knew about Chalmer's Creek, got us there in a flash.

"What's here?" he asked.

I stood at an outcropping of rock, looking down at the blue-black water. "This is where Lana Robinelle went over," I said. "Drowned."

I picked up a heavy rock, held it in two hands. Dropped it over the side into the water. Watched it disappear, the circles spreading out from the center, wider and wider, reaching

"What's it look like to you?" I asked him.

He looked down, eyes following my pointing finger. "A bull's-eye," he said.

"You're in it now," I told him on the drive back. "That's what you wanted, right?"

"Yes."

"All right, kid. First rule—you don't talk. Understand?"

"Yes."

"Anybody you talk to, regular?"

"Just . . . Wendy."

"Nobody knows your secrets? Not your mother? Nobody?"

"Nobody."

"Okay. Keep it that way. Meet me at the garage tonight. Eleven o'clock. We're gonna do some work."

"I'll be there," he said, face set in harder lines than I thought it had.

Back in the apartment, I found the microphone and pulled it loose. Whoever set it up would have to come back. I checked the rest of the place. Couldn't find anything new.

Eight o'clock. I took a shower, wrapped a towel around my waist, lay down on the bed and closed my eyes. I didn't even try and sort things—I'd be talking to the Prof soon enough.

A tap on the front door glass woke me up. I flicked off the towel, slipped into a pair of pants, walked through the dark house. My watch said 10:05.

It was Randy, standing outside the door, hand poised to tap again. I opened the door. "What?"

He stepped past me, agitated, moving quick, words tumbling out of his mouth too fast for me to follow.

"Hey!" I said to him. "Hold it down. Get it together, all right? Something happened?"

"No. I mean, yes. I don't know. It didn't *just* happen. I have to tell you—"

"Randy, sit down. Relax."

"I can't. I . . ."

"Breathe through your nose," I told him. "Close your mouth and breathe through your nose. Deep breaths. Slow."

He followed orders, working at it until he stopped gulping air, sat down on the couch. I sat across from him. The only light was a moon-spill through the windows, enough to see his shape, not his face.

"Now . . . what is it?"

"I . . . lied, Burke."

"About what?"

"When you asked me, about secrets. Did I talk to anyone . . . ?"

"Yeah?"

"Charm. I talked to Charm. That time she was here. When she went into the house by herself."

"You already told me about that."

He mumbled something, head down.

"Randy, work easy now. Speak so I can hear you. Come on."

"Charm asked me about you. What you were doing here."

"You told me that."

"I didn't tell you that I . . . told her about Crystal Cove."

"That's all right. It's not much of a secret now, with all the running around I've been doing."

"Charm said to . . . keep an eye on you. I'm supposed to call her, tell her what you do."

"And you said you'd do that?"

"I told her no. But she . . . took me inside the house."

"I don't get it."

He started to cry then. First a bubble, then a dry sob . . . then it all went loose. Shame radiated off him like heat. I let it go for a while, saw it wasn't going to stop. I got up, walked around behind him. Put my hands on his shoulders, working the piano-wire muscles with my thumbs the way you loosen up a fighter before he gets it on. "Let it go, kid. Nothing's gonna hurt you now. It's pus, like from a wound. Squeeze it out."

I kept working until the sobbing slowed down, stumbled to a stop. I stepped back away from the kid. He shook himself violently, trying to throw something off his back—sweat flew off his body, spraying fear. When that stopped, he trembled. Sat there trembling.

I went back to my chair. "Tell me," I finally said.

"Charm was like my . . . babysitter. When I was a kid. I really . . . admired her. She's so tough. One time, she was jumping horses and she fell off. Broke her leg. We were all there, watching. Charm didn't say a word. I mean, you could *see* it hurt . . . her face was all white and sweaty and her leg . . . it was bent all funny. But she didn't say a word."

"When . . . ?"

"In the seventh grade, that's when it started."

"What did she do?"

"If I told my friends, they would have thought it was great. So great. Like a dream come true. That's what Charm says, the trick is to come true."

"You had sex with her?"

"I . . . guess it was sex. What she did. It made me . . . excited. But I was scared too. I didn't know what to do."

"I know."

"I wanted to do it. I mean, after a while, I wanted to do it. All the time. All she had to do was touch me. The handle, that's what she called it. Charm says everybody has a handle. I thought she meant my . . . cock. But that wasn't it. The handle, it's the way you twist people."

"How did it start?"

"I was in my room. In my bathroom, taking a shower. And she just came in there. I was . . . embarrassed. But she did something . . . with her mouth . . . and I got excited. Then she did it. With her hand. Then she . . . hit me. Hard. It hurt. I was . . . crying. And she kept hitting me. She told me I was a dirty little boy. I was scared of her, but she did it again, later. Then she told me I had to do what she said."

"Did you ever tell? Tell anyone?"

"I . . . couldn't. I was . . . guilty, like. Like it was my fault. Dirty. I started . . . fucking up. Everything. I used to get all A's—I really liked school, once. And I was . . . beating off. All the time, even in the Boys' Room at school. I had bad dreams. Then I got caught . . ."

"In school?"

"At the mall. Shoplifting. The security people, they made me sign something, then they called my mother. She came down, all mad. She went in their office with them. Alone. When she came out, she took me home. And she showed me the paper I signed. Tore it up right in front of me. It was okay, she said. All fixed. But she wanted me to . . . see someone."

"A therapist?"

"Yeah. Dr. Barrymore."

"From Crystal Cove?"

"Yes. But I didn't have to go into the hospital. He has this house, right on the grounds. And he has an office in the back. That's where I saw him."

"You didn't tell him about Charm?"

"I kind of . . . did. But not for a long time. He's my mother's friend. I'd seen him in the house. A couple of times. I could tell from the way she talked to him . . . I thought he'd tell her."

"Why didn't you just tell her yourself?"

"Charm showed me . . . pictures. Pictures of her and my mother, naked. Together . . . you know?"

"Sure. You thought they were lovers?"

"They were! You could see . . . what they were doing. In the pictures. They were . . . disgusting."

"Because of what they were doing?"

"Because it was my mother!" He started crying again. "And Charm told me . . . Charm said my mother told her to do it. With me. So I'd know how to do it. With girls, like."

"And you believed her?"

"My mother always hired people to teach me things. To play the guitar, or ride horses. Dancing. She always paid people to teach me. Charm said I would be . . . a homosexual unless she helped me."

"That's got nothing to do with her," I told him.

"I know. I mean, I think I know. But I never . . ."

"With girls?"

"Yeah. Except with Charm."

"Still?"

He looked down, quiet for a minute. "Yes," he finally said. "That's what happened the last time she came over. I didn't want to do anything, but . . ."

"It's okay. It takes time, to get strong enough."

"I'll never be strong enough. I thought I was. She . . . hasn't come around for a long time."

"Yeah you will. And soon, too. She was conditioning you, understand?"

"No."

"She started with you early, so you got used to . . . certain things. After a while, you feel like that's the only way you *can* do it, see? But it's a trick . . . a cheap, dirty trick."

"How could I . . . ?"

"You already are, kid. If her stuff was really working, you wouldn't feel anything for Wendy."

"What do you mean?"

"How do you feel about Wendy? Like she's your sister?"

"No. But I never tried to—"

"What? Have sex with her? Don't worry about it. You feel like you want to be with her. Close. To protect her, right?"

"Yes."

"The rest will come, kid. I promise you. You may have to talk to somebody . . . some pro who knows what they're doing—some places you can't get to all by yourself. But it's already happening. You got a good throw of the dice now—let it ride."

His head came up, eyes on me now. "What do I have to do?" he asked.

"For now, you have to drive—we got a meet to go to."

I showed the kid how to park so we could cover the whole lot with one eye-sweep while we waited. A couple of minutes before midnight, Clarence's Rover glided past the gas pumps. They spotted us, rolled over to where we were parked. I was already stepping out of the car. The Prof came over to where I was standing, leaving Clarence at the wheel. He was carrying a dark green canvas duffel in one hand. We naturally rolled into a prison-yard position, shoulder to shoulder at a slight V-angle so we narrowed the exposure of our backs and could watch the maximum vista. The way it's done, your mouth hardly moves but your eyes never stop.

"What you got that's hot, schoolboy?"

"A nest of snakes, Prof. I need to show you a few things. We'll take my car, okay?"

"You say, we play, bro," the little man said, waving Clarence over.

The Prof took the shotgun seat next to Randy, Clarence and I sat behind. Randy cruised through the quiet streets as I ran it down. The Prof gave me a quick glance over his shoulder, tilting his head toward Randy. I nodded—it was all right for the kid to hear.

"The Mole showed the printout to some other people. Israelis," I said. "They got somebody they want on that list."

"Don't be downing the Mole, man. Everybody's got a button, something to push."

"I know," I said. Thinking of Charm—and her handles. "That's not the thing. I saw the list too. Here's one of the names on it," I said, pausing to give it weight, "—Angelo Mondriano."

"Damn! He's been *long* gone, youngblood. Word is he's holding up a bridge somewhere, inside a slab of concrete."

"I don't think so."

"I remember it now," the Prof mused. "He went canary, then he jumped the cage, right? Didn't some of the wiseguys ask you about running him down?"

"Yeah. He must have dropped a couple of dozen heavy hitters when he testified. He was in the Witness Protection Program, then he went over the Wall. Six-figure bounty on his ass. Open contract—the money for his head."

"That's not like the new Italians. What about all the cash he was supposed to have swiped?"

"There's Italians, and there's Italians," I said. "The guys who came to see me, they were the old guys, you understand? *Vindicata!* The money wasn't the thing for them. It was blood. You know the rules."

"Yeah. You turn, you burn. You roll, you pay the toll. But I thought . . ."

"No. Couldn't be. They dropped him, they'd want to make it public. Put his head on a stake, send the message."

"That's right enough," the little man agreed. "So what we got, somebody in the ID business?"

"Sure. That's where the money's coming from. It was a long list, Prof."

"And the Israelis, they're going in?"

"Yeah." I gave Randy directions, told him to cruise by Rector's. "And that's ours," I pointed.

Without being told, the kid swept into a slow series of figure 8's, passing back and forth around Rector's from different angles.

"It don't look like much—a real soft touch," the Prof said, evaluating with his eyes.

"I got a way in. Front door," I told him. "That's not the work."

"Okay, bro. Take the point—let's eyeball the joint."

"Drive over to Crystal Cove," I translated for Randy.

The kid drove the way a pro diver hits the water . . . without a splash. Fingertips light on the wheel, taking the corners just the quiet side of tire squeal, braking so smooth he wouldn't have spilled a full cup of coffee.

"My man can *drive*, can't he, Prof?" I asked.

"Fine as wine," he replied, holding out his palm for me to slap.

Clarence never said a word.

"What can you tell me about the grounds?" I asked Randy, talking over his shoulder.

"I was never inside the hospital itself," he said, not turning around. "Just inside the doctor's house, near the front. There's a stone wall all around it. Not a high one—you could jump it with a good horse."

"Any guards?"

"I never saw any."

"Okay. When we get close, let me know."

We drove in silence for a bit. Then the Prof said, "We going in?"

"If it looks right. You got your works?"

"It's in the bag, and that's no gag."

"Righteous."

The road turned narrow, trees arching over the top of the car as we drove. No houses. The car started up a grade. "It's about a half-mile up the road," Randy said.

"Find a place to pull over. Where we won't be seen from the road."

He slowed the Plymouth, watching the landscape.

"No," I told him. "Someplace with a strong sight-line. Can you do it?"

"Sure." He slowed down again for a deep J-curve, still climbing. When he finally stopped the car, we were standing on a bluff. "Down there," Randy said, pointing.

We got out of the car, walked to the edge, looked down. I could see where the hospital got its name. The cove was landlocked, nestled in a natural triangle of hills and woods, with one side open to a road below. It was a series of low, interlocking buildings, all flat-topped except for a glass spire rising several stories from the part closest to the entrance.

I popped the trunk, found the night glasses, held them to my eyes. Most of the buildings were old stone, with small multi-paned windows. Along the back part of the triangle there was a long, narrow structure, built into the rest of the hospital but obviously constructed much more recently. Gray, smooth-finish granite, with seamless slits of dark glass. Probably one-way—I couldn't see any lights behind them like I could in the rest of the place.

The stone wall was in place, just like the kid said. It didn't completely circle the grounds. Instead, it ran in a sharp V from a meeting point at the front, where a wide opening was guarded by a black metal gate, hinged in the middle. I tracked the right-hand wall to its end—it seemed to merge into the underbrush at the base of the hills behind the hospital.

I handed the glasses to Randy. "Can you get the car close to the rear . . . where the wall comes against those hills?"

"I think so."

"Okay, let's get it ready," I said to the Prof, turning back to the trunk. I took out a pair of Connecticut plates, special-made for me at the Mole's. Handed them to Randy. "Put these on, front and rear," I told him. "It's just wing nuts—you can do it with your fingers." He held the plates in his hands, tracing the heavy seam on the reverse side of the embossed numbers, looking a question at me.

"You take two plates, cut them down the middle with a torch, then you weld the two halves together. It gives you a cold plate—won't bounce any of the Law's computers."

He nodded, went to work. I took a wide roll of tape, Day-Glo orange, peeled it open, and handed one end to the Prof. We taped a line across the back bumper—headlights would pick it up hundreds of yards away. We left a big piece loose and dangling. When we were done, I handed the Prof a big orange circle of plastic with a peel-off back, took one for myself. We pasted one on each of the back doors. The Prof took off his long duster—underneath he was wearing black jeans, a black sweatshirt, black sneakers on his feet. When my jacket came off, I looked the same. Added a navy watch cap for my head. We each slipped on a pair of thin black kid gloves. The Prof took a flat leather case from his duffel, slipped it into a side pocket.

Clarence got in the front seat—I took the back with the Prof. Randy started the car, then he motored slowly down the rise, nosing around until he found the right spot. We were maybe twenty yards from the end of the stone wall.

"You want to run the jungle?" the Prof asked.

"I don't think so. Don't know what's back there. Maybe a trip-wire . . ."

"So let's do the wall, Paul."

"Hold up a few minutes," I said. "See if there's a guard on the circuit."

Nobody spoke for a while.

We gave it fifteen minutes or so.

Nothing.

"You ready, Clarence?"

"You're covered, mahn," he said, pulling a long black tube from under the seat, holding it pointing down.

"Randy," I said quietly, leaning forward. "We're gonna commit a crime here. All of us. Prof and I are going in, Clarence's gonna hold our place, understand? Your job, you start the engine, leave it running. The back doors stay open. Don't worry, no light will show. If we come back walking, you move off slow, okay? But if we come back smoking, you have to *go*, understand?"

"Yes."

"You up for it?"

"Yes."

"Randy, you don't have to do this, okay? We can drop you off somewhere, pick you up when it's done. Reason we need you, it's for the driving."

"Count me in," he said, voice steady, looking me in the face.

The Prof and I walked off, Clarence right behind us. "No shooting," I told the young man. "No matter what."

Clarence ignored me, his handsome West Indian face totally trained on the Prof. The little man nodded. "Your play, your way," is all he said. Clarence walked back toward the car. The Prof and I strolled toward the wall, stepping carefully, eyes on full sweep.

"You strapped down, schoolboy?"

"I'm empty."

"So what's the game, son? This ain't no B&E we doing, is it?"

"No. What we're gonna do, we're gonna go over the wall, look around a little bit. Worst that happens, we get busted, it's a trespass, that's all."

"Say why, Sly."

"We wait a bit, okay? Then we come busting out, tell the kid to *fly*. I gotta see what he's made of . . . give him a chance to stand up without us taking a risk on a fall."

"He's a little tight, but he'll be all right."

The wall was not quite chest-high, but wide across the top. I couldn't see any sensors. Would they have cameras this far out?

I went over first. Waited on the ground, listening. The quiet was thick, like it had been around a long while, settling in.

The Prof came next. With our backs against the wall, it was more than a football field's run to the nearest building.

"Too easy," the Prof whispered.

He was right. I could feel the buildings standing across the broad expanse of neatly trimmed lawn, bristling with . . . what?

"This is enough," I whispered back. "Give it another five minutes and we're off."

We settled back against the wall, watching, nerve endings throbbing, fully extended.

It was quiet as a congressman's conscience.

I threw a hand signal at the Prof. We climbed over the wall, him first. When we got to the other side, we took off running.

The Plymouth was standing, ready to roll, the back doors open, Clarence down on one knee by the front wheel.

"Go!" I barked at Randy as the Prof and I piled into the back seat with Clarence a step ahead of us in front.

The kid came out of the chute like a rocket sled, straight and true, making the adjustment from grass to pavement perfectly. The Plymouth's monster motor was wound tight in seconds, holding in low gear with a baritone scream. Randy felt his way into the J-curve, running without lights, working the big car into a controlled skid, goosing it through with the throttle.

"They're coming," I said into his ear, leaning over the back seat. "Let it out."

The Plymouth gobbled the straightaway in humongous gulps, the engine singing a different harmonic as Randy upshifted. We came to a switchback—the kid braked and downshifted in one motion, staying on the gas with his other foot, keeping the spring coiled. He was a skater on black ice, leaning into the curves with the Plymouth, *being* the car. We hit another straight stretch and I looked over his shoulder—the tach was at five grand and climbing, way over a hundred miles an hour.

"You bought us some time, kid," I told him. "Quick—find a place to pull over."

He hit the brakes, snapped the Plymouth into a turnoff as neatly as a tongue-in-groove carpenter, stayed alert at the wheel as we all jumped out. The Prof and I each pulled one of the Day-Glo circles off the black doors, Clarence stripped the tape from the bumper. The license plates took only another minute . . . and we were legit.

"Speed limit now, Randy," I said, getting back into the car. "Lights on."

He drove the rest of the way like he was taking the final in Driver's Ed.

"Follow us," I told Clarence through the window. His Rover was standing next to the Plymouth, motors running, side by side, like getting set for a drag race.

"This is not no race car, mahn."

"We'll do it slow and easy," I assured him. "If we get stopped, just roll on home—I'll call."

He threw me a half-salute. I nodded to Randy and he dropped the Plymouth into gear.

The kid watched the rearview mirror for a minute, making sure Clarence was in position. I lit a smoke, leaned back.

"You did good," I told him. "Drove like a veteran."

"Thanks. I know about the plates . . . but how come you put those orange stickers on the car?"

"It changes the appearance. It's the one thing anyone chasing you remembers. Like when you do a stickup—a fake scar on your face or a phony tattoo on your hand, that's what the mark will fix on. If we had to, you could reach out and pull off the tape even with the car going, see?"

"Yeah. That's why the brake lights don't go on? And why there's no light when you open the door?"

"Sure. But I didn't expect you could drive that fast without head-lights."

"Well, I knew the road pretty good. And I can see in the dark fine."

"Had a lot of practice, haven't you?"

He didn't answer. Concentrated on his driving like he hadn't heard me.

Clarence was right on our rear bumper in the driveway. When the headlights went off, we were in darkness, the only light coming from the kitchen window of the big house.

"You leave the light on?" I asked the kid.

"Yes. I always do."

"Okay. Let's go someplace where we can talk."

"Can't we just go upstairs?" he asked, nodding his head in the direction of my apartment.

"Better not. Somebody's been playing with microphones."

"The . . . intercom. From my mother's—"

"I don't know. Somebody. Can't take chances," I told him, opening the trunk. I took out a couple of heavy army blankets.

"We going to have a picnic, mahn?" Clarence wanted to know.

"Close enough."

"Then I got some stuff too," he said, going into the Rover's trunk and pulling out something that looked like a small toolbox. The Prof stood in one spot, turning a full 360, smelling the ground.

I opened the garage, pointed. Clarence got behind the wheel of his Rover, drove it inside. I pulled the Plymouth in too.

"You know a decent spot?" I asked Randy.

"I . . . guess so. The back pasture, okay? I mean, there's no more horses there or anything."

"No bulls either, mahn?" Clarence said, looking around suspiciously.

"No."

We walked a short distance past the wood fence, found a spot on a grassy slope, spread out the blankets, sat down.

I lit a smoke. Clarence unsnapped the top of the box he was carrying, took out a dark bottle, offered it to Randy.

"You have a beer with us, mahn? To celebrate success. You sure earned it."

"I . . ."

"Go on, mahn. This is Red Stripe. Best beer in the world. From the Islands, where the air is sweet and the women are sweeter."

"Thanks."

Clarence took out a church key, popped the cap, handed the bottle to Randy.

"Long as it's free, how's about me?" the Prof piped up, reaching in to help himself.

Clarence took one too. "Got your poison right here too, Burke," he smiled, handing me a screw-top bottle of pineapple juice. It was cold. Clean and good.

"To Randy," the Prof said, holding his bottle high in a toast. "My man can drive, and that ain't no jive."

"Word!" Clarence acknowledged.

"You got my vote," I said, tapping my bottle against theirs.

Randy hung his head. I could feel the blush. But when his eyes came up, they were heavy with regret.

"What?" I asked him.

"It's . . . gonna sound stupid."

"Ain't no 'stupid' among friends, mahn," Clarence encouraged him.

"What's it about? Spit it out," said the Prof.

It was quiet for a minute. Then Randy looked somewhere into the open space between the Prof and me, blurted out, "I *hate* my name."

"Randy? Or . . ."

"Randy. It's a kid's name. A baby name. Everybody always calls me that. Randy. I mean, nobody would say *Randall*. That's a name on a business card."

"You don't like the game, you turn up the flame," the Prof told him. "A man don't pick his mother. Don't pick his father neither. But a man can choose his family, right?"

I reached over, tapped bottles with him again. Underlining the bond.

"You a man, cuzz. You old enough to play, you old enough to say, okay?"

"I . . . suppose so."

"*We* give you a name, mahn," Clarence said, caught up in the idea. "Like a baptism."

"You came through tonight," I told the kid. "What do you want your name to be?"

"I don't know. I mean . . . I never thought about it."

"Ain't but two names for the outlaw game," the Prof said. "You a bad man behind the wheel. Drive like a hell-hawk tracking a mouse. Got to have a bad man's name."

"Like what?"

"Like I said: whatever you do, it's one of two. It's Junior. Or Sonny. Got to be either Junior or Sonny."

"Those don't sound like a bad man's names."

"What I gonna do with this rookie, schoolboy?" the Prof said to me. "True-clue him, all right?"

"It's the way things are," I said to Randy. "You meet a man named Junior or Sonny, you know you're dealing with serious stuff. Those are heavy-duty names."

"I knew a man named Junior Stackhouse back home," Clarence said. "Baddest man in town. Junior would get himself drunk, nothing he liked better than to fight the police, mahn. He was a terror."

"Junior . . . sounds like . . . I don't know. Like it should be Randall Cambridge the Second or something lame like that."

"Well, maybe Junior's too slow around all this dough," the Prof said. "Sonny it is."

"I never knew a man named Sonny that wasn't a stone dangerous stud," I put in. "Like the name was a brand so people could tell."

"Rhymes with honey, too," the Prof added. "That seals the deal."

Clarence held out his hand, palm up. Randy slapped him five.

"Damn, cuzz," the Prof told him. "You look badder already."

The night didn't have a chance against the kid's smile.

"Here's what we got so far." I ran it down. "Somebody's doing ID switches—big money in that. And we got the suicides too. I can't see the connect, but there almost has to be one. If there is, Crystal Cove is the link."

"The link stinks, bro," the Prof replied. "Kids off themselves. Do it all the time. Don't take much, 'specially out here. The beds are soft, but the life could be hard. Out here, they whip their kids with words. Cuts just as deep."

"I know."

"I don't see going in, Jim. What we need, we need to talk to the boss. The list . . . that's the key to that lock."

"I may have another one," I said. "Few more days, I'll know for sure."

"Company," Clarence whispered, his hand going inside his jacket. I stubbed out my cigarette. Headlights cut the night, bluestone crunched under tires. A pearl white Rolls-Royce sedan pulled to a stop just past the garage.

"Charm," the kid whispered. "That's her car."

Minutes passed. A car door opened and a person stepped out. I couldn't see anything about them—whoever it was wore a long black coat with a hood covering their head. The hooded figure walked confidently over to the big house, unlocked the back door and went inside. Lights went on.

"She has a key?" I asked.

"I guess so," the kid replied, not sounding surprised.

She was inside maybe ten minutes. Then she went back to her car. There was nothing in her hands that I could see. The Rolls purred off, as unhurried as its driver.

We spent some more time out there, talking things through.

"Follow me back to the highway," I told Clarence. "I'll get you pointed toward home."

The kid got up, reaching in his pocket for the keys. "I'll drive," he said.

He pulled over just before the highway, Clarence right behind. We stood together in the dark.

"Be cool, Sonny," Clarence told him.

"I will."

The Prof gave him a light punch on the shoulder, waved at me, and climbed into the Rover.

In a minute, their taillights vanished.

"**B**urke?"

"What?"

"Is it okay . . . I mean, are you going to go to sleep?"

"I don't know. Why?"

"Well, I thought . . . if it was okay . . . I'd go over and see Wendy."

"It's almost four in the morning, Sonny."

He blinked a few times at his new name, found his voice. "She doesn't sleep. At night, I mean. That's when I go over. Around the back. I toss some dirt against her window and she comes out."

"Go for it," I told him.

I took a quick shower, changed my clothes, and headed the Lexus toward Fancy's. Halfway there, I reached for the car phone—tossing some dirt against a girl's window, you can do that when you're young—when you still *believe* in things.

"Hello." Her voice was thick with sleep.

"It's me. I wanted to be sure you were awake."

"I . . . guess I wasn't. I didn't think you were coming."

"I said I was."

"I'm sorry."

"Don't be sorry for your thoughts. See you soon."

All three cottages were dark. Lights on in the main house, different dots of brightness in the blackness. Like a constellation.

Fancy's NSX was parked in the long driveway, carelessly sprawled, like it was abandoned. I didn't see a white Rolls-Royce anywhere. I walked past the fender of the Lexus, pulled the pistol free, slipped it into my jacket pocket.

Fancy opened the door, her face scrubbed clean of makeup, hair tousled. She was barefoot, dressed in a short blue nightie. The only light was a soft spill from somewhere in the back of the house . . . maybe the bathroom door standing open? I took off my jacket, draped it over the back of the couch. She walked over, reached for it.

"Don't touch that," I told her. "Just leave it where it is."

"Yes sir."

"Fancy . . ."

"Tell me what to do."

Christ. I was tired. In my body, in my heart. Tired of games. Guessing games. "Turn around," I said.

She did it, her back to me, head slightly bowed. I found an amber glass ashtray standing on one of the broad arms of the couch—it hadn't been there the last time. I picked it up, looked around. In one corner, a bright red steamer trunk with two heavy straps wrapped around it, a thick pillow on top, like a gym mat. In the opposite corner, a four-legged, round-top wooden stool.

All set up.

I put the ashtray on top of the stool, picked them both up and carried them over to the side of the only easy chair in the room. I took out my cigarettes and a box of wooden matches, put them next to the ashtray.

I sat down in the chair, stretched my legs out. So tired.

Fancy was still standing, back to me. "Come here, girl," I said.

She walked over slowly, head down, hands clasped in front of her. When she got close enough, I reached up, took her left hand and pulled her down. As she tumbled forward, I kept pulling, turning her around so she spun into my lap. She made a purring noise as I put both hands on her hips, shifting her weight so she was sideways, her face in my neck. I patted her hip with my right hand, settling her in.

"Should I— ?"

"Ssshh," I soothed her. "Just be still." I reached for the cigarette, got it lit, lay back, Fancy's springy girl-weight spread across me, sweetly balanced. I blew some tension out with the smoke.

Closed my eyes.

Fancy wiggled her bottom, just a mild tremor.

"Burke?"

"What?"

"Is this . . . yours?"

"What?"

"Is this the way you like to do it?"

"I'm too tired for word games, bitch," I said gently. "What are you talking about?"

She turned her face so she was speaking right into my ear, baby's-breath soft.

"Sitting down. Like in your car. I like that too. I'm all wet. See?" grabbing my hand, pulling it toward the triangle between her thighs.

"Fancy, I want to hold you on my lap. Understand?"

"Just hold me?"

"Just hold you, now."

"I thought—"

I lifted the hem of her nightie, slapped the side of one sleek cheek. "Shut up. *I* thought you were going to do as you were told."

"I am."

"Then sit still, bitch."

She snuggled into me obediently, a clean, moist smell rising off her tawny skin. The cigarette burned itself out in the ashtray as I closed my eyes.

I woke up, feeling the change of light in the room. Almost daybreak. Fancy was asleep in my lap, breathing through her mouth. I bounced her lightly on my knee to bring her around.

"Wha . . . ?"

"Wake up, Fancy. It's morning."

"Morning?"

"Yes, girl. You had a good sleep, but if I leave you here much longer my leg's gonna be paralyzed."

"I'm sor—"

"Shut *up*, bitch. I'm tired of hearing that. Come on, get up. I'm going to get you into bed before I go."

"Go?"

"Ah, come on," I said, shifting my weight, boosting her up. She got to her feet, rubbed her eyes with her fists, as unselfconscious as a child. When I got to my feet, my right leg was asleep. I stomped it a few times on the carpet, feeling the pins and needles, getting the life back. Fancy stood in one spot, eyes heavy-lidded, still dopey from sleep.

I took her hand, led her back toward the bedroom. I half pushed her onto the bed. She lay on her side, looking up at me standing there. I bent over, kissed her next to her mouth.

"I'll see you tomorrow," I told her.

"You could sleep here," she said. "Stay with me."

"I've gotta . . ."

"Please. Just for a little bit. Till I fall back asleep."

I sat down on the bed, slipped off my boots and socks. I took everything else off except my shorts, dropped onto the bed on my back. Fancy rolled into my chest, licking gently, making little noises. She curled her legs at the knee, feet up, like a teenage girl talking on the phone. I stroked her back through the nightie, drifting.

Fancy put her hands flat on my chest, pushed herself up so she was facing me on her knees. Her hands dropped to the hem of the nightie, then she pulled it up and over her head, tossed it over the side of the bed. Her breasts stood out sharply from her body, unnaturally cantilevered, so heavy they almost met in the center, dark nipples standing out from the bronzed skin. She arched her back, emphasizing. Proud.

I reached for her, held the back of her neck as I pulled her down, rubbed my face against one of her nipples, feeling it grow hard as my light beard stubble scratched her. I moved my face, took the nipple in my mouth, bit down lightly.

"Yessss," she moaned.

I let go of the back of her neck. Still kneeling, she bent so deeply I could sight down her back to the separation of her buttocks, the twin peaks flaring out from her tiny waist into a perfect heart shape as she arched her back into a deep curve. Her glossy dark hair shone in the early light as she reached for the waistband of my shorts, tugging. I lay flat on the bed, not helping her, but she kept tugging until she got them down.

"Hah!" she grunted, her face up, grinning at me. She kept pulling, working her way backward toward the foot of the bed, finally pulling the shorts off, flinging them hard in the direction of the bureau. She lowered her head and came forward fast, head down, charging like a bull. I could feel her tongue licking my balls, then rooting deeper, a muffled grunting noise coming from somewhere past her throat.

I reached out, took hold of her hair and pulled. She didn't move, resisting. I pulled harder. She wiggled her hips, shifting the pitch of the noise she was making, staying where she was.

"Fancy!"

She looked up, a wicked grin on her face, gray eyes wide open now. Then she lowered her head again.

I felt swollen, like a blood vessel was going to go, every vein full. I sat up, put my hands under her armpits and hauled her up until her face was right against mine. She fitted herself over me, taking it deep, trying to sit up. I kept my hands on her, holding her against me, forcing her to straddle. Her hips bucked, thrusting almost to full lock with each stroke. I ran my hand down her smooth back, tracing her spine with my fingers until I found the little spur at the end, right between the dimples on her bottom. I pushed the spur like it was a trigger. She muttered something in my ear, something I couldn't make out.

Her hard breasts bounced against my chest, slick with sweat. I kept my finger at the base of her spine, forcing her hips into little spasms. She was still saying something, harsh short breaths separating the words.

"Tell . . . me . . . what . . . to . . . do!"

I put my hands on her hips, driving her toward me as I shoved upward. "Come, bitch," I told her. "Do it now."

She popped off so hard I could feel the temperature change inside her. Her teeth were closed at the side of my neck as I caught her rhythm, followed her home.

When I came around again, the sunlight was slanted across Fancy's back. She was still on top of me, propped up on her elbows, looking down into my eyes.

"You're awake?" she asked.

"I guess I am."

"I didn't want to move—didn't want to wake you up."

"Thanks."

"You want a shower?"

"In a minute."

"A cigarette?"

"Sure."

She slid off me, a faint crackle between her legs as we pulled apart. She stood up, stretched. Then she padded off to the living room. Came back with an ashtray and my cigarettes, sat on the bed, lit one for me. I took it from her, dragged deep.

"I never did that before," she said.

"That?"

"Sex. Like that. Before last night. I mean, before *last*, last night, in your car."

"Like what?"

"With a man. Inside me."

"I seemed to fit easy enough."

She took the cigarette from my hand, pulled on it, exhaled. I watched the smoke fire from only one nostril, feeling her eyes, not connecting with them.

"I . . . put things inside myself. To get off. After I was done playing dom. Or sometimes, just thinking about it. And a couple of times, she did it to me . . . with a vibrator."

"Who?"

"It doesn't matter," she said. "I'm going to take a shower. There's another one, down the hall, if you want."

"**W**e can go. Sunday night," she said, standing at the door, her hand on my sleeve.

"Where?"

"Rector's. Sunday night, Monday's the next day. It doesn't open until late. Like you wanted. Okay?"

"Great."

"Do you have any tattoos?" she asked.

"What?"

"Tattoos. On your body. I . . . couldn't see in the dark."

"No."

"Nowhere?"

"Nowhere," I told her, remembering. I'd wanted one, all right. Not during the kiddie camp bits I served when I was a juvenile, but my first felony fall. There was a great tattoo artist in there, TKO Tony, a burly Irish prizefighter doing time for assault. He'd drunk himself out of the ring, but he was working himself up to number one contender status as a bar brawler when the Law took him down. He did beautiful work—

panthers, dragons, snakes, anything you wanted. Going rate was four crates of cigarettes or a lid of grass. I wanted a hand of playing cards— Aces and Eights. I was a kid. The Prof pulled me up quick, crooning the truth.

"Skin art is for gangbangers and gunfighters, schoolboy. Not for professionals. You gonna work the stealing scene, you gotta stay clean."

He was right and I knew it. Tattoos were for those guys doing life on the installment plan.

"They're not for me," I told her.

"Could I get one?"

"A tattoo?"

"Yes."

"I . . . guess so. Why do you want one?"

"I want a brand. Your brand."

"Hold up, girl. It wouldn't look so sporty on the tennis court."

"Please!"

"Let me think about it, okay?"

"Okay. Where are you— ?" She caught my look, stopped in her tracks. "I'm sorry. I . . ."

"I'll call you," I said. "Stay here."

Sonny was working in the driveway as I pulled in. He had the Plymouth opened to the bright sun, airing it out, doors and windows all wide open, front end assembly and trunk standing up, a hose in one hand, big bucket of suds nearby.

"Good idea," I told him.

"I'm going to do the undercarriage later. I've got a pressure attachment for the hose—it'll be like steam cleaning."

"You're a natural," I said. "Some people, you have to tell them to clean their tools after they use them. You know what to say? If the cops ask you where you were last night?"

"I . . . guess I don't."

"Okay, listen up. You always want to tell the Law something as close to the truth as you can. Their game is to catch you in a lie, like a loose thread in a weave, see? They pull the thread, the whole thing starts to unravel. So always keep it as simple as you can. Last night? You were cruising all around the area, testing the car, working on your moves for the races Sunday, see?"

"Yeah. So even if we were spotted . . ."

"Sure. I was gonna do some work around here, if I needed a car, I wouldn't use this one."

"'Cause it doesn't blend in, right?"

"Right."

The kid nodded, looking at the Lexus. I could almost see the gears mesh in his head, but he didn't say anything.

I went upstairs, changed my clothes. When I came back down, the Plymouth was still open to the cleansing summer breeze, but the kid was gone. I found him at the house, at the kitchen table.

"You want some food?" he asked.

"I could sure use something."

"I got some rye bread. Fresh from the bakery. And some pineapple juice."

"You're on the job, Sonny."

He ducked his head. Put a couple of slices into the toaster as I pulled out my vitamins. We ate in peaceful silence. I could see he had something to say—decided to let him get to it in his own time.

He waited until I was done, watching out of the corner of his eye. Then he pulled a piece of pale blue paper from his pocket, neatly folded.

"Burke?"

"Yeah?"

"Wendy gave me this. Last night. It's a poem. About Lana. Do you want to see it?"

"Sure."

He handed it over. It was handwritten, the letters precise, small, unslanted . . . almost like printing.

LANA
CAN I COME OVER?
NOT YET.
BUT I MISS YOU.
THERE'S TIME.
ARE YOU STILL SO SAD?
A DIFFERENT SAD.
BUT YOU'RE NOT LONELY?

NOT HERE.
THEN WHY ARE YOU STILL SAD?
BECAUSE I CAN'T COME BACK.
DO YOU WANT TO?
NOT TO THAT.
OH, LANA, WHY DID YOU GO?
I HAD TO GO. WHY, YOU ALREADY KNOW.
I HAVE TO GO TOO.
YES. BUT YOU DON'T HAVE TO GO HERE.
THEN WHERE?
YOU'LL SEE.
BUT I DON'T.
THEN LOOK! LOOK AT TOMORROW.
WHAT'S TOMORROW?
TOMORROW IS EVERY DAY.
THAT'S A CLICHÉ
NOT FROM HERE.

I looked over at Randy. "She gave you this . . . or you took it?"

"She gave it to me. Why?"

"You understand what she's telling you, then?"

"I . . . think so. She said Lana's mother was always beating on her. Not like . . . punching her or anything. Telling her she was a piece of garbage. Ugly. Stupid. Always in the way. Her mother, she used to leave stuff around where Lana could find it. If a girl killed herself in the newspapers, her mother would leave the article. She had real long hair, Wendy told me. Lana did. Real long. She never cut it from the time she was a little kid. One day her mother cut it off. While she was asleep. She thinks her mother put something in her food, knocked her out. When she woke up, it was all hacked off. Her mother had always been after her to be . . . fashionable. She wanted her to have short hair, but Lana never would. So she cut it all off. Then she took her to the beauty parlor so they could fix it."

"Fucking freak."

"She was, you know. I never met her, but Lana told Wendy stuff. The poem, it's like Lana saying maybe she should have run away instead. You can always do that."

"You think Wendy wants to run away?"

"Yeah. Not like . . . to the streets or anything. But out of . . . here. Around here, I mean. This is a dead place, Wendy says. I used to think she was . . . a little nuts, you know? But I can see it, see what she means."

"Me too," I told him.

"You don't think she's . . . I mean, that poem, you don't think it's crazy to be talking to a dead person?"

"It's just a poem, Sonny," I said. But it didn't feel like that. Maybe the channels were open. Maybe they were close enough, the emotionally abused girl and her pal who explored death with her soul. I hadn't spoken to Wesley in a long time. "I don't know where I'm going, but you better not send anyone after me." His suicide note. Just before he blew himself into the Zero. The ice-monster's voice is still in me when I hunt. Wesley, singing his killer's song in perfect pitch. The best, he was. Nobody could touch him until he got tired. So tired he touched himself. With a few sticks of dynamite. Even his name spreads terror from the grave.

And the last time I listened to his song, a baby died.

"It's time to crank this up," I told the kid. "And I need you for backup."

"To drive?"

"No. Not yet, anyway. I need to see this Dr. Barrymore. Talk to him a little bit. I'm gonna give him a call straight up, make an appointment if he'll see me. And I need you to cover me—tell him your mother hired me, you know the story."

"Okay. When are you going to do it?"

"Now," I told him, heading for the phones in the living room.

The Yellow Pages had two numbers listed for Crystal Cove, local and 800. I tried the local, asked for Barrymore.

"Hold please," a woman's voice, pleasant-efficient. Some sort of New Age Muzak kept me company. Then:

"Dr. Barrymore's office." Another woman, sounding like the pleasant-efficient balance was tipped a little toward efficient.

"Good morning. I wonder if I might speak to Dr. Barrymore."

"Who may I tell him is calling, please?"

"My name is Burke. I'm calling on behalf of Mrs. Lorna Cambridge."

"Let me see if he's available."

"Thank you."

No music-on-hold this time, just an expensive fiber-optic hum.

"This is Dr. Barrymore."

"Good morning, Doctor. My name is Burke. I'm a private investigator, retained by Mrs. Cambridge. She and some others have been concerned about some youth problems in the community, and I'm told you're the leading expert. I wonder if I could impose on you for a few minutes of your time, at your convenience."

"I'm not sure I understand the scope of your investigation, Mr. Burke."

"Well, it's a bit difficult to describe on the phone. If I could come and see you . . ."

"Let me check my calendar and have Lydia get back to you."

"I'd appreciate that. I'm staying at the Cambridge residence temporarily. The number is—"

"Oh, that's all right, Lydia will look it up. We'll be back to you in a day or so, will that be all right?"

"Absolutely, doctor. And, thank you for your time."

"No problem," he said, ringing off.

"Y ou have an answering machine?" I asked the kid.

"Yeah. It's around here someplace. I never use it."

"Well, let's hook it up. I want to be sure to get the message if this Barrymore calls."

"I'll take care of it."

"Okay. You gonna be around for a while?"

"Yes. Wendy said she might . . . come over. Besides, I want to do some more work on the car."

"Yeah. Listen, Sonny, okay if I take the Miata?"

"Sure," he shrugged. "How come?"

"I was someplace last night, while you were at Wendy's. Looking around. I wouldn't want anyone who was watching to make the connection so quick."

"The keys are in the ignition," he said.

The Miata was nothing like my buddy's old Alfa. It didn't look so different, but it felt solid as a little ingot. I went through the gears a couple of times, getting the feel, but there was nothing special about it, no quirks to deal with. I thought the kid might have tricked it up a bit, but it drove like it was bone-stock.

I got Fancy on the pocket phone. "You up and around yet?"

"I've been up for hours. I feel wonderful."

"Yeah, you do. I'm on my way."

"I'll be outside. Around back. By the greenhouse. Just come around, okay? I might not hear the door."

The grounds looked as deserted as they always seemed to. Fancy's car was in the same place it was last night. I parked the Miata in front of her cottage, walked around to the back.

She was in the greenhouse, wearing a short yellow pleated skirt, with a white button-front blouse, barefoot.

"This is over a hundred years old," she greeted me, pointing to one of the bonsai trees. The tiny trunk was thick, gnarled with age. The branches all went in the same direction, as if in obedience to a strong wind.

"What kind is it?"

"Cypress. That's one of the standards."

"Where'd you learn about this?"

"I took a course. At the college. And I read some too. The thing about bonsai, you have to be in control. Ruthless. You have to keep cutting back, keep the wires tight, stay on it. If you don't watch them close, they grow too big."

"They're beautiful."

"Strong, that's what they are. They live much longer than we do. In Japan, they pass them on from generation to generation."

"What's that one?" I asked, pointing to a hanging pot with a fragile network of stems and leaves.

"That's a bromeliad. They're epiphytic . . . air plants. They grow without roots."

Something flashed on the screen in my mind. I changed channels quick—I'd already seen the movie.

I watched her for a while. She pruned branches with a tiny scissors, reset the wires she was using to train them to hold a position. She finished with a light mist of water, bending close, using her own breath to distribute the moisture once it settled. When she was finished, she made a little bow in the direction of the bonsai.

"You want to sit outside for a while?" she asked.

"Sure."

She led me over to a small, elaborate deck. The wood was a weathered white, like a beached sailing ship. Flowering plants were set into the corners, in tubs built into the structure. We each took a chair next to a round table with a pebbled glass top.

"I want you to do something for me," I said.

"What? I mean, yes."

I explained what I wanted.

"I'll have to make some calls," she said. "But I can get the perfect thing, I know."

"In time?"

"Oh sure. All that ever costs is money."

"How much?" I asked, sliding my hand toward my pocket.

"Oh, I'll take care of it."

"No you won't. You can front the cash if you want to, but I'll make it up soon as you tell me the toll."

"Is that like an ego thing?"

"Huh?"

"Because you're the man, you have to pay? That's what my tricks think too. The man pays."

"It's not that. I have to pay for this because it has to be from me, understand? And as for your tricks, that's not a man-thing either. When you do women, they pay too, right? That's what lets them call the shots."

"When I'm a domina, *I* call the shots."

"Do you? Then you'd be the first one I ever met who did. That's all bullshit, Fancy. Just a game. Whatever you do, it's what *they* want . . . or they'd go someplace else. If money's in the game, you're the one dancing to their tune—they hold the key to their own handcuffs. It's more complicated than you think it is."

"Or less than you do—if you'd just close your eyes, you could see me better."

"Fancy—"

"I don't want to argue," she said, standing up and walking over to the railing, facing away from me. "I want a tattoo," she said, right-angling her body at the waist, standing on her toes so her elbows rested on the railing. She flicked up the yellow skirt in a sassy gesture. I first thought she was nude underneath, but then I saw the black thong barely covering her sex, the string buried deep in her buttocks. "Right here," she said, looking over her shoulder, patting her right cheek. "Can I?"

"Come over here," I told her. She padded over obediently, light dancing in her gray eyes. I pointed at the chair. She sat down, keeping her skirt up so her bare bottom was on the seat, a little pout on her face.

"A tattoo is permanent, Fancy."

"I *want* one," she said, a stubborn little girl, insisting.

"Okay, I got an idea. How about if . . ."

We both heard the tap of high heels, coming toward us from inside the house. I turned just as a woman stepped through the back door onto the deck. A willowy woman, in a skimpy pair of tight white shorts, long legs ending in a pair of red spikes worn over little white anklets with a border of red hearts on the cuff. She had on a white bippy top ending just below her breasts, exposing a flat stomach. Her hair was long, worn brushed straight back from her forehead, trailing past her shoulders, dark with reddish highlights from the sun. Her skin was a rose-flushed white. She looked about twenty-five.

"Oh, you've got company," she said to Fancy.

Fancy didn't move, didn't take her eyes off the other woman. "Burke," she said, "meet my sister. Charm."

I got up, held out my hand. She took it, looking straight at me, a knowledge-glint in her china blue eyes, like the glimpse of a shoulder holster under a coat. A slip? Or a warning?

I returned her look. My own eyes were flat, but I had some knowledge of my own—I'd seen this woman before.

Across Fancy's lap, with her skirt up.

It was a long minute before anyone said anything. "I just came over to see if you wanted to go shopping," Charm said to Fancy.

"I'm busy right now," Fancy told her, looking off into the distance.

"I see," Charm said, her eyes glancing down at her sister, taking in the yellow skirt bunched in Fancy's lap, the exposed hips. She stepped behind Fancy, stroked her sister's hair, bent over and gave her a kiss on her cheek. "Sure you won't change your mind?"

"I'm sure," Fancy said, still looking away.

"I thought you guys were twins," I said to Fancy, trying to break the spell.

"We're not monozygotic," Charm answered for her. "In fact, there were originally three of us. If our bitch of a mother had gone for an abortion, it would have been megacide. As it was, only two of us made it out alive."

"So you're fraternal twins?"

"It's not a fraternity," Charm said, her voice deeply veined with something flirting with contempt. "It's a sorority. Sisters, not brothers."

"I get it."

"Right," she said dismissively. "You know him long?" she asked Fancy.

"Long enough," Fancy told her, shifting her shoulders, turning away from Charm's touch.

"He been behaving himself?" Charm smiled. "Your Mr. Burke looks like a bad boy."

"You sure you know the look?" I asked her, holding her eyes.

"You're not from around here," she said, as if that was the answer.

"I work here, now."

"Oh yes? Doing what?"

"This and that."

"Oh, you have secrets, do you?"

"Lots of them."

"I'll just bet," she smiled again. "See you later, sis," she said, bending forward to give Fancy another kiss. She went out the way she came, swaying her hips, not wiggling. A threat, not a promise.

reached over to the table for a cigarette, caught Fancy in the edge of my vision. She was nibbling at her lower lip, face bathed in sweat.

"What is it?" I asked her.

"She always . . . thinks she knows. You're very good. I didn't know things were going to be like this. I mean, I knew you'd meet her. That's why I showed you the video. I thought it would be a good trick. On her, for a change. But you didn't show a thing on your face. Didn't you recognize . . .?"

"Sure I did."

"Oh. Burke? Can we . . . go somewhere?"

"Where?"

"Anywhere. Away from here. Could we?"

"Let's go," I said.

She climbed into the front seat of the Miata, strapped herself in without a word. I started the engine, drove off. She held her silence, looking down at her lap. I headed toward town, found a place to park.

"Stay here," I told her. She didn't reply.

I was about a half hour putting together everything I wanted. Nice thing about rich towns—the deli displayed a massive selection, and the art supply shop had just what I needed. I carried it back in a couple of environmentally correct paper bags with store logos plastered on them, put it all in the trunk.

Fancy was just where I left her, still looking down at her lap, her seat belt still buckled. I opened her door, reached across her and unsnapped the belt. "Come on," I said, taking her hand, pulling her up. "Give me a hand with this," I told her, pointing at the canvas top to the Miata.

She dutifully unhooked her side of the top, helped me fold it back behind the seats. We climbed back inside and took off. Out of town, meandering until I found the back roads that led to Crystal Cove. I played with the Miata on the curves a little bit—the little car seemed happier higher up on the tach.

Fancy still hadn't said a word. We were on a smooth straight stretch of blacktop. "Unbutton your blouse," I told her.

"What?"

"Unbutton your blouse, bitch," I said again, smacking my hand lightly against the side of her thigh.

She undid a couple of buttons, not speaking. "Do another one," I said, reaching inside her blouse as she obeyed, feeling for the clasp. It was in the front, a solid notch between her heavy, thick breasts. I popped it open and they came free.

"Very nice," I said, reaching my hand under her loose skirt. She looked straight ahead. I found her plump sex under the cotton, pinched hard. She made a little squeal. I pinched harder, feeling the wetness come.

"You gonna behave yourself?" I asked her.

"Yes sir," she said, still looking down.

"You gonna do what I want?"

"Yes, sir. Oh!" she yelled as I pinched her harder.

"What I want, I want a bouncy, merry girl to go on a picnic with me, see?"

"Yes."

"Then *act* like you understand. Close up your top. And give me a kiss."

She closed the bra, buttoned the blouse, twisted in her seat and kissed me on the cheek. I patted her knee, kept driving until I found the same spot we'd watched the hospital from. I pulled the Miata off the road. If anyone ever asked me another time, I'd been there before, legit.

I opened the trunk and took out some of the stuff I'd bought. There was no blanket back there—I guess rich kids didn't use them.

We walked away from the car until I found a spot under a tree. I took off my jacket, spread it out on the ground. "Sit, bitch," I told her. "I hope this is big enough to keep your fat butt off the grass."

"Close enough," she giggled, some color back in her face.

I unpacked the big paper bag. Handed Fancy a thick, stuffed croissant.

"What is this?" she asked.

"Halibut salad. The guy at the deli assured me it's the latest craze."

"Ummm," she said, taking a deep bite. "It's delicious. What did you get for yourself?"

"Roast beef and chopped liver," I said, biting into my pumpernickel bread sandwich.

"Ugh. Cholesterol City!"

"Shut up—it's good for you."

"Oh sure," she said, her mouth full of sandwich, gray eyes alive again.

I handed her a small bottle of champagne, opened a bottle of Ginseng Up for myself.

"You don't ever drink?" she asked me.

"No."

"How come?"

"I was overseas. In Africa. During some stupid war, a long time ago. I got malaria and some other stuff. Damaged my liver. Booze feels like acid running through my guts."

"Oh, you poor man."

"Because I can't drink alcohol? Big deal."

"No, I mean . . . a war. And all those diseases. It must have been terrible."

"It's over," I told her. "That's what happens with things. You survive them, then they're over."

"Some things," she said.

I held up my bottle of soda, acknowledging the truth.

The sun was warm. We finished the meal. I lay on my back, head in Fancy's lap, smoking a cigarette, watching the clouds. Waiting.

"She always thinks she knows everything," Fancy said. "She always has to be on top. Charm . . . she's had a charmed life, all right."

"What was bothering you so much?"

"Did you see the way she looked at you? At me?"

"Yeah."

"That's what I hate about the scene so much—you can't ever have anything private. Anything to yourself. That's why the videos don't matter—they all know about you anyway. They say it's like a family . . . the hanky-spanky people say that, anyway. Us against Them, you know?"

"Yeah."

"Well, it isn't. It just isn't. It's a way of having . . . sex, I guess—it isn't *all* you are. But with them, that's all there is. That's the way Charm sees it—if she knows what you like, she knows *you*. She saw me, sitting there like that . . . I wanted to confuse her, just for once."

"Why couldn't I just be a friend of yours?"

"I wouldn't have a friend at my house. Not a man friend. I never had one, anyway."

"Not a boyfriend? Even in school?"

"Sometimes. But never for long."

"Why would it bother you so much if Charm thought I was a trick?"

"Because you're *not*, that's all. She always wants to find out about things. How they work. Keys, she calls them. She's a biochemist. She even has her own lab."

"Where?"

"In her cottage. She has one just like mine, but she doesn't live there. She lives in the house."

"All alone?"

"Except for the staff."

"Your parents are . . . ?"

"Dead. My mother had a stroke of some kind. A blood vessel broke in her head. It was a long time ago."

"What happened to your father?"

"He killed himself," Fancy said, fingers playing idly in my hair. "He left a note. On the computer. Then he took sleeping pills. A lot of them."

"I'm . . . sorry."

"Don't be," she said.

She had her door open almost before I brought the Miata to a stop in her driveway.

"Where's the fire?" I asked her.

"I forgot," she said, sounding forlorn. "Remember what you asked me to do? I have to get going, make some calls, find out—"

"Slow down, little girl. It's not a matter of life and death."

"It is to me. I said I'd do it. I told you I'd do it. I want you to trust me."

"I do trust you," I said, grabbed the front of her blouse, pulling her close for a kiss. Thinking about other videotapes she'd starred in—

ones she'd never showed me. I handed her the other paper bag I'd picked up. "Put this in your front room. And don't open it, bitch."

"What's in there?"

"You'll see."

"When?"

"Tonight. After dark."

The Plymouth was missing. I went upstairs. Found a note neatly taped to the outside of the door.

"Be back by 5," it said. Signed: "Sonny."

I changed my clothes, glad I hadn't been wearing anything Michelle bought—I wouldn't want to face her with grass stains on the fancy duds. I took the Lexus, drove till I found a pay phone. Dialed the Mole. He answered the way he always does, with silence.

"It's me," I said. "Best time to go in is this Sunday. Anytime between eleven in the morning and four in the afternoon. I'm going to leave a car in the parking lot of the Three Trees Mall, right outside of town. Terry's seen it—he's got the key."

The Mole grunted—I couldn't tell if he was surprised.

"Tell them to take that car when they go in. Return it to the same spot when they're done. Anyone sees it in the driveway, they won't get excited."

"Okay."

"I'll come back, late Sunday, all right?"

"Yes."

"I've had it with take-out," I told the kid. "How about if we go someplace, have a meal for dinner?"

"Okay, sure. Where do you want to go?"

"Anyplace someone else does the cooking, preferably right on the premises."

He flashed me a grin. We took the Lexus. "It's only a couple of days until the races," he said by way of explanation.

"You giving the beast a rest?"

"It's not that. I just don't want anybody to see her until . . ."

"I got it."

The place he took us to looked like a giant diner from the '50s, all glass and chrome, every seat near the windows. The parking lot was half-full, mostly with the kind of sports cars rich people buy their kids. We found a booth near the back. The joint was packed with twenty-something children, all working hard to be too hip for the room.

"Did you see Gaby? She's all glam'ed out. That cat's-eye makeup, it's so *razor*," one girl twittered at another. "I just *skeeve* her, the bitch!"

"Yeah, that's wicked cute, all right. But, that makes me, like . . . what?" her pal replied.

I sure as hell didn't have the answer.

The menu promised Steak in Twelve International Styles as well as a Complete Selection of Gourmet Beers. The kid wanted hamburgers. I opted for the meat loaf, prepared for the worst.

The waitress was a skinny dishwater blonde with heavy black makeup around her eyes, giving her the much-coveted raccoon look. She took our order smoothly and moved off, not wasting a motion. The food came on heavy white plates. Big portions. The meat loaf was a deep rich slab, with a fine thick crust. The mashed potatoes tasted like they came right out of the skin. Even the mixed vegetables looked fresh, but I didn't taste them to find out. The kid wolfed his food, hold-ing the burgers in both hands, juice running down his chin.

The waitress cleared our plates, asked if there'd be anything else.

"Is the lemon pie good?" I asked her.

"You like the meat loaf?" she replied.

"Sure did."

"The pie's better. They bake it fresh every day."

"That's for me," I told her. "Sonny?"

"A hot fudge sundae," the kid responded, showing impeccable taste.

I was working on an after-dinner cigarette when I saw the kid look up, watching something behind my back. I didn't turn around.

"Hey, there's my boy! What's shaking, Randy?" Brewster. With a flunkie on each side. Expanding his chest, grinning. He stepped for-ward, so he was standing between us, looking down.

"Brew," the kid acknowledged him.

"Heard you were gonna be running on Sunday. Why don't you dump that little kiddie car of yours so you and me can hook up?"

"I'll be running the Open Class," the kid said, level-voiced.

"Is that right? What're you gonna bring?"

"I'm still working on it," the kid replied.

"Still got your bodyguard, I see," Brewster sneered.

The kid ignored him.

"How's the caretaker business?" the big dummy asked me, leaning over.

"Interesting," I told him, holding his eyes until they dropped.

"Hey," he said. "No hard feelings, right? How about I buy you guys a beer? Waitress!" he shouted. "Come on over here!"

The blonde made her way over, pad in hand. "Where's your table?" she asked.

"Right here," Brewster said, sliding in next to the kid. One of his flunkies pushed against my shoulder, telling me to move over. I looked him over, not budging. Then I stood up, pointed to the inside. The flunkie moved in, sitting across from Sonny. The other one faded.

"Well?" the blonde asked.

"Coors," Brewster said. "Draft. For me and him," pointing over at his flunkie. "What about you?" he asked the kid.

"Do you have any Red Stripe?" he asked the waitress politely.

A quick grin lit up her face. "We don't get much call for that here, but I think there's some in the cooler." She looked at me—I shook my head.

She came back with a tray. Gave Brewster and his flunkie each a bottle and a clean glass. "I told you draft," Brewster glowered at her.

"All out," she said, unimpressed. She handed Sonny a big mug, frosted. The waitress poured the Red Stripe into the mug, taking her time, watching the head.

"Okay?" she asked Sonny.

"Perfect," he said, throwing her a smile.

"Hey! How come he gets the special treatment?" Brewster asked her.

"He's a special guy," the waitress said, winking at Sonny. She moved away with an extra twitch to her hips.

Brewster had a confused look on his slabby face, puzzling it out. "I gotta order that stuff next time," he muttered.

Sonny worked on his beer right, not sipping it, not chugging it either. Enjoying it. Brewster was talking a blue streak . . . something about new tires he got for his Corvette, whether it was going to be good weather for the races, yak-yak. The kid listened, responding in monosyllables. "We gotta go," he finally told Brewster. "Got a lot of work to do."

He got up to leave. I was right behind him. I carried the check over to the register, not wanting to leave cash on the table and deal with Brewster's sense of humor. The check came to a little over thirty bucks. I pulled on the kid's sleeve, handed him a pair of twenties. "No change," I told him.

I watched as he handed the check and the bills to the waitress. Saw the grin split her face at something he said. He walked out tall.

"**C**ould I use the Plymouth tonight?" he asked on the drive back. "Sure. You gonna burn it in?"

"No. I think it's okay, except for the tire pressures. I can't fix that until I see the track. I'm taking Wendy out. To a drive-in," he said, ducking his head. "She loves monster movies, and there's a couple of good ones playing near Bridgeport. I thought it'd be more comfortable, the seats and all."

"Works for me," I told him.

I took a nap. It was almost ten when I woke up. I called Fancy from the phone in the apartment—anybody listening wouldn't get anything they didn't already know. I told her I'd be there soon.

I took the Lexus. When I got to a straightaway, I punched up the kid on the car phone. He answered on the first ring.

"It's me," I said. "I forgot to ask you . . . you set up the answering machine?"

"Sure. Tested it too."

"Any calls?"

"Just some junk. Not the . . . guy you were expecting."

"Thanks. Keep the channel open, okay?"

"You got it."

I tapped lightly on Fancy's door. She was right there, snatching it open.

"Hi!" she greeted me, bouncy.

"You look sweet," I told her.

"Sweet?" she challenged. "Maybe you'd better take another look," she said, turning to walk away. She was wearing a pair of electric blue spandex bicycle pants, molded to her tighter than most people have skin. "It took me half an hour . . . and a whole bottle of talcum powder to get into these. You ever see anything so tight?"

Sure I had. When I was a kid, there was this girl who used to run with us, Brandi. She was famous for her tight pants. She told me how she did it—she'd buy a pair of jeans a couple of sizes too small and cram herself into them. Then she'd stand in the shower until she got them soaked all the way through, and let them dry right on her. Brandi always carried a razor. Not because she was a gang girl—because it was the only way to get the pants off. Money was tight then, for all of us. Buying a pair of pants you could only wear once, making that kind of commitment . . . it was worth what it cost. I looked over at Fancy, posing in her spandex. For the privileged, life is a karaoke machine—even if they can't sing, the background's always there for support.

"No," I told her. "Not for a long time."

I put my jacket over the back of the couch. "Where's the package I left?" I asked her.

"Right there," she said, pointing to the wooden stool.

"You didn't open it?"

"I swear I didn't. I didn't touch it."

"Good," I told her, tearing open the top. "Do you have a strong light? One that's portable?"

"I think so," she said. "Just a minute."

She came back with the black floor lamp, the one with the gooseneck top.

"Perfect," I told her, kneeling to plug it in. I bent the head down, stepped on the button in the base to turn it on. A narrow cone of bright white light shone on the top of the stool. I took things out of the paper bag, lining them up neatly.

"What is all that?" Fancy asked.

"This," I told her, holding up a pen with a point that looked like a hypodermic needle, "is a Tombow. With a two-X nylon point. Kind of a drafting pen. And this is black dye—that's what it uses instead of ink."

I unscrewed the pen, put one end in the long narrow bottle of dye, and let capillary action do the rest. I smoked a cigarette through while I was waiting. Then I adjusted the point. "Have you got a piece of paper?"

She brought me a pad of pink squares with a little butterfly design around the top. I ran the pen over the paper—the line was thin, but so dark you could see it easily. I took out some more stuff: sharp-pointed #2 pencils, a calligraphy-point felt-tip pen, a package of pre-moistened towelettes, individually wrapped in foil.

I carried the stool over next to the couch, setting it up so it was readily to hand when I sat down. Then I unplugged the lamp and moved it over to the couch, adjusting the cone until it fell on just the right spot. Fancy watched me, fascinated, not saying a word.

When I had it all arranged, I sat down on the couch.

"Come over here," I told her.

She walked over slowly, uncertain. I took her hand, pulled gently. She came willingly enough. I kept pulling until she was sprawled across my lap. I yanked the spandex pants down over her rump, almost down to the back of her knees. Her panties were black silk, matching the patent leather pumps on her feet. I slid the panties down to her thighs, moved her bottom slightly toward me with my hand.

"Hold still," I told her.

"What did I do?" she wanted to know, a pouty tone to her voice.

"You opened your big mouth," I said. "Now don't do it again."

She lay still, her face in the couch. I rubbed the residue of baby powder off her bottom with my hand. Then I took the #2 pencil and lightly traced what I wanted on her right cheek. I took a close look—no good. I rubbed it off, tried again. Finally, I got it right.

"What are you doing?" she asked, voice muffled.

"I told you to shut up," I said, smacking her hard on the rump. A red spot the size of my palm flared in the intense light from the lamp. "Don't move," I told her.

I traced the penciled design with the Tombow, working carefully so I didn't puncture her skin with the sharp point. My hands are surgeon-steady, but I'm no artist. It took me a long time before I was satisfied. I held her there, one hand resting on her thigh, waiting for it to dry.

"Okay," I said. "Get up."

She struggled to her feet, red-faced, adjusting her panties, hauling the reluctant spandex into place.

"You have a good mirror?" I asked her.

"Yes. In the dressing room."

"Show me."

She stalked away from me, moving quickly. The dressing room had a full-length mirror, but the lighting was all overhead—I wasn't sure if it would work.

"Take those pants off," I told her. She practically ripped them down, kicking off her shoes, dropping the pants sullenly at her feet. I walked her over to the mirror, holding her by the shoulders. Then I turned her around so her back was to it.

"Pull down your underpants," I told her. "Take a look."

She did, craning her neck to see over her shoulder. She touched the black dot on her rump wonderingly. "What is it? I can't see it good."

"It's a tattoo, Fancy. Like you wanted. Only it's not permanent. This way, you get to see what it looks like. Feels like."

"Oh, I want to *see* it," she squealed, pulling up her panties and running from the room.

I followed her down the hall into her bedroom. She was standing in front of a makeup mirror on her bureau. The mirror was bordered by a string of tiny light bulbs, glowing a soft, rich yellow.

"It reverses, see?" she said, flipping the mirror to its back side. The new mirror was magnified, distorting the image unless you were real close. She pulled the panties all the way down to her ankles, stood on one leg as she kicked them off. Then she turned around so her back was to the mirror, bent over and thrust her bottom at the magnifying glass, looking over her shoulder.

"It's a little bomb!" she said.

I took a look for myself. Not bad, I thought. A little round bomb, complete with fuse, sparks coming off the end like it was going to go off any minute.

"You like it?" I asked her.

"Oh, I *love* it. But shouldn't it be . . . bigger?"

"No. Anyone getting near enough to see it, it should be something just between you and them, right?"

"I guess so."

"This way, it's like a beauty mark, unless you look real close."

"It's great," she said, wiggling her bottom hard. "Does it mean something?"

"Sure. It means you're an explosive girl. Tick . . . tick . . . tick . . ."

"You want to . . . take a closer look?" she asked softly, walking over to the bed, bending over.

"I love my tattoo," she said later, lying on her side, touching it with one finger.

"You get to decide this way," I told her. "For now, it'll be a secret."

"I have lots of secrets," she whispered. Sad, not teasing.

"We all do."

"Charm does too. Charm has more secrets than anyone."

"You seem to know some of them."

"You mean the video? That's not a secret. She doesn't care what she does."

"It wasn't her idea?"

"It was . . . a long time ago. When it started." Fancy shifted her hips, throwing one leg over mine, warm wetness against my upper thigh. "She got to watch. When we were kids. I never did."

"Watch what?"

"Spanking. My father would spank me. All the time. For anything. For nothing. He'd call me and Charm into his den. He had a special chair for it. A chair with no arms. He would tell Charm to stand still. Then he'd put me over his knee and spank me. Hard. He always made me tell him why I was getting it. If I didn't tell him, I'd get it harder. It hurt. And it was . . . embarrassing. With Charm watching me and all. If I cried, I'd just get it more. Then he'd tell me to pull up my pants and go to my room, think about what I did. When I went out, he'd close the door behind me."

"He never spanked Charm in front of you?"

"No. I guess he always waited until I was gone. I hated her for that—it wasn't fair."

"How old were you?"

"When it started? I don't know. I was real little. Maybe first grade? I'm not sure. But it didn't stop until I was a senior in high school."

"How did you get him to stop?"

"I didn't. That's when he committed suicide."

"Did you ever tell anyone?"

"My mother. I told my mother. She tied me up. In a chair. She slapped me and slapped me, screaming. She told me I was a little slut. I didn't even know what it meant, then. She said if I ever told her filthy stories again, she'd burn me. She held a candle right up to my face. I was so scared I wet myself. She just left me there like that. For a long, long time. I never told her anything again."

"Christ."

"When I was about thirteen, Charm came into my room. When they were out for the evening. I was still sore. From what he did. She said she was sorry, asked me if I wanted her to rub some witch hazel on it, to take out the sting. I told her to get away from me—I hated her so."

"Did you think she was—?"

"She went away," Fancy continued like I hadn't said anything, "but she came back in a little while. She had her nightgown on. She laid down on my bed and pulled it up. She asked me, did I want to spank her? To make up for what happened?" She took a deep breath—it caught somewhere in her throat. "I did it. Harder and harder, but she never made a sound. When I was done, I was so tired I couldn't move my arm. My hand was sore from doing it. She turned over, said she was sorry. About what happened. I was crying by then, but she wasn't. She . . . kissed me. I was all . . . excited, but I didn't know what it was. Charm knew. She . . . kissed me there too. Until I came."

"And now she—"

"She still does it. I still . . . hit her. And she makes me come. She was the one . . . with the vibrator. She put it inside me, held it there. She taught me to do it."

"Why did she make the video with you?"

"For my business. It was Charm who got me into it. Right after my father died. She knew people, she said. Men mostly. I could do what I liked, and they'd pay for it."

"You didn't need the money . . . ?"

"No. We have lots of money. In a trust. Just the income, not the principal. But it's a lot. Enough for anything. I just . . . got into it. I always liked doing the men . . . Charm said we should do the video together because men like to see stuff like that. Two women. It's a real turn-on, she said. Besides, I had to have a thing."

"A thing?"

"Yes. Like, 'it's your thing,' see? Some people's thing is painting. Or riding horses, or whatever. Charm said, if you don't have a thing, you have no thing. Get it? No thing . . . nothing?"

"So what's her thing?"

"Charm is a scientist," Fancy said, a hint of pride in her voice. "Everything is building blocks to her. Like DNA. Little blocks. You take them apart, see how they work. That's her thing."

She reached one hand toward my face. I stroked her right arm, feeling the hard biceps muscle.

"Pretty powerful, isn't it?" she whispered.

"Sure is. From all that tennis?"

"From all that whipping," she said. Then she started to cry.

"I shouldn't have done it," she said, much later, cuddled against me so close I could hardly hear her.

"Done what?"

"Hit Charm. She was just trying to make up for something that wasn't her fault. She couldn't do anything about my father. He was too powerful. Everybody knew him. Everybody respected him. I could understand why he loved Charm—she always kept his image. Made him proud. In school, she got the top grades. And she was beautiful, not like me."

"You're a beautiful girl, Fancy."

"Charm fixed that too. I . . . wasn't. I was chubby as a kid. Fat, even. Charm looked like a model—me, I looked like a butterball. But she told me that I could be in control. Started me exercising. And she watched everything I ate. But I was still . . . I don't know. Not ugly or anything, but . . ."

"That was in your head, girl."

"No it wasn't. It was in my mirror. Every night. In my mirror, I could see what I was. My nose was too big. And my chin was, like, pushed in. When I was nineteen, on my birthday. I remember it like it was yesterday. I wanted to get Charm something special. To show her how much I loved her. You can't buy anything for Charm—we all have money, it wouldn't mean anything. I got her a cat. A special, special cat. An odd-eyed white, it's called. He had one blue eye and one orange—he's so magnificent. When I gave him to Charm, she broke down and cried,

she said he was so beautiful. She loved the idea that he was special—
nobody knows exactly how you get one, they just show up in a litter.
Most of the time they're born deaf, but Rascal wasn't. He's a stud, Rascal. Charm always breeds him."

"Did she ever get any more?"

"No. Not yet. And you know what she got me? For my birthday gift?
Plastic surgery. They fixed my nose and my chin. They even pinned my
ears back a little bit . . . so they wouldn't stick out. When the bandages
came off, I was different."

"You just looked different."

"No, I *was* different, Burke. A different person."

"Where did you get the plastic surgery done? In Europe?"

"No," she said. Something in her voice, something I couldn't figure
out. I left it there.

"I thought you said you hated her, Fancy."

"I do. I mean, I did. Before I understood. We're sisters. Twins.
There's nothing closer than that. I'm not stupid—I know she's a manip-
ulator. But if it wasn't for Charm, I'd be a basket case. She stopped me
once . . . from killing him."

"Your father?"

"Yes. You could never understand how he made me feel. Like I was
nothing. It wasn't just the spanking. Not even in front of Charm. He
was always . . . teasing me, he called it. I was fat. I was stupid. I was
lazy. I made him ashamed of me—that's what he always said. 'You
never make me happy.' He said that all the time."

"You were really going to kill him?"

"I came back once. After he was finished with me. The door was
closed. Charm was in there with him. I . . . wanted to hear her getting
it too. I know it was wrong, but I just wanted to know . . ."

"What happened?"

"Nothing happened. I waited and waited. Finally, Charm came out.
She snuck down the hall, to her room. I opened the door and I peeked
in. He was asleep. On the leather couch he had in the den. Sleeping
like he was dead. I wished he *was* dead.

"I told Charm what I did, how I tried to spy on her. I always told
her everything. She said it always happened the same way—after he
was finished, after she left, he would go to sleep. We had some men
working out back. Building an extension on the pool. They always left
their tools outside. One of them, he liked me a little, I think. He was
always talking to me. He had a hammer. A sledgehammer, with a short

handle. I stole it. Kept it in my room. They never found it—I could hear them shouting out back, looking for it. I showed it to Charm. I told her, the next time it happened, I was going to go into his den and smash his skull until he was dead."

"Wouldn't they figure . . . ?"

"That's what Charm said. That I'd get caught. I didn't care about being caught. You know what Charm told me? She said he had a fatal disease—she saw a doctor's report. In his desk. Cancer. He was going to die in a year or so, that's what she said. So, if we could wait, we'd have everything. And he'd be gone. Later, I figured out she must have been making it all up. When he . . . killed himself, the note he left, the one on the computer, it just said he was depressed. Sick of everything. The lawyer who read us the will, he said they had done an autopsy— there was nothing wrong with him."

"Not with his body, anyway."

"He wasn't sick—he was mean. Pure mean. If he was sick, he would have treated Charm the same way he did me. Now the only way I can feel like I'm somebody is when I'm role-playing."

"With the whips?"

"Yes, with the whips. Men *pay* me to do it. They wouldn't pay if they didn't want it. *Want* me. Money, that's the proof."

I lit a cigarette, blew smoke at the ceiling. Every little street hooker I'd ever known had a name for their pimp. Daddy.

"Charm was the one who taught me," Fancy said. "The power of a fetish. Do you know how strong that can be?"

"Yeah," I said, thinking of another kind of fetish—the kind they use in voodoo.

"You *don't*," she said fiercely. "It controls everything. Charm showed me. A man who needs to beat a woman to become aroused . . . that controls him. If you offered him a night with the most beautiful woman in the world . . . straight stuff, plain vanilla . . . he'd pass it up for the chance to whip any old ugly beast."

"But when it's over . . ."

"It's never over. It just comes and goes, see? That's the power. It's inside them, not me. I just learned how to see it. How to be it."

"So what do you get? You don't need the money."

"I get . . . wanted. I'm a star. In the scene, everybody knows me. I have slaves—they do whatever I tell them."

"So why . . . ?"

"Why you? I listened to Charm. Better than even she thinks. The power of a fetish, like I told you. It had a power over me too. I wanted to . . . see the other side."

"What do you mean?"

"S&M, it's different from hanky-spanky. S&M, it's about pain. You take enough of it, the endorphins just start *flying* around inside you. It opens up the nerve endings, changes your temperature . . . everything. That's what they tell me."

"Who?"

"My . . . clients. It's more than just a turn-on, it sets you free. But hanky-spanky, that's a *scene*, you understand? What you feel, it's all inside you. Everything's important—the way you dress, the words you use . . . everything. It's not about pain. Not real pain. When it works, you get out . . . I don't mean you come, I mean you . . . get to what the real *you* is. The doms, they never really get it. I never got it—I just heard about it. They say it's a search for the truth. A line you step over. I wanted to see. To be free."

"Did you?"

"Not enough. You don't play hard enough."

"I'm not a trick, girl."

"But you like it, right?"

"I like you."

"But you wouldn't let me . . . discipline you?"

"No."

"Why not? I know how it works. I studied it. Guilt, that's what it is. They feel guilty about something. I punish them. It works out. Balance. Haven't you ever done something you feel guilty about?"

I got up from the bed. She said something—white noise. I didn't listen. Couldn't listen. I walked out of the house. Onto the deck in back. I looked down, but it wasn't high enough. I couldn't find the Zero.

The next thing I remember was Fancy, wrapping me in a blanket, walking me back toward the bed. I was shaking so bad my legs didn't work right. She pushed me down on the bed, piled covers on top of me. I was so cold.

When I came around, I was drenched in sweat. Fancy was sitting next to me, legs in the lotus position, watching, her gray eyes alive in the candlelight.

"Burke . . . Burke, are you okay?"

"Yeah."

"You stood out there forever. With no clothes on. Like one of those statues in a museum. Just standing out there. What happened?"

"I don't know," I lied. "I need to take a shower."

"No you don't," she whispered, lifting the sodden covers, sliding in next to me. She wrapped her arms around me, hugged me close, pushing my head toward her breasts, nestling me against a chill she couldn't warm.

"What am I?" Fancy asked later, still holding me. "Remember I asked before? If . . . playing that way, if that was yours? I don't know what's *mine* anymore. What am I, anyway?"

"You're a plum," I told her. "A ripe plum."

"What does that mean?"

"A plum, little girl. A rich, dark plum. You squeeze it right, you get sweet juice. You tear it apart, all you get is the pit."

"Tell me what to do," she said.

I leaned over, kissed her. Hard. Her mouth blossomed under mine, yielding, finally opening to me.

I left at first light. Fancy was still asleep. A lush deep sleep, a woman's sleep. Soaking in her own sweet juices.

I stood in the dawn, looking across at the big house standing like a fog-shrouded fighter plane, locked in by enemy radar.

The light was on in the kitchen as I pulled up. I went over. The kid was working on some concoction in a blender, pouring in ingredients.

"What's that?" I asked him.

"I'm not exactly sure. Wendy gave me the stuff. It's supposed to . . . clean you out or something."

"Clean you out from what?"

"Drugs, booze . . . anything that's toxic."

"So how come you . . . ?"

"From the tanking. I don't do it anymore. Wendy says, there's no point taking this stuff unless you really stopped. It flushes everything out, but you can't be doing it every day."

"Sounds good to me."

"You want some?"

"For what?"

"Uh . . . cigarettes?"

"I think I'll pass."

He flashed me a grin, one with some strength in it. "Guess what? We got a call. From Dr. Barrymore. He said you could see him . . ." looking at his wristwatch, "today. He said he had a cancellation at eleven, and you could have the time he was gonna use."

"You spoke to him?"

"No, it was a message. On the machine."

"Good." I looked over at the kid. He wasn't asking to come along.

I dressed carefully, went downstairs. Then I pulled the pistol loose from its housing under the fender of the Lexus, stashed it back in the Plymouth.

By a quarter of eleven, I was at the gate. The guard was casually dressed in a dark maroon blazer over steel gray slacks. He didn't look like a rent-a-cop, something ex-military about the way he strolled over to the driver's window.

"Can I help you, sir?"

"I have an appointment. With Dr. Barrymore."

"Yes sir. Your name, please?"

I told him. He walked back to the guard shack standing to the side of the gate. There was a window, but I couldn't see inside. One-way glass? He was back in a couple of minutes.

"If you'll just go straight up the driveway and turn right at the stanchion, you'll see Dr. Barrymore's residence about a hundred yards away," he said, pointing. It was an old house, dark wood with shuttered windows.

"I got it," I told him. "Thanks."

His eyes were unreadable behind tinted lenses. I had a hunch they wouldn't be any more open if he took them off.

I drove slowly, watching for speed bumps, checking the manicured grounds. The house looked as if it had been airlifted from some other location and plopped down—nothing about it synced with the austere, clean hospital corners of the surrounding lawn. I walked up three wooden steps onto a wide porch, rang the bell. The door was opened by a young woman in a burnt orange business suit, chestnut hair piled on top of her head in something a stylist had worked on to look careless. A diamond glittered on her left lapel—some kind of stickpin.

"Hi! Can I help you?"

I told her my name, said I had an appointment.

"Oh! You're just a bit early. Can I ask you to sit in the waiting room while Dr. Barrymore finishes his session?"

"Sure."

"Just follow me." When she turned around, I could see her dark stockings had black seams. It didn't fit, somehow, didn't match the tightly controlled sway of her hips. She ushered me into a small, comfortable-looking room, offered me coffee. I passed.

"I'll be back as soon as he's ready," she said, stepping out of the room. I looked around, didn't see any ashtrays, took the hint.

Before I could really check out the room, she was back, her hand full of papers. "Will you come with me?"

I followed her down a corridor, around a right-hand turn, all the way to the end of the building. She stepped aside, making a graceful sweeping gesture with her hand. A man stepped from behind an antique desk to greet me, holding out his hand. I shook it—his grip was firm and dry. "Have a seat," he said, nodding toward a mahogany rocking chair canted at an angle in front of the desk. We sat down simultaneously and watched each other for a minute.

He was tall, slender, with a neat haircut of tight golden brown curls. His skin was almost the same color, eyes a pale blue. His features were fine, sharp-cut, a cross between handsome and exotic.

"Trying to figure it out?" he asked with a smile, showing perfect white teeth, leaning forward, elbows on the desk, hands clasped.

"Genetics is too complicated a subject for me," I said.

Another smile. "I'll help you out," he said. "My mother was half Norwegian, half British. My dad was Samoan. They met during World War Two, on the island."

"Looks like the meeting was successful."

"They surely thought so. They celebrated their fortieth anniversary last year. What about you?"

"Me?"

"Well, Burke, that's an English name, isn't it? Or Irish? But your features are more . . . Mediterranean. Perhaps you have some Latin blood?"

"I don't know."

"You were never curious?"

"There's never been anyone to ask," I told him.

"I'm sorry. I didn't mean to pry."

"It's okay—I didn't come here to search for my roots."

"I understand." Therapist-speak, acknowledging aggression, mollifying it when it surfaces.

I let him stay uncomfortable for a minute, using the opportunity to look around the office. It was something out of the last century, all heavy dark furniture and paneling. The ultra-modern clock was the only discordant note, a duplicate of the one in Cherry's bedroom.

"Your message was a little unclear," he finally said. "If you'll tell me how . . ."

"I guess I'm a little unclear myself, Doctor. Mrs. Cambridge . . . you know her?"

"Yes. Quite well. She's been a patron of the hospital for years, serves on the board as well."

"Well, she was concerned about the suicides. Some of them were peers of her son. I'm not sure what I could do—this isn't exactly my usual line of work. But I thought, the least I could do was get an expert opinion."

"I see. About suicide, then?"

"About youth suicide in particular. What would make them do it? How come they seem to do it in clusters? Like that."

He leaned back in his chair, flicking one hand against the white turtleneck he wore under a camel's hair sport coat. "Tell me what your take on it is," he said. "It might be more helpful if I tried to fill in the blanks."

"Seems to me it's real hard being a kid. Not a baby, like a teenager, young adult, whatever. Hormones, peer pressure, uncertainty about the future, all kinds of messages about the environment, war, religion, society . . . tough to process. Kids are impatient, that's part of being one. They work hard at being cool, but they feel things real strong. And they don't get it . . . that death is forever."

"What do you mean?"

"It's like . . . they can experiment with dying. See if they like it. Try it on the way they do clothes. Kids don't see the future real well . . . mostly because they don't look. It's all *right now* for them."

"That's true enough. But most suicides have their root in depression."

"Lots of people get depressed."

"There are different forms of depression, Mr. Burke. Reactive depression . . . like being sad over some personal tragedy . . . cancer, flunking out of school, a death in the family. And there's a depression of the spirit too. A profound sadness, very deep. But some youth suicide is anomic."

"Anomic?"

"Simply put, it means having no special reason to live. Anomic suicides don't feel the same sense of loss the others do. It's more like an emptiness at the core. You see it a lot in borderline personality disorder . . . a sense of a void within yourself."

"Don't some of them just want to check out of the hotel?"

"I'm not sure I understand you."

"Life can be intolerable, all by itself. It's not so much that there's a better place, just that this one's no good. You see it in prison, sometimes."

"You worked in a prison?"

"I was in one. More than one."

"Oh. Did you ever think about suicide?"

"Not then. Not for those reasons. But there's a . . . Zero, you know what I mean? A deep black hole you can dive into. Where people all go when they die."

"People don't *go* anywhere when they die. A person's spirit lives past death. That's as close to them as you can get . . . you can't join them."

"I know."

"But you've . . . thought about it."

"Yeah."

"Do you want to tell me about it?"

I felt a twig snap in the jungle of my mind—the enemy flirting with the perimeter, closing in. "No," I said. "I'll deal with it—it'll pass."

"It always does?" he asked, leaning forward.

I nodded, holding his eyes, wondering how he knew. I moved to deflect the probe, going on the oblique offensive. "The kids who killed themselves, they were all treated here?"

"I guess it's no secret," he said. "But literally hundreds of young people have been treated here. We've already pulled their records and I can assure you of this much . . . there is no common denominator among them psychiatrically, none. They presented with different behaviors, their diagnoses were not similar . . . although depression was a factor in most. Therapeutic modalities varied according to their individual needs. Some were drug or alcohol abusers, others abstained. Some had gender identity problems, sexual or romantic issues. Others did not. Some were discharged to individual treatment, some to a group, some with a pharmacological regimen. Some had supportive, caring parents. Some had parents I would characterize as downright abusive. Emotionally abusive, certainly. There was no similarity in EEG . . ." He paused, looking to see if I was following him. I nodded, encouragingly.

"Some had apparently good peer relationships," he continued. "Some were quite isolated. And there's no question but that patients with almost precisely similar profiles were discharged without incident."

It had the air of a prepared speech, but he delivered it as though he was doing the work as he went along. "I guess you're way ahead of me, Doctor," I said.

"I don't think it's a question of that, Mr. Burke. Suicide prevention is like all other forms of viable therapy—it requires participation for its success. The patient has to *engage* in treatment, not just passively accept it. Mechanical compliance never works. The problem is, unlike any other form of mental illness, we don't have the opportunity to interview the patient once they've made their decision."

"Don't some make suicidal gestures?"

"Yes, and some have suicidal ideation we can pick up early. But the truth is, if they decide to kill themselves, there is literally no way to stop them."

"I know," I said, thinking of all the dead prisoners who defeated a suicide watch, how easy it was. "How long did it take?"

"Take?"

"From the time they were discharged."

He nodded thoughtfully, tapping his long, slender fingers on the desk top. "That's the wild card," he said. "They all killed themselves within ninety days of being discharged."

"Every one?"

"Yes. Every one. I've gone back over our screening mechanisms, especially our pre-discharge summaries. If they were carrying that virus, it seems we should have seen it. I'm telling you this in confidence. It disturbs me, but we're no closer to an answer."

"Maybe there isn't any," I said.

"Maybe not," he replied. "But we're not going to stop looking."

I hate the idea of "vibes." The only time I saw an aura in my life was around the face of an intern as I was coming out of a concussion. Turned out it was the broken blood vessels in my eyes. But . . .

I know freaks. I know how they hunt. I can track their spoor through the best camouflage, the heaviest perfume. I'd been prepared for Barrymore to be . . . something like that. And he was slick, all right. Sharp, on the job, focusing in. He had the best psychologist's mind— telling you he didn't exactly know your secrets, but, whatever they were, he'd work something out. They can't teach that. Top professional interrogators all have it—they can open a vein with their soft voices, probing around until they find the carotid, pinching it just enough to let you know what they *could* do.

Maybe I was slowing down. Getting old. Maybe the Zero was pulling me, tunneling my vision. But . . .

Barrymore didn't seem as though he was lying. He didn't waste time with layering a glop of thick-troweled "concern" on me. Kids killed themselves—he didn't deny it, didn't minimize it. It seemed like some piece of him really wanted to know. But . . .

That clock in his office bothered me. Maybe Cherry gave them as gifts to her friends. Maybe that was part of her patronage.

But why would the digital window be set the same way hers was . . . to three hours ahead? That would be the middle of the Atlantic Ocean.

Soon as I got back, I pulled the pistol out of the Plymouth. Not to switch it to the Lexus again—I wanted it close at hand.

It wasn't until I heard some radio announcer blathering about how it was a beautiful summer Saturday that I paid attention to what day it was. I steered the car toward Fancy's.

She wasn't home. I turned to leave just as her black Acura sailed into the drive and nose-dived to a skidding stop. She bounded out, running toward me.

"Burke! Wait!"

I stood where I was. She started to run to me, stopped suddenly, charged back to her car. She opened the door, reached behind the back seat, and came out with a big white box in her hands.

"Come on inside," she said, as soon as she got close. "I got it."

I followed her inside. She was wearing her tennis outfit, a white sweatband around her forehead. "Take a look," she said, handing me the box.

red knitted waistband and matching collar. The back was blank, a broad expanse of white, just waiting for a billboard. On the front, right over the heart, a name in red script.

Sonny.

"TKO in the first round," I told her.

She threw me a "What the hell are you talking about?" look.

"It's just right," I explained. "Exactly what the kid needs," I told her, kissing her just to the side of her mouth. "You did great. How much was it?"

"Couldn't it be my gift too, Burke? I think it's so great he's going to be doing something . . . for him*self*, you know?"

"We'll split it," I told her. "How much?"

"Well, it was a rush job. And I really had to stay on their case. I know it's his right size . . . I got one of his jackets from—"

"How much, Fancy?"

She shifted her feet, like a guilty little girl. "About three hundred."

"Jesus!"

"Well, you said—"

"It's okay, girl," I said, reaching in my pocket. I handed her a yard and a half, thinking she didn't care enough about money but she sure knew other people did. A sweet and classy thing for her to do. For her to feel.

"You really like it?" she asked.

"He'll get pre-orgasmic just putting it on," I assured her.

"Ummm . . ."

"Never mind, bitch. You coming to the races?"

"Oh, could I?"

"Sure. Don't you want to see how he likes the jacket?"

"Yes. But I didn't want to—"

"You won't. How about if you keep it with you? Until then? I don't want him to see it up front."

"Okay. Uh . . . Burke?"

"What?"

"I got you something too."

"Fancy . . ."

"Just wait, all right? Come on out back. To the greenhouse. It'll look better there." She held out her hand, then pulled me along like a kid wanting to show off a school project. "Close your eyes and hold out your hand," she said as soon as we went into the greenhouse. I gave her a look, but went along. "Not that one," she said, pushing my left hand away, taking my right. I felt her run her fingers gently over my hand, exploring.

"What are all these little white scars?" she asked. "Around these two knuckles?"

"I broke it open once."

"How?"

"I hit a brick wall. Hard."

"Oh God! Because you were angry?"

"Because I missed—the other guy ducked."

"Ugh! Well, this will make it look better. Hold still."

I felt her slip something on my right ring finger, kept my eyes closed as she turned my hand back and forth. "Look!" she said.

The ring was heavy, a soft, dull silver-gray. Platinum, I guessed. Supporting a fat, glistening diamond set in its center.

"Damn!"

"You like it, honey?"

"I . . . don't know *what* to say. It's a monster."

"Just over two carats. I put a string around your finger while you were asleep."

"Fancy, something like this must have—"

"So what? It's my money. I want you to have it. You don't wear any jewelry . . . at least I've never seen any."

"It . . . wouldn't go with what I do."

"That's not it, is it? Not really. It's like the tattoo—you don't want to mark yourself. You don't want people to know anything about you just by looking."

"Maybe."

"Well, this is just *like* the tattoo, honey. The one you gave me. You can try it. And you can always take it off, yes?"

"Yeah, but . . ."

"You're worried that it would make people . . . greedy?"

"No. Hell, it's so big, it doesn't look real. Any decent mugger would take it for C.Z."

"C.Z.?"

"Cubic zirconia. Man-made."

"Not a chance. Here—hold it up to the light."

It was like someone put a stick of dynamite inside a rainbow and set it off—the colors exploded in lancing shafts of brilliance. I held it almost at arm's length, hypnotized by the icy flames.

"See the fire?" she whispered. "The fire inside?"

"There's no fire inside," I told her. "That's a myth. Diamonds don't have any light of their own. They bend the light—that's why they don't work in the dark."

"I don't get it."

"Only living things have light," I said. Thinking: *Living things have dark, too.*

Back inside, on her couch, shades drawn. "Do I smell . . . musty to you?" she asked, leaning close.

"You smell like a lot of perfume."

"I know. I was trying to cover it up."

"What?"

"I didn't want to take a bath. Like I always do. Soaking in the tub. I was afraid it would come off . . . the tattoo."

"It'll come off eventually, no matter what you do."

"I know. But it worked. Already. It made Charm crazy. Early this morning, when she came over."

"I don't get it."

"Remember when you met her? How I was sitting out back with my skirt up? The look she gave me? I told you, that look wasn't about me, it was about you. I hate that. She thinks she knows everything about everybody."

"It bothers you so much, that Charm would think I'm a trick?"

"Not just that. I mean, it's bad enough, she would think that. Like I couldn't have someone unless I . . . dominated them. You understand?"

"That nobody would want you unless you did a domina routine? That's insane, Fancy. You're a beautiful woman, and you—"

"But she knows me. She knows I don't have sex. I have . . . male friends. But they're friends, you know? I have a good friend, Reggie. He's gay, but he doesn't flame—you'd never pick him out of a crowd. *That* doesn't bother Charm."

"Because she knows you don't have sex with him?"

"Because she knows *about* him, okay? She knows the handle. What buttons to push."

"And you didn't want her to know mine?"

"She *doesn't* know yours, does she? I let her see it. The tattoo. Not up close, just enough. I let her stay here, right where you're sitting. I went back to the bedroom, like I was in the middle of changing clothes. I knew she'd follow me. She saw it. Asked me what that was, on my butt. I just told her, 'Never mind.' Then I kept getting dressed. I put on a thong under my skirt. Instead of underpants. She told me it looked slutty—I should put on something nicer. I told her, I was following orders. Your orders. It got her real upset. She asked me, was I working as a switch now. Flipping it around. I told her, I wasn't working at all— you were my boss. All the time."

"Why'd you do that?"

"Just to upset her. She's so in control, Charm. I could have her tied up, be whipping her, and she'd be smiling. Not because she likes it, she doesn't care. Because she was getting me to do things. Opening me up, seeing inside. Sometimes I feel like one of those dogs."

"You mean like with a collar and a leash?"

"No. I make the others do that, not me. One of those Pavlov dogs, where they ring the bell . . . ?"

"Yeah."

"Did you ever do that, Burke? Hear the bell."

"I've heard that sound all my life," I said, reaching for her, the diamond on my hand sparkling against the bronze flesh of her thigh. "It always sounds like the bell for the next round."

On the drive back, I raised the kid on the car phone.

"Where are you?"

"In the parking lot," he said. "By the deli. I wanted to pick up—"

"I'm heading back now. Meet me there."

He was waiting as I arrived, doing something with the Plymouth, peering into the open trunk. He looked up as I approached.

"Why didn't you tell me your mother was a patron of Crystal Cove?" I asked him, quick, before he could get set.

"I . . . didn't know. What's a patron?"

"A supporter. Financial."

"Oh."

"Yeah, 'oh.' What's between her and Barrymore?"

"I don't know."

"But you know there's something, right?"

"I . . . guess so. He used to . . . come over to the house. A long time ago."

"Sonny, listen good, okay? Your mother never told you to get in touch with Barrymore? If there was any trouble . . . ?"

"No. She never said. Just you."

"Okay, kid. It's probably a false alarm anyway. You gonna be working on the car for a while?"

"Yeah. The fuel cell, how can you tell if it's full? I mean, does the gas gauge—?"

"It works just like a regular one. Look, there's a videotape I want to look at . . . you got a VCR over at the house, right?"

"Sure, it's—"

"I'll find it," I told him.

I went through the house slowly, but there was just too damn much of it. I'd need days to do a decent search—it was a job for the Israelis. Cherry's bedroom looked the same—no patina of dust even though I'd never laid eyes on a housekeeper all the time I'd been hanging around. It wouldn't be the only safe drop she had anyway. The clock in her bedroom mocked me. Three hours *ahead* . . . what the hell was that all about?

"First run's at nine," the kid told me as I was moving back across the driveway to my apartment. "I'm gonna get there early, burn things in."

"I'll come by later," I told him. "You don't know what time you go off?"

"No, not really. They usually run the Open Class last, but . . ."

"I'll find you," I said.

I was at Fancy's before dark. "I tried the parents of Troy and Jennifer," she told me. "The kids who . . . did it together?"

"And?"

"I figured, they'd be . . . together too, you know? Seeing as how their kids loved each other so much. But, Jennifer's father, he jumped right on me. He said he'd heard about you. About checking things out. And he and his wife, they just wanted to be left alone. So I called Troy's house. His mother wanted to know if I spoke to Jennifer's parents. I told her, not yet, like it was going to happen, right? She said she thought Jennifer was pregnant, and her parents wouldn't let her have an abortion. They're Catholic. But she wouldn't let me make an appointment either."

"Could that be true . . . what she said?"

"I kind of . . . asked around. Don't be mad—I was careful. It wouldn't be true. First of all, her parents aren't Catholic. And besides, lots of girls get abortions around here—it's a common thing. And Jennifer wasn't underage—she wouldn't have needed anyone's permission. They could have even gotten married if they wanted."

"But they were both in Crystal Cove . . ."

"I know. That's the funny thing—I think that's where they met. They really didn't know each other all that long . . . to be doing something like that."

"How long does it take?"

"Don't make fun of me, Burke. It's such a serious thing, doing what they did, I just thought . . ."

"I wasn't making fun of you, girl. That's the thing about suicides— you can never ask them."

Fancy drove us to a Thai restaurant in town in her NSX. I ordered skewered beef, seared in hot oil in a fondue pot they brought to the table. Fancy asked for stir-fried vegetables over sesame noodles.

"What do you drink with Thai food?" she asked, looking over her menu.

"Beer," I said. "At least that's what everyone says."

"Could I have one?"

"Sure. Why not?"

"Well . . . you don't drink. I thought maybe . . ."

"What?"

"Well, I don't know. Maybe you don't like the taste of liquor . . . on me. You know, how some people who don't smoke can smell it on you?"

"Is that a hint?"

"Oh no! Honest. I don't care. I just didn't want to do anything you—"

"You don't, Fancy. Have a beer."

She ordered a Bud Light. Knocked it back like she was used to it. Halfway through the meal, she held up her hand and the waiter came over. "One more?" she asked me.

"Go for it. I can always drive back if I have to."

"Oh, I'm not *that* bad," she giggled. "I've been drinking since I was little. Wine, mostly. We used to have it at dinner."

"Does Charm drink?" I asked her.

She gave me a shielded look. "She plays with a drink. Like at parties and stuff. But she doesn't really like it."

Sure.

The captain ushered a portly man in his fifties past our table. He was dressed to the teeth, a dark suit just this side of a tux. The woman with him was taller, bone-thin, with straight auburn hair that looked too stiff to touch. The captain seated them somewhere to my left, just out of my line of vision.

Fancy started fussing with her food, not talking. "Something wrong?" I asked her.

"Burke, could you . . . oh, never mind."

"What?"

"It's too complicated. I . . ."

"Fancy!" My tone was sharper than I intended. Her face came up, gray eyes widening. She pushed her seat back, got up. She walked around the little table to her right, bent over where I was sitting, her lips right against my ear. "I'm going to the Ladies' Room. When I come back, I'm going to give you something. Will you take it? Put it in your pocket without looking at it? Please?"

I nodded, looking straight ahead. She stayed where she was, bent over, her lips still against my ear, but not saying anything, just getting her breath under control. Then she straightened up and walked off in the direction I was facing, an exaggerated twitch in her stride.

The waiter cleared the plates. I lit a cigarette, feeling the eyes, not turning around. Fancy came back, a high flush on her face, walking more stiffly, eyes downcast. She took her seat.

"Here," she said, leaning forward, extending her right hand around the edge of the table. I reached out with my left, holding her eyes. Felt silk. Bunched it up, put it in the side pocket of my jacket.

I paid the check. Fancy got up to leave before I could move. She walked around behind me, slid the chair back for me like a maitre d'. As we walked out together, I saw the portly man watching. His face was blotched with patches of white.

I opened the door to the NSX and Fancy climbed into the passenger seat. I turned the key and drove out of the parking lot, feeling the turbine-smooth power of the engine just waiting for a tap on the gas pedal to kick in.

"What was all that about?" I finally asked her.

"Could you light a cigarette?"

"What?"

"Light a cigarette . . . so I could have a drag?"

I did it. Handed it to her. She put it in her mouth, played with it, not inhaling. Handed it back to me.

"Tell me," I said.

"Look in your pocket."

I put my hand in, pulled out a pair of red silk panties trimmed with black lace.

"They're mine," Fancy said. "I took them off in the Ladies' Room."

"I don't get it."

"Did you see that fat man? The one who came in with that skinny lady?"

"Yeah. I mean, I didn't get a real good look, but I saw him."

"He's one of my . . . clients."

"So? I mean, that has to happen a lot, right? It can't be the first time."

"It's the first time it happened when I was with someone. I don't . . . date. Not in public. I go out and everything, but not just a man and me."

"I still don't get it."

"It's like it was with Charm, Burke. I saw him looking. Like he *knew* something."

"Fancy, he *does* know something. So do you, right? Sounds even-up to me . . . why should you be embarrassed?"

"It's not me, it's you. He saw me with you. I saw the way he was looking. It's like he knows you, see? I never talk about a client. Never, never. That's why I never date them. This kind of thing . . . like before . . . it could happen."

"Huh?"

"Don't you *get* it? If one client saw me with another, the one I was with, he wouldn't know anything. But the other one, *he'd* know. It's a real . . . advantage to know about someone like that."

"Are you talking about blackmail?"

"Kind of. That's one of the most disgusting things in the world, selling secrets. Nothing would make me do that."

"You worried about someone blackmailing me?"

"No. How could they? Even if they saw you, they'd have no proof. That's not what I mean. It's so much power, to know what a person needs. Charm knows it. She used to always ask me who I was . . . doing. You know."

"What about the videos?"

"That's different. That's professional, not personal. Charm was always like that—she had to know secrets. That's why she joined Rector's. If you come there, you have to be into it."

"So she has to—"

"She doesn't have to do anything. There's lots of ways to be into it. Hanky-spanky isn't the same as B&D. Or S&M. Rector's has all kinds of rooms. Private rooms, like bedrooms. A couple of dungeons. All kinds of toys, equipment. A big room too, for group stuff. Some people pitch, some catch. Some switch, go both ways. And some, they just like to watch. That's Charm. She just watches. Mostly in the group rooms. One girl, a long time ago, she told us she was going to get it good that night. Her owner was going to really give her a session. Charm wanted to watch, but they wouldn't let her. She really got mad. I mean, I knew she was mad . . . I know her. You couldn't tell from looking at her."

"Charm's a voyeur?"

"No. She really doesn't care. It's not like she likes to look at porno or anything. She's a . . . collector. She collects information. It's from her science, I think. Knowing how things work and all that. She was always like that. I know she read my diary. That's where I learned. To trick her. I'd write stuff in there that wasn't true, just to throw her off."

"Does she go on dates and stuff?"

"Oh sure. But nothing serious. She wouldn't ever get married—she told me that when we were little."

"Okay. So why the scene in the restaurant?"

"The man who saw me . . . with you. He was going to think you were . . . like him. So if you ever met him, he'd have that. An edge, like. I made out like you ordered me to do it . . . go in the Ladies' Room and take off my underpants. He saw me hand them to you. Like you were embarrassing me . . . to teach me who's boss. You wouldn't do that—you couldn't do that—if you were a submissive."

"So it was just to throw him off? About me?"

"About me too," she said, looking straight ahead out the windshield. "Why should people be so sure they know me when I don't even know myself?"

Much later. In Fancy's shadowed bedroom.

"Is there anything you want from me?" she asked.

"How about some of this?"

"Stop that!" she giggled, slapping at my hand. "That's not what I mean. A big thing. Money . . . ?"

"I'm . . . not sure," I told her. The truth.

"If you'll figure it out for me, I'll do anything you want."

"Figure what out?"

"The mystery. My mystery. I'm not a mysterious woman, but I'm caught in a mystery. All my life, in a mystery. Charm's so sure she knows me, but she doesn't know me. Not at all. She doesn't know me. That's what I want."

"To know yourself?"

"Yes! That's what I want. I can't . . . do this forever. Not *be* anything. She was right, you know. No thing. That's nothing. But she's wrong too. This . . . domina stuff isn't me. It's what I do. It makes me feel . . . things. But it isn't me. Not the whole me."

"What makes you so sure I—?"

"You *could*, Burke. I know you could. Will you . . . ?"

"I'll try, girl."

Fancy came out of the bathroom in a sheer nightgown, the radical curves of her body illumed in the backlight. She was holding something in her hand, a long, thin wand.

She came over to the bed. I was lying on my back. She took the cigarette from my hand, held it to her lips, took a deep drag, put it out in the ashtray. She lay across me, her heavy breasts against my chest.

"Do you want to . . . do something else?"

"What?"

"I told you . . . how Charm did it to me . . . put . . . things inside me . . . where a man goes," she whispered.

"I remember."

"She put it . . . other places too. With this," she said, holding up the wand. "Do you want . . . ?"

I shook my head. Fancy climbed on top of me, pulled up her nightgown, fitted herself over my cock, lowered herself. She put both hands behind her. I saw the upstanding wand, felt her soft grunt, heard the insistent buzz of the vibrator as she got herself over the top, anchored at both ends.

She was sleeping when I got up in the dark. The greenhouse was cool, thick with humidity. I looked through the glass at the stars.

Fancy didn't know where she wanted to be. I thought about the Zero.

And for the first time, I knew I didn't want to be there. It didn't wash over me peacefully, it hit like a crowbar, making me dizzy.

I leaned against the shelf in the greenhouse. I wanted to be in a hillbilly bar someplace. Holding Blossom in my arms, slow-dancing so slow it was something else. Blossom. If somebody started a fight, she'd drag you away from it—but if you got pulled along, she'd be right there.

I went into that house to kill what they did to me. Told myself a lot of lies about it before it happened. None since.

People say you can't heal until you can forgive. Fucking liars. Cowards and collaborators. A beast steals your soul, you don't get it back by making peace with him. You make peace with yourself.

I went into that house to do that. With a gun in my hand. And I killed a baby.

Say it! I killed a baby. I didn't mean to, but he's just as dead. Surrounded by the bodies of humans who tortured him.

Would he forgive me if he knew why I walked that walk?

I got it then. Really got it. The Zero isn't where you go when you die . . . it's where you go when you volunteer for the ride.

I could feel the dead child inside me—like Wendy's poem, talking across the barrier. The Zero was no good to me—I wouldn't find the kid there. But maybe he could hear me. I heard Wesley sometimes, maybe . . .

I will always hate them, I promised the child I'd killed. Always. I swear on my true family I will never forgive. And if I could find them, I would kill them.

Quick. Not like they did me.

Like they did you too, child.

I'm sorry, kid, I said inside me. *But you're no place I can go to tell you—I can't make it right.*

I sat down on the cold floor and dropped below the Zero. Cried myself to sleep like I did when I was a kid myself.

Before they taught me nobody was listening.

The sun woke me, burning through the greenhouse. I was naked, cold, sore.

I didn't want to go into the Zero anymore. Didn't want to be in this rich ghetto anymore either.

I wanted my family back. The family I helped make for myself. I would die for them, but I'd die trying.

I missed Pansy. I felt sick inside. Not sad anymore, sick with knowledge.

A hundred years ago, I was standing on the prison yard, listening to the Prof tell me I couldn't use a shank to settle some petty beef I had with another con. Telling me to chill, get icy, pick my shots. I didn't want to hear it—what I wanted to do was stab the miserable motherfucker who sold me the tickets. "Do it like I say or get on your way," the Prof said, then.

I stayed. I was going to stay now. Stay the distance.

Fancy was sprawled on her stomach, face buried in a pillow, sleeping drained. The tattoo I'd drawn was almost gone. Fading away like the shroud around the mystery of her life.

I slid in next to her, covered her body with mine. She muttered something, still under. I nuzzled at the back of her neck until she stirred. As soon as she was sure it was me, I held her until she went back to sleep.

I was chewing on a granola bar I'd found in her kitchen, washing it down with some ice water. So calm I could count my heartbeats. Fancy walked in. "How's this?" she asked, posing.

She was wearing hot pink stretch pants with a thick black stripe down the side of each leg. The pants ended at mid-calf. Shiny black spike heels. A black cotton bra with wide straps that crossed behind her back. She was holding a black sweatshirt in one hand.

"You going to put that on?"

"Well, of course! I just wanted you to see what's underneath first."

"I didn't see what's underneath those pants," I told her.

"There isn't anything," she said, sticking her tongue out at me. "There wasn't room. Is this okay?"

"Dynamite."

She turned sideways, shot a rounded hip, gave herself a hard smack on the rump. "Boom!" she whispered.

I drove the Lexus to the parking lot where I'd promised it would be waiting, Fancy following in her NSX. She didn't ask any questions when I took the wheel from her.

By the time we arrived, there was already a long line to get in. A young girl in a set of bright orange coveralls was walking down the line, taking money, making change.

"How much?" I asked her when she got to us.

"Ten dollars per car to get in. It's another ten if you want a pit pass."

I handed her a twenty. "We'll take both."

She peeled off two stickers, one white, one blue. "You can paste these on your dashboard," she said. "Make sure they're visible through the windshield. Here, I'll . . ."

She bent over, put her head inside the car. "I'll take care of it," Fancy snapped at her, snatching the stickers out of her hand.

"Easy," I told her, pulling off.

"Oh, *I'll* take care of it," she mimicked, dripping sarcasm.

"She's just a kid, playing around."

"I'll give her something to play around with."

"That's enough."

"That's enough, what?"

"That's enough, bitch."

She unsnapped her seat belt, reached over and gave me a quick kiss.

We found the pit area. It was jammed. I parked Fancy's car over to the side and we starting looking around. The whole joint looked like a Concours de Cash . . . the occasional Mercedes stuck out like a poor relative, only invited to the wedding for the sake of form. Ferraris, Maseratis, a gullwing Lamborghini. All toothbrush-polished, shrieking status.

Fancy's sweatshirt draped down past her hips. We didn't get a second glance as we strolled through the grounds, even in that sea of Laura Ashley and country barn chic.

"There he is!" Fancy yelled, pulling at my arm. If a Mercedes looked out of place, the Plymouth looked like it was from outer space. The kid was standing next to it, a clipboard in his hand. A tall, slender girl with him, long reddish blonde hair almost to her waist, dressed all in black. But instead of the pasty indoor skin I expected, her face was porcelain, with a faint rose undertone.

"Burke!" the kid shouted, looking up and spotting us. "And . . . Fancy. Wow."

"You ready?" I asked him.

"Yeah. Burke, Fancy . . . this is Wendy."

The tall girl offered her hand. Black nail polish. I held it for a second, but even the strong sunlight didn't fluoresce wrist scars—if she'd ever secretly tried to visit her dead-and-gone friend, it hadn't been that way. Her eyes were a gentle gold-flecked copper, cheekbones prominent in a thin, patrician face.

"I love your hair," Fancy told her. "I wish I had it."

"Thank you," Wendy said. Not blushing, not arrogant either.

"Give it to him," I told Fancy.

"Here!" she bounced out, handing the kid the white box.

"What is it?" he asked.

"Just open it," Wendy told him, standing close, her hand on his shoulder.

He put it on the hood of the car, opened it slowly. Took out the jacket. "It's beautiful!" he said, holding it up. Wendy took it from him, gestured for him to turn around, helped him into it. The fit was perfect.

"I love it," he said softly, running his fingers over his name in the red script.

"Hey, Randy! They said you were over here. Where's your car?" Brewster, with half a dozen kids trailing him.

"This is it," the kid said, patting the Plymouth's flanks. I admired the big numbers whitewashed on the back door: 303. I guess they assigned them at random.

"This? You're kidding me, right?"

"Nope."

"Far fucking *out!*" one of his boys said.

Brewster rolled his head on the column of his neck, like he'd just taken a punch. "Whose jacket you borrow?" he asked the kid, standing close.

"It's mine."

"So who's Sonny?"

"That's me, too."

"Sonny? What kind of fucking name is that?"

"It's what his friends call him," Fancy said, stepping up like she was measuring Brewster for a right cross.

"That's sick, man," Brewster said, laughing. "One of your psycho ideas?" he sneered in Wendy's direction.

"There's one kind of sickness you'll never get, Brewster," she replied, gently.

"Yeah? What's that?"

"Brain fever," she said. Two of Brewster's boys slapped a high five. His face flushed. "Don't even think about it," I said to him real quiet.

"See you out there, wimp," he said, stalking off.

Sonny swung the front end of the Plymouth forward, exposing the engine and upper suspension. A guy in a little cloth cap stopped by, stood off a few feet checking things out. I watched his face for that superior-snide look, but he was rapt with respect.

"Is that a four-thirteen?" he asked.

"It's a four-forty," I told him. "With sixty over."

"What a monster!" the guy said, open admiration in his voice. "I haven't seen one like that since I was a kid. You going to run her?"

"He is," I said, indicating Sonny.

"I guess you got enough torque for a short course," the guy said to Sonny. "But it's got to be carrying a couple of tons unsprung weight."

"Yeah," Sonny said. "But it loads to the outside wheels pretty good."

"Can you lock it up? Hold it in low gear all the way?"

"That's my plan. The automatic's just a three-speed—it probably won't even red-line."

"Good luck," the man said, offering his hand.

"Thanks," Sonny acknowledged.

The man walked away. "You know who that was?" Sonny asked me, answering his own question without waiting for my response. "That was John Margate—he used to race Formula One. Even did the Grand Prix . . . damn!"

"I guess he knows the real deal when he sees it."

"John Margate . . ." the kid mused, chest swelling.

We watched the races from the roof of the Plymouth, legs dangling down across the windshield. Mostly sports cars: I spotted a sprinkling of Alfas, old Triumphs, an MGA coupe. Most of them handled the course pretty well, with only an occasional spin-out. An electronic board at the finish line flashed the time of each car as it came through. After a while, the course attendants went out on the track, moved the cones around, set them wider, opening things up. The next wave was stronger stuff: a white Nissan 300ZX, a blue Mazda RX-7, even an NSX like Fancy's.

"Pretty soon," Sonny said. He looked about as nervous as a pit bull facing off against a cocker spaniel.

We all climbed down. Sonny walked around the Plymouth one more time, stroking the big car, saying something I couldn't hear. Wendy took her long black chiffon scarf from around her neck, tied it carefully to the Plymouth's upright antenna, gave Sonny a kiss. He put on his driver's helmet, donned a pair of leather gloves, and started the engine. The Plymouth growled a warning, ready.

Sonny put it in gear and pulled off toward the staging area.

"He's gonna be fine," I told Wendy.

"I know," she said.

I looked around for Fancy, couldn't see her. Before I could puzzle it out, she strolled up carrying a cardboard tray with big paper cups carefully balanced, a white cowboy hat on her head.

"Where'd you get that?" I asked her.

"There's a concession stand on the other side," she said, handing an iced Coke to Wendy, another to me.

"I mean the hat."

"Oh. Some young boy was wearing it—he gave it to me."

"Come on," I said to both women. "Let's get over to where we can see it."

The first car through was a lipstick red Dodge Viper. The P.A. system gave the guy's name, drawing some polite applause. He couldn't drive to save his life, wiping out on the twisting backstretch, spinning out of control. The car skidded harmlessly to a stop.

"You get three runs." I looked over at the speaker, a guy in his forties, wearing one of those suburban safari jackets. He looked fully equipped—a clipboard in one hand loaded with crosshatched paper, a monocular on a cord around his neck. "Most of them push too hard the first time through," he said knowingly. I nodded my thanks for the information.

The next car was a one-seater with some kind of boattail—I didn't recognize it.

"Herbert Carpenter. Driving a D-type Jaguar," the P.A. announced.

Whoever he was, he was good. Real good. The dark green car zipped through the pylons smoothly, making a sound like ripping canvas. The electronic scoreboard flashed . . . 1:29.44.

"Best time of the day," the guy next to me said.

Wendy tapped my forearm. "I'll be right back," she said.

"Brewster Winthrop. Driving a ZR-one Corvette," the announcer told us.

The 'Vette was Darth Vader black, bristling with aero add-ons right down to a useless rear spoiler that hovered over the tail like a stalking bird of prey. It charged around the course like an enraged bull, all brutish power and noise. But the jerk could drive, I had to give him that. He smoked past the finish line as the board flashed . . . 1:29.12.

"All right!" the guy next to me cheered, marking something on his clipboard. He wasn't alone—Brewster got himself a heavy round of applause as he stepped out of his car. He pulled off his helmet, took a little bow.

"John Margate. Driving his famous Lola." The P.A. wasn't needed—everybody there seemed to know the car. Margate's blue beast slipped through the course like rushing water, fiber-optic thread-ing, glass on Teflon. I didn't need the scoreboard to tell me he was faster than anyone else, but it showed the numbers for all to see . . . 1:27.33.

"The best!" the guy next to me said.

It was three more cars before they called the kid's name. "Sonny Cambridge. Driving a . . . Plymouth."

"He's gotta be kidding," my tour guide remarked sourly, the monoc-ular screwed into his eye.

"At least they got his name right," I said to Wendy.

"I went over and told them," she replied. "I wanted him to hear it."

Sonny launched out of the starting gate like a dragster, threw the big car into a long, controlled skid, sliding from pylon to pylon like a bootlegger on a dirt road, a rooster-tail of smoke and pebbles behind him. He kept it high on the tach, braking against the gas pedal, crank-ing the wheel between extremes of full lock. Wailing!

The timer told the story . . . 1:28.55. The crowd went wild as Sonny stepped out. He kept his helmet on, climbed back inside the Plymouth and motored off to the side.

We found him in the pit area. "That was great!" I told him. Wendy and Fancy each kissed a different cheek. The kid's face was a sweet shade of red. "I'm gonna skip the second run," he told me. "Unless somebody beats my time. The last run is just two cars—I think John Margate's gonna wait too."

"Good plan."

"It was . . . wonderful, man. I can't tell you . . ."

"Let's go back and watch," I said.

We found a place to stand off to the side. "I can't *see*," Fancy said. I hunted around, found a sturdy-looking wooden crate, stood it on end. "Try this," I said. She stepped up, posing gingerly on her spike heels, one hand on my shoulder. "It's perfect," she said. "Can you find one for Wendy too?"

I took a quick walk around, looking. The Viper was getting ready to try again. I caught the glint of sun on glass somewhere to my right. A man in an army field cap, binoculars to his eyes. He took them down. It was Blankenship. I turned my eyes back to the course. The Viper was heading for another DNF. I turned back toward Blankenship. He was gone.

I found another crate, carried it back. Wendy climbed aboard, balancing herself without difficulty.

Brewster was the last to run. He rammed the 'Vette through, clipping a couple of cones, but he didn't make the cut . . . the timer said 1:29.04.

"It's me and John Margate," Sonny said, fingering the car keys.

Sonny went first. As soon as I heard the Plymouth on the starting line, I knew he'd bypassed the mufflers—the sound was as ominous as an earthquake tremor. The muscular machine gave off a sustained guttural scream as Sonny slashed through the course. Wendy and Fancy were both yelling something, but I couldn't make it out. Fancy whipped off her sweatshirt, waved it around her head like a flag. Sonny came across the finish line sideways, slid almost off the course.

1:27.52.

"Soonnnny!" Fancy screamed, waving the sweatshirt. This time, everybody looked.

Margate's Lola didn't look like it was going any faster. He razor-sliced the cones, as sure-footed as a tightrope walker.

1:27.44.

"Fuck!" I said to myself.

They awarded the trophies at the edge of the course. Seemed like most of the crowd stayed around to see it. Brewster took his third-place cup like the surly bastard he was. Then they called Sonny's name. The applause was sustained, heavy. The kid took his second-place trophy, held it up for a second to more applause, and walked off. Margate took his first-place prize like a man accepting the mail.

We all stood together, watching the rest of the presentations. There was a trophy for everything: longest distance traveled, oldest car competing, you name it. The announcer was a jolly-looking fat guy with a full beard. He had a deep, rich voice, like he did it for a living. Then he said: "And now for the crown jewel . . . Outstanding Driver of the Meet. The vote was unanimous. And the winner is . . . Sonny Cambridge!"

Sonny staggered forward, a dazed look on his face. He took the huge silver trophy in both hands, turned to face the crowd. John Margate stepped up, extended his hand. Sonny shook it. Margate raised Sonny's hand high. The cheers sounded like what you'd hear at a prizefight.

We waited for Sonny by the Plymouth. He was surrounded by people—I could barely make him out in the throng. When he finally walked over, he had a trophy in each hand. "This is for you, Burke," he said, handing me the second-place cup. "Thanks, man. For everything."

I shook his hand, not saying anything.

"You know what?" he said. "John Margate said he wants me to run SCCA. In his car! He's got a couple of Nissans he's been preparing, says I can drive one of them. Isn't that amazing?"

"Not to me. Class knows class."

He nodded, not fully absorbing it yet, dumb with happiness. "Wendy," he said. She stepped next to him, copper eyes alive.

"This is for you," the kid said, handing her the big silver trophy.

She hugged the cup. I made a motion to Fancy. We started to move off when Brewster walked up.

"Not bad, wimp," the dummy said. "Maybe someday we'll do it for real, you and me."

Sonny turned his eyes to Brewster. Different eyes, now. Gunfighter's eyes—calm and hard. "You know the Old Motor Parkway, Brewster? Where it goes off-road, past the tannery? There's a bridge at the end of the dirt road. A rickety old wooden bridge . . . only room enough for one car at a time. Tell you what . . . you meet me there tonight and we'll go down that road. First one over the bridge wins."

"You're fulla shit!"

"Midnight, okay?"

"Crazy fuck!" Brewster said, walking off.

"Sonny . . ." I said.

"He'll never show up," Sonny told me. Not a kid anymore.

It was almost four in the afternoon when we finally pulled out of the airport lot. Sonny and Wendy were going their own way. Me, I needed a pay phone.

"It's me," I told the Mole. "They get in and out?"

"Yes."

"They find it?"

"I don't know yet."

"About time you put your top back on," I told Fancy as I climbed back into the NSX.

"Oh, come on. It looks just like a halter, doesn't it? Anyway, I got excited—I wanted a flag to wave, you know?"

"Yeah. It worked out great."

"Sonny's so different," she said. "He's really changed."

"He hasn't changed at all, girl. What happened was he's just starting to be himself."

"That's how it works?"

"Sometimes. For some people. Like what you do in your greenhouse—seeds to buds to flowers, right? Depends on the soil, the weather . . . parasites, crop dusters . . . the whole works."

"Is that going to happen to me, Burke?"

"It already is."

The scenery swept by the windows of the low-flying car, a green blur. Fancy was quiet, playing with the band of the cowboy hat in her lap.

"You promise?" she asked.

"Promise what?"

"That I'm changing . . . getting to be me."

"Yes."

We neared the turnoff for her street. Fancy put the cowboy hat back on her head, reclined her seat until she was lying almost flat, looked up from under the brim.

"Can we go back to your place?"

"It's not a good idea."

"How come?"

"People could be . . . listening, like I told you before. I'm not sure or anything, but I want to play it safe."

"Is that why you took me . . . outside that first time?"

"I guess it was."

"I . . . liked it there. Outside. Could we . . . ?"

"After it gets dark," I told her.

T he parking lot at Rector's was empty, as deserted as yesterday's hot restaurant. I nosed the Lexus through a full circuit, checking, Fancy following in the NSX.

"I don't see why we have to take two cars," she'd complained, hands on hips in her living room.

"If someone . . . a member, say, just happened to pass by, it wouldn't spook them to see your car, right?"

"Of course not. I told you."

"Yeah, okay. But if they thought you were with a . . . client, they wouldn't expect just one car, would they?"

"I . . . didn't think of that. Are you always so careful?"

"That's the real me," I told her.

The back door was thick, with enough steel plate to do credit to a crack house. Fancy opened a metal box, pushed some buttons, waited.

Then she inserted her key. I heard heavy tumblers click as the deadbolt snapped open.

We walked inside. The front room was what you'd expect from a private club for rich people: heavy dark red velvet drapes, a long, plain wooden bench directly across from a checkroom with waist-high Dutch doors. The place was musty with that perfume-smoke-sweat smell . . . reeking of Last Night.

Fancy's heels tapped on the varnished hardwood. "What do you want to see first?"

"It doesn't matter."

"Okay, this is . . . what's that?" she yelped, looking at my right hand.

"It's a gun, Fancy."

"I can *see* that. What's it for?"

"For whatever."

"I don't like guns."

"I don't like them either. Come on, let's just do it, all right?"

She gave me a sad-puzzled look for a second, then turned on her heel and played tour guide. Some of the rooms were spare, almost Oriental in furnishings, others were lush, Victorian. One even had a fireplace. The dungeon was garden-variety B&D—racks and restraints, even a metal bar set into the floor, with hooks for the ankle cuffs. I couldn't see a closet anywhere—no place to store what I was looking for.

"Does she have an office here? A private office?"

"Who?"

"Cherry."

"Just a little one. We're not supposed to go in there," she said.

"Show me."

"Burke . . ."

"Bitch, I'm done playing. *Any* kind of playing, understand? Where is it?"

The door was behind a set of floor-to-ceiling royal purple drapes. The knob was tiny, a delicate piece of faceted crystal with a keyhole in the center. The lock was a joke. I loided it with one of Juan Rodriguez' numerous credit cards—the only thing he ever used them for. Fancy stayed outside. It was just as well—the room was a small, windowless box, the walls lined with thick acoustic tile. The ceiling was covered with the same tile, the carpet industrial dark gray.

The only furniture was a slab of butcher block held up by sawhorses at each end and a simple swivel office chair. On the butcher block: a plain-paper fax machine, a three-line phone, a calculator, some kind of ionizer to keep the air clean. Another one of those dual-zone clocks, set the same way. And a laptop computer. Underneath it all, an anti-static plastic mat.

I sat down, pulled on a pair of surgeon's gloves, opened the laptop, turned it on, smoothing out the cheat-sheet the Mole had given me with one hand. The screen ran through a whole bunch of nonsense I couldn't understand, finally settled down into a menu.

WP
Optimize
AntiVirus
Park

I followed the Mole's road map, used the arrow keys, highlighted WP, hit the return. The computer cycled, and I got a blank screen. I hit F5. The screen listed one directory: DATA. No documents listed. I tried the C:\ prompt. All I got was:

AUTOEXEC.BAT	20	02/03/91	6:31AM
CONFIG.SYS	11	02/03/91	6:35AM
COMMAND.COM	29851	05/06/90	1:00PM
DOS	<DIR>	02/03/91	5:44AM
WP51	<DIR>	02/03/91	6:47AM
NORTON	<DIR>	02/03/91	7:04AM

I checked all the directories—they were all legit, no subdirectories, hidden or otherwise. The thing was empty—probably vacuumed before Cherry took off. I tried the other menu items in order, but they just performed as advertised. I finally hit Park, heard a couple of electronic beeps. The screen said: HEADS PARKED ON ALL DRIVES. POWER OFF THE SYSTEM NOW. I turned it off.

"Are you done yet?" Fancy asked from outside the door, tapping her foot.

"I'll tell you when I'm done—just keep quiet."

The fax machine was empty of incoming. There was a row of direct-dial buttons on its face, sixteen of them. I took out a piece of paper, tapped the keys one at a time, writing down the numbers as they appeared in the liquid crystal display, then hitting the Stop button before the call could go through. They all started with 011—international calls.

The phone didn't have a display—I left it alone. Nothing taped under the butcher block. No loose tiles. The carpet was all of a piece, tacked down tight at the corners.

"Is there another place?" I asked Fancy.

"What do you mean?"

"Another private place. Like this one."

"No."

I walked through again anyway, Fancy trailing behind, more at ease now that I wasn't looking anyplace she hadn't been. In a back corner, I spotted a circular staircase, black wrought iron.

"Where does that go?"

"It's just a room I . . . use sometimes."

"Let's see."

"It's just a room, Burke. A trick room, okay?"

"Get up there!" I said, pushing her toward the staircase, punctuating the order with a smack on her butt. I followed close behind. The room stood on a small landing, built-out walls along the sides, nothing else there. She opened the door without a key, and stepped over the threshold.

It was the white room—the room I'd seen in the video I took from Cherry's safe.

I stood in the doorway, sweeping with my eyes. The foot of the bed was a few feet from a pure white wall, the seamlessness broken only by a shadow box, black glass in a white wood frame.

"How does this work?" I asked her.

"It's like a light show," she said, flicking a toggle switch at the side of the box. The black screen sparkled at the center, a burst of red-centered yellow. Then the colors flowed into a series of comet trails, mostly shades of blue and purple. Soundless explosions burst new colors into the box, waves of different colors swept them away.

"I don't get it."

"I . . . make them watch it, sometimes. It helps them get out. Let go."

"You always turn it on? When you . . . ?"

"No. Some of them like it, some don't."

So the camera worked right through it. It wouldn't matter if she turned it on or not—if she was telling the truth.

Time to find out.

"Turn that off," I said. "And come over here."

She did it. Walked over obediently enough. I slapped her hard enough to make her sway on her high heels. Her hands flew to her face. "What . . . ?"

"Shut up, bitch. Put your hands down. Put them behind your back."

Her gray eyes widened. I slapped her again, harder. "It's about time you learned the truth about yourself," I told her, my voice flat and hard. "Are you going to do as you're told?"

"Yes."

I slapped her again.

"Yes sir," she said that time, in the zone where she wanted to be—somewhere between turned on and scared—but maybe just a little too close to the far edge.

I grabbed her shoulders, spun her around, pushed her forward until she was bent over the bed. I pulled her skirt up roughly. "Don't you move," I warned her, unthreading the belt from my slacks, doubling it up in my hand.

It took a long time before I was through. Then I stood in the corner, my shoulders past the shadow box's camera-eye, watching Fancy, her wrists lashed to each corner of the bed, her bottom elevated by a couple of pillows stuffed under her pelvis, harsh red stripes from the belt standing in bold relief for the camera's eye.

I smoked a cigarette all the way through. Then I untied her. I opened her purse, stuffed her bra and panties inside, told her to put her dress on. Then I walked her out of the room holding the back of her neck.

Outside, I waited till she locked the back door.

"Follow me in your car. Don't say another word. Don't get out of your car, understand?"

"Yes sir."

I found a pay phone on the highway, dialed the Mole.

"It's me. Was it there?"

"Yes."

"Everything worked?"

"Yes."

"They're still around?"

"Yes."

"I did them a favor. A big one. There's something they could do for me. That's fair, right?"

He didn't answer. I told him what I needed. "Can you get them in now?"

"Soon," he said.

I told him where to leave the package.

W e drove back to the apartment in a two-car caravan. Fancy pulled in behind me. I got out, gestured for her to come to me. I held the door to the Lexus open for her, watched while she fastened her seat belt. Then I pulled off again.

She didn't say a word on the drive, but her face registered surprise when I turned off into the grove by the creek. I hit the power window switch, watched the glass whisper its way down the track into the door. I pushed another button and the seat slid back. Satisfied, I got out, went around to her door and opened it. I held out my hand. She took it, hesitating, still not meeting my eyes. I led her gently around the back of the car down to a soft patch of grass. I took off my jacket, spread it on the ground for her. "Sit, honey," I said. "It's okay now."

She sat down placidly. I sat next to her, my arm around her waist. We didn't say anything for a while, looking out at the gently moving water, taking the calm.

She slumped against me. I kissed the top of her head. "Lie down, baby," I told her.

She rolled across my lap, face down, pulling at her skirt. I grabbed her hand, pulled the skirt back down. I reached up to her shoulders, held her in place as I slid along the grass so her face was in my lap. I stroked her back until she relaxed.

"Close your eyes, girl. Just let it go . . . it's over, now."

It took a while, but finally I felt the muscles in her back unclench, heard her breathing smooth out. She nuzzled at the base of my cock through my pants, then turned her head. "Can I . . . ?"

"Turn over," I told her.

She did it, lying on her back, face up, gray eyes open and alert in the shade my upper body cast.

"Why did you . . . do it like that?" she finally asked.

"Like what?"

"Just . . . whip me. No sex. I thought you . . . didn't like that."

"There was a good reason, little girl. I promise you."

"What reason?"

"Ssshh, baby. You'll see."

"What reason, honey? Please tell me. I mean, I didn't . . . mind. But I thought . . ."

"Fancy, remember what you asked me before? About your mystery?"

"Yes."

"That was part of it. I can't tell you any more now, but real soon, okay? Will you trust me that far?"

"I'd trust you with anything, Burke."

"Close your eyes," I told her.

I watched the brook's current as she slept, watched as it broke over the rocks into a white froth, smoothed out again. Fancy went down deep, the heavy muscles at the backs of her calves relaxing. She turned her head to the side, snuggled into a better position, breath rattling sweetly through her one open nostril. My fingers played with her hair. She made a high-pitched sound I couldn't place, put her thumb into her mouth, sucked deeply, content.

It was just starting to get dark when she stirred.

"Wha . . . Burke?"

"I'm right here, girl."

"I must have fallen out."

"It's okay."

She shivered, rolled into a sitting position, hugging herself. "I'm cold."

"Okay. Come on." I helped her to her feet, walked her back to the car, my arm around her.

"Where are we going?"

"Just come on, Miss Motormouth. That's enough questions for one day."

I found a good spot in the parking lot of the mall. Told Fancy to get us some take-out. Instead of waiting in the car, I walked over to an outside phone.

"It's me. They do it?"

"Yes."

"Would anyone know they'd been there?"

"No."

"They left it where I said."

"Yes. They said to tell you—it triggers off a sensor when anyone goes in there."

I rung off. Pulled out the cellular, dialed.

"Hello?" Sonny answered.

"It's me," I said. "Where are you?"

"At the diner. Remember where—"

I could hear the noise in the background. "Yeah. You headed back to the house?"

"No, not for a while. We were gonna—"

"Do that. Whatever. Understand? Can you stay past midnight, stay away from the house?"

"Sure."

"Okay, champ. See you tomorrow morning."

By the time Fancy came back with her arms full of take-out, I was watching her through the windshield of the Lexus.

It was dark when we got back. I sent Fancy over to the big house, told her what to do. I went upstairs to the apartment, turned on the radio and a couple of lights. Then I came back out, walked over to the house. No lights on in the kitchen. I kept going through to the living room. Fancy had the floor set up like a picnic, the glow from some candles casting murky shadows.

"It looks great," I said, sitting down on the floor.

"How come you didn't want any lights, honey?"

"Don't talk with your mouth full," I told her.

"But my mouth isn't full. I didn't start to eat—I waited for you."

"Now I'm here," I said, helping myself to what looked like a deli plate: chunky tuna, potato salad, cole slaw.

We ate quietly, in companionable silence. I complimented Fancy on her choice of food, listened with half an ear as she ran through all the mall choices she'd had to make, why she settled on deli instead of Chinese, how it wasn't good to eat a heavy meal so late, something about cholesterol . . .

It was nearing ten o'clock by the time we finished the meal and cleaned it up. Fancy insisted on wrapping whatever we didn't eat, putting it away in the refrigerator. "Maybe Sonny'll want a snack when he comes home," she said.

While she was bustling around, I looked under the pillows in the living room couch. I found the videocassette, turned on the VCR, shoved in the cassette, started it running and hit the Pause button. The screen was all visual static, like dirty snow.

Fancy came back in. "Blow out the candles and come over here, girl."

She did it quick enough, sitting next to me expectantly.

"What, honey?"

"Watch," I said.

I hit the Play button on the remote. A brief flicker and it snapped into life. Fancy walking across the threshold of the white room.

"Burke! What *is* this? Where—?"

"Just watch for a minute," I said, holding her hand tight.

The whole scene played out from a few hours ago. Now that I knew how it worked, I could see the camera shots were mechanical, the zooms unplanned. The tape ran back into gray trailer right after we exited the room. Fancy burst into sobs, trying to pull away from me.

"Oh God! Why did you *do* that? You . . . who was *there*? How could you? I would have . . . if you'd just asked . . ."

"Come here, girl. Listen to me."

"*No!* You filthy bastard!"

"Fancy, it's *all* on tape. It's got nothing to do with me."

"I don't believe you. If you didn't set it up—"

"Stay here," I told her. "Don't move." I walked over to the VCR, popped out the cassette, shoved in the copy I'd had made from the video I'd lifted from Cherry's safe. I hit the Play button again, walked back over to the couch. As soon as Fancy saw herself facing the camera, unzipping her skirt as the man on the bed behind her watched, she broke.

"That was over a year ago, that tape," she said, later. She was sitting on the floor in front of the couch, her back between my legs, my hands on her shoulders.

"There'll be a whole lot of them, Fancy. Every time you went into that room. The camera setup works automatically—it doesn't need an operator."

"I'll kill her."

"Who?"

"Cherry."

"It wasn't her, baby."

"Who else could it be?"

"Can I tell you a story?"

"I've heard enough stories. Especially from you."

"You'll appreciate this one, honey. I promise you. In the city, we got three different police departments. The regular cops, NYPD. Then there's Transit, they mostly work the subways. And Housing, they cover the Projects. They're really the only ones who still walk a beat—Vertical Patrol, they call it. The Projects, they're like a neighborhood. Everybody knows everybody else. It's bad out there. Not as bad as Chicago, where the gangbangers take over whole buildings, but dangerous, you know? More for the people who live there than the cops. The kids go elevator surfing, people fuck in the hallways, the rooftops are a good place to get raped. Or die. It's a strange mix—you got old people trying to make it on some lousy Social Security, you got Welfare scammers, you got decent, hardworking folks . . . everybody. Anyway, this old Housing cop I know, he was working a string of push-in muggings . . . where the skell follows an old lady up in the elevator, gets off on the floor below, runs up the stairs and shoves her into her own apartment. Then he works her over, loots the place, and disappears. So this cop, he watches. Real close. He finally bags this mugger, snatches him right on the stairwell. Takes him into custody. And the dirtbag can't *wait* to talk—admits to maybe a dozen of his 'jobs.' The cop's all excited, naturally. He brings the old people down to the precinct, but not a single one of them can ID the mugger. Not one. It was too dark, it happened too fast, he hit too hard, they were scared . . . whatever. So now he's stuck. Without an ID, the DA won't even consider the case. He's thinking about it and thinking about it and he comes up with this dynamite idea . . . a Reverse Lineup. Now listen to this. He rounds up a whole bunch of old people from the Projects, okay? Then he puts *them* up on the stage, under the lights. And he puts the skell behind the one-way glass, like he was the victim. Guess what? The skell *loves* it. He stands there, picks out his victims. 'Yeah, I did her. No, not that one.' And he's on the money every single time! He knows which one had jewelry in a dresser, which one had some cash hidden in the refrigerator, which one he punched in the face. All they had to do is match up the original police reports with what the skell said, and they had it all. Nobody else could have done it. Pretty slick, huh?"

"Oh, it's just a wonderful story. So what?"

"So this—the tape you just looked at, I picked it up from a hideout, where it was stashed. I made a copy, and I put it back. I wasn't around when that tape was made—you said so yourself. Now listen—when I went back to the hideout, the tape was gone. And the only person who was anywhere around it was Charm. Charm, you understand? Cherry isn't even in this country. Hasn't been for quite a while. You said it yourself—Charm always wants the handle. She needs to know how things work . . . and how to work people. You didn't want her to think she knew about me, right? Well now, if I'm right, she thinks she does."

"You mean you . . . knew?"

"Yeah. At least I thought I did. That tape . . . the one with you and me we just saw . . . that's a copy too. The original is right back where it came from."

"At Rector's?"

"Sure. You think Cherry's gonna stop by, pick it up?"

"Maybe Charm just . . . works for her."

"Sure, girl. Maybe she does. But what would Cherry want with a tape of me and you? Who's she gonna blackmail? Especially behind that fairy story she told you—about me being a hitman and all. That's why I stood where I did . . . when you were tied on the bed. I was out of camera range—it's behind that shadow box on the wall. It's that super-safe sex you talked about . . . Charm'll read it that I was masturbating, watching you. And sooner or later, she'll drop it on me."

"It doesn't make sense," she said, turning to look up at me.

"How much truth do you want, little girl?"

"All of it," she said, taking a breath. "Just do it."

I slid off the couch, lying down on the carpet next to her. I lit a cigarette, took a deep drag, offered it over. She took it the way I saw a woman take a wet rag in her teeth in the jungle a lifetime ago . . . biting down so the sounds of childbirth wouldn't alert the enemy soldiers nearby.

"You and Charm have the same room? When you were kids?" I asked.

"No. I mean, just when we were real little . . ."

"But you were real close to her, right? You didn't keep secrets from each other?"

"*I* never did. Charm wouldn't let me. She hated secrets—she had to know everything. We had a bathroom, for the two of us, between our rooms. She would just walk in there and start talking to me, even when I was sitting on the toilet."

"Why didn't you lock the door when you were in there?"

"We didn't have any locks on the doors. Not in the whole house, except for—"

"The room where your father took you."

"Yes. But—"

"When you were growing up, did you get your period first, or did Charm?"

"What?"

"Your period . . . who had it first?"

"Me. I was way ahead of her."

"And you didn't have it at the same time after that, right? Not the same time of the month?"

"I . . . don't know. I don't know *when* she had hers, but—"

"She knew when you had yours."

"How could you *know* that?"

"When your father took you in that room, it was never when you were having your period, was it?"

"Burke!"

"And he always did it the same way, right? Said the same words, made you do the same thing. Did he have something special he hit you with?"

"His hand. And a . . . paddle. A black one. With holes in it."

"Yeah, he's perfect. A ritualistic scumbag."

"No. He never . . . you mean, like Satanism and that stuff?"

"It's *all* ritual abuse, girl. Got nothing to do with Satan. Child molesters love their rituals, their secret ceremonies. You remember how you told me Charm never got punished in front of you? That's because it wasn't punishment that was going to happen once the door closed. Not like you got, anyway. Your father was having sex with her. For years and years. You were just the appetizer."

"Stop it!"

"Where do you think she learned it, child? You weren't getting punished, you were being used. Spanking kids . . . the way he did . . . it's erotic for them. Foreplay, that's all. That's why you hate people who do it—you've always known the truth."

"Noooo . . ."

"Yes. Trauma is scar tissue over memory, but nobody ever really forgets. Charm showed you how to flip things over. Get powerful yourself . . . at least that's what you thought. You see it in the kiddie joints all the time. The weaker ones get taken off. Raped. You do it to somebody else, you're not the target, see? Sex in prison, it's not really sex. Any more than rape is. You get to beat on somebody else, it doesn't happen to you. Remember how you said it made you feel? Strong?"

"She was just—"

"Playing. Sure. Playing *you*. For your father. With him. He picked her out from the beginning, Fancy—she never had a chance. She's doing the same thing. Getting powerful. Drinking blood."

"I don't believe you."

"Yeah you do. Charm set you up in business. So you'd have a 'thing' of your own, isn't that what you said? Instead, you've been a Judas goat, staked out so the prey comes sniffing around. And Charm's always there. With her cameras."

She made a moaning sound, dropped her shoulders. I reached over, held her hand. It was damp.

"There's more," I told her. "Charm used Sonny too. When he was just a kid. Got him involved in sex way before he was ready, and it really fucked with his head. She may have been with his mother too . . . Cherry's gay, right? There's a wire on my phone, in the caretaker's apartment. That's her work too. I thought it was you at first, when I saw the tape. But there's money floating around here. Big money. More than Charm could score from some lousy little blackmail scheme."

"But why . . . ?"

"Your mother knew it too, Fancy. Remember when you told her, what she did? She gave her daughter away. Handed her over like a present."

"I saw that once . . . what you said. On 'Oprah.' How people get abused when they're kids and they remember it all of a sudden, years later."

"I know."

"But there's like nothing they can do, right? I heard it on the show, the Statute of Limitations. It's too late to make them go to jail . . ."

"Yeah. They need to call it the Statute of Liberty instead. The freak does his work good enough, he makes the kid block it right out . . . and then he walks away giggling."

"You think Charm . . . doesn't remember?"

"I don't think she ever forgot. That's what turned her. Into whatever she is, now."

She was quiet a long time, all inside herself. Then she looked over at me, gray eyes in the dark. "My own sister," she said. "My twin. Now I don't have anybody."

I made her come back to the caretaker's apartment with me. Showed her the tiny microphone that had sat inside the phone until I pulled it loose.

I took her to the bedroom. Undressed her slowly. We made love. A deep, rich vanilla.

"I want you to stay with Sonny," I told her the next morning. "All day, no matter what, wherever he goes. Whether he likes it or not."

"Okay."

"Don't 'okay' me, Fancy. It's important. Make a promise."

"I swear," she said, her hand over her heart.

I puffed on my smoke, absently, wondering if she knew. "Fancy, what happened to your other sister?"

"My other sister?"

"Charm said you were originally triplets, remember?"

"Charm tells stories," she answered, looking somewhere else.

I walked over to the big house. Sonny was awake, at the kitchen table. "I think I'm close now," I told him. "I need you to do something."

"You got it."

"Fancy's upstairs. Over in the garage apartment. I want you to stay with her. No matter what she does. Don't let her out of your sight. Don't take no for an answer. Stay with her until I get back."

"I'll take care of it," he said. In a man's voice.

The junkyard was shrouded in what passes for morning mist in Hunts Point—a nasty mix of industrial pollution and half-burnt garbage no converter could ever recycle. Terry was right near the gate, as if he was expecting me.

"Mole had a fight," he said.

"A fight? Is he okay?"

"Oh sure. It was, like, not a physical thing. With Zvi."

"The Israeli?" I asked, climbing aboard the shuttle.

"Yes. He didn't want you to know anything about . . . whatever they took. I couldn't follow it all. He said you weren't one of them. But Mole said, you were one of *him*, and he was going to show it to you. They had this big argument. Then this Zvi guy, he offered Mole money. For the information, he said. Mole got *really* mad then. They started arguing, in Jewish, I guess, I couldn't understand. Then this Zvi guy left."

"Don't fuss about it, kid. They won't do anything to the Mole."

"Oh, I know that. I just never saw him, like, *mad* before."

The Mole was in his bunker. If the argument with the Israeli had him worked up, you couldn't see it on his face.

"You cracked the code?" I asked him.

"Yes. It was what I thought—a sort program. It matched all the names—before and after."

"You have a copy?"

"Yes."

"Any trouble. With . . . ?"

"No," he said, handing me a thick sheaf of papers.

"They do plastic surgery there," I told him. "It's the perfect cover for the ID business."

"They do something else, too."

"What?"

"I'm not sure. See this?" he said, holding up a clipboard covered with calculations.

I nodded, waiting—the Mole had already used up his supply of words for the week and I didn't want to throw him off the track.

"This was an experiment, like I told you. A double-blind, with a probability matrix."

"Huh?"

"Don't play stupid, Burke—I don't have time. There was a group of subjects, all right? It was divided in half. Half received some . . . input. A substance, a treatment, exposure to radiation . . . I can't tell. The other didn't—maybe they got a placebo, maybe nothing. Again, I can't tell. Now for the group which got the input, there was a certain result predicted. That's the probability matrix . . . the experimenter was looking for a result, and that result was something you would *expect* to get in a certain percentage of cases anyway, understand?"

"You got a group of a hundred people. You give fifty of them a pill that causes headaches—you give fifty of them nothing. In the first group, ten of them get headaches. But you gotta figure, people get headaches without the pills. So the question is . . . how many more? Is that it?"

"Yes. The difference must be statistically significant for the input to be the cause."

"But you don't know who . . . or what?"

"No."

"Did the . . . experiment work?"

"I don't know. It's not in the data. The running time was ninety days. They run it four times a year, with different split groups. Whatever they expected to happen, it did happen. But I don't know the probability of it happening without the input."

"Wouldn't they know it?"

"They made . . . educated guesses. It seems they don't have hard data on it."

"So after ninety days, the . . . input . . . it's not gonna work."

"That's what it seems. If it works at all."

"It fucking fits," I muttered.

"You think you know . . . ?"

"Mole, you know all about the experiments in the camps. Remember you told me about them?"

"Yes," he said, Nazi-hate blazing behind his thick glasses.

"They were just experiments for the sake of experiments, right? Not science at all."

"Not science at all," he agreed bitterly. "Sadism. Torture. Freakish ugliness."

"But . . . even if someone wanted to do real experiments, like for cancer or whatever . . . you couldn't do it on humans, could you?"

"Not legally. I've heard . . . about places in the Third World where you can . . . buy subjects."

"Mole, listen for a minute. Is there a drug that could make people suicidal? Make them kill themselves?"

He stroked the side of his face, took off his glasses, polished them on a greasy rag lying on his workbench. "There are drugs that cause depression, drugs that interfere with cognition, affect mood. All kinds of results. But to actually make people kill themselves . . . no. If they were already disposed, maybe . . ."

I drove out of the junkyard dazed, brain spinning crazy, info-pinballing, colors and numbers bouncing off the corners. Trying to pick a drop of mercury off a slick Formica surface through a cloud of smoke.

Until I faced it. The same way I did with the child I killed in that basement. Just looked at it and looked at it until it told the truth.

Only one question left—who else was in? And how deep?

The Plymouth was wedged in the driveway like a roadblock. The garage doors were closed. I jumped out of the Lexus, headed inside. They were in the living room: Sonny, Wendy . . . and Fancy. She was on a padded chair in the living room, knees together, hands in her lap.

"Hey, Burke! We've been playing a game. You want to play too?"

"What's the game?" I asked her.

"Bondage," she said, holding up her hands, wrists together, as if she was wearing invisible handcuffs.

Sonny's face reddened. Wendy stretched her long legs out on the couch, protective and watchful, not saying anything.

"I don't get it," I said.

"Well, it seems like your young friend here got it into his head that I wasn't supposed to leave."

Sonny nodded agreement with the accusation. Hard to believe this was the same kid Charm had slapped into submission such a short time ago. "Good work," I told him as I took Fancy by the hand and pulled her out of the room.

Back in the caretaker's apartment, Fancy sat on the bed as I changed my clothes. "Why did you do that?" she asked.

"Do what?"

"Play that trick. To make me stay there . . . with Sonny?"

"It didn't have anything to do with Sonny. I just wanted to be sure you didn't wander off somewhere."

"Where would I go?"

"To Charm."

"But you told me—"

"Some things, not the whole thing. I've been stupid. This suicide thing, it didn't start when I came out here. I didn't get it because I was *in* it. Me, not them. I came here with too much baggage, and the weight made me blind. There's one more thing I've got to tell you . . . and then it's up to you."

"Tell me what?"

"The truth, Fancy. The truth about Charm, and your father."

"You already *told* me," she wailed. "I don't want to—"

"It doesn't matter what you want anymore. Things are gonna happen. Happen soon. I don't want you making any more offerings."

"I don't know what—"

"Offerings. Like the way your mother served you up to your father. Like the way Charm uses you for her blackmail videos. I'm not here for the same reason now."

"In Connecticut?"

"On this earth. I am going to fix things. This time. This one time. I looked into the Zero and I saw it. You know what I got, little girl? Another chance."

"Burke, you're scaring me."

I lit a cigarette. Handed it to her. "Blow me a smoke ring, Fancy."

She pursed her lips, puffed gently. The smoke billowed but didn't form itself into rings. She tried again, working harder. "I can't," she said. So much sadness in her voice—a little girl who couldn't do the trick.

"Watch," I told her. I took the pack of cigarettes, pulled the cellophane wrapper down so it was anchored to the pack only by a thin strip. I held the glowing tip of the cigarette against the cellophane, carefully. When I pulled it away, there was a neat round hole in the cellophane— it looked like an entrance wound. I handed it to her. "Draw in some smoke," I said. "Then blow it into the pack, right through the hole."

She did it, puzzlement in her eyes. The cellophane filled up with smoke, thick and cloudy. "Now tap the back of the cellophane, Fancy. Gently."

She held the pack straight up, tapped a long fingernail against the back. A perfect smoke ring bubbled out of the hole, hanging in the air. "Oh!" she giggled, doing it again.

"That's what we need, girl. A trick. To make things work. You gonna play with me?"

She nodded, as gravely as a child promising to be good.

"**D**o you recognize my voice?" I said into the phone, low-pitched and calm.

"Yes," he replied. I could hear the gears switch in his head, down-shifting to someplace familiar. Getting *back* there in a snap-second, alert and ready.

"I have something. *May* have something. Will you meet me?"

"Say where and when," is all he said.

Fancy led him into the room. I was seated on one side of a desk I'd cobbled together from a door laid across the seats of two chairs. He sat down on the other side. Fancy walked out.

Blankenship was clean-shaven, jungle close. Wearing an old set of army fatigues, camo-patterned. Lace-up black boots on his feet, saddle-soaped, not shined. Ready ever since he got my call.

"Thanks for coming," I said, lighting a cigarette, resting it in an ashtray I'd made out of aluminum foil.

"Please don't be fucking around with me," he said quietly, taking a .45 out of a side pocket. It looked like a custom job, all flat black matte finish, with a short-tube silencer that probably cost more than the gun itself.

"I'm not. I wouldn't. Hear me out, all right? Show me the respect I'm showing you."

His face was empty. No expression. Nothing in his eyes. The patience of a sniper. His nod of agreement didn't travel three inches.

I told him a version of the truth. Left Charm out of it, concentrated on Crystal Cove. "You see where I am," I concluded. "I don't know if the stuff even works. And I can't know . . . I'll never know . . . if it worked on Diandra."

"The army did that," he said. "Experiments. I heard about them, in the field. Drugs to make a man brave. Or to make you focus. Most of them backfired—the VA hospitals are full of—"

"It isn't the army doing it here," I interrupted nervously. He was too close to the edge—if he decided it was a government conspiracy . . .

"Okay," he said. Flat, no heat coming off him, safe even from thermal sensors if the enemy had them working.

"I'm close," I said. "Real close."

"What do you need from me?"

"I'm going to go inside. See the head man. Barrymore. The doctor. He could deny everything. He does that, I'll go back to working the corners. Or he could make it right—then we're done. But he might decide to get stupid . . . that's your piece."

"Say what."

"Backup. I'm going in the door. The front door. He's got a squad all over the grounds. They wear maroon blazers, look like servants from a distance, but they're all pros. I need to get off the grounds. You know the place?"

"I've been there. Every night. In and out. There's a good piece of high ground. And I've got a night scope."

"You'll do it?"

"Over there, I did my job. Just my job, understand? I never took ears, I took eyes. One shot . . . pop! Right through the cornea. I don't know how many I got—I never kept count. After a while, they had a bounty on me. Not my face—they never saw my face—but they knew my work. If this Barrymore helped . . . kill my Diandra, he's gone. There's no place he can go. I'll wait as long as it takes. I don't care. About anything. He did that to her, I'm going to put his heart on her grave."

I spent more time talking with him. Soldier to soldier, the way he saw it. Defining the mission, making sure he wouldn't go hunting on his own. He agreed to stay at his base, wait for my call.

He got up, didn't offer to shake hands. I let out a long breath as Fancy came back into the white room.

Back in the caretaker's apartment, I opened a fresh videocassette, plugged it into one of two slots in the front of the high-tech VCR Fancy had bought. I handled the used one like it was a stick of dynamite floating in nitroglycerin.

"I never knew there was another room there," Fancy said. "What do you call that . . . opening?"

"A pocket door. Whoever built it knew what they were doing. The craftsmanship was incredible. If the . . . other people hadn't told me about it, I wouldn't have found it even though I knew it was there."

"You switched the tapes?"

"Yeah. And I re-tripped the sensor. When Charm goes to check it out, she'll just find a blank, figure nobody used the room for a while."

"Did it work?"

"Just sit still, girl. We'll know in a minute."

I pressed the switch. It showed me and Fancy setting up the make-shift desk in the room, Fancy walking out, me sitting there alone. Her coming back with Blankenship. And all the rest. "Perfect," I said. "Now we edit a piece off onto the fresh tape."

"For what?" she asked.

"Bait," I told her.

"You're not going back for a while," I told her. "I want you to write a note, leave it for Charm."

"Where?"

"At her house. I'll drive you over."

"I can't do that."

"Fancy . . ."

"Burke, I *can't*. It would make her suspicious. I never go in her house. I'm not allowed."

"Okay, I get it. We'll leave it in your place. She'll see it when she comes snooping around."

I rehearsed in my head, running it through, smoothing out the edges. When it got too loaded, I took a break, looked through the list of numbers I'd copied off the fax machine in Cherry's office at Rector's. Something . . .

"Fancy, is there a phone book around here?"

"I don't know—I'll look."

She came back with two of them—yellow and white. I pored through the white pages until I found it: "International Country and City Codes."

011 was the international access code. Okay, next step: 61 was the country code. For Australia. So 011-61-2 was Sydney. 011-61-3 was

Melbourne. They were all Australia, all Sydney and Melbourne except for one in Perth.

Australia. I checked the International Time Zone chart in the phone book. Sydney was fifteen hours ahead of us. Six in the afternoon on Tuesday would be nine in the morning on Wednesday over there. Fifteen hours . . .

If you showed fifteen hours ahead on a dial clock, it would look like three hours. One full spin, twelve, plus three more for fifteen.

Did Cherry have a passport? Dual citizenship? Another identity?

And that clock, that special clock. Twin clocks, one in Barrymore's office.

It was late when I heard the crunch of tires on the bluestone. Charm's white Rolls, sitting in the driveway, pointing the wrong way, like she'd driven in the exit. I watched for a minute—she didn't get out. I couldn't see her face behind the driver's-side glass. Fancy stood next to me. I could feel her breath against my cheek.

"Too late for that note," I said.

"I'll fix it," she replied, yanking her dress over her head, stripping frantically. Nude, she ran into the back room. She was back in a second, hopping on one leg as she fitted a pair of spike heels onto her feet. "I'll be right back," she said, and went out of the door before I could stop her.

I watched as Fancy negotiated the stairs, as she walked over to the Rolls, stepping carefully in the spike heels on the loose stones. The driver's window slid down. Fancy bent at the waist, her face inside the window, her naked backside white sculpture in the night.

It didn't take long. The Rolls pulled off slowly. Fancy stood there watching it for a minute, then she turned and climbed back up the stairs.

"**W**hat was that all about?"

"I told her I was being punished. That you made me go outside like that."

"What did she say?"

"She asked if I turned you out yet."

"Huh?"

"Turned you out . . . into the scene. I told her you were my master . . . I wasn't going to be doing anything without your permission now."

"Why was she coming around?"

"She said she was worried about me. What a joke. When I told her . . . about you . . . she was happy, I could tell. She kissed me. Deep, like a lover. She hasn't done that in a long time."

"You really handled that perfectly, girl. How'd you know it would work?"

"I just . . . knew. It worked on me too. I was all . . . embarrassed. And excited too. Charm said she could smell it on me. Can you smell it, Burke?"

"Come over here and I'll tell you."

I waited two more tight days, perfecting the pitch. Then I made the call.

"Dr. Barrymore please."

"Who may I tell him is calling?"

"Mr. Burke."

"Hold please."

"Mr. Burke, this is Lydia, Dr. Barrymore's personal assistant. You may remember we met the last time you were here . . . ?"

"Sure." The woman with the improbably seamed stockings and the controlled walk.

"I'm so sorry, but Dr. Barrymore really has quite a full schedule. He said to give you his regrets, but it may be some time before—"

"Tell him I have something I need to show him. A tape."

"As I explained—"

"I don't mean to be discourteous, miss. But please just tell him what I told you—I believe he'll understand the urgency of my request."

"Very well. If you'll hold for another few moments, I'll try and track him down."

I lit a cigarette, smoked it down while I held the receiver to my ear. If this card didn't play, there was always the bottom of the deck.

"Mr. Burke?" It was Barrymore's voice, blue-tinged, loaded with resignation.

"I'm here. Sorry to disturb you from your practice, but I really think you should see this tape."

"Yes, I'm sure. There's really no need. If you'll just—"

"It's not what you think, Doctor. I'm coming to you in friendship, believe me."

"All right. Can you come this evening? Say at nine?"

"I'll be there. And, Doctor . . ."

"Yes."

"Please believe what I just told you. I am coming in friendship. You're a professional—so am I. Understand?"

"Yes. Yes, I do."

"**I**'m going in," I said into the phone. "Tonight. Nine o'clock."

"I've got your back," Blankenship replied.

He let me in himself. The house felt empty, the phones quiet. I followed him into his office.

"You have a VCR here?" I asked.

"Over there," he pointed. "But, as I told you, it's not necessary. Just tell me what you want."

I ignored him. Slid my cassette into the machine, turned it on. I saw Barrymore's face twitch as the picture came into focus.

"Over there, I did my job," Blankenship was saying on the screen. Barrymore sat straight up, eyes riveted, head cocked to hear every word.

I let it play through. Right up to a tight closeup of Blankenship's nobody's-home, truth-telling eyes:

I don't care. About anything. He did that to her, I'm going to put his heart on her grave.

"You see why I had to show this to you, Doctor? He's out there. Right now. Waiting."

"God! I didn't . . . I mean, I thought . . ."

"Yeah, you thought it was a blackmail tape, didn't you? You and Charm, getting it on. Or was it you and Fancy?"

"I don't know what you're . . . I was never with either of them."

"Sure. And it's a big surprise to you, isn't it? That Charm would be in the blackmail business."

His head slumped forward. "No. I knew that. That's how she . . . got in here. To work. I thought—"

"It doesn't matter what you thought. Not anymore. This is out of control. Charm's a nasty, mean little bitch all right, but you're running with the big dogs now. I'll be sure to tell Angelo Mondriano how good you keep secrets."

The blood drained from his face but he kept his professional mask on, fighting for control. "Who's that?"

"Well, seems like now it's plain old Robert L. Testa, of Seattle, Washington. We've got all the names, Doctor. Before and after. The new addresses too. I know you changed the faces. Probably got all-new documentation too. A beautiful job you guys do. But this is your lucky day—that's not why I'm here."

"You . . . don't understand," he said. "This place was my dream. We have the finest facility in the country. We can do things for children that are truly remarkable. But it costs a fortune."

"Don't these rich kids all have some kind of insurance?"

"Insurance doesn't begin to cover some of our work. We don't just take children from this area, we have a sliding scale. Some scholarships too."

"So when Cherry came up with the idea . . . ?"

"She . . . stores information. Like a computer. I know it's . . . illegal. But, the way she put it, it's as though some foundation was funding our work."

"Yeah, that's nice. You help people lose themselves, the money helps kids find themselves, right?"

"You make it sound so—"

"Your pal Charm's been killing kids," I told him. "Or trying to, anyway. I can't tell. Take a look."

His hands were shaking—he gripped the edge of his desk to steady them, a shot fighter, lying back on the ropes, waiting for the ref to stop the contest. I tossed the Mole's calculations on his desk. He looked at the papers without moving his hands, frozen, watching the scorpion twitching its tail on the polished wood.

"What is—?"

"Charm's been doing experiments. On kids. Your kids. The ones who come here for help. She's got a drug she thinks induces suicide. And she's managed to make sure half of the kids who come here get it. Double-blind experiments she's running. Now tell me . . . tell me she doesn't have access to them."

"She . . . does. But I never—"

"No, I don't think you did either. You're in business, aren't you? You and Cherry. What's the tariff, doc? For a new face? For a new life?"

"It . . . varies."

"I'll bet. You're down to two choices now. You live, or you die."

"What do you want?" he whispered, his face so stark it looked X-rayed.

"The truth. Some cash. And silence. You put that on the table, you stay alive. And in business too, if that's what you want."

"What do you want to know?"

"Charm was doing experiments?"

"Yes. With psychotropics. I knew about it. But she told me it was an antidepressant. Something she'd developed herself. She didn't want to go through the FDA maze—it takes too long, costs too much. You have to wait forever, to get human subjects. A real breakthrough, that's what she called it. We don't know very much about endogenous depression . . . depression from the inside. I thought—"

"How do they get it? The drug?"

"It's an injection. Intramuscular. One dose, five cc's."

"And she gave it to them herself?"

"No. She doesn't come here. She . . . gave me the . . . material. And I did it."

"And you kept records?"

"I didn't keep them. I turned my notes over to her. Every week. To a post office box. They were coded—nobody could know which . . ."

"Where is it?"

"What?"

"The drugs, Doctor. Where's your supply?"

"Right over there," he said, pointing to a mini-refrigerator with a black face built into the bottom of the bookcase, right next to the VCR. "It's . . . unstable. You need a fresh supply every couple of weeks. She just dropped some off, the day before yesterday."

I moved over to the refrigerator, opened it up. It was full of those little cartons of fruit juice, the kind you pierce with a plastic straw. Two little bottles at the back, full of clear fluid, with flat rubber screw-on tops . . . for the hypodermic needle to draw through.

I pocketed the bottles. "Did Cherry know?" I asked him.

"She knows Charm is . . . dangerous. Sociopathic. And she always suspected she might hurt Randy in some way. But she doesn't know about this . . ."

"How does she know . . . that Charm is crazy."

"*I* told her. Charm never wanted me to treat her—she had her own agenda. Still, she wasn't a difficult case to diagnose. Classic. She doesn't see people as people—they're just objects to her. Things to be re-arranged, like furniture."

"Why did you let someone like her into your life? I mean, she's got some hanky-spanky films of you, so what? You're not running for office."

"I told you . . . it's nothing like that. I first met her as a patient. She self-referred. I probably wouldn't have seen her personally, but Cherry asked me to. My profession is founded on secrecy—I figured it out—Cherry wanted to learn Charm's secrets . . . through me."

"Did you?"

"Oh yes. At least I thought so. Charm is . . . capable of anything. Anything at all. She has no superego at all, no moral controls. She doesn't *feel* anything. Inside or out. Her pain threshold is incredible. I saw her once, right in this office, I saw her hold a finger over a burning match until I could smell the flesh burn. She never changed expression."

"You were afraid of her?"

"Everybody's afraid of her. She is a person utterly without limits."

"A lot of crazy—"

"Charm is not crazy, Mr. Burke. She's well oriented in all spheres; she has excellent reality contact. She's not psychotic . . ."

"Just dangerous."

"Yes."

"Dangerous enough to kill?"

He got up from his desk, walked in tight, agitated circles, dry-washing his hands. I watched his walk, timing my voice so it hit him as he circled just in front of me. "You remember the tape I just showed you, doctor? Diagnosis is your business. The question for you isn't whether Charm's dangerous, it's whether the man I just showed you is. The man on the tape. There's only one way out for you now."

He reached inside of himself, got a grip somewhere, sat back down. "She killed her father," he said. "Maybe her mother, too. I don't know that for sure, not about her mother, but she has the . . . knowledge to do it."

"Was that revenge? For the incest?"

"You know about that? How could . . . she would *never* tell anyone."

"She didn't. I put it together. From other stuff. Stuff Fancy told me."

"It wasn't for revenge. At least I don't think so. He was in the way, her father. That's what she said. That's all it takes. For Charm, that's all it takes. She told me . . . all about it. Sat right where you're sitting and laughed about it—she knows all about doctor-patient privilege—I could never testify against her."

"So you thought I was working for her? I was here to blackmail you?"

"I guess I expected it. I've been expecting it for years. I was trying to . . . protect someone."

"Who?"

"It doesn't matter."

"It does to me. I'm going to tie up all the loose ends, or I'm not. If I don't, you can talk to Blankenship."

"Blankenship?"

"The man on the tape," I said. "Diandra's father. You don't believe me, check your own records."

He didn't say anything for a minute. I waited. Like Blankenship was waiting.

"Randy," he finally said. "She said she'd destroy him. I know she had a . . . relationship with him. When he was just a boy. I got her to promise to leave him alone."

"And she did?"

"Yes. Absolutely. I probed it fairly deeply. When he was in treatment with me. For a long time. He's very close to working it through. Once he finds something to connect with . . ."

"He already has," I said. "But what's the kid to you?"

"He's my son," Barrymore said, meeting my eyes for the first time. "When Cherry wanted a child, she didn't want to go near a sperm bank—all those stories about tainted blood. Looks as though she was right too—look what's happened since. Bad screening for HIV. And that doctor who used his own sperm on dozens of his own patients. She was afraid. So I . . . did it myself."

"And Charm found out?"

"Yes. I don't know how, but she did. She swore she'd never tell, if only I'd . . ."

I stood up. "The experiments are over," I told him. "Charm's out of business. *Your* business, you go and do what you want with it—it's not my problem. This cost me and my associates a lot of money. You have to make it good. But it's a one-shot tap—I won't be back."

"How much do you—?"

"Half a million. Cash. It's a small bite—I got a good idea of what you all take in with this operation. You'll get a call—somebody'll be using my name. They'll make all the arrangements for the pick-up. You keep nice and quiet, so do I. You say one word, to anybody, and the list gets into circulation. Then people will die . . . and they won't go alone, understand?"

"Yes."

"Don't say one word to Charm. Not one word."

"I understand."

"Doctor, listen to me now. I'm going to walk out of here. And out of your life. You pick up that phone, it won't help you. You swallowed some poison—I'm the antidote. Got it?"

"Yes," he said, head down, looking at his desk.

I drove the Lexus away from the grounds, feeling Blankenship's thermal track all over my back. I kept driving all the way to his house. Parked in his driveway and waited.

He was maybe fifteen minutes behind me. We went into his house. I almost didn't recognize it—the dump I'd seen before was transformed, as poison-neat as a monk's cell.

"It's not Barrymore," I told him. "I've got it down to a short list now. Few more days, couple of weeks at most. I'll be in touch."

"Take your time," he said. "Be sure."

Half a million was just the right amount. Enough so Barrymore would think it was the score of a lifetime for a small-time operator like me—not so much that he might think about other alternatives. I drove straight into the city. Told Mama as much of the story as she'd want to know. Michelle would make the call, get Barrymore to come into our territory with the money. Check into a hotel, go out for a walk. The Prof would do the rest. Very simple.

"Gems worth much more," Mama said reproachfully.

"Smooth is better," I told her.

More calls. More arrangements. More deals.

"I need the Plymouth," I told Sonny.

"Sure. You want me to drive?"

"No, it's just a pick-up. I'll be back tomorrow."

"You want me to keep looking after Fancy?"

"No. She's going with me. But, Sonny, if Charm comes around, tell her that. Fancy went someplace with me. Nothing more. Got it?"

He nodded.

I made another call from a pay phone. Listened to the arguments, ignored them.

"Where are we going?" Fancy asked, squirming around on the Plymouth's front seat.

"To pick up my girl. It's not far."

"Your . . . girl?"

"Shut up, Fancy. You like to play at being a bitch—you're about to meet the real thing."

I t wasn't a long ride. Elroy's shack up in Dutchess County hadn't changed . . . maybe it sagged a little more. I pulled into the yard just as one of his pit bulls charged the car, running right up on the hood to glare through the windshield. Elroy came out in a minute, shambling forward, his prize beast on a chain. Barko, a white demon with a black patch over one eye.

I cracked my window carefully. "I came for my dog," I told him.

"Hey look, man, she never got pregnant. I mean, she won't even *tie* . . . even when she's in heat. I think maybe she's gay. But I got an idea. I know this vet—"

"Now, Elroy. She's coming with me now. Call off your mutts." As soon as he gave the signal, I stepped out of the car, crouched, cupped my hands, shouted "Pansy! Come here, girl!"

The monster cranked around the corner of the house like a rhino on methedrine, pounding toward me, ears flapping, huge mouth open, yipping like a pup. She piled into me, knocked me over, stuck her enormous snout in my face, nuzzling, tail wagging out of control.

"Pansy! Good girl! You look great!"

She finally let me up, running around in circles, a hundred and forty pounds of joyous muscle and bone.

"Pansy! Jump!" I snapped at her. She hit the ground prone, waiting. I opened the back door of the Plymouth, made the hand signal. She piled in. Saw Fancy on the front seat, parked her massive head on the seatback, drooling. I made a signal for "friend" and she growled happily. Fancy was rigid, eyes huge.

"This is my girl," I told her. "Pansy. The world's finest puppy, aren't you?" I said, rubbing the back of Pansy's neck.

"What *is* it?"

"Pansy's a Neapolitan mastiff. The best, sweetest, most loyal dog in the whole world."

Pansy growled agreement. "Go ahead and pat her," I said to Fancy. "She's cool."

Fancy gave the dog a halfhearted pat. Pansy immediately licked the entire side of her face in one huge swipe.

"Eeewww!" Fancy responded. I couldn't tell if she was happy or disgusted.

"You ready to do what I asked you?" I questioned Elroy.

"Okay, man. But look . . ."

"We'll talk later," I told him, gesturing for Fancy to come over to me.

We walked into Elroy's shack. It was all set up, the assortment of working tools I'd told him to buy on a flat table next to a chair. I sat on the couch, told Fancy to come to me. I pulled her across my lap, lifted her skirt, pulled the hem of her panties toward the center of her buttocks, off one cheek. "Right there," I told Elroy, pointing.

The tattoo needle hummed as Elroy did his work. He'd never done one before, but he had world-class hands, a master engraver, specializing in commercial artwork—stock certificates, bearer bonds, twenty-dollar bills . . .

Fancy lay still for the whole thing, holding my hand.

"Looks pretty good," Elroy said, admiring his work. "It'll probably scab up—better keep the bandage on for a few days. And try to stay off it."

"Thanks," I told him, helping Fancy to her feet.

Elroy walked over to the driver's window. "Look, man, I'm telling you—"

"It's not gonna happen," I told him. "You'll have to find some other way to breed your super-dog. The experiment's over."

I stopped at a deli, left Pansy and Fancy together while I went shop-ping. Back at the apartment, I dumped a quart of chocolate chip ice cream into a giant mixing bowl Fancy brought over from the big house. I added a couple of pounds of gingersnaps, all crumbled up for a topping. Pansy watched the preparations, her eyes screaming with desire.

"Speak!" I told her. She hit the mixing bowl like a jet-fueled bat-tering ram. Fancy watched, transfixed, as the huge dog made the whole concoction disappear.

"God!"

"Yeah. Isn't she beautiful?"

"I never saw anything like it."

"I had her with Elroy, that guy you met? He was gonna breed her, but I guess it didn't work out. But now she's back with me. Back home, right, girl?"

Pansy put her head in my lap, making her downshifting-diesel noise of contentment as I scratched behind her ears.

The next night, in the apartment.

"You ready?" I asked.

"Yes." Fancy was nude again, standing in the high heels, the white bandage stark against her right cheek. She bent over, dialed the phone.

"Charm? I'm back!"

. . .

"No, it's perfect. You were right. I'm really *out* now."

. . .

"No, he went off somewhere. I'm not allowed to move from the corner where he put me. He's . . . perfect, now. That's why I called. I want to . . . give him something. He's really into it now, the scene. He wants to do a double. The whole thing. Over the barrel. I have to bring him . . . another slave. I mean, maybe I don't *have* to, but it would be—"

. . .

"Yes! Do you think Sybil would—?"

. . .

"Really? Charm, you'd do that for me. Oh, that's perfect. Can I—?"

. . .

"Okay. It has to be late, though. He's not ready for a group thing. After it closes, all right?"

. . .

"And I'm in charge, Charm. You might have to really take it. He's—"

. . .

"Oh, that's great. Thank you so much. I'll see you."

The parking lot at Rector's was dark. A little past four-thirty in the morning. The white Rolls was the only car there, standing right next to the back door. I pulled Fancy's NSX in next to it.

She opened the door and we stepped inside. Fancy unzipped her dress. Underneath, she was wearing her domina outfit—all black leather—restraining, displaying, threatening. Her spike heels clicked on the floor as she walked over to the cabinet just past the long bench. She came out with a black whip, a cat-o'-nine-tails with a short stock.

She walked beside me, flicking the whip lightly against her hip. All the way down the hall to a room with a red door. I started to reach for the handle. She pulled at my hand, pointed to the back of her thighs, nodded emphatically. I took the whip she handed me, watched as she bent over, cracked it across the back of her muscular thighs a few times, more sound than fury, being careful to stay away from the bandage. She let out a moan, turned and winked at me. Then she took the whip from my hand and opened the door.

Charm was sitting in a straightback chair, facing the doorway, dressed in a schoolgirl's sailor suit, blue top over a white pleated skirt. She had on the Mary Jane shoes with straps, plain white socks. Her long hair was combed into pigtails, each one anchored with a white ribbon. Right out of the fetish catalog.

I nodded at Fancy. She stalked over to Charm, every scene-freak's fantasy, the domina turning submissive, following orders. Turning the tables.

"You're a bad, disobedient little bitch," she said. "Aren't you?"

Charm hung her head.

"Answer me when I speak to you!" Fancy snarled, grabbing Charm's hair, pulling her face up.

"Yes," she said, looking just past Fancy's hip, catching my eye, in control. That's how she thought this was going to end . . . with a cluster fuck.

"Yes what?" Fancy demanded, slapping Charm hard across the mouth.

"Yes, mistress."

"You know what happens to bad girls?" Fancy said, slapping her again.

"Yes, mistress."

"All right, miss. Get up. Right now!"

Charm got to her feet. Fancy pointed at a barrel standing off to one side. It was full-size, standing in a shallow wooden cradle so it wouldn't roll. Charm lay on the barrel, face down. Fancy fastened the wrist and ankle straps, pulling them tight. Then she lifted Charm's skirt to expose the white cotton schoolgirl panties.

"You're a bad girl!" she said again. "And now you're going to pay for it." Fancy picked up the little whip and held it high—I could see the hard muscle flex in her arm. She cracked it across Charm's bottom, again and again. Charm groaned.

"You better keep your smart mouth shut, bitch. Or I'll really give you something to cry about," Fancy said, whipping her more.

It went on and on. Longer than I thought anyone could take it, but Charm didn't make another sound. Finally, Fancy stepped back, tossing the whip aside. Then she pulled down Charm's panties, displaying the violent red stripes.

"She's ready for you now, master," she said to me.

I stepped behind Charm, put one hand on the small of her back. My right hand flashed.

"Aaaargh!" It was a scream of rage.

I walked around the barrel, facing her. She looked up, craning her neck, tendons standing out, psycho eyes dry iced.

"Did that hurt?" I asked her.

"Yes!"

"The pain's not over," I told her, holding up the hypodermic needle so she could see it.

"What . . . what is that?"

"Don't you recognize it, Charm? It's your serum. Your special little suicide drug. Time to find out if it works."

"You . . . !" she snarled, her body rigid with strain as she fought against the straps.

"Forget it," I told her. "It's too late. You got ninety days, Charm. That's the way you set it up, right? Ninety days. To find out the truth. Maybe it works, maybe it doesn't. If it works on you, it'll work on anybody, wouldn't it? You never even *thought* about killing yourself."

"I'll kill *you*," she said. No emotion—a viper's promise.

"No, you won't do that. See, the same scientist who cracked your code, he's working on an antidote. Maybe he'll get it done in time, maybe he won't. You can't take that chance, can you? Here's the deal. The last deal you'll ever make. I'm walking out of here now. When I get the antidote, I'll call you. And it'll cost you. I figure you can scrape up some serious money pretty quick, especially if you're motivated. How's about two million bucks, you miserable blackmailing bitch? Two million bucks, for your life?"

"I can get it," she said, calm.

"I know. My man says he's close. Couple of weeks, at the outside."

"How would I know—?"

"You won't. You never fucking will. What I want is the money. It's up to you."

"But what if I—?"

"I'll stay with you," Fancy said. "I'll stay with you, Charm. Every minute. I won't let you . . . kill yourself, I promise."

"I love you, Fancy," Charm said.

"I know," Fancy told her, stroking her sister's face.

It only took me a few minutes to pack the next morning. Sonny was standing outside, patting the Plymouth like he was saying goodbye to it. I gave the command and Pansy jumped inside.

"This came for you. Yesterday, by messenger," he said, handing me a heavy buff envelope, sealed tight.

"Thanks," I said, slipping it into my pocket.

"Burke, I can never—"

"Shut up, kid," I told him. "I'll be watching for your name in the Grand Prix."

"Or Daytona, I haven't made up my mind yet."

"It doesn't matter, Sonny. You found yours, that's what counts."

He grabbed me in a bear hug, almost cracked my ribs.

I didn't look back. Neither did Pansy.

B ack in my office, Pansy prowled her old haunts as I slit open the envelope Sonny had given me. A short note, on thermal fax paper.

Jubal told me. Everything. You did what I asked you to do. I don't know what you think of me, but I love my boy. I know he's safe now. I didn't mean for things to happen like they did. It was just business. We're all square, you and me. No hard feelings.

It was signed "Cherry."

T en days later, a knock at the door of the motel room I was renting in New Rochelle, just south of the Connecticut border.

Fancy stepped in, wearing a severe black business suit, low-heeled pumps, a black pillbox hat on her head. An alligator briefcase was in one hand, as thick as a book bag. She gave me a chaste kiss, walked over and sat on the bed.

"Here it is," I said, handing her a hypo-ready bottle of blue liquid. "Draw five cc's, give it to her in the butt."

"Will it really work?"

"That's what the man says," I told her.

She nodded, handed me the briefcase. I opened it. Stacks of neatly banded bills, all hundreds. I'd already told them—no sequential serial numbers, used bills. I didn't count it.

"I have to get back soon," Fancy said. "I left her tied up. There's no way she could kill herself, but it could get real uncomfortable after a while."

"That's okay."

"Well, I guess this is—"

"Not quite yet," I told her. "There's one more thing."

She looked a question at me with her deep gray eyes.

"I'd sure like to see how that tattoo turned out," I said.

I met Blankenship in the parking lot of Yonkers Raceway, the spot behind the paddock where the overhead fixtures cast more shadow than light.

"It wasn't the doctor," I said. "Like I told you before. Nobody at the hospital. Nobody who legitimately works there, anyway."

"Who?" is all he said.

I told him about Charm. Not the whole thing, just enough. "She's taken off," I told him. "I got word she's heading for Switzerland. We're looking. Sooner or later, she'll turn up."

"I'll get a passport," he said.

I thought it was over then. That shot I'd given Charm when she was posed over the barrel, it was a dummy. As useless as the phony antidote she'd just bought. Her fangs were pulled.

I was done.

And the Zero wasn't pulling.

I had time after that. But it didn't feel like the kind of time a judge gives you anymore.

I used the time. Thought about that bromeliad I'd seen in Fancy's greenhouse—the one without roots. Plants die in pots, but they never die in gardens. Not really die. They return to the ground, to nourish their brothers and sisters coming up.

The cash all went to a laundry I know. For thirty percent off the top, we got back clean money—some mob-run movie house was going to do boffo box office in the next few weeks. I split the take with my family, equal shares. "Slick as ice, but twice as nice," the Prof praised me. "And you did it without the gun, son."

Clarence said he was going to buy some ground. On the Island. So he could always go home.

Michelle counted the cash in her perfectly manicured hands. Told me about a new place she'd found. In Colorado. Where they'd take her the rest of the way back to herself.

The Mole grunted.

Mama's face lit up, her faith in the world's balance restored.

Max didn't say anything.

Me, I went across the barrier. In my mind. Talked to Belle. To the boy who died in that house of terror.

I'd always have the pain. I made it for myself, like Fancy's tattoo. And I'd carry it around the same way.

I'd always feel sad. But I felt something else too.

Forgiven.

I had me back.

Belinda was still writing. Maybe I'd answer her someday, find out what the game was.

Or maybe I'd go find my Blossom.

I remember the day. It was in September, crisp, with the winter hawk's promise far in the distance. I sat in the back booth of Mama's restaurant, checking the mail her driver brought over from the warehouse. The envelope had no return address. Inside, a clip from a newspaper.

TWIN SISTERS TRAGEDY! the headline said. Twin sisters were vacationing together in Maine, near the coast. They went rock climbing. One of them jumped or fell from a high cliff. Dead on impact. Her sister was inconsolable. Told the cops Charm had been depressed. They'd gone climbing to get away from all the pressures of business. Just the two of them.

I put the newsclip in an envelope. Mailed it to Blankenship—flowers for Diandra's grave.

wondered if Charm saw the Zero on the way down. And if she blinked.

■

·

A NOTE ON THE TYPE

This book was set in Caledonia, a face designed by William Addison Dwiggins (1880–1956) for the Mergenthaler Linotype Company in 1939. It belongs to the family of types referred to by printers as "modern," a term used to mark the change in type styles that occurred around 1800. Caledonia was inspired by the Scotch types cast by the Glasgow typefounders Alexander Wilson & Sons circa 1833. However, there is a calligraphic quality about Caledonia that is completely lacking in the Wilson types.

Dwiggins referred to an even earlier typeface for this "liveliness of action"—one cut around 1790 by William Martin for the printer William Bulmer. Caledonia has more weight than the Martin letters, and the bottom finishing strokes of the letters are cut straight across, without brackets, to make sharp angles with the upright stems, thus giving a modern-face appearance.

W. A. Dwiggins began his association with the Mergenthaler Linotype Company in 1929 and over the next twenty-seven years he designed a number of book types, the most interesting of which are Metro, Electra, Caledonia, Eldorado and Falcon.

Composed by Graphic Composition, Inc.,
Athens, Georgia
Printed and bound by R. R. Donnelley & Sons,
Harrisonburg, Virginia
Designed by Virginia Tan